He never saw the shadowy figure who slipped in beneath the rising door. His head was turned away, his eyes focused on the car beside him as the figure slid alongside. A .32 caliber American Derringer "Ultralight" came up in line with the back of his head. When it was directly behind his left ear, the shadowy figure pulled the trigger.

He never heard the report of that shot, but inside the house where his wife was, it sounded like somebody had pitched a fire cracker into the garage. She hurried to peer out. There was still enough light for her to see the sparkle of shattered glass . . . and to create a soft glow behind the crimson sheen coating the inside of the windshield. Then she started to scream.

Also by Christopher Newman
Published by Fawcett Books:

MIDTOWN SOUTH
MAÑANA MAN
KNOCK-OFF
SIXTH PRECINCT
BACKFIRE

MIDTOWN NORTH

Christopher Newman

FAWCETT GOLD MEDAL • NEW YORK

This one is for
Bernadette, Jack, Pat, O'B, Frank,
Bob, Mary, Pete, and Tom.
Siblings.

Closely I peered ahead and seemed to see
The shadowy shapes of lofty towers rise
And asked, "What city's battlements are these?"
My master then: "Because you strain your sight,
Seeking to pierce too deeply through the fog,
Your concept wanders widely from the truth.
When closer we approach you may perceive
How senses cheat when objects are remote."

Dante, *The Inferno*
Canto XXXI
18–25

ACKNOWLEDGMENTS

The author would like to thank the following people for their kind assistance in both the research and preparation of this book: Capt. Bob Cividanes and Capt. Steve Davis, NYPD Public Information, for the access granted to the inner workings of the "big building"; Sgt. Ray O'Donnell, for his generous tour and crash course in how the bureaucracy of New York's Finest functions; Sgt. Janet Greco, for a look at Spring 3100's inner sanctum; Lt. Bill Caunitz, NYPD (ret.), for finding the many places where I screwed up procedure and terminology; Knox Burger and Kitty Sprague, for their guidance and patience from inception to completion; my wife, Susan, for that treasured first edit; and Daniel Zitin, my editor at Fawcett, for his insight and support.

ONE

To strut the strut, each step demanded that Lawrence Kipp plant on the ball of his front foot. That plant allowed him to swing his entire body around in a slow, rolling arc, his hip socket acting as pivot. After years of practice, his follow foot never failed to float effortlessly into position. And plant. And roll. It was an art; the thighs flexed just so, the tightening buttocks ground, and the hips swayed seductively.

At four-thirty on a Tuesday morning, it was too late for much action, but Lawrence Kipp didn't mind. He had a head full. He was lost in the depths of an idle meditation, his rumination wandering to whether it was ever *truly* night in New York City. If it was, he didn't believe he could remember seeing it. Not that his memory was all that good anymore. Kipp mostly slept through the hours of sunlight and emerged only in the hours of streetlight to stroll midtown, west of Times Square. In his stiletto heels, lace panties, garter belt, seamed net stockings, and brassiere bulging with proud silicone breasts, he worked like any craftsman at any other trade. Those hours became his days. And each day, a moment like this arrived. The moment when the trickle of john traffic finally died; when mid-Manhattan

1

yawned like a bored insomniac and paused to briefly shut her eyes. Lawrence Kipp was left alone with his thoughts.

And so he was wrapped, snuggled deep in a warm, heroin-cocaine haze, when the sharp crack of a pistol discharge, close at hand, snapped him out of his reverie. At the time, Kipp was headed west across Eleventh Avenue on Forty-fifth Street. It was a track that would soon see him joining the rest of the girls in the backseat of Honey Lucas's Jaguar Vanden Plas for the ride back uptown. Now his head snapped right around, those mincing steps doing a quick freeze. The noise was so close that if he weren't so blitzed-to-the-tits stoned, he might even have jumped. It was followed by a scream of rage. Deep, definitely male, and fueled by pain, it was punctuated with abrupt finality by a second gunshot.

From the direction toward which the transvestite hooker's head was turned, a shadowy figure emerged from the mouth of a dark depression between buildings. It staggered, got itself righted, and started directly toward him. The heroin's warm haze was now supplanted by the cold, damp dew of panic. Lawrence couldn't run in those shoes. Any effort to do so would only draw attention to his presence. There was a doorway directly behind his left shoulder; not much more than a niche and not much of a hiding place, even for a man of his slender build. His panic propelled him toward it. Before the shadow had developed the actual form of a man, Lawrence was pressed into those uncertain depths, naked shoulders, buttocks, and thighs kissing the cool metal of an unadorned steel-clad door. Footsteps and labored breathing were all Kipp knew of that passing presence. Heart pounding and streams of icy sweat running from his armpits, scalp, and down the backs of his legs, he stood as inanimate as the building itself, eyes squeezed shut.

An eternity seemed to pass before the prostitute lifted

his lids and peered once again into the street. It was empty; the shadow had passed. Some summoning of courage was required before Lawrence could force his head to move. Forty-fifth Street was empty to the east, in the direction the shadow was moving. And to the west, from where it had come. The loudest noise to be heard was the sound of Kipp's own pounding heart. Cautiously, he crept forward a step. With a painful slowness, his hunched shoulders relaxed. Not a car passed. Not another of Lawrence Kipp's sisters of the night was anywhere in sight.

As the level of adrenaline ebbed in Kipp's bloodstream, his heart rate eased off. He struggled to regulate his panicked breathing. Slowly, curiosity crept in where terror had just been; curiosity and another kind of trepidation. There was a small, dark-colored car parked at the curb directly opposite that alley down there. The driver's door was ajar. A trick's? Kipp had seen enough violence in his line of work to know it could be one of his sisters lying mortally wounded in that alley. Or worse, Honey Lucas with his tiny vials of sweet sanity. Kipp forced his feet into the short-stepped hurry that was all his shoes would allow. As he progressed, the cheeks of his exposed ass glistened with fear's sweat, twitching and rolling in the mercury-vapor light of his day.

A junkie is not unduly upset by the sight of blood. With every injection of a hypodermic needle, a certain amount of blood is drawn back into the syringe. When the works are later cleaned, that blood is mixed with water and ''backwashed'' with a thrust of the plunger. The walls of an urban shooting gallery are covered with the bloody spatter of a thousand backwashings. What Lawrence Kipp was *not* prepared for was the *amount* of blood splattered at his feet and across the walls at the mouth of that alley. In the streetlight, the features of the man's face were difficult to make out. Still, Kipp was sure it was no one he would recognize. The light-

3

colored suit and dark tie were too square for anyone
working Lawrence's side of the street. They were john
clothes. The shoes were john shoes. But the blood,
where it soaked the front of that shirt and bubbled over
a sucking chest wound, was the same sort of blood any
dying animal's heart might pump. And dying was what
this man, eyes wide and staring sightlessly at their own
private terror, was doing. The rasping breaths drawn in
and pushed out of his lung wound came like the quick
pantings of an overheated dog.

As Lawrence Kipp stood staring, the dying man began to convulse. The heel of one shoe snapped as Kipp
stumbled backward in revulsion. To hell with the shoes,
and the seamed stockings which would surely be ruined
in the process; Lawrence kicked free of his sling-back
pumps and ran hell-bent for the Hudson.

TWO

Just minutes before receiving that homicide squeal from Midtown North, Detective Lieutenant Salvatore Onofrio had idly thanked God that the cool summer weather was holding. The wee hours had been quiet ones for Onofrio and his Task Force detectives at Manhattan South Borough Command. Working the Night Watch detail was not often like that, but today the citizens of their sector seemed content with catching up on a weekend's lost sleep. Onofrio was setting up to shoot the moon in this, the most recent of a dozen games of hearts, when Detective Second-Grade Howard "Crime Dog" McGraff handed him the phone.

"Lieutenant Fennema, Lou."

Onofrio scowled. Twice tonight he'd attempted to shoot the moon and was forced to take points. This time, he had a lock on it.

"Who he?"

"New Operations lieutenant at MTN. You don't read the orders?"

"Fuck you, McGraff." And slapping his cards to the surface of the squad room table, Onofrio grabbed the receiver from Crime Dog's hand. As the new exec up there, Lieutenant Fennema would be commanding the

5

Midtown North Precinct's patrol officers on the midnight-to-eight shift. There was no way he could be calling with good news.

"Yeah, Lou. What can we do for you?"

"We've got a stiff. Male Caucasian. Middle age. Well dressed in a tan summer-weight suit and tie. Two of my guys found him in Hell's Kitchen, way over by the river. Bullet in his chest."

Silently, Onofrio cursed his luck. It was coming up on six-thirty, and in a mere hour and a half, the Task Force day shift and Midtown North's regular squad detectives came on duty. At eight, he'd be on his way home to Staten Island and the loving arms of his wife. Now he and his boys were going to have to drag ass across town, oversee the initial Crime Scene investigation, and probably miss breakfast. Why did these things always turn up at the *end* of his shift?

"They ID'd him?" As Sal asked it, he had to stifle an irritated yawn.

"No wallet," Fennema reported. "Nothing in his pockets. Hell, the street creeps had already stolen the poor bastard's shoes."

Onofrio told the lieutenant that they'd be along presently and avoided stating the obvious: that the poor bastard didn't have much need for shoes anymore. Within five minutes, he had his four-man squad rolling in two separate Plymouth Fury sedans. Over in the eastern sky, the sun was already well up on a morning surprisingly cool for late July. With the dog days of August a mere week away, the men of this and every detective squad in the five boroughs knew that a homicide today was only a taste of what late summer had in store.

Forty-fifth Street, where it stretches west from Tenth Avenue to the Hudson River, reflects none of the glitz of nearby Times Square. Here, Midtown moves beyond several insulating blocks of ancient tenements to become a decaying waterfront in transition. The pavement is pitted and patched, both sidewalks lined with weathered brick and neutral-painted stucco facades. Just west of Tenth, there is a public school, its outward appearance more suggestive of a house of detention. Clustered around it, warehouses teeter on the brink of extinction. The area is changing fast, with the nearby Hudson waterfront being actively re-claimed, and close at hand, the spires of new luxury towers rising like phoenixes from the ashes of old Hell's Kitchen. At that hour, this stretch of one-way street was still quiet, while the streets running parallel, north and south, were already clogged with early rush-hour traffic. Onofrio, riding with Sergeant Wally Mansker at the wheel beside him, saw huge piles of shiny, black-bagged refuse lining the lengths of both curbs. He concluded that today was garbage day.

"I wanna get this mess bagged an' outta here," Sal growled. " 'Nother geek comes inta town for a little convention fun an' frolic. He steps out t' get his pipe cleaned an' some crack-crazed hooker rolls him. The pros in Dubuque . . . or wherever the fuck he comes from . . . don't play dirty like that. He gets indignant. Fights back an' blammo. The little missus an' kiddies don't have a daddy no more. Tough fuckin' break for them, but then, Daddy should'a kept it zipped."

Mansker chuckled. The Gospel according to Saint Sal. He'd heard it before, and in Onofrio's testament, neither Lazarus nor any other dead guy was ever brought back from the grave.

Midtown North had three squad cars deployed at the scene. Onofrio was relieved to see that the meat wagon had arrived as well. If he was going to get this thing wrapped and have any hope of making it home before noon, he didn't want to have to wait around for the people from the Medical Examiner.

Lieutenant Cecil Fennema was easy enough to pick out of a small crowd of uniforms gathered off to one side in front of a narrow alleyway. While the beat cops all wore their uniforms like work clothes, Fennema wore his with a crisp air of authority. The single silver bars

7

of his rank glittered with a high polish. While other shoes in the group were scuffed, his were buffed to gleam in the morning sun. He was young for a lieutenant, at maybe thirty-four or -five, and that fact, as much as his ramrod-straight bearing, was enough to cause Sal Onofrio to groan. Young, ambitious cops who'd already climbed into the ranks were ball-busters. This Tuesday, after starting off innocently enough, had turned ornery on him.

Once Mansker parked and the two of them emerged from the car to approach, Onofrio could feel Fennema sizing them up. That fact, in itself, was no cause for resentment. Hell, any watch commander with a homicide on his hands wants to see it handled by the Guide. He'd have to have his thirty in and a down payment already made on a condo in Orlando before he'd risk bungling the investigation of *any* major crime by not paying attention to detail. *All* the detail.

Onofrio supposed that at first glance, Mansker was the easier of them to peg. Wally was big, at better than six foot, with those heavy shoulders, the lumpy peasant's face, arms like stovepipes, and sandy hair going prematurely gray. They made him look like the beat-walking, apple-stealing flatfoot of yesteryear; a look that belied a clever brain and excellent eye for discrepancy. Onofrio, on the other hand, looked more like a *consigliere* for the mob than a cop. Shorter than Mansker, at no more than five-ten, he seemed taller because of his slight shoulders, a pair of bony, oversize hands, and a wasp-skinny waist. A mop of unruly steel gray curls was a stark contrast to glinting obsidian eyes. While Wally Mansker dressed in rumpled off-the-rack suits from the Johnny Carson collection at Sears, the wise-guy-slick image Onofrio projected was bolstered by Givenchy and Giorgio Armani knockoffs.

Onofrio greeted the watch commander with a brusque nod.

"Mornin', Lou. And to think, it was startin' t' look like such a beautiful day."

"Not for him." Fennema nodded toward the entrance of the alley, where one bare, bright white foot could be seen protruding out beyond the corner of the nearest building.

"Still no ID?" Onofrio was already stepping over, Mansker in his wake.

"Nope. We're assuming that's his car, and we've requested a plate run on it, but still not a peep." Ten yards down the block, a lone Ford Escort, navy blue, sat parked at the curb. "The suit's from Barney's, so figure he's probably local. I've got my guys out lining up the few hookers left working the area . . . see if they heard anything." Fennema paused. "Not that I hold out any hope there. It was a Monday night. Theaters all dark. Half the restaurants closed. Most of the die-hard blow-job trade gets paid Thursday. They're broke by Sunday afternoon."

Onofrio's Night Watch guys had long admired the way their boss could give a corpse a cool, dispassionate once-over. Even the most brutal butchering rarely seemed to cause Onofrio distress anymore. It came as a surprise, then, when he reached the mouth of the alley, peered in, and straightened suddenly with a quick intake of breath.

"Jesus *Christ*!"

"What, Sal?" Wally was craning his neck, trying to get a look. "What is it?"

"That's Warren fucking *Mott* in there."

Cecil Fennema was right there at the mouth of the alley with them. He'd seen the Night Watch whip's reaction and heard the name. It was obvious from the look on his face that it meant nothing to him. "You *know* that guy?"

Mansker, after finally getting a look over Sal's shoulder, rolled his eyes and grunted. "He sure as hell *ought* to know him. That back-stabbing son of a bitch was his brother-in-law.''

Onofrio, oblivious to all but Fennema's question, looked the man straight in the eye and took a deep breath. ''We've all stepped in it this time, Lou. I suggest you get on the horn, call in a ten-thirteen to the Third Division's duty captain, an' then brace yourself. In the next hour, you're gonna see more braid an' scrambled egg hat brims than you've seen since Academy graduation.''

''A ten-thirteen?'' Fennema was clearly stunned. ''That's a *cop* in there?''

Onofrio was already advancing into the alley, easing in alongside the body and moving to slowly squat on his heels.

''A *dead* cop, Lou. Captain Warren Mott. Detective Bureau Field Internal Affairs Unit.'' The Homicide commander's voice had taken a quieter, more reverent tone. He slowly shook his head in wonder. ''A shoofly, Lou. A dead fuckin' shoofly.''

For a change, Detective Lieutenant Joe Dante was already showered and had grabbed his first cup of coffee when the Operations Desk at One Police Plaza called. In one corner of his Manhattan apartment's tiny kitchen, Dante's geriatric cat was yeowling for the food being spooned into his bowl. The pathos in his tone suggested he hadn't been fed in a fortnight. Not true. All cats are natural-born liars. Still, once that bowl hit the floor, the gruel he was getting would do nothing to improve his ornery disposition. As Dante had tried to explain to him many times, old cats eat old-cat food, a scientifically formulated blend of unappetizing ingredients guaranteed to evoke scorn. And while they were intended to prolong an elderly cat's years by means of healthy diet, they no doubt made the prospect of any added years on this planet a miserable proposition. In a gesture of solidarity, the lieutenant had taken to eating from an ever-increasing variety of disgustingly healthy high-fiber and vitamin-charged breakfast cereals. That way, the two of them could spend a few miserable minutes bonding before the boss emerged from his Greenwich Village digs to fight crime and keep the world safe for pampered, aging felines.

Receiver wedged between cheek and shoulder, Dante lifted the food bowl from the counter and set it on the floor.

"Yeah." He offered it in lieu of greeting.

"Lieutenant Dante? Op Desk. Sergeant Lewis."

"Sure, Phil. What's up?" As whip of the Detective Bureau's Major Case Squad, Dante was on a first-name basis with most all job personnel assigned to Operations Division.

"C of D is en route to the scene of a ten-thirteen homicide, midtown on Forty-fifth between Eleventh and the river. Your name is at the top of the list of people he wants there with him."

C of D meant Chief of Detectives Gus Lieberman. A 10-13 was the worst sort of news. They had a police officer victim on their hands. Dante thought quickly.

"How long before the PC and mayor make the scene?"

"They just got the call. If you hurry, you can beat everybody. The chief made it clear that he wants you to kick in the afterburners."

"Get me all my people, Phil."

"Next on my list, Lou. You're rolling?"

"Ten-four, Phil. I'm already gone."

As Dante hurried from his ground-floor apartment and out into the bright sunshine of Perry Street, he didn't have time to reflect on how gloriously this July Tuesday had dawned. His Department sedan was in a garage three blocks west, and the distance was covered at a brisk trot. They always kept his wheels parked up front for him, and after wedging his thermos between windshield and dash, he made tracks. At only a few

minutes after seven, it was still early on in his neighborhood's daily work-force migration. With the exception of a few briefcase-bearing eager beavers and the
usual dog walkers, pedestrian traffic on the sidewalks
was light.

The drive north up Eighth and then Tenth avenues
went easy enough until he hit crosstown commuter traffic streaming into the city from the Lincoln Tunnel and
off the Westside Highway. Entering the low thirties,
Dante eased his flashing red gum ball out onto the roof
and gave the cars in his path periodic blasts of the siren.
By the time he reached Thirty-ninth Street, the traffic
moving east and west was creating minor gridlock conditions at every intersection.

The little gray Honda Civic parked directly in his
path at a green light crossing Forty-second Street was
the last straw. When three screeching yelps of the siren
failed to produce the desired effect, Dante snatched up
the handset and got on the public-address hailer.

"What is it, buddy? Are you fucking *brain-dead*?!
Pull that piece of shit the hell out of the road!" He had
the gain knob cranked up high and didn't doubt apartment dwellers in the high-rises on either side of him
could hear it loud and clear on the thirtieth floor. In
another city, the mayor's office switchboard would be
flooded with irate complaints, but this was New York.
Flustered, the driver of the Civic jumped it forward, his
front bumper crunching hard into the back end of a
commuter bus. Dante didn't wait around for the upshot.
The gap in traffic that opened before him was narrow
at best. He put his two left wheels up on the curb and
scraped a mailbox squeezing through.

Forty-fifth Street was barricaded at the west end of
Eleventh Avenue. The scenes both in front of and behind the barriers were circuses. Dante couldn't be bothered trying to drive through. That was best left to the
commissioner, job brass, and the mayor. Instead, he
pulled it around into the southbound lanes of Eleventh

Avenue to park at the curb just ahead of a Channel 7 "Eyewitness News" van. All the local stations were here, network and independent. The news of a 10-13 cop-shot tended to get out the press in legions; video-cam snouts hopefully hunting for just the right shots of heavyweight politicos; hand-held microcassette recorders extended to catch every pearl dropping from those anointed lips.

"Whata'ya got, Lieutenant?" It was Jake Horowitz from the *Post*, spotting him and pressing the advantage. Horowitz was one of a corps of news hounds who infested the News Bureau and Public Information offices at One Police Plaza.

Stone-faced, Dante gave him a quick shake of the head. "A call to the scene of a ten-thirteen, same as you, Jake. I'm sure, once the mayor gets here, all's gonna be revealed."

"What happened to 'no comment'?"

Dante flashed him a tight little smile. "No fun anymore, babe. You ruined it for me."

The Major Case whip pressed ahead, flashing his shield at the patrol officer on the south end of the barricades and slipping inside. The scene on the street here was no less crowded, but at least it was a bit more subdued than the media sideshow without. Behind the barriers, groups of uniforms stood in clusters; many from Midtown North, and others flown in from the nearby Tenth and Midtown South station houses. Just beyond, a host of vehicles from the forensics labs, Medical Examiner, and job command were parked in roughly ordered ranks. Because Dante was the only member of his Major Case squad living in Manhattan, he wasted no time wondering whether any of his guys had shown yet. Instead, he set out in search of the man currently in charge of the scene.

Manhattan South's Third Division duty captain, Conroy "Connie" Beck, was a man of immense proportions, both by genetic predisposition and a fondness for

13

rich foods. He was an easy enough figure to pick out in a crowd, and as Dante worked his way toward him, Beck spotted the Major Case whip's approach. Pushing his way through personnel surrounding the command post, Beck extended one of his beefy mitts in greeting.

"You made good time, Joe."

Dante acknowledged the comment with a nod, eyes flickering out over the scene. "What's the situation here, Cap?"

Beck jerked his chin toward the mouth of an alley less than fifteen yards away. A horde of Crime Scene techs swarmed inside an area sectioned off with yellow plastic *crime scene* tape. Deep in the alley's gloom, a photographer's strobe flashed.

"From the top?"

Dante nodded. "In your best *Reader's Digest* condensed form."

Beck turned toward Twelfth Avenue and the river. "Two of ours in a radio unit were flagged by one of the homeless. Guy told them that there was a dead man in this alley . . . and sure enough. Middle age. Well dressed. Shot once in the chest."

"Heart?"

"Nope. Lung wound. Judging from the amount of blood, it took him a while to die. ME's man says he drowned in it. No ID on him when MTN called Night Watch. It was Sal Onofrio recognized the dead guy. That's when the ten-thirteen went out."

"Who?" Dante pressed.

"Deep shit, Joe. He's a shoofly. Captain Warren Mott."

Dante wasn't sure just what he was set for, but this slipped his guard. A career Internal Affairs investigator, Warren Mott was most recently assigned to run the Detective Division's Field Internal Affairs Unit. He had an office in the Police Athletic League headquarters on East Twelfth Street, just down the hall from Central Robbery. Joe hated his guts.

Watching Dante's eyes, Beck saw the impact of the news he'd just delivered. "You knew him?"

"Not to speak to. He tried to get my shield a few years back."

The duty captain's memory hit on a vague recollection of circumstances surrounding that event. "The unauthorized wire. A hooker got killed."

"Yep. Mott campaigned hard to see them hang my ass. The most he could get was six months without pay." Dante paused to shake his head, his eyes wandering back to the mouth of that alley. "It's funny. I cursed the fact of that asshole's existence every day of that suspension, but I never actually met him, toe to toe. So what about this homeless guy? What kind of witness is he?"

Beck didn't look hopeful. "Wino. Maybe fifty. It's hard to tell when they've lived that hard. The corpse was found missing its shoes and God knows what else. Man swears he saw nothing, that he was down at the piers, digging through trash dumped by crowds off the Circle Line boats. Says he came back here, where he's been sleeping lately, to find the dead man in his living room. There's a whole pile of his stuff back there. Crime Scene's going over it now."

"Where's Onofrio?"

"Right over there." The captain pointed to indicate a small knot of men on the sidewalk, just a dozen feet from the mouth of the alley. They were evenly mixed, a handful each of uniformed and plainclothes cops. "The uniforms are Fennema, my MTN midnight-to-eight commander, and the two guys who caught the squeal."

Dante had excused himself and was on his way to hook up with the Homicide squad for a forensics update when the barricades at the east end of the block came down. Among the cars entering, Joe recognized Chief Lieberman's Buick. It would only be minutes now before the C of D relieved Beck of responsibility for the

Command Post. Then, with the mayor, commissioner, and chief of Department, Lieberman would deal with the media and the *public* ramifications of a cop killing.

As Dante approached Sal Onofrio's Night Watch squad, it was hard to miss how glum they looked. They were stuck out here with a hot homicide and only fifteen minutes left on their regular shifts. Onofrio spotted him, lifted his chin in recognition, and moved to intercept. By the time Joe reached the opposite curb, Sal had fallen into step alongside. Unlike Dante, who'd grown up in the same Brooklyn neighborhood, Sal's speech was distinctly Canarsie.

"What gives, paisan? What's Major Case doin' here? I thought Homicide was *my* beat, Joey."

To get away with calling him Joey, a man had to have known Dante for quite some time. Joe and Onofrio went at least that far back. Sal was in his late forties and five years older than Joe, but both men had fathers who were cops and mothers who were members of the St. Clement's Altar Society. Sal's wife, Viki, was a year younger than Dante, and once upon a time, Joe had escorted her to her junior prom.

Dante shrugged. "They call, I come. From what I hear, this ain't any garden-variety homicide."

"You can say *that* again. Somebody swatted a shoofly. It's your old buddy Warren Mott we got in there. One in the fucking lung. Drowned, bleedin' out like a stuck fuckin' pig."

"And no weapon's been recovered."

Sal shook his head. "Nope."

The two of them pulled up in front of the tape barrier, with Dante scanning for the Crime Scene Unit commander. Onofrio waved back and forth, indicating the street from Eleventh Avenue to the river.

"This kid they got working the midnight-to-eight at MTN . . . Fennema? Works a little like somebody cinched his asshole with an end-wrench, but he's thorough. Him an' me had our people go over every inch'a this block, and we ain't turned nothin' but his car an' a pair'a high-heeled shoes." He nodded to a navy blue Ford Escort, parked at the curb and swarming with forensics technicians.

"Beck says there wasn't any ID found on him. That *you* recognized him." Dante had turned from a brief scrutiny of the car to confront Onofrio face-to-face. "How's that, Sal? Fucker tried to have me tarred and feathered, and I wouldn't know him from Adam."

Onofrio showed surprise. "You tellin' me you don't know?"

"Know *what*?"

Sal broke into a broad grin. "I just assumed, Joey. You remember my wife Viki's little sister Theresa? Little Miss Goody Two-shoes? She met Mott out on Fire Island a couple years back. Whirlwind sun-an'-sand romance, an' then she *marries* the fucker." Sal paused to chuckle as Dante's jaw dropped. "Hey, *paisan*. Nobody was more surprised than this guy . . . or *less* surprised when it finally come apart, this past Christmas."

"They split?"

"Some kinda trouble in paradise. Warren was what when they tied the knot . . . forty-three or -four? Career bachelor an' kinda set in his ways. Theresa was twenty-nine. That crazy clock that all women got was startin' t' tick on her. Love is blind. Either that or she thought she could civilize the asshole."

"Kids?"

"Baby girl. Bonnie. It's a damn shame, y'know? Ain't easy these days for a thirty-two-year-old broad with a baby t' find another man. An' what a waste, Joey. That skinny little kid you remember? Blossomed inta the fuckin' *flagship* of the Caravaglia line."

Dante was only half listening now as he got a leg over the yellow tape and moved to peer into the mouth of the alley. There was a tremendous accumulation of blood on the pavement and walls in there. In the middle of it lay the corpse of Captain Warren Mott. A half dozen forensics people were stepping gingerly around it, picking objects off the pavement with tweezers and sealing them in clear plastic bags. No question, the dead man had suffered an agonizing death if he was at all conscious while the blood filled his lungs. Contemplating the blank, empty look of neither panic nor agony frozen on that dead face, Dante supposed Mott *hadn't* been conscious. Because no cop deserved to die like this, he knew his heart should be warmed by a sense of relief. Warren Mott was that one exception to every rule.

As Joe moved deeper in, the stench of urine filled his nostrils. Bitter irony gnawed at him. Just yesterday he might have contended that the memories of Mott's campaign for his shield, and that resulting suspension, were buried in the past. This was obviously not so. Now, five years after Mott tried to destroy his career, he was going to be asked to find the party who hated Mott enough to want to see him dead. There lay the irony. On a list of suspects hundreds of names long, any other investigator would place Dante's right up at the top.

THREE

Detective Sergeant Deborah Glenmore didn't put much stock in picture-postcard days. The fact that this Tuesday in late July had dawned cloudless and without the usual humidity of the season was lost on her. Already this morning, the lanky Internal Affairs investigator had spent two hours on the iron, her trainer urging her through uncounted light reps in a workout designed to improve endurance. The resulting physical exhaustion did nothing to assuage an anger that had been boiling inside her for better than a week.

Glenmore parked her company Plymouth on the street and started off on foot toward Internal Affairs Division headquarters on Poplar Street, beneath the looming superstructure of the Brooklyn Bridge. En route, she tried once again to assign each pressure in her life a priority. Once again, she failed. For the past six months, the upcoming National Tae Kwon Do Championships in Cleveland were her primary preoccupation. Last year she'd placed third in the women's 135-pound division, and this year, she intended to win it. Every spare minute went into her training program. And then, a month ago, came the allegations of sexual misconduct against two patrol officers at the Four-Four in the South Central

Bronx. The initial gripe, turned over to the IAD by the Civilian Complaint Review Board, alleged that two officers had raped a prostitute arrested for crack possession. Raul Escobedo and Timothy Ahern. Glenmore's investigation turned up five subsequent allegations, made by other women on the partners' female arrest list. Each woman claimed to have been sodomized with a gun to her head. Each was threatened with death if she talked. Sergeant Glenmore suspected that there were more such victims refusing to come forward out of fear for their lives.

The alleged crimes themselves, while loathsome, were not what fueled Glenmore's current outrage. Friday a week ago, she'd filed her final report. Every day last week, she'd checked to see what actions were being taken. Yesterday afternoon, with the hierarchy still sitting on its hands, Glenmore finally blew her cool. When she stormed into her unit commander's office to protest, Captain Rick LeFevre could offer nothing in the Department's defense. He promised to have some sort of information for her by this morning, and she'd spent all last night stewing over it. Once she arrived at her dojo in Kew Gardens this morning, she took out her frustrations on the equipment in the weight room. Those karate championships were less than a month away. She knew she had to buckle down to fine-tuning her form pretty soon if she wanted to have a prayer.

IAD headquarters, here on the fringes of very fashionable Brooklyn Heights, was once the station house for the Eighty-fourth Precinct. The beige stone structure was recently repainted and in decent repair, with the ground-floor windows all covered with heavy wire mesh. The guts of the place were typically beat-up, starting right at the lobby. Its gloomy interior was painted over the hundredth time in battleship gray tones. The elevator Glenmore now approached had more rattles and less speed than a derelict oil tanker. As she flashed her ID at the uniformed man at the battered metal desk, she wondered what sin he'd committed to draw duty in this dreary little hell.

Each such building, and each office within it, has its own subtle personality. Cops seem to thrive on working in shopworn conditions. Crummy old desks and squeaky-wheeled chairs are standard issue throughout the job, but at each NYPD outpost, they take on a life of their own. The surrounding walls are generally painted a glaring white with bright blue trim: the same colors the public sees on radio cars. And inside these walls, the comfortable squalor of the frat house common room prevails. Glenmore hated it. She'd been inside enough cops' homes to know that few of them lived their private lives like this. Still, the job was the job, and over the years, she'd grown numb to the rat's-nest nature of her working conditions.

It was eight-forty when Glenmore reached her cubicle office on the third floor. No one else had arrived yet, and it fell to her to start the daily ritual of setting coffee to brew in the squad-room machine. The aging Norelco was just beginning to gurgle and spit into its stained Pyrex carafe when Rick LeFevre entered and headed toward his office door.

"Morning, Ricky. You look like hell. Baby keeping you up?"

The captain glanced down at his clothing and then back up, irritation flashing in his eyes. The shoes had a bright shine to them, the pants a razor crease, and the shirt an impeccable press.

"Like hell?"

"Not your clothes. Those bags under your eyes."

The forty-eight-year-old LeFevre had recently married a former high-powered ad exec. This past spring, his wife presented him with a baby boy. These developments seemed to catch him off guard. Now he grunted and started to turn back toward his office.

"Baby's still got colic. I think I'm beginning to understand what's behind infanticide."

"Don't say I didn't warn you."

The fact was that Glenmore *had* warned him . . . back when LeFevre first started acting the love-struck fool. He'd taken a second mortgage on his co-op apartment to pay for the big wedding his fiancée had always wanted. At the time, Deb told him he had rocks in his head. Then, when Rick's new wife promptly managed to get pregnant on their honeymoon—while swearing she'd been faithfully using a diaphragm—Deb gave up. On the job, LeFevre was a precise, detail-oriented unit commander. In his private life, he was ignorant of even what sort of birth control device he and his wife employed. Six months into the pregnancy, Rick's wife quit her high-paying job. By all appearances, she had no intention of going back. Still, she expected them to make the increased mortgage payments on their Kips Bay apartment. She still shopped at Bergdorf's and Balducci's. LeFevre found himself trying to support a two-income Manhattan life-style on a detective captain's pay. The strain was starting to tell on him.

Once the coffee was brewed, Glenmore filled two cups, doctoring LeFevre's with Cremora and Equal. While she was in the process of doing that, the captain's phone rang. By the time she could carry both their cups over, he was on his feet beside his desk and shrugging back into his jacket.

"Whoa, Ricky," she protested. "Where do you think *you're* going? You promised me I'd get some answers this morning."

LeFevre didn't break stride. "And you promised *me* that if you *didn't* have them, you'd take it across the river and confront Jerry Liljedahl personally."

Jerome Liljedahl was the Department's Chief of Inspectional Services. His command included IAD, the Intelligence Division, and other specialty functions.

"I wasn't kidding, Rick."

LeFevre was moving toward the door. He pointed to the cup in Glenmore's hand. "That's gonna be cold by

22

the time we get back, Sergeant. I suggest you drink up.''

"Wait a sec. Get back from where?" Glenmore was already turning to follow, bringing the cup of scalding liquid to her lips in little jerks.

"That was Operations. We're wanted on the West Side of Manhattan, ASAP.''

"What's up?''

LeFevre opted to forgo the elevator and headed for the stairs. His reply was thrown back over his shoulder as he descended, taking steps two at a time. "Warren Mott's been murdered. On West Forty-fifth Street in Hell's Kitchen.''

Chief of Detectives Gus Lieberman appeared while Dante was still getting the Crime Scene overview. From the alley, Joe and Onofrio had moved to watch as Crime Scene Unit techs dusted Warren Mott's three-year-old Ford Escort, found parked less than fifty feet away.

Lieberman, a bulky, tough-looking customer in his early fifties, had donned the full-dress regalia of his rank in anticipation of a media spectacle. As he ambled toward Joe's position, the job personnel in the street gave him wide berth.

He greeted Onofrio with a curt nod. "Sal.'' Then he turned to the Major Case commander. "So what've you two been able to piece together, Joey?''

There was too much history shared here for any formality to be enforced. Fifteen years ago, Lieberman was Dante's first squad commander once Joe earned the gold detective's shield. Just last year, when the previous Major Case commander moved on to direct the Manhattan and Bronx section of Central Robbery, Lieberman moved Dante in to fill the vacancy. Dante had a long history of being unafraid to act on good instincts . . . and to speak his mind. The latter trait had gotten him into his share of hot water, but Dante's free-spirit approach helped power him through investigations in much the same fashion as a plumbing snake churns through a clogged sewer. His methods weren't necessarily pretty, but they got results.

Dante nodded back toward the mouth of the alley. "Couple of unexplained curiosities. Other than the obvious questions, like what he was doing here, we're curious to know why there are fresh scratches on his face. Looks like he tussled with his killer before he was shot."

"Stripped of his ID and even his shoes," Onofrio added. "No way to tell how much other shit the perp took, and what was stolen by the bums. We been all through a pile'a crap we found at the back of the alley. Didn't turn a thing."

"We've got Ballistics and the labs sending over everybody they can shake loose," Dante said. "As soon as I can break free here, I want to get a look at his calendar and his office; see if they shed any light."

The chief patted his pockets in search of his cigarettes as he nodded his approval. "Nasty mess here, Joey. Media an' the mayor's office are gonna be watchin' us like hawks on this one. Let's give it everything we've got."

Onofrio excused himself to confer with a batch of uniforms who'd just returned from searching the nearby riverfront for the murder weapon. Lieberman glanced down in that direction, saw that the barriers at that end of the block had created a zone of relative tranquillity, and started toward it. With Dante at his side, Gus held the lit butt cupped in one hand and walked with his brow knit deep in thought.

"Wouldn't be surprised if you were actually glad to see the son of a bitch dead, Joey. Man put your pecker through the wringer."

"Let's just say I'm not grief-stricken, boss. Then again, you and I'd be out of work if we only investigated the homicides of *nice* guys. Sure I hated him. That ain't the point, right?"

Gus stopped and turned to confront his old friend directly.

"All the job hates a shoofly, Joey. I got a bad feeling about this."

"Maybe we'll get lucky, Gus. Me? I'm hoping it was something as simple as a whore, tried to rip him off."

Lieberman took a drag and held it a moment, shaking his head.

"Wouldn't it be nice if all'a life was that easy, huh? Mott was a cool character, secretive, but I can't see him as a man who cruised whoors in the wee hours. It don't feel right. He was the sorta customer who liked to get his teeth inta somethin' and shake it like a pit bull. My gut feelin' tells me he was onto something."

"And you think that *something* might be dirt on a cop."

"Findin' it was his job, wasn't it?"

Dante grimaced. "I'm still hoping it was a whore. If not, if we don't turn something quick, we're gonna end up with a list of suspects a thousand cops long. I speak from experience, Gus. It wasn't just finding dirt that Mott was into. He enjoyed pissing on people."

What Gus hated most about trying to launch this type of investigation were the political games and the media spectacle. He'd barely had time to huddle up with Dante before Commissioner Tony Mintoff's arrival demanded his presence at the command post. It rankled, having to wear the hats of both public-relations smoothie and competent, high-level field commander. The duties involved in wearing the former never failed to interfere with the function of wearing the latter. For the past half hour, Gus had been in conference with Mintoff, the mayor, the chief of Department, and Inspectional Services Chief Jerry Liljedahl. By the time they'd delivered their first statement to the press and Gus was finished with those silly white gloves, Warren Mott's body was already removed to the morgue.

He found Dante sitting with one thigh hoisted up onto the rear fender of an MTN radio car, sharing coffee from his thermos with Sergeant Beasley "Jumbo" Richardson. Gus thought maybe it was the grim set of his jaw; both seemed to pick up on his mood. He and Jumbo, Dante's second-in-command, hadn't yet crossed paths that morning and now exchanged nods. Joe filled a Styrofoam cup and handed it over.

"Want to get it off your chest?" Dante asked.

Gus scowled, set the coffee on the roof of the car, and dug into his jacket pocket for cigarettes. "You guys ain't gonna like it."

"Try us."

"That square-head Jerry Liljedahl is throwin' a real roadblock in front of us."

Both detectives bristled. Because they were the people who policed the police, a real animosity existed between shooflies and the rank and file. The mere mention of Chief Liljedahl's name had nearly as much impact as the fact that he was trying to make trouble.

"How's that?" Dante growled.

"Jerry's pointed out to our esteemed PC that he can't possibly grant the investigation access to IAD files. He wants a couple of his people included on board."

Alongside Dante, Richardson groaned and shook his massive head. Until recently, the big black detective was grossly overweight. After putting himself on a medically supervised liquid diet, he'd lost 110 pounds. The diet ended over a year ago, but a program of rigorous exercise and continued self-discipline was keeping the lost weight lost. Still, the nickname "Jumbo" was sticking.

"I hope you told him t' go fuck himself. We ain't interested in startin' no witch-hunt. This is s'posed t' be a homicide investigation."

"The concerns are legitimate," Gus countered. "The IAD opens its files, and a lot of internal investigations are potentially compromised."

"Investigations into the activities' a *potentially* innocent cops," Jumbo muttered.

Gus tapped a new pack of butts against the back of his hand and glanced skyward. "All of that potential aside, Beasley. I'm demanding you guys be granted *direct* access to anything Warren Mott worked on over the past two years. Jerry wants his people to *screen* that fucking material first, to work as liaisons with Detective Bureau."

"Liaisons?" Richardson wasn't amused. "It's fuckin' obstruction, Gus. If it ain't some pro did him out here over the price of a fuckin' blow job, then all our prime suspects is gonna be in them files."

Lieberman tore the foil wrapper and shook a Carlton from the pack. Once he got it lit, it felt good and calming to take a deep lungful of smoke. After pushing it out with a whoosh, he shook his head. "I hope not. The mayor and PC hope it, too. Still, we gotta consider all the possibilities, an' that's where it gets sticky. Warren Mott was technically assigned to my command, but Liljedahl considered him to've been under Inspectional Service's overall umbrella. We got us a classic tug-o'-war goin', and that puts the ball in Tony Mintoff's court. When I left him just now, he was straddlin' the fucking ditch."

"That's good," Dante muttered. "The stiff isn't even on ice yet and already it begins."

"You're gonna see whatever you gotta see, Joey. You get the ball rollin' and leave the head bangin' t' me." Gus paused, took another deep drag on his butt, and waved it at the scene around them. "So what's new here?"

As if on cue, Rusty Heckman, one of Dante's five Major Case Unit detectives, trotted over to interrupt. "Got something you might want to take a look at, Joe." He paused to acknowledge the chief's presence before continuing. "I was going over the notes made by the guys who dusted the cap's car. They found the passenger-side door slightly open. Struck me as sort of funny, so I took a closer look.''

Rusty, generally regarded as the unit clown, with his bushy Bozo hair and quick wit, was all business. A recovered alcoholic, he'd been seen as all washed up before Dante took him aboard last autumn. He had a history of doing brilliant work before a nasty divorce pushed him over the brink. Dante, made aware of Heckman's progress in rehab by Rusty's current partner, Don Grover, decided to take a chance. It was a decision he didn't regret.

"What do you mean by slightly open?" Dante pressed. "It was actually ajar?"

Heckman shook his head. "Negative. The latch mechanism was only half-engaged. The door was closed but not shut tight. I doubt Mott was driving it that way. On these streets, with a chuck hole every eight feet, it would have made an awful racket.''

The foursome ambled across the street to where Mott's car stood parked at the curb. On reaching it, Rusty tugged the passenger-side latch handle and swung the door wide.

"What do you see?" he asked.

"The inside of a car," Jumbo replied. "I don't get it.''

The interior of the Escort was covered with a film of print-dusting powder, making a nasty mess. Rusty ignored it to reach in and grab hold of the automatic seat belt. It rested in the fully open position, just like the one on the driver's side. There was a cool confidence in Heckman's tone as he explained.

"Normally, this would roll forward in its track when I open the door. It would stay that way until the car was started. Sal Onofrio's people say they only touched the driver's-side door. The Crime Scene guys missed the significance of the belt position when they found it like this, but luckily logged it in their notes anyway.''

Dante was standing a step back and regarding the

proceedings with his arms folded, one fist pressed to his lips. "He had a passenger."

"That's right," Rusty replied.

"How could you know that for sure?" Gus demanded.

"The seat's got a pressure switch in it," Heckman explained. "Connected to a simple electronic memory. If a passenger's just departed the vehicle, the belt stays in the forward position until the ignition is switched on again. Once the car is started, the belt retracts, same as on the driver's side. The position of the belt, *before* we opened the door, tells us that Mott didn't arrive here alone. He had a passenger with him. Crime Scene and Homicide guys think it was a hooker. The shoes they found might support it."

"Shoes?" Lieberman glanced back and forth between Dante and Rusty. "What and where?"

Dante gestured up the block toward Twelfth Avenue. "A pair of sling-backs. Gold glitter. One with a broken heel. Found the busted one in the gutter and the other half of the pair about twenty feet further along . . . out in the street like it was maybe tossed off by someone in a hurry." He shrugged. "Then again, they could belong to some Jersey girl who threw them out the window after a night on the town."

Gus nodded toward the interior of the car. "What about latents?"

Rusty shook his head. "Dozens. Sorting them is gonna be a real needle-and-haystack proposition."

"Anything else?" Gus included all of them in this question. It was Dante who answered.

"Not a helluva lot. Organized search of this and the immediate three-square-block area didn't turn the weapon. Crime Scene unit didn't recover so much as a shell casing."

"Real problem with that alley," Richardson added. "Outta the weather like that, it's a prime spot for vags t' call home. Been at least one livin' there recently. Lab

29

boys ain't holdin' out much hope that they'll get any useful hair or fiber evidence.''

"What about witnesses?" Gus asked. "Any luck there?"

"Pickings are slim in a neighborhood like this," Joe replied. "Especially with the time of death put at five or six hours after midnight. Right now, Midtown North is getting assistance from both the Tenth and Midtown South. We've got a dozen uniforms dividing the Coles Directory between them and making calls to every phone listed in these three square blocks. Don Grover's got another dozen guys organized and conducting a door-to-door.''

"What about the hookers? How you doin' there?''

"Nothing so far. People from all three station houses have rounded up as many stragglers as they could find at this late hour. Monday's never been much of a night, and they only managed a handful. I've got Mel Busby up on Fiftieth, questioning one bunch, and Guy Napier down on Thirty-ninth, doing the same. Napier just called in. To hear him tell it, they've found him a real pack of sweethearts. Combined, he says they're high enough to keep the Hindenburg flying. Of course, none of them saw shit.''

"Tell me who or what else you need.''

Dante thought a moment before shaking his head. "It's too early yet. Let me get some of this sorted out. Sal and his Night Watch guys just left to work with the Task Force day shift on an expanded weapon search. For right now, I can't see what we don't have covered.''

"You said you wanted a look at Mott's calendar.''

"You bet. Calendar, office, whole ball of wax, as soon as we can break free here. Then I want inside his apartment. It was news to me, but until just this past December, Mott was married . . . to Sal Onofrio's sister-in-law. Since the divorce, he'd been batching it out in Bay Ridge.''

"Chief Lieberman?''

The voice came from twenty feet off, over Lieber-man's left shoulder. He turned to see Inspectional Services Chief Jerry Liljedahl approaching. He had two plainclothes people in his wake, one male and one female, each with shields hanging from the breast pockets of their jackets.

"Yeah, Jerry." A weariness invaded Lieberman's tone, and he could see Liljedahl's jaw muscles struggle to tighten at the informality. Gus really loathed this man, peer or not. Gray-fleshed and seedy in his appearance, from those turned-in arches to the liberal use of hair cream and a light dusting of dandruff across the shoulders of his jacket, Jerome Liljedahl seemed the antithesis of a man in command. Gus had no idea how a top cop could expect respect from his subordinates when he appeared to have no *self*-respect.

"Meet Detective Sergeant Glenmore and Detective Captain LeFevre." Jerry pronounced the captain's name *la fever* instead of *le fave*, and Gus watched LeFevre wince. "They're the people I'm assigning as liaisons between IAD and your investigation."

The captain appeared to Lieberman to be like any one of the several hundred middle-aged detectives working those cushy ten-to-six shifts for Inspectional Services. In a word, with his bland face and overfed softness, he was forgettable. But Sergeant Glenmore was another story altogether. At maybe five foot ten or eleven, she was as tall as he was, with good facial bones and long, gracefully proportioned lines. She carried herself with the spring of an athlete in her step. There was scar tissue on the knuckles of both hands. Her entire bearing had an air of cool challenge to it.

"I wasn't aware that there'd been a resolution on that issue," Gus replied. He tried to keep his tone measured, allowing only the slightest edge of displeasure to leak into it.

Liljedahl's return smile could have frozen brine. "There is a meeting scheduled for after lunch, this af-

31

ternoon. In the commissioner's office. Meanwhile, until the matter *is* resolved, your investigation team will no doubt be wanting access to Captain Mott's office and files. I'm insisting that Captain La-Fever and Sergeant Glenmore be present . . . to review all materials for sensitive information not pertinent to this case.''

''And *they're* gonna decide that?''

''For the moment, yes.''

Gus glared. ''We'll see.'' He then turned to introduce the men standing behind him. With the interruption, Heckman had hurried off. ''This is my Major Case Unit whip, Lieutenant Joe Dante; and his second, Sergeant Beasley Richardson. You are correct on that one count, Jerry. They *will* be needing access to Mott's office. The sooner the better.''

''You're a fighter.'' Dante addressed this out-of-the-blue comment to Glenmore, and Gus watched curiously as Joe got a cool, level stare in return. Those eyes of hers would have had an unsettling effect on anyone less confident. Blue eyes, but bright with the hot fire of challenge in them. Gus also noticed that the way she wore her dirty-blond hair, cut short and off her face, accentuated a hard-edged but undeniable beauty. Beside her, Liljedahl scowled.

''What the hell is that supposed to mean, Lieutenant?''

LeFevre, to that point a detached observer, spoke for the first time. ''Perhaps what Lieutenant Dante is referring to is the fact that Sergeant Glenmore won the bronze medal in her weight division at the National Tae Kwon Do Championships last year. *SPRING 3100* is profiling the sergeant in the upcoming issue.''

SPRING 3100 was the glossy magazine published by the Department's Public Information Division. Gus watched Dante as he shook his head.

''Afraid I wasn't aware of that,'' Dante admitted. ''I was looking at the sergeant's hands and the way she carries herself.''

Gus was amused to see Liljedahl's eyes narrow and sneak a peek down at the hands. Meanwhile, from the subject of this scrutiny came an unmistakable twinkle in eyes that had not lost contact with Dante's for an instant.

"Jae Doo Roh's dojo on Sixth Avenue and Waverly Place, isn't it, Lieutenant? I worked as Warren Mott's assistant five years ago; during his investigation into the deaths of that prostitute and your ex-partner."

The pronouncement seemed to catch Dante by surprise. "Do tell," he murmured.

"Oh, there's not all that much to tell, Lieutenant. Once Warren got warmed to an investigation, he worked it until he was satisfied he had *everything*. As I recall, your karate instructor told him that you were good. *Very* good. High praise when it comes from a man who's a seventh-degree black belt. Don't I also recall that you've never been rated? That you refuse to enter belt competitions?"

Dante nodded his compliments. "You've got a good memory, Sarge. Any rocks Mott *didn't* look under?"

"If you *are* that good, why won't you compete?"

"I'm forty-two years old, Sergeant. And then there's the possibility that Jae Roh was pulling Mott's leg. Maybe I'm *not* that good."

Glenmore dismissed the suggestion with a smirk. "Nice try. I can read the same things in you that you can read in me."

Ten-thirteen homicide or not, Deb Glenmore still had another matter to clear up. Dante and that bruiser of a partner of his had huddled up with another guy from their unit who looked like Bozo the Clown. While they were busy, she intended to take full advantage of the respite. This was Tuesday; she'd been promised some answers and had yet to see any. It wasn't often that a unit detective got the Bureau chief's ear, and while she had it, she was going to chew it. She saw her opening

33

and went for it while Rick LeFevre shifted nervously from foot to foot beside her.

"It's better than a week and a half since I filed my report on those two jerks up in the Four-Four, sir. So far, I haven't heard word of any action being taken. I'd like to know what gives."

"What *gives*, Sergeant?"

"That's correct, sir. I'd like to hear it from your mouth. I'd like to know why it hasn't been passed along to the Bronx district attorney."

Liljedahl's face colored slightly, and Glenmore knew she'd pushed him dangerously close to the edge. Up close, the man was even less impressive than he seemed from a distance. Scuffed shoes. A spot on his tie where someone, probably his wife, had tried to remove a stain, without much success. He didn't actually smell bad, but he looked like maybe he might.

"It's your job to investigate allegations made against police personnel, Sergeant. It's my job to determine how the Department proceeds on the results of such investigations. Both of those officers are family men, with wives and kids. A prosecution based on hearsay allegations made by prostitutes and drug addicts could destroy lives. We have to proceed very carefully here."

"Destroy lives, sir? What about Maria Guitterrez? What's her life worth? More, or less, than a rapist's who just happens to be a police officer?" Glenmore was hot with rage. "Those *police officers* held a gun to her head and told her that she either performed fellatio on them or they'd dump her in a vacant lot with a bullet between her eyes."

"Hearsay, Sergeant. The cuts and bruises in those pictures could just as well be the result of some accident."

Glenmore pulled up short like she'd been kicked in the gut. "Ac-accident?" She stammered it, momentarily at a loss for more words. Taking a deep breath, she seemed to look inward for a moment. Then she shook her head. "It wasn't any accident, sir. You couldn't have read my report and still be able to say that. She was *raped*. We've got other pictures: of teeth marks around Maria Guitterrez's nipples. We have semen smears. If a court forced those two men to submit to DNA printing, you'd have absolute proof of *who* raped her. I personally interviewed twenty-seven of their female arrests. Timothy Ahern told three of my interviews that if they'd suck him off and do a decent job of it, they'd live to tell their *bastard kids* about it. Two more claim that they were pinned to the backseat of a cruiser while Escobedo and Ahern first beat and then raped them. I've talked with Maria on three different occasions, for a total of six hours. Her story never changes. It's consistent with the other stories I've heard."

As she hammered home the graphic nature of the alleged sexual abuses, Deb watched Chief Liljedahl visibly lose his grasp on the high ground. His face and ears had gone red. Still, she didn't let up. "Accident? The public is supposed to be able to *trust* those guys, sir. Three nights a week I teach a self-defense class to women who are terrified of being mugged or raped. I've felt firsthand the sort of trust they place in me. A uniform and job tin don't give any man the right to go on a job-condoned rampage of sexual terror through the South Bronx."

"Hold it right *there*, Sergeant!" the chief snapped. "This Department condones no such thing."

"Then turn the results of my investigation over to the Bronx DA, sir. To *hell* with those men and their families. Raping helpless women on the backseats of squad cars does more than destroy a few lives. It makes a mockery of the entire social contract."

With a quick about-face, Glenmore reached to grab LeFevre's sleeve and left Chief Liljedahl standing rooted.

"C'mon, Ricky. Let's make ourselves useful."

FOUR

The early morning rush of construction workers had finally subsided, and Fouad Hanafi was catching his breath. Ever since the ground breaking for the new luxury hi-rise going up diagonally across Ninth Avenue, Fouad and his brother Rifaat had experienced a business boom to match their wildest dreams. Every morning, from the moment they unlocked the street door of the Qadr Deli/Grocery, a horde of foulmouthed, roughneck heathens descended on them to purchase nearly fifty gallons of coffee and often as many as five hundred donuts. To meet this demand, increased coffee-making capacity had been purchased. Fouad and Rifaat worked like galley slaves. Two weeks ago, to keep up with the lunch-hour demand for sandwiches and sodas, they'd done the once unthinkable and hired a young black man to deliver take-out orders to the construction site. Since coming to New York City eight years ago with little more than the shirts on their backs and a small inheritance, the two brothers had worked tirelessly to breathe life into their little shop. Today, they were taking in so much cash that the register could no longer hold a morning's proceeds. Every half hour between six and nine, it was Rifaat's duty to empty most of the drawer cash into a paper sack kept out of sight beneath the front counter.

Fouad had just removed his apron in exchange for a new one and splashed water into his face when he heard the bell installed above the street door, alerting him of customer traffic. Rifaat was minding the register. Fouad, having just completed the last of five resupply trips downstairs to the basement, now leaned exhausted against a stack of soda cases in the cramped back room. At thirty-seven, Fouad still had a bit of his youth left, but lately, those trips up and down the cellar stairs left him more exhausted than in past years. Perhaps it was true what the surgeon general said about the effect of cigarettes. Fouad smoked two packs of Camel straights a day. For months, the younger Rifaat had been suggesting he switch to a filtered variety. Fouad resisted, feeling that smoking cigarettes with filters was a sign of weakness. Today, after that fifth trip downstairs, with sweat stinging his eyes and breath coming in labored gasps, he was rethinking his position.

". . . your mutherfuckin' *head* off! *Now!*"

Suddenly the blood ran cold in Fouad's veins. The morning's exhaustion disappeared. From where he stood, he could see out into the store and into a convex mirror mounted high in the corner above the cold case to the rear. Within that mirror he watched the distorted image of his brother behind the counter and a black man directly in front of it. Rifaat had his hands in the air, and the black man, dressed in a yellow warm-up suit with black stripes, had a gun.

"I said *now!*" This time it was not so much a shout as a low, guttural snarl.

Fouad was already on the move as Rifaat's left hand lowered slowly to push the release button on the register. The drawer could be heard to spring with its neat little electronic chirp.

"Okay, *asshole!* Back off!" In the mirror, Fouad saw the black man reach over the counter and into the

37

drawer. Rifaat eased away and up against the cigarette rack behind him. Both of his hands were in the air again. Fouad knew there was no possibility of his brother getting to the .357 Ruger revolver secreted inside the soda-straw box.

As he lifted the cut-down twelve-gauge from the stock shelf, Fouad's head swam. He realized that he was holding his breath, and hot shame set the skin of his face and scalp burning with a sudden, flushed itch. So many times, he had rehearsed the possibility of this event in his mind. And countless more times, he'd relived the horror of masked Christian Lebanese Militiamen murdering his defenseless father in their Beirut dry goods emporium. Then, there had been no shotgun close at hand; no weapon of any kind. Not now. Fouad Hanafi forced himself to expel and then draw air back into his lungs.

Four years ago, a Syrian cabbie from Astoria, moonlighting as a gunsmith, had cut back the barrel of the Ithaca Model 37 Ultralight to a point just forward of the forestock. When he fitted it with a pistol grip, the result was a weapon similar to those factory versions of the Model 37 manufactured for law-enforcement use. Slowly, Fouad wrapped the fingers of his right hand around the butt grip, never losing sight of both his brother and the man who held Rifaat immobilized at gunpoint. In his heart, he prayed that Allah give him courage.

It didn't make much sense to Dewayne Muncie that there should be so little cash stuffed beneath the bill-and-coin tray of the Arab's cash register drawer. Everybody always parked the big bills out of sight under there, leaving the tray with just enough cash to make change. Dewayne had been watching the Qadr Deli/Grocery on and off for over a week. He'd seen those hordes of hardhat assholes from Brooklyn and Jersey wander in there every morning to top up their thermos jugs and to indulge the old sweet tooth. Hundreds of them, each and every one making heavy union bread. Infuriated, Dewayne brought the flat of his free hand down hard on the counter, stared intensely into the Arab's eyes, and lifted the pistol with new, menacing focus. It was a nice piece: a Colt .38 Detective Special with two-inch barrel and some heft to it. It made him feel good to see this sorry fucker jump at the noise of his hand and then swallow hard, that gun barrel staring him in the face.

"You-all fuckin' with me? Fuckin' with me 'cuz you don't *believe* I'd shoot your sorry ass?" And with calculated cool, Dewayne eased back the hammer. That Colt blue was as hot in his hand as the heart of flame.

Something he caught in the Arab's eyes caused Muncie to glance back over his shoulder. The glance spotted movement, up high to the rear of the store. He forced his attention to ferret it out. There. Up above a wire rack stuffed with potato chips and pretzels, backlit by fluorescent beer signs . . . in a goddammed *mirror*!

But from where? It was close to two minutes now since Dewayne had entered the store. More like five since he'd smoked that last pipeload in the doorway around the corner. The crack still stoked a full-tilt glow between his ears, his heart was big in his chest, and the world was puny in comparison to the power in his young, fine-tuned being. Weren't *no* motherfucker going to step between him and his prize. There was more bread here. Lots more. There *had* to be. And because he had the gun on the skinny dude with the big, fear-filled eyes, it was his. That was the law of the jungle.

"Wha . . . ?" his lips demanded, unbidden from within. His eyes left the mirror, abandoning the search for the lurking interloper's whereabouts to check on his prey. The Arab's eyes weren't so big anymore. Dewayne had a cocked gun on him. It made no sense.

What made less sense was the image confronting him when he turned his attention back to the mirror. This time, it wasn't *in* the mirror anymore. The same fuck-

39

ing Arab who stood behind the counter with his hands raised, stood in the middle of the main aisle, fifteen feet away. Same pants. Same shirt. Same apron. Same receding hairline and short-cropped black beard.

Back in the Alawite sector of East Beirut, people often remarked that the Hanafi brothers, two years apart in actual age, looked enough alike to be identical twins. Dewayne Muncie had spent a week watching *outside* the Qadr Deli/Grocery, mistakenly assuming from a distance that the two brothers were one man. Now, while one brother had his hands raised, the other had a shortened Ithaca .12-gauge pointed at Dewayne's gut.

Muncie never saw the muzzle flash, nor did he hear the deafening report when the identical Arab with the shotgun pulled the trigger. Before anything could register with his crack-charged senses, the sledgehammer effect of twenty-seven no. 4 buckshot pellets, impacting with his lower abdomen over a ten-inch area, propelled him backwards through the air like a discarded rag doll. Neither did Dewayne hear the shattering of glass as he crashed into the front counter's horizontal deli case.

As Dante and Richardson pulled up to park in the tow-away zone out front of the Police Athletic League building on East Twelfth Street, the car carrying the IAD captain and his karate champ partner appeared in the rearview. For Dante, the whole idea of being forced to cooperate with them chafed. Before he could get the direction of this investigation established, get it rolling, it was already loaded up with deadweight. For the moment, his efforts would be aimed at establishing turf control as much as at solving a homicide. Ground given now might be ground lost forever. Like it or not, the chief of these shoofly clowns had forced him into a hardball position.

Warren Mott's third-floor office turned out to be something less than he expected, but looks often deceived. Tucked away in a backwater like this, well off the beaten tracks of precinct, Borough South, and Detective Bureau life, it exuded a certain free-reign atmosphere. Scuffed linoleum. The requisite metal desk: chipped and gray. Antique wooden desk chair. Low bank of three double-drawer file cabinets. Mr. Coffee. Every surface neat as a pin. Dante got the feeling that Mott relished working in this sterile atmosphere. It was the lair of a predatory beast, unencumbered by warmth or sentiment. Joe also got the feeling that Mott had been trying to hide something behind this monklike facade. Fanatic neatness, like extra starch in a dress shirt, was presumed to bespeak virtue. In his gut, Joe thought this office screamed overcompensation. But for what? What was it that Mott was trying to hide?

Accompanied by Sergeant Glenmore, Richardson went to work on the desk while Dante and LeFevre hit the files. Jumbo located the dead man's desk calendar only to discover that each and every entry was made in an abbreviated personal code.

"Lotta help this is gonna be," he muttered in disgust. "Last entry here is for three-thirty, yesterday afternoon. Says: *Call bk D.L.D.* Ain't a thing for any time last night."

With LeFevre having positioned himself before the files in a manner aimed at blocking Dante's view, the lieutenant elected to let him have it. This wasn't yet the moment to wage war. Instead he used the time to call Operations, report his position, and check for updates from the members of his squad. As he cradled the receiver, he nodded toward the Rolodex.

"Check the listings under 'D.' Any with the first initials D.L.?"

LeFevre glanced up. "Help the sergeant with that, will you, Deb?"

Jumbo already had the card file in his hands and was starting to paw through it. Glenmore couldn't very well tear it away from him, so she took pains to remind him of Chief Liljedahl's ground rules.

"We haven't screened that file for sensitive materials yet, Sergeant. I believe that was the agreement."

The big black man turned, hackles suddenly up. "Sensitive materials? Gimme a fuckin' break here. Not even a shoofly'd be shit-for-brains dumb enough t' put the names of people he's investigatin' inta his fuckin' *Rolodex*."

The drawer that Captain LeFevre was inspecting crashed closed as he spun to confront Richardson in red-faced fury. "Give her that goddammed Rolodex, Sergeant!"

Richardson stood his ground. "They're splittin' hairs here, Joey. This here cooperative collaboration's only a few minutes old."

Dante stepped up, took the card file from Richardson's hands, flicked through to the Ds, and located the name of a Detective Dennis L. Donaldson. Removing his pen and notepad from his jacket pocket, he scribbled the name and accompanying phone number. An incredulous LeFevre watched in outrage. When Dante was finished, he handed the Rolodex to Glenmore with a curt nod. He then turned to her boss.

"About those files, Cap. When do you think you and Sergeant Glenmore will've finished inspecting them?"

LeFevre's reply came through tight-clenched teeth. "I'm impounding every scrap of paper in this office, Lieutenant. You don't see *shit* until Chief Liljedahl clears it. And seeing as we're all so shit-for-brains dumb at IAD, that could take some time."

Dante took a step forward, shaking his head. When he spoke, he was standing no more than three feet from LeFevre, addressing him head-on. "It's funny, Cap. I'd think you people would be more eager to see this case wrapped than us cops from the rank and file . . . losing one of your own and all. You're an investigator. You ever try to run an investigation one-legged? If you have, then you know how important that *shit* there could be.

Right now, you're wasting my valuable time. What say we see who can pee higher some other day, huh?''

While LeFevre sputtered and Glenmore played it cucumber-cool, Dante opted for a trip out to Warren Mott's Bay Ridge residence. As they got under way, he reached Gus Lieberman's office by car phone, got the chief's exec, and reported the trouble they were having along lines of inter-Bureau cooperation. Then, with Joe at the wheel and Jumbo lounging in the seat alongside, a brooding silence prevailed as they rode toward the southern tip of Manhattan. It wasn't until they'd reached the Brooklyn-Battery Tunnel that Richardson ventured to break it.

"She's got a certain appeal, though, don't she?"

Dante shot his second a confused glance, and Jumbo hurried to clarify.

"Glenmore. That other moron got hot as a pistol an' she stayed cool as jazz. That's discipline."

"Or disposition," Dante countered. "Hotheads don't make good fighters. They're too headstrong and they make too many crucial mistakes."

"Young for a detective sergeant, wouldn't you say? What? Maybe thirty? Thirty-one?"

"Around there somewhere."

"So you agree."

Dante snorted. "To what?"

"That the woman's got a certain appeal."

Joe let it sit in the air a minute as they emerged into daylight at the Brooklyn end of the tunnel. At the toll booth, he flashed his shield and kept rolling. Bay Ridge, sitting above the Verrazano Narrows at the mouth of New York Harbor, was most quickly accessible by taking the southern leg of the Brooklyn-Queens Expressway to the Gowanus. Late morning traffic was as light as it ever got during the daylight hours, and they made good time. As Dante eased into the speed lane of the highway and accelerated past a lumbering semi rig, he returned to the topic at hand.

"A certain appeal. That's subtle, buddy. Would you mind telling me why you, your wife, and every other friend I've got, inside and out of the job, seems so concerned about my marital status lately? That *is* what we're talking about here. Right?"

"C'mon, Joey. I seen the way you two eyeballed each other back at the crime scene. And I couldn't help but notice how good-lookin' she is, for a white woman."

Dante chuckled as he shook his head. "You remember what the man said about shitting where you eat?"

"Never seemed t' bother you before."

"Maybe my tastes have changed. You know, older-wiser."

Richardson got a good chuckle of his own.

Within ten minutes of pulling onto the Gowanus, they'd left it at the approach to the Verrazano Bridge and were headed northwest toward Ridge Boulevard. Eventually, they left Ridge to go west toward the water on Seventy-fourth and started watching the addresses.

"There it is."

They'd traveled less than a block, and Jumbo pointed at a redbrick two-family just ahead on his side of the street. The neighborhood was one of those solid Brooklyn bastions of mixed white- and blue-collar middle class. Each house was evenly spaced from its neighbor at intervals of twenty feet. All were in excellent repair. The cars parked on the street in the middle of this, a workday, were mostly late model. Tiny postage-stamp lawns and gardens were lovingly tended.

As the detectives slowed to pull to the curb and park, the door of a van sitting directly ahead opened. A young Hispanic in coveralls emerged and waved. Dante had asked Operations to send a locksmith once they'd ascertained that no one on the premises had a key to Mott's second-floor flat. The kid approached, toolbox in hand, as Jumbo climbed from the car.

"You Lieutenant Dante?"

"Not in my worst nightmares, amigo. You think you can get us inta that upstairs apartment?"

"No sweat, bro." The kid rubbed the tips of his fingers together, an amused twinkle in his eye. "Name's Ramon. We split fifty-fifty, right?"

"Great," Jumbo growled. "We radio for a locksmith an' they send us a fuckin' comedian."

Dante joined them, leading the way up the drive. From his jacket pocket he extracted the electric garage door opener that the Crime Scene techs had found clipped to the visor of Mott's little Ford. "This help?" he asked the locksmith.

Ramon wiggled his eyebrows. "Good thinking, bro. Most of these places, a lotta people screw the real front door shut an' use the garage entrance t' get upstairs. You leave your house all day, go to work, it makes it harder on the burglars."

The lieutenant gave him a deferential tilt of the head. "We're on a schedule. Whatever'll take the least amount of time."

"You don't know how lucky it is you got this," the kid told them. Taking aim, he depressed the transmit button. "Used to be they only made 'em with a couple frequencies. One'd open half the doors on the block. Now they got digital. Eight switches, eight codes, each with two positions." From behind the door came the clunk of the mechanism kicking in. The door started up with a high-pitched squeal. "Needs grease," Ramon advised. "Hope the inside door ain't a Medeco." He'd squatted next to his toolbox and retrieved a set of picks. "Them locks is a pain in my ass. Anything else, Ramon'll get you dudes inside it, five minutes tops. It's all in the amounta practice. I put in at least three hours a week."

Once the big double door was raised, all three men proceeded slowly into the garage interior.

"Uh oh. It don't look like you need Ramon, bro."

Dead ahead, the door leading to a set of stairs at the

back of the garage hung ajar, its lockset bent at a crazy angle in splintered wood. All around them, a dozen or so cardboard cartons, emblazoned with the logo of a major national mover, lay overturned. The contents, mostly clothing and household goods, were strewn over the painted concrete floor.

Dante held up a cautioning hand and gestured back toward the driveway. "Right back out the way we came in, gents. Beasley, let's get the Crime Scene Unit out here and call Gus." He turned to the locksmith. "Sorry, Ramon. Maybe next time. You got something I'm s'posed to sign?"

Melissa Busby, the Major Case Unit's lone female detective, had spent the last three hours talking to hookers. It was the sort of activity that would give most women new and unusual insight into the nature of commerce, but Melissa wasn't most women. In her twelve years on the job, six spent as a uniformed patrol officer and six more working plainclothes, she'd already seen many of the more unusual things money could buy. Perhaps she was jaded, but few of them surprised her now. Tastes in New York ran the gamut.

Less than an hour elapsed between the moment the compact, high-energy detective received Dante's urgent summons and the time she arrived at his Bay Ridge location. Pumping any further information from a dozen irritable, stoned-out streetwalkers was the sort of thankless task she was glad to leave to the Midtown North squad. The scene she had found in Brooklyn was something of a surprise. Expecting a few detectives and maybe a lab van, she found a multitude of uniformed and plainclothes cops crowding the street in front of the dead IAD man's residence. There were radio cars, unmarked units from the Six-Eight, a couple cars from the Brooklyn/Staten Island Robbery Squad, and a Crime Scene Unit station wagon, all jamming the street. Down the block, she spotted Chief Lieberman's driver leaning against the front fender of the chief's gleaming black Buick.

Beside Melissa in the front seat, her partner, Guy Napier, was also digesting the scene. As she parked, she shot him a glance.

"What say, Boy Wonder? Any hunches?"

"Robbery Squad's here. That says something."

Napier was the newest addition to the squad, a rangy, easygoing kid of only twenty-seven who'd compiled an impressive record of taking initiative as a uniformed officer. Five years after graduating City College and the Police Academy simultaneously, he was awarded the Gold Shield and recruited by Lieutenant Dante into Major Case. Melissa figured their ages to be the only likely reason he'd been assigned as her partner. Eight years Napier's elder, she'd been the baby of the unit before his arrival.

Together, the partners emerged from their car and started into the crowd, heads moving in search of the boss. The taller Napier spotted Dante emerging from the open garage and nudged Melissa with an elbow. As they approached him, the lieutenant stood with his head bent in conversation with Chief Lieberman.

"Could be just the break we're lookin' for, Joey."

"We'll see," Dante replied. His tone suggested doubt. "Right now, we need to talk about the wild hair Chief Liljedahl's got up his butt. That asshole LeFevre's impounded all of Mott's papers and carted them off to Poplar Street. You've got to get this monkey off my back, Gus. I can't have free access to those files, I can't conduct this investigation. It's that simple."

"That's gonna be resolved this afternoon," Lieberman promised. "By tonight, you'll either have a free hand t' look at *all* that stuff or I'm pullin' Major Case off it. I won't ask anyone in my command t' work with his hands tied."

Dante was turning to acknowledge the arrival of his two squad detectives when his attention was diverted by something behind them. Melissa watched as his eyes left her face to go wide, nostrils suddenly flaring. God, he was a hunk. Even today, a year and a half after he'd taken command of the unit, he could still get her blood racing.

"Speak of the devil," he murmured.

Melissa and Napier turned and saw ISB Chief Liljedahl striding purposefully toward them up the drive. Without acknowledgment of the others gathered, he pulled up short before Lieberman.

"Gus. Speak to you a minute?"

Lieberman turned to Dante. "You all set here?"

"Covered, boss. Buy me some room to move."

Liljedahl reacted with an irritated glare and turned without further word. As Chief Lieberman followed, Melissa thought he looked tired. In the two years since he was named the new Detective Bureau boss, his face had aged five.

"What's going on here, Lou?" Napier asked.

Melissa couldn't help but smile slightly. Guy, ever conscious of the generation gap between him and his boss, was the only one on the unit who wouldn't call Dante by his first name.

"Good question." Dante jerked a thumb toward the house. "Mott moved in here last year after a divorce. Somebody broke in, probably either last night or this morning. Forced the upstairs front door. Inside of the place is a mess. Right now, we're trying to figure out what he might've been after. TV and all the other usual stuff is intact, but the place is really torn—"

"Joey. We've got somethin'."

It was Richardson, hurrying down a flight of stairs at the back of the garage. He'd been fat when Melissa first met him, but even then he'd been as agile and light on his feet as Jackie Gleason. With her own stocky girl-athlete's build and the daily battle she waged with her bathroom scale, she saw him as a shining example of what willpower could achieve.

48

Dante lifted the tape barricading the garage opening and ushered Melissa under it while addressing Napier. "Keep an eye on things, will you, Guy?" Just inside, two lab people and a photographer were busy dusting and shooting the disarray of the garage interior. "Nobody gets inside without my personal okay."

The upstairs flat into which Richardson led the way seemed, at least to Melissa's sensibilities, to be the sort of place a cop might keep on the side as a splash pad. She wondered if, before his divorce, Mott had done just that. The furniture and decorations were volume-merchandiser variety, each room bought as a package and utterly devoid of personality. Right now, half a dozen Crime Scene guys were dusting it and looking none too thrilled about being called out so soon after the earlier summoning to midtown.

Jumbo wasted no time moving them down a short hall, past a bath done in a hideous mint green, to the bedroom. On entering, they found Rusty Heckman standing alongside a gray laminate captain's bed, looking smug.

"It must be good," Dante commented. "He's still got feathers stuck in his teeth."

"The deeper we got, the less it looked like a burglary," Rusty announced. "More like some sort of search. Most every place where something might be hidden is torn apart. Cereal boxes dumped with coffee and flour on the kitchen floor. Outlet covers removed. Clothes all torn off their hangers, and pockets turned inside out. It seems sorta surprising, with such an enthusiastic going-over, that anyone managed to miss this."

With a flourish, he produced a large plastic evidence bag. It contained a nine-by-thirteen manila envelope with the Internal Affairs Division return address printed in one corner. From where she stood, Melissa could see it contained something between a quarter and a half inch thick. She could not see what.

"And?" Dante prodded.

Heckman lifted his eyebrows. "It's full of cash, Joe. We didn't want to count it till the lab has a look, but it looks like all big bills. Fifties and hundreds. Thousands of dollars worth. One of the lab guys noticed that the wall-to-wall was loose from the tacking strip in this corner . . . between the closet and the head of the bed. He found a rectangle of the padding cut away underneath and this envelope tucked in its place."

For the moment, Dante appeared lost in thought. Melissa used the break to voice the obvious. "I guess there isn't much doubt that's what our man was after."

Heckman shrugged. "He did a damn thorough job to have missed it, but that *is* a nifty hiding place. None of the rest of the carpet is loose, anywhere in the house, so maybe he just didn't think of looking there."

"Get it to the lab pronto," Dante told him. "And have them put a rush on it. You got anything else?"

"Else?"

The boss smiled and clapped him on the shoulder before turning to leave. As he started back downstairs, Richardson hurried ahead and Melissa trailed behind.

"We haven't talked about what you and the Boy Wonder got from the hookers, Mel. Anything?"

"Not much," she admitted. "One of them mentioned that a showboat pimp named Honey Lucas was running his string of four transvestites up and down that block of Forty-fifth and the one between Ninth and Tenth. I gather Mondays aren't much of a night in the trade. Most of the usual players stay home, but Lucas is breaking in a new talent."

At the landing, Dante stopped and met her eye to eye on the step above. In a reaction of pure self-consciousness, she reached to pull the left side of her short-cut red hair back behind one ear. The fringe of it framed a freckled face that might have been called cute on a high school cheerleader. After studying it for years in a makeup mirror, Melissa long ago concluded that it made her appear too open and vulnerable for this kind of work. It was more than once that she'd thanked God for giving her the sort of bloodhound brain a specialist unit like Major Case found invaluable. At thirty-five, while most of her Academy class were still pounding a beat, Melissa Busby had carved out a niche for herself in an elite squad. She worked for a man respected by many, including Chief Lieberman, as the best investigator in the entire job. That man respected her abilities. Then there was the fact that he was so easy on her single woman's eyes. That didn't hurt either.

"You think this Lucas might be a lead." It wasn't a question.

Melissa nodded. "It's a crap shoot, Joe. Lucas has been put in the vicinity. The time sounds right. There couldn't have been much traffic. One of his people may have tried to pull something cute and found she had a tiger by the tail . . . uh, *he*. At the very least, one of them may have seen something. We should check it out."

Dante grinned. "Why do I feel like the prince in a macabre Cinderella? Complete with golden slipper. So how are you and Guy working out?"

"He's a puppy dog. You throw the ball, he fetches and then slobbers all over it while he brings it back." She got a twinkle in her eye. "I hear he's hung like a stud horse."

Dante feigned shock. "You *hear*?"

"From Shirley Reed. Personnel Orders Section. She and our Boy Wonder went through the Academy together. To hear her tell it, she fucked half the guys in that class."

Chuckling, Dante turned to continue his trip downstairs while shaking his head. "I want you to run with this pimp angle, Mel. And go easy on our boy, huh? He just got engaged."

* * *

It had been a busy morning on the Ballistics Unit. First there was the murder of the IAD captain. Then some crack-crazed stickup artist gets one kidney blown halfway to Hoboken. On the first, they had one homicide bullet and no gun. On the second: one cut-down shotgun, no registration; one .38-caliber Colt Detective Special revolver, medium-frame snub-nose, fired twice, one bullet. There was evidence that the stickup guy's gun had discharged once during the attempt. A matter of some curiosity was where the other shot was fired. Meanwhile, there was a rush on the bullet recovered from the 10-13 homicide. Once the Medical Examiner dug the slug out of the dead man's lung, Major Case Detective Donald Grover had hurried it downtown from Thirtieth to Twentieth Street.

The tall, gangly Grover took a lot of ribbing from the rest of his squad about a prodigious appetite and the fact that he never seemed to gain an ounce. His partner, Rusty Heckman, contended that Grover had a hollow leg. This morning, Don had missed breakfast, and right now his stomach was rumbling like the LL train. All morning, he'd asked a lot of repetitious questions of an irritated citizenry and gotten a lot of nothing in reply. Right now, he was feeling a bit irritable himself. Still, there was a rush on. To ensure that rush meant *rush*, he'd hustled his fanny down here with that slug and now loomed persistently over a senior lab tech's shoulder. Food was going to have to wait, and for Grover, there was no greater sacrifice he could make for the job. The lab guy was working with that bullet now.

Little more than a misshappen chunk of lead, the thing wasn't much to look at. Clamped there beneath the lens of the microscope, it was already determined to be a .32-caliber hollow-point, and that at least was a start. For the past hour, the tech had culled slug profiles of .32 bullets recovered from crimes dating back as far as five years. Each bullet, once fired, bears the signature striations of a particular gun barrel's rifling grooves. One by one, he'd tried to match them with the sample there to the left in his viewer.

The tech straightened, backing away from the microscope and wincing as he massaged the small of his back with both hands.

"No, huh?" There wasn't much hope in the way Grover asked it.

The tech shook his head. "And that's the last of them."

Grover grunted, already tasting lunch in the now foreseeable future. "It's always a shot in the dark anyway. Appreciate the hustle, pal." He retrieved his jacket from the back of a chair and started to slip into it.

"Holy *shit*, boss! You got to *see* this!!"

It came from across the lab, where another technician was busy poring over computer printouts. She was looking up now, the glow of triumph on her face.

Coming off his stool, the senior man was still trying to stretch some of the kinks out as he moved to her position.

"See what?"

"You aren't going to believe this." The lady technician was leaning forward, one stockinged foot wedged beneath her on her stool as her boss arrived. "The gun they took off the stickup guy, Dewayne Muncie? The make, model, and serial number match the gun registered to Detective Captain Warren Mott. It's the dead IAD guy's *service revolver*."

Across the room, Grover's jaw literally dropped. Any notion of lunch went out the window as he rushed over. "You're *sure* of that?"

"Of course I'm sure. Look for yourself. Here."

Grover ignored the invitation, his face suddenly lighting up. "Pay dirt. Holy Jesus. You just made the Major Case Christmas list, sweetheart."

FIVE

In Captain Bob Talbot's eyes, the police commissioner was some unique piece of work. When the captain watched his boss in action, he saw a cocky little bastard with a mean streak a mile wide and the confidence of King Kong strolling Broadway. Big Tony, as the Palace Guard at One Police Plaza referred to Anton Mintoff behind his back, was a five-foot-inch, 160-pound confluence of absolute confidence, hyperactivity, and an expertly managed short man's rage. Only a fool crossed him, and nobody was crossing him right now.

The atmosphere in the PC's office was colder than any air-conditioning could effect. Chief Jerry Liljedahl, Talbot's former boss when the PC's exec ran the Action Desk at Internal Affairs, sat in one of two leather-upholstered armchairs facing Mintoff. Beside him, Gus Lieberman sat with the jacket of his dress uniform unbuttoned, a cigarette going between yellow-stained fingers, and the knot of his necktie tugged loose. Talbot stood behind them, leaning against the wall alongside the inner sanctum door. From there, he was afforded a good vantage of the players and the proceeding. Liljedahl and Lieberman had both stated their cases. Mintoff appeared to take a moment to digest the pros and cons of each. Then that head, with its heavy-lidded eyes and jet, slicked-back hair, turned in Jerry Lilje-dahl's direction.

"You'll grant that this Department, wanting to avoid accusations of foot dragging from any quarter, wants this investigation brought to a successful resolution as quickly as possible?"

Chief Liljedahl seemed nonplussed by the question's implications. "Within reason, absolutely."

From where he sat, Lieberman leaned forward to butt his smoke in the ashtray on the corner of Mintoff's desk. "Within reason?" he grumbled. "What the fuck does that *mean*, Jerry? You restrict my investigation's access to Mott's files, you leave it hog-tied. The smart money says our killer is somewhere in those files."

Liljedahl's gaze flickered only momentarily to his ad-versary's face. Talbot, always concerned with how the Department brass looked in the public eye, was no fan of his former boss's slovenly appearance. Still, he re-spected him. Dandruff and stained tie aside, the man was a tough nut. After a brief pause to gather his thoughts, the chief addressed the seat of power directly.

"I'm still standing by the objections I just raised, Tony. Those files are sacrosanct. Sensitive ongoing in-vestigations could be compromised. Anyone familiar with Lieutenant Dante's past history knows that he's anything but sympathetic to IAD and its concerns."

Lieberman's face clouded with sudden fury. "Is *that* what the issue is here? *Dante?*"

Liljedahl's eyes never left Mintoff's face. "Let my people conduct this investigation and we won't have this problem."

Cool and deliberate, Mintoff shook his head. "An-swer Chief Lieberman's question, Jerry."

"Fine. Joe Dante had reason to hate Warren Mott's guts. The captain campaigned hard to see him stripped of his shield. You want me to open Mott's files to a man like that? He's a loose cannon. A maverick."

"He's got the best fucking street sense and instincts in the job," Lieberman retorted. "Maverick my ass. There ain't a man in your command who could hold—"

"Gentlemen!"

Talbot watched with amusement as all eyes shot forward toward the source of this rebuke. Once he had their attention, Tony Mintoff leaned forward to plant his elbows on the desk blotter and slowly fold his hands.

"Granted, Lieutenant Dante has something of a reputation, but today he's commanding officer of the Major Case Unit. I personally endorsed his assignment after reviewing the lieutenant's record. Frankly, I was and still am impressed with both his arrest record and his selfless dedication to the job. This morning I assigned the Mott homicide to Detective Bureau jurisdiction. Just now, I asked you to state your cases. I've listened to them. So far, they haven't changed the way this office chooses to act." He paused to look directly at Chief Liljedahl. "Internal Affairs will grant Lieutenant Dante and his investigation unrestricted access to Captain Mott's case files. Thank you for your input."

Lieberman stood, buttoning his jacket, while Jerry Liljedahl sat riveted. As he watched them, Talbot was distracted when the intercom line buzzed on the phone in his adjoining office. The exec slid reluctantly into the anteroom to pick up. A moment later, he leaned around the doorjamb, the receiver extended in his right hand.

"Chief Lieberman. Detective Grover. Dante's in transit somewhere and he says it's urgent."

Talbot handed the phone over and opened the door to the big outer office with its half dozen desks and din of activity. Once Liljedahl gathered himself, he drifted out behind the captain, through the outer office and into the hall beyond. It was clear from the way the big boss delivered his last remarks that they were parting remarks. Whether or not Jerry agreed with Mintoff's decision, he knew enough not to argue further.

"You're angry," Talbot observed. Ten years the chief's junior, Bob had known Liljedahl for the better part of his own tenure within the job. Unlike most job personnel, Talbot hailed from a background of prep schools, Ivy League colleges, money, and political clout. Groomed since childhood for a life of public service, Talbot had chosen the police department. The choice was unorthodox for a man of his ilk and therefore attention-getting. In another year, Talbot would have his twenty in. His plan was to use his job experience as a springboard into politics. Being an astute political animal himself, Jerry Liljedahl was among the first to spot the gleam of bigger ambitions in Bob's eyes. It was fifteen years since the chief, then a deputy inspector, gave a young uniformed patrolman from the Dignitary Protection Detail his first desk job at Internal Affairs.

"Angry? I just got pissed on. You ask me, that son of a bitch Dante should be a prime suspect. Instead, that Jew bastard's got him heading up what should be my investigation."

Talbot sat hard on a wave of disgust and gave the slovenly chief a sly wink. "Careful what you say in these hallowed halls, Jerry. They've got ears. Besides, Tony's Maltese, not Jewish."

Liljedahl scowled and forged on toward the elevator lobby.

"You know who the fuck I mean. Keep an ear out, Bob. I've got no idea what Warren was up to last night, and I sure as hell don't know what that money they found means. One thing I sure as *shit* know is that Warren Mott wasn't dirty. Something stinks. If I can get to the bottom of it before Lieberman, I intend to rub his face in it."

Once Rusty Heckman was sent off to hand-carry that envelope full of cash to the lab, Dante left Mel Busby in charge of wrapping up the Bay Ridge scene. He and

Richardson had an early afternoon appointment at the morgue. With a deli sandwich clutched in one hand, Jumbo took his turn at the wheel.

"Which way you leanin', Joey? You think Mott was dirty?"

The midday traffic was light enough to allow speed. The Plymouth was rolling north on the FDR at a good clip. Dante, slumped in the passenger seat, was staring out the window to where a tug towed an oil barge up the placid waters of the East River. He was grateful for the moment's respite and a chance to organize his thoughts.

"*Think* he was dirty? I don't know what the fuck I think, Beasley. I *want* him to be dirty, sure. He was always on some self-righteous moral crusade, while out on the street, we're trying to hold the city together with chewing gum and mirrors. Everybody upstairs, from the mayor down, is hoping we can justify calling this prick a martyr."

"I don't hold no grudge like you do, Joey, but that cash he had squirreled was as green as the stuff in my wallet. Somethin' stinks here. Mott was hidin' it, and somebody didn't want us t' find it."

At Twenty-fifth Street, Jumbo eased it onto the exit ramp and eventually caught First Avenue going north. Five short blocks past Bellevue Hospital, the Medical Examiner's office and the City Morgue are wedged up next to University Hospital at the corner of Thirtieth Street. Richardson eased it to the curb out front, taking advantage of the yellow tow-away zone. He flipped the vehicle ID onto the dash and followed Dante toward the street-level entrance.

Rocky Conklin, Assistant ME, was awaiting their arrival in his basement office. Rocky even *looked* like a forensic pathologist. He was tall and slightly stoop-shouldered, and his skin had that eerie translucence associated with lock-aways in mental wards, regulars on the late night club circuit, and others who never saw the light of day.

"Okay, Dante. What kept you? I thought this was supposed to be a *rush* job."

Conklin had one of his ever-present Bering Imperials going, with three more visible in the breast pocket of his lab coat. Dante reflected that a visit to the morgue just wouldn't be the same without the heavy odor of cigar smoke fouling the air.

"So much to do, so little time, Rock. What've you got for us?"

The pathologist picked a manila folder up off his desk and was suddenly all business. "You saw the scratches on his face?"

Both detectives nodded.

"They look to be made by fingernails. The lab guys at the scene took scrapings from beneath Mott's nails, on the chance that he gave a little of what he got. Cause of death? Just what it looks like. One slug in the right lung. Asphyxiation caused by an accumulation of his own blood. No other contusions or evidence of trauma. I'm putting the time of death at approximately five A.M."

Before either cop could react to this information with the usual barrage of questions, Dante's beeper went off. The call-back number in the display window was that of Gus Lieberman's direct-access line.

"Use your phone, Rock?"

Conklin nodded toward the instrument on his desk. "Knock yourself out, Lieutenant." And then an amused grin spread across his face. He glanced to Richardson and shook his head. "*Lieutenant* Joe Dante. I still can't get over that. Time was when I figured a man this hard-headed was doomed to retire at no higher than detective first-class."

As he dialed, Dante looked up. "You can be replaced, Doc. A pathologist of preference is a lot like having a favorite butcher. You ought to be thinking about all the business I've thrown your way. Scorn is all the gratitude I get?''

The glow of Conklin's lighter reflected amusement in his eyes as he relit that well-chewed butt. ''Little does he know, Sergeant. There's folks here *still* talk about them three bikers he and Scruggs shipped us, five or so years back. Set all kinds of records. Most tattoos in one delivery. Highest gross weight. Most—''

''Spare me, Doc,'' Jumbo pleaded.

On the phone, Dante listened a lot and spoke only a few words before hanging up and reaching for his file copy of Conklin's report. ''Big happenings,'' he announced. ''Ballistics just got a match on a gun used this morning in a robbery. Thanks for the hustle, Rock. Hate to break up the party.''

''What gun?'' Jumbo demanded. He had to race to keep up as Dante surged out into the corridor and summoned the elevator.

''Mott's. His service revolver. They took it off some bad guy who got himself shot trying to take off a deli.''

''They know how he come by it?''

Dante stepped forward as the elevator doors opened. ''That, my friend, is the sixty-four-thousand-dollar question. Conklin puts Mott's TOD at around five. Nine-one-one got the deli owner's call at nine thirty-five. The store's on the corner of Fiftieth and Ninth. We're playing with four and a half hours and half a mile, separating the first scene from the second.''

Jumbo still had the keys. He took the helm and pushed the gum ball out onto the roof as they got under way. The way Dante got the story from Gus, the perp shot in the holdup had been stabilized in the Emergency Room at St. Clare's Hospital on West Fifty-second. He was hanging on by a thread in Intensive Care. A squad detective from Midtown North was awaiting their arrival. He'd update them. Traffic, midtown at midday, was the usual snarl of delivery trucks parked helter-skelter and smaller vehicles attempting to crawl between them. Richardson avoided the narrower west-bound streets, opting instead to thread his way along the double yellow line down the middle of Thirty-fourth. Twice he narrowly missed jaywalkers.

Sergeant Dave Brickman was an old hand with better than thirty years on the job. He and Dante had crossed paths at least a dozen times over the years. When the Major Case detectives stepped off the elevator on the third floor, Brickman was there to greet them and lead the way toward ICU.

"You twose are quick," the gravel-voiced cop complimented. "C of D just called t' say youse was on the way."

"What've you got here, Dave?" Dante pressed.

Around them, hospital personnel moved at a sedate, controlled pace which belied the urgency of individual circumstances in the surrounding rooms. Like most New York hospitals, St. Clare's had undergone a series of transitions, each calculated to enhance the quality of its interior atmosphere. Gone were the drab colors and utilitarian but uninspired furniture of decades past. Today, everything was pastel-bright and cheery.

"Only had a sec t' glance over his sheet, but it looks like this guy's a real fuckin' mutt, Joe."

They passed through a pair of double doors to approach the ICU's Nursing Station. There, Brickman retrieved the contents of an open manila envelope from a chair and quickly shuffled them.

"Let's see," he growled. "Dewayne Muncie. Born: Bronx, New York, June 6, 1972. That'd make him just nineteen. His sheet reads like a veteran low-level street crud's. First arrest for burglary at fourteen. Caught breakin' an' enterin' a TV repair shop onna Grand Concourse. Probation. More'a the same shit, 'bout every six months, until two years ago. Nineteen eighty-nine was the year Muncie discovered Manhattan. 'Tween May of eighty-nine and now, he was arrested five times for crack sales, once for suspicion in a mugging, twice for possession of stolen property. Only two convictions: one on a sales rap; one for sellin' hot watches on'a street. Not exactly Billy the Kid stuff, right? Probation an' probation. Dewayne Muncie never done a day's hard time."

"God bless the criminal justice system," Jumbo murmured. "Nice kid like that; why put him in jail?"

Brickman grinned. "The only place they'll be puttin' this mutt is in the *ground*. Docs say there ain't a snowball's chance in hell he'll live the night. Tried t' take down the wrong A-rabs an' got himself a bellyful of genuine Islamic Jee-hod. The shot from that twelve-gauge took out a kidney, most'a his liver, an' his gall bladder. Looks like the little fuck was on a homicidal rampage an' ran smack up against a piece'a his own. Blood tests they run on him put his cocaine toxicity levels through the fuckin' roof."

Dante shook his head in wonder. "He was working all alone? Mott's was the only gun he had when he walked in the deli door?"

Brickman nodded emphatically. "One brother was behind the counter an' the other was inna back room. It looks like this is our lucky day, fellas. You get your cop killer an' we got one less creep crawlin' our beat."

"Maybe," Dante allowed. As always, there was caution in it.

"Maybe?" Brickman pointed down the hall to a doorway guarded by a baby-faced lady cop. "Fucker's gaspin' his last on a respirator down there. Go take a look."

Dante shook his head. "I'm not afraid he might be pulled back from the brink of death, Dave. Where's my *murder* weapon? The thirty-two-caliber gun used to kill Warren Mott? For all we know right now, Mott *gave* Muncie his service weapon as a token of his esteem."

"So Muncie threw the other gun inta the fuckin' river," Brickman countered. "He liked Mott's better.

More firepower. With its two-inch barrel, maybe he liked the way it was easier t' conceal.''

"That's one possibility."

"How many more you need?"

Dante shoved his hands deep into his pockets and started to pace. "I need a motive, Dave. We were thinking maybe it was a whore. If it wasn't, then I need to know why an Internal Affairs cop was out meeting this street rat at five in the morning. Right now, it doesn't make sense. We know Mott drove to the scene with someone else in the passenger seat of his car. Muncie? Or were Mott and his mystery passenger coming out there to *meet* Muncie? I don't see how it makes sense that a guy as cautious as Mott would drive a street-smart thug into deepest, darkest Hell's Kitchen just to have a chat.''

"*And* be fool enough t' get outta the car," Jumbo added.

Brickman was thinking hard. "It *would* make sense if his passenger was a whoor, huh? Some streetwalker workin' in cahoots with Muncie to rip off unsuspectin' johns. Maybe she snatched Mott's wallet, pitched it out the window t' Dewayne, an' Mott gave chase."

The idea gave Dante pause. He turned it over quickly in his mind, looking for holes. "That's not bad, Dave. It's a street punk's prank, all right. It's not likely that either a hooker or Muncie would know Mott was a cop. But even if you're right, we're still missing half the equation. We still need that murder weapon. For starters, I'm going to order a residue scrape of Muncie's hands; see if he's recently pulled a trigger."

Brickman shook his head. "Dead end there, I'm afraid. His gun discharged when the Arab shot him. Between that and the powder from the shotgun, there's gonna be residue all over him *and* his clothes."

By the time she and Guy Napier finally dragged themselves back to the Major Case offices late that afternoon, Melissa Busby was dead on her feet. She was also sick of Harlem jive. Honey Lucas, the elusive Harlem pimp, was nowhere to be found. Mid-afternoon, the partners got a call from Dante, telling them about Dewayne Muncie and emphasizing the urgency of their current assignment. To no avail, they'd tracked down the address of Lucas's crib on 118th Street and Adam Clayton Powell, obtained the necessary warrant to enter when he failed to answer his bell or phone. They found the place cleared out.

Collapsed into one of the armchairs pulled up around the table in the unit's squad room, Melissa was assembled with the rest of the squad, her shoes off and stockinged feet up, crossed at the ankles. "Two hours of nothing but bullshit," she concluded. "To hear it from the neighbors, nobody saw Lucas, talked to him, or knows where he went. One thing's pretty certain, judging from the way he left the place: The man's taken his string and gone to ground."

Dante, taking notes on a yellow pad, paused to nod his thanks.

"Let's get out an APB, tonight. First thing tomorrow, I want you to assemble what you can by way of pictures and profiles. Get them out to every station house north of Central Park . . . including the Bronx. In my experience, a pimp's a creature of habit. He doesn't break routine like that without motivation. Honey Lucas is a priority. Right now, we want very much to talk with him; find out what spooked him so bad."

Rusty Heckman was next. He and Grover had spent the afternoon at the police lab, overseeing progress made on the evidence gathered at the Mott homicide, Mott burglary, and Muncie stickup scenes. When Dante glanced to him, Heckman opened the folder set before him on the table.

"Funny thing about that money. The lab found Mott's latents on three of the bills, but none on either the inside or outside of the envelope."

"Three out of how many, and what denominations?" Dante asked.

Rusty didn't need to refer to the file. "Three out of three hundred twenty-six. Fifty-two C notes, two dozen Franklins, and the rest, twenties. Total of eleven thousand four hundred bucks. The bills with the latents on them were all hundreds."

For the squad clown, Heckman had one hell of a memory.

"Only eleven thou," Richardson marveled. "It looked like more'n that, didn't it?"

"What else, Rusty?" Dante asked.

"Not much. Hair and fiber ended up with so many bits and pieces of crap from the homicide scene that they've thrown up their hands. Right now, they're busy giving it all classifications and feeding it into their computer. We get a suspect, they'll try and get us a match. The scrapings from under Mott's nails were all his own skin. The canvassing efforts, both phone and foot, weren't much help either. There's a Fire Department Investigation Unit headquartered just up the street from the scene, and we thought we might get lucky there. No soap. They didn't get a call all night, and their unit commander went home with the flu."

"Anything new on Muncie?"

Grover fielded that one. "Midtown South located the room he was renting in a flophouse off Times Square. Real dive, I guess. It's above one of those theaters playing kung fu flicks round the clock. That guy Brickman you talked to is circulating his picture, trying to get some idea of who his connections were and maybe reconstruct his movements earlier this morning."

Dante looked ready to wrap it as he tossed his pad onto the table and yawned. "Okay, people. They can't ask for any more than we gave today. Tomorrow we hit it all over again. Mel, Guy, I guess it's back uptown. Let's find this son of a bitch Lucas. Rusty, Don, I want to organize a more detailed search of the area for the murder weapon. Maybe we're ready to call out the Harbor Unit and have 'em put Scuba into the river. Use your imaginations. I'll talk to Gus about getting you some legwork assistance from the rookie ranks.''

Twenty minutes later, as Melissa Busby left the unit, she found Napier waiting for an elevator.

''Any problem with the APB request?'' she asked.

He shook his head. ''Nope. Within the hour, they'll be looking for Lucas in five states. If we need it expanded, all we've got to do is call.''

Whether he was the unit greenhorn or not, Melissa was beginning to enjoy her partnership with this guy. He knew how to get things done quickly and efficiently. On the street, he was careful whose toes he stepped on but wasn't afraid to exert authority when it was called for. Uptown, she'd felt safe in his company.

''You look as whipped as I feel, big guy. What's on tap tonight? You going out or staying in?''

Napier rolled his eyes. ''Out with who?''

''Whom.''

''Kiss mine.''

''Maybe some other time. What's the deal? You're in the prime of life. You just got *engaged*.''

''To a workaholic. They've got some sort of big push on, with the sales force flying in from all over hell and gone. Jenny's one of the buyers who's supposed to make a presentation. At least that's the story *this* week. If it's not one thing, it's another.''

The elevator came, and both stepped in. It was crowded, the trip downstairs taking forever. When they finally stepped out into the lobby, Melissa glanced at her watch.

''Listen,'' she said. ''I don't feel like fighting rush-hour traffic in the state I'm in, and it isn't gonna get much better for another hour yet. How about you and me wander over to the Seaport? I'll buy you a drink.''

* * *

Dante finally got a chance to ride the two floors upstairs to see Gus once his people had cleared out for
the day. He found the chief's outer office crowded with
stringers from the News Bureau down on the mezzanine
floor. The girl reporter from AP was the first of them
to spot his arrival and hurry over. It was pretty obvious
from the way the rest of them turned to descend on him
like a school of piranha that their presence here had
something to do with the Mott case.

"The chief's playing his cards pretty close to the vest
on this Muncie thing," the woman blurted. "What do
you think, Lieutenant?"

Dante beamed her a big smile. "There's no question
this budget crunch hurts. Not just us in the public service sector, but every citizen of the City of New York.
I happen to know that Chief Lieberman feels exactly
the same way."

Dante moved as he spoke. By the time he'd finished
making his statement, he was at Lieberman's inner-
office door. Opening it, he walked in without knocking
or looking back. The besieged chief was staring out the
window overlooking the East River, his jacket hung on
the coat tree to his left. Without prying his eyes from
the view, he reached to rub the flat of one big hand over
his face. Slowly, he shook his head.

"Somebody in the mayor's office got wind of the
Muncie connection. Right now, City Hall's crowing
about what a wonderfully efficient PD this city's got.
Dead cop at dawn, an' before the sun sets, we got our
perp on a respirator, all signed an' sealed."

"Sorta jumping to conclusions, aren't they?"

Gus glanced Dante's way. "We got a green administration just gettin' settled in, Joey. This mayor's yet to
suffer the first crisis of his incumbency, an' he's scared
shitless that it's gonna blindside him. Somethin' real
nasty, like corruption inside the cops. You an' me are
havin' trouble believing that the perp would just surface
like that. The mayor? He thinks it's a fuckin' *miracle*."

"I guess you've gotten an earful from Mintoff, huh?"

"At least. He hates t' hear it from Hizzonner's stooges that we've made a major case. He comes t' me to find out why that is, an' I've gotta tell him the truth. My man on the front line don't believe we *have* made the case. Not yet, anyway. Then he asks me why, and I can't answer with any specifics. Feed me some now, Joey."

Dante tried to bring the jumble of that day's revelations into focus. "Granted, Dewayne Muncie had Warren Mott's gun. But look at the condition Mott was in when MTN found him. His gun was missing, but so were his ID and his shoes. A free gun, lying on the pavement next to a dead man, would be hard for a street punk to pass up. It's nice we've recovered it, but it isn't the *murder* weapon. The residue tests of Mott's hands tell us that he fired a gun in the very recent past. At whom? And did he *hit* them? The gun we recovered was discharged during the robbery. We've established that. But when MTN found it in that Ninth Avenue deli, there were *two* empty shells in the chamber."

"What you're tellin' me is that you got a whole lotta inconclusives. You know as well as I do that they ain't enough t' get Mintoff an' the mayor's office off my back."

Dante wasn't abandoning his position. "What about motivation, Gus? Dave Brickman at MTN has a nifty little theory about Muncie and a prostitute maybe working as a team. What we don't have yet is evidence that Mott ever patronized pros in the past. Then there's the problem of a nickel-and-dime street punk making all those career leaps in one day. First he murders and robs a cop. Then he turns around four hours later to commit an armed robbery. Who did he think he was? John Dillinger?"

Gus sighed. "I know the old saw about zebras an' stripes, just like you do, Joey. But the medical workup says he was higher'n a kite on crack. Them crazies are capable of thinkin' they're just about anybody.''

''I'll shoot when all my ducks are in a row and look like they're going to *stay* there, Gus. I want to find that pimp. I want a look at Mott's case files. And then there's his ex-wife. If anybody suspects anything about our victim's propensity for getting his ashes hauled on the highways and byways, it would be her. I'm too good a cop to let you pull the plug on this now. Let me finish it.''

Lieberman swung slowly around in his chair to confront Dante head-on. Curiosity was evident in his eyes. ''You hated Warren Mott's guts, Joey. I *know* how good a cop you are, and I ain't gonna tell you how t' do your job unless I think you're way outta line. What I ain't gettin' is *why*. You could be out there with them news hounds right now, baskin' in the glory of a job well done.''

''But it isn't well done. Somebody killed a cop, Gus. Maybe not a cop I liked, but a cop who did the job he was asked to do. Nobody deserves to die like that. We owe it to him to turn over every rock we can find. Dewayne Muncie isn't gonna last the night, let alone confess to anything. Until we turn this theoretical whore or find the gun with Muncie's prints on it, this case stays open.''

A grin of admiration spread slowly from the older cop's mouth to those heavy jowls. In rising to the top, the chief had accumulated a lot of weapons in his arsenal along the way. One of them was an absolute confidence in his judgment of character.

''The door's open tomorrow mornin', over the bridge on Poplar Street. I can't guarantee them two IAD people you pissed off are gonna be *glad* t' see you. And in light of recent developments, I can't say how long that door'll *stay* open. If I were you, I'd get there first thing an' make the best possible use of my time.''

SIX

When Joe Dante was a kid, the locals described this strip of Ocean Parkway running through Bensonhurst as the Beverly Hills of Brooklyn. Growing up in Brooklyn, a place he'd thought of as the center of the universe, Joe hadn't been able to imagine that anywhere in California could be this nice. It made him smile to think that now. He'd since been to Beverly Hills.

Like Dante, Theresa Caravaglia Mott was raised five miles farther east in Canarsie, but both had strong ties to Bensonhurst. Joe had two uncles on his mother's side and an aunt on his father's who were from here and nearby Bath Beach. Bath Beach was bent-nose territory: Mafiosa. Here, with the exception of that upper-crust section of Ocean Parkway, the area was solid, working-class paisan; a people welded together by the familiar social order of the Old World. Two, three generations after arriving here, a fierce pride prevented them from leaping into the melting pot of a less predictable New World.

The Personnel Bureau had tracked Theresa Mott to the same residence she'd occupied before her divorce. Her Avenue N address was located three houses off the parkway. The redbrick single-family, with its glassed-in veranda and neatly groomed front yard, was typical of the area. There were two cars parked in the drive, a late-model Cadillac Seville with its rear bumper hanging almost into the street, and an older Toyota Camry. The Camry was parked deeper in, between the subject house and the one next door. Dante eased his Plymouth to the curb, shut it down, and took a deep breath. A half hour ago, just as he was leaving the Big Building, the skies had opened in earnest. By the time he emerged on this end of the Brooklyn-Battery Tunnel, the deluge had broken off. Bits of blue sky were now visible between departing clouds. As the late day sun poured through, there was a rain-cleansed tinge to the air.

Joe climbed out to approach the house, already knowing what it would look like inside. Some things never changed. His own mother, God bless her, insisted to this day on protecting the fabric of her living room sofa and chairs with clear vinyl coverings. The new generation didn't do that so much anymore, but the furniture styles often remained the same. Some of the trendies were going with a lot of beige leather and chrome, but that would be a bit fast-lane for the sort of woman Warren Mott would marry. The dead captain wasn't Italian, but the house would still be Bensonhurst. The basement would be fitted out like a social club lounge, complete with elaborate bar, sound system, little café tables and chairs. Every basement on this block would embrace some variation on that same theme. One would have a jukebox; another, an Hawaiian motif. That was Bensonhurst.

"Yes?" Spoken softly. Joe was stunned by the beauty of the woman who answered the front door. She wasn't tall, at maybe a touch under five and a half feet, but her brother-in-law Sal Onofrio hadn't reported on her development so enthusiastically out of pure family pride. Those loose-fitting gray slacks nipped in at a tiny waist. The dignified white blouse, also loose, couldn't hide the way she'd blossomed from the waist up. But most striking was her face. Framed by short-cut black hair, its beauty was pale and precisely sculpted. There was warmth there in full, pouting lips, and mystery in dark, unreadable eyes.

"Theresa Mott? I'm Lieutenant Dante. NYPD. I know this isn't the best of times, but could I have a few minutes?"

"*Joey* Dante?" It wasn't from her, but came as an excited squeal from somewhere within the house. Theresa Mott turned, the confusion evident on her face, as her sister Viki Onofrio came rushing forward. "Holy Mother, it *is*!"

The contrast between the sisters was marked. Theresa embodied a delicate, classic beauty. Viki was overwrought. The elder sister was ten or fifteen pounds too heavy, her designer jeans a size too tight. Perched precariously on a pair of open-backed heels, she minced rather than walked. Masses of hair were tortured and teased into a nightmare of lacquered submission. Where Theresa wore little makeup and no jewelry, her sister's entire image was contrived of such stuff.

"Victoria," Dante greeted her. "Long time, no see."

"No *shit*. Damn, Sallie told me you was some sorta muckie-muck downtown now. So what's this? You come callin' t' ask Terry about that asshole ex-husband of hers?"

Theresa turned, sudden anger flashing in her eyes. "Viki, *please*. The man is dead. He's the father of my daughter."

Viki flashed her a big, tight-lipped smile. "Oh, right. I forgot. Now that he's dead, we gotta sanctify his memory for little Bonnie's sake. Come on in, Joey. Damn, you still look good enough t' eat. What's your secret? You work out or somethin'?"

Ignoring her, Dante turned to the lady of the house. "I'm sorry to barge in here like this. It'll only take a few minutes. You understand that when something like this happens, we've got to cover all the bases.''

Theresa Mott forced a smile. When she spoke, her voice came out quiet and subdued again. ''I wasn't a cop's wife for all that long, Lieutenant, but between Warren and Sal, I think I managed to get the picture. You're married?''

''No.''

''Good. I hope you'll keep it that way. Spare some poor woman the grief.''

Viki, who'd started to lead the way into a well-ordered, brightly decorated living room, whirled. ''And just what the hell is *that* s'posed to mean?''

The ground was shifting precariously beneath Dante's feet. The decor in here was nothing like he'd expected. It was contemporary but not harsh. Imaginative. He was surprised by it in the same way he'd been caught off guard by Theresa Mott's beauty and the presence of Viki Onofrio. It was time to take the situation in hand.

''Ladies, please. Can we move ahead here?''

Theresa indicated seats. ''I'm sorry, Lieutenant. I'm afraid that since my divorce, my sister's been put through as much by Warren as I have.''

''You're goddamn right I have. It ain't like Sallie was the one caught him fucking around, but it was Sallie's balls he decided to break over it.'' Viki had left something in a highball tumbler on the coffee table. As she delivered this broadside, she took a huge gulp of it.

''I'm sure that's not my business.'' Dante directed it toward Theresa. ''I came here to ask you about your ex-husband's behavior in the last few months before you split . . . or since. We've got a few things we've uncovered that we're trying to make fit. I don't want to lead you with speculation, so I'll leave the question open-ended. Did you notice anything strange about how he acted?''

''Strange, Lieutenant?'' The woman's tone, to that point measured and cool, now faltered. ''Only if you

73

consider the splash pad he kept in Bay Ridge strange. Or his behavior when I walked in there and caught him screwing his investigative assistant. I'd say that was strange.''

"Don't forget to mention what went down *after* that," Viki piped up. "Don't forget that after you threw his two-timing ass out and filed for divorce, he launched a corruption investigation into Sal and his whole squad.''

Dante, swimming upstream through this torrent, hoped that he'd managed to keep a straight face. "He did *what*?''

Viki looked to him in disbelief. "You don't *know* about this? Warren all but accused Sal and his guys of fucking *extortion*. It was *crazy*. He finally had to give it up when he couldn't prove a goddamn thing. It was like he got so pissed off at our whole family that he went haywire. Sal never liked his shoofly ass, and when Warren couldn't hurt Terry no more, it was like he tried to get at her by hurting me.''

The existence of such an investigation was news. As Dante shifted to the discovery made in Mott's bedroom, he made a mental note. Once he got to Poplar Street tomorrow morning, he could check into it further. "Your ex-husband's apartment was broken into early this morning, Mrs. Mott. You wouldn't know anything about that, would you?''

Theresa bristled. "Are you implying that I had something to do with it?''

Joe smiled, trying to put her at ease. "I'm not implying anything. The intruder appeared to be searching for something. I'm curious to know if you have any suspicions . . . about what that something might be.''

Poise recovered, Theresa turned thoughtful. "No, Lieutenant. I can't imagine what. It was rare, even when we were married, that Warren would talk to me about the job. I have to admit that until I discovered the apartment and then the affair, I never paid much attention to where he went and what he did in the course of his work.''

''He was making all his support payments on time?''

''The first of every month. I believe he genuinely loved our daughter, just like I believe that in his own twisted perception, he even loved me.''

''Did you ever have money troubles, outside the usual ones?''

''Is that any business of yours, Lieutenant?''

Dante nodded. ''We've subpoenaed the captain's financial records, Mrs. Mott. I ask because you've got a different perspective than a sheet of numbers can provide.''

''Fair enough. I teach courses in fabric design at Pratt. Warren had his captain's salary. Combined, our incomes were around a hundred thousand a year. We weren't getting rich, but we were doing better than most people. I had some money saved. We used it to make a substantial down payment on this house. The monthly payments were and still are manageable. I don't believe the five hundred dollars a month child support left Warren badly strapped for cash. I've suspected since the divorce that he's always had a nest egg. How big? I don't know.''

''I appreciate your frankness, Mrs. Mott. This next question isn't an easy one to ask, but we need to know. You mentioned an affair. Was that sort of thing a habit of his?''

Theresa seemed to sense something in the question. She swallowed hard and sat up a bit straighter. ''What are you trying to say, Lieutenant?''

''Specifically? I'm asking you about prostitutes, Mrs. Mott. The area where the captain was found this morning is a prime prostitution area. We're trying to determine why he would be there.''

''Prostitutes, Lieutenant?'' Her voice was tight now, without a trace of warmth in it. ''How would I know that? It's not the sort of thing a man confides to his wife."

"Did you have reason to *suspect* it?"

"No. But then, maybe I was being naive. I didn't suspect he was screwing Sergeant Glenmore either. So let me put it this way; if he was in the habit of patronizing prostitutes, I never *caught* him at it. Now *you* tell *me* something. There's an AIDS epidemic on. Should I be concerned?"

Dante was reeling, Deborah Glenmore's name still ringing in his ears, as he searched for an answer to this frightened woman's question. "Concerned? We don't have any specific evidence yet, Mrs. Mott. And you seem to have more information than I do. An affair with his ex-partner is news to me."

"That I'm *sure* about. I caught them at it, Lieutenant. It never occurred to me that there might be *others*."

Imagination now working furiously, Joe shook his head. "Everybody's fair game if he's out there playing the field: gays, junkies, and unfaithful husbands alike." He rose to go. "I'm sorry I had to put you through this. I know this is a trying time."

Theresa stood with him. "For me, the trying time started months ago, Lieutenant." When she offered him her hand, Dante was surprised by the strength of her grip.

"Check this guy out," Viki bubbled. "This is the fucking *hunk* who took me to my junior prom. Goddamn, Joey. How many years it been? More than twenty."

Eager to escape, Dante eased toward the front door. "Twenty-five, Victoria. You see your mom and pop, give 'em my best, huh?"

The fresh air felt good as he pushed through the veranda's storm door to descend the stoop. It was dead in the middle of rush hour now, and while he wasn't eager to join the bumper-to-bumper flow, it would beat spending even another minute in Viki Onofrio's company. In the years since he left Canarsie, Joe had worked hard to become a synthesis of the strong Old World ethic and the newer, more homogenous American society in which he lived. Viki had stayed behind, building walls around herself. Hers wasn't the solution to any of the current problems plaguing their city; it *was* the problem.

The new dimension now added to Mott's sexual profile was probably of no concern to this investigation. All it indicated was a willingness and perhaps an inclination to dabble. Joe couldn't fault the man in his choice of bedmates, and Mott wasn't the first cop to hit the sheets with his partner. What seemed a bit odd was the actual fit. Dante had trouble imagining it.

That Fire Department shift commander who'd gone home last night with the flu was somebody Dante wanted to see. Trained investigators tended to see their worlds differently from other people, and that Fire Unit was headquartered less than a block from the homicide scene. Operations had provided a phone number and Forest Hills, Queens, address. Apparently it *was* a flu bug, and the man was still laid low. A check with the unit revealed the fire captain had called in late in the day to make sure somebody could cover for him. It wasn't looking like he'd be able to return to work for at least another day. Dante was reluctant to wait any longer for the man's input, and here he was, already on the east side of the East River. He caught the Kings Highway going north toward Queens instead of heading back into Manhattan.

Traffic was nasty. It was six o'clock before Joe left Woodhaven Boulevard in Forest Hills and began searching for Sixty-eighth Avenue. Yesterday he'd promised a buddy he'd stop by after work tonight and help with some heavy lifting. Right now, it looked like he might not make it until as late as eight o'clock. At a light, he lifted his cellular handset from the console and punched in the number.

"Hello?" The female voice sounded slightly out of breath.

"Diana? Joe. I know Brennan is expecting a hand from me tonight, but right now, it looks like I'll be a while. You got plans or can it wait a couple hours?"

"Could be your loss, copper." Diana Webster's tone was taunting. "I don't know where he finds them, but if I know you, you'd love to see the one he's got in there now."

"Do I detect a note of sarcasm?"

"From who? Me?"

Brian Brennan was a sculptor who'd made his name and fortune doing slick, high-definition nudes. In recent years, he'd gone off in other directions, returning only when a combination of market demand and mood took him. He'd met his wife, Diana, gritty-voiced lead singer of the rock band Queen of Beasts, when she'd come to work for him as a model during her hungry years. Dante's friendship with the pair dated back to those same years and the investigation of a brutal homicide Brennan had witnessed.

"Maybe you could encourage him to work late?" he wondered.

From down the line, he heard her chuckle. "Chances of that are nearly as fat as your head, copper. If you're going to be late, how about dinner?"

His light turned green as Dante accepted the offer and broke the connection. The address he was searching out proved to belong to the left half of a one-story house. It was a two-family built in a side-by-side configuration and done in the area's predominant mock-Tudor style. Parking on the street was getting tight, so he eased his car into the drive to park bumper to bumper with a late-model Ford Thunderbird. Once he rang the bell, there was a delay of at least two minutes before he heard movement behind the door.

"Yeah?" The muffled voice came through the panel just as he was getting set to ring again.

"Captain Schoenfeld? Lieutenant Dante. PD's Major Case Unit."

When the door heaved open, Dante found himself confronted by a solidly built, heavy-jawed man, maybe forty, with close-cropped graying hair and bloodshot eyes.

"What can I do for you, Lou? Gotta warn you about getting too close. Got one bitch of a nasty bug."

The velour bathrobe and sleep wrinkles creasing Schoenfeld's face told Dante that he was dragging this poor guy out of his sickbed. "I'll try to make it quick."

"Wanna step in?"

Dante gave him another quick once-over, grinned, and shook his head. "Right here's fine, I think. I'd love to share your flu with you, but right now, I'm in the middle of a high-pressure investigation."

"This about that IAD guy? Mott?"

"That's right. How'd you guess?"

Schoenfeld shrugged with effort. "Happened right down the block from my unit, right? I call in this afternoon and the Day Watch tells me you fellas been crawlin' all over the neighborhood. Rough way to go. You know him?"

Dante shook his head. "Only by reputation. You?"

"Naw. Never heard of him till today."

"According to my information, you called it a night sometime around . . . what? One, one-thirty?"

"Somewhere in there. I didn't pay much attention to the exact time. I was feeling like shit. It'll be in the log."

"Not important. What I want to know is what it was like on the street when you left. It's a heavy prostitution block. What kind of night was it? Business brisk, normal for a Monday, or was it unusually slow? And did you see anything that struck you as being out of the ordinary?"

"Like what, Lou? That stretch of midtown in through there is a fucking cesspool. It chokes you at first, but after a while, you get used to the stink. Right after we first moved in there, one of my boys got so upset about what he was seeing that one night a bum pisses on some steps he'd just cleaned and he held a gun to the poor bugger's head. We hadn't stopped him, he'd probably be upstate cooling his heels right now. Wasn't suited to the duty. Not temperamentally, that is."

"Warren Mott was driving a three-year-old Ford Escort. Dark blue."

Again, Schoenfeld shook his head. "I'd like to help you, Lou. But believe me, I went back over it in my mind when I first heard the news and drew a complete blank. If I'd remembered seeing anything strange or offbeat, you would have heard from me already. As it was, I barely made it home here before I puked my guts green. Thought it was something I musta ate, but it's hung on."

"Summer bugs," Dante sympathized. "Sometimes they're the nastiest."

Schoenfeld forced a grin. "I'll get on top of this sucker. One, maybe two more days, and I'm back in the pink."

Dante reached out to shake hands. "Thanks for your time, Cap. Feel better."

"No problem. I'm sorry I can't be more help."

At seven-thirty, sculptor Brian Brennan lifted his arm, pointed to the watch on his wrist, and set down the sketch pad. "If you want to get to work by eight, I guess we'd better wrap it, Linda."

Linda Fletcher, one of those rare creatures who is both curvaceous and extraordinarily long-limbed at the same time, lay sprawled in the buff across the hood and windshield of a new Nissan 300 ZX sports car. The work in progress, to be executed in life size and tentatively titled *Aerodite*, was being commissioned by Nissan, Japan, for the lobby of its corporate headquarters in Tokyo. Brennan, looking every bit the man who enjoys his work, stepped up to hand the model her robe.

"Sorry you can't stay for dinner," he told her. "Your favorite rock star cooks at least as well as she sings."

Linda groaned. "*You're* sorry. I haven't eaten since breakfast, and the smell of whatever's cooking in there is making my stomach growl." As she spoke, she slipped off the car and reached to grab the terry garment from his hand.

Once the model disappeared to dress, Brennan busied himself with tidying his pencils and charcoals. The sketches from today's session were culled, the best hung on the studio wall for future study. He'd just finished pinning them up when he heard the elevator bell. Out beyond the studio, Diana hollered that she'd get it.

Brennan's work and living spaces were immense. Half a decade back, after a divorce from his first wife, he'd purchased this warehouse building on the corner of Twenty-seventh Street and Eleventh Avenue. The ten-thousand-square-foot top floor became his home, with the four floors beneath rented to commercial tenants. Half that ten thousand feet was work space, complete with wood and metal fabrication shops, drawing studio, small foundry, and kiln. When his work called for the casting of large pieces, he took them to the large-scale foundry he'd built at his place on the Sound, west of New London, Connecticut. Most sculptors of his income and reputation preferred to farm their casting out to specialty houses. Not Brian. To him, the hands-on pouring of molten metal was the payoff for weeks and even months spent here in the studio.

Departing the drawing studio for the larger workshop beyond, Brennan grabbed a couple of cold beers from the refrigerator. He was closing the icebox door when Dante and Diana entered from the living room, arm in arm. When Brian handed his buddy a bottle of Beck's,

Dante clicked it with his, raised it in silent toast, and took a long pull.

"Ah!" He set the bottle down on the nearest bench, disengaged his arm from Diana's, and shed his jacket, hanging it on the back of a chair. "God, you've got no idea how good that tastes right now."

"Long day?" Brennan asked.

Joe retrieved his drink and started to wander, searching out progress made since his last visit. It had gotten so his friends hardly noticed the compact automatic he carried clipped to his belt, back of his left hip. It was part of him. "Long? It seems like this morning was sometime last week." He paused to glance around again. "So. Diana tells me it's still another half hour before dinner's gonna be ready. What're we moving?"

Brian pointed to the north side of the main work area. "Waxes. My new project is going to need some room. The best light area is all backed up."

Dante was headed in that direction when he passed the drawing studio door. The sight of the new 300 ZX parked in there, illuminated by a battery of work lights, brought him up short. "Wait a minute. What the fuck is *that*?"

"What the fuck does it look like?"

"C'mon. We're five floors off the street. How the hell'd you get it *in* there?"

Brennan nodded toward the back corner, to the gate of an ancient freight elevator. It was much larger than the one in which Dante had arrived. "She's slow, but she's huge."

Joe turned again to step toward the car and stand there in open admiration. He was oblivious as Linda Fletcher emerged from the cubicle next door, now fully clothed.

"They're sure getting this design thing together now, aren't they?" Dante marveled. He stooped to peer in the driver's-side window. "God, she's a beaut."

"Depends on your taste. I think it's a sad day when

a man ignores a beautiful woman to ogle a beautiful car.'' Brennan punctuated the comment with a drama-drenched sigh. ''Then again, I wasn't raised in *Brooklyn*.''

Catching his friend's tone, Dante straightened and turned.

''Linda Fletcher, meet Brooklyn's own Detective Lieutenant Joe Dante.''

Dante scowled at him. ''Let's lay off this Brooklyn crap, huh? You didn't have to spend half your day over there like I did.'' And then he smiled, all the wattage of his considerable charm behind it. ''Hi, Linda. Nice to meet you.''

''Linda has a job right around the corner from your place,'' Diana told him. ''She's a waitress at the White Horse.''

''You *live* in the Village?'' the model asked. ''Where?''

''Perry Street. The *other* side of Bleecker.''

''God, I *love* those blocks. Why haven't I seen you at the restaurant?''

Joe shook his head, smiling. ''The yuppie-per-square-foot density's gotten a bit too much for me. They still got a decent burger?''

She nodded eagerly. ''A *great* burger. You should come by and try one sometime. Listen, I've gotta run. Nice meeting you, Lieutenant. Thanks, Brian; Diana. I'll see you tomorrow at ten.''

No sooner had the elevator gate closed and the car started down than Dante turned, a look of disgust on his face. ''Linda works right around the corner from your place,'' he mimicked. ''Jesus *Christ*, Diana. She's beautiful, sure, but she's young enough to be my daughter. I'm paid to protect her from people like me.''

''She's an adult,'' Diana countered. ''So are you. And let's face facts. You'd hate us if we *hadn't* introduced you.''

Joe chuckled. ''Damn. Isn't it great to have friends

who know you so well? All right. Let's move this crap, Brian. I'm starving.''

Guy Napier thought of himself as a pretty smart fella, and he couldn't quite figure how this had happened. And so fast. One minute he was feeling sorry for himself; that Jennifer was always so busy. The next, he and Mel Busby hit the Seaport to have a couple of drinks. That couple had turned into half a dozen beers, while Mel guzzled at least that many dry martinis. It tickled him at first to watch her get drunk. After all, *nobody* drank martinis anymore. She was half in the bag as they walked back here to the Big Building's parking garage. Then, up on the second level, Mel found the rear door of an EMS ambulance unlocked when she reached out to tug at it. When the door swung wide, she got a mischievous grin on her face.

"How do you feel about older women, Detective?"

Flustered, Napier glanced nervously back and forth. "For Crissake, Mel . . . we're in the fucking *parking garage.*"

"That's one of the things that makes you so attractive, Boy Wonder. You're observant."

"We're drunk."

"Right. Neither of us should be driving right now." Instead of backing away, as the voice of conscience advised, Napier took a hesitant step forward. The ambulance door shielded them from the view of anyone who might step onto Level Two off the elevator. He *liked* Mel. A lot of old hands would be busting his balls while he learned the ropes in his first special unit assignment. Mel had been gentle. And there was definitely something sexy about this crusty, compact little detective with freckles across the bridge of her nose. He was intrigued and had the erection to prove it.

"Jesus *God,*" he murmured. And then their lips met.

Her eagerness was suddenly surging up against him, hands groping, fingertips probing the muscles of his back and then his buttocks. Her fierceness inspired him; the way she pulled them hip to hip, grinding herself against him.

"Oh my," she purred. She'd half climbed him, arms wrapped around his neck and feet clear of the ground. Her breath was hot in his ear as her tongue flicked in and out of it. "What have you *got* down there?"

Napier somehow managed to get them into the back of the ambulance and to get the door closed. All other events then blended together in one long, rushed blur. The way Mel produced that condom, she must have been holding it palmed, all through drinks. The way she slipped it onto him and took control until he reached release with her writhing atop him was the stuff of fantasy.

They left the ambulance at intervals, Napier going second. He approached his car to find Mel leaning against the trunk. Her entire demeanor had changed. She wasn't drunk anymore but radiant, even in the shadowy atmosphere of the ill-lit garage interior.

"I—I don't know what . . ."

A surprisingly long and gracefully tapered finger reached out to touch his lips, stopping him in midutterance. He'd never noticed that about Mel before. She had great hands. Beautiful, like the ones pictured wearing rings in DeBeers diamond ads.

"This was something between just us, all right? I don't honestly know what got into me. I've never fucked my partner before."

"That's *it*?" he demanded, suddenly angry. "You don't know what got into you?"

Eyes still sparkling, she moved her head slowly from side to side. "You don't understand. I thought it might be fun, but you sort of took my breath away. If I'm sorry about anything right now, it's that you're getting married next spring."

Before turning to walk away, she stood on tiptoe and kissed him gently on the cheek.

* * *

At quarter of eleven, as Dante pulled away from the curb out front of his friend's place, it struck him that he hadn't thought about the Mott homicide in nearly four hours. The evening's conversation instead ranged from the contemporary music scene to baseball's divisional races. To Brian and Diana, Joe was a close friend first, and a cop second. The three of them lived divergent professional lives, but an enduring, solid friendship kept them together. For so many of Dante's brother officers, the fraternity of cops became their entire social sphere. They not only worked the job, but drank it in cop bars, lived it in bedroom communities packed with other cops, and came to view all society outside their own as the enemy. Today, Viki Onofrio had brought the reality of that all-too-common life-style into sharp focus. She and her husband, Sal, lived in just such a community on Staten Island. For years now, Sal had written Dante off as an oddball because Joe refused to live within some job-exclusive circle. And oddball or not, the glimpse Dante got of his old prom date this afternoon had vindicated many decisions of the past twenty years.

The cool front that arrived around rush hour and caused all that rain was continuing to dominate as Dante left his car with the garage attendant. He started east along Eleventh Street on foot, his hands plunged deep in his pockets, and looked forward to sleeping with the door to his back garden thrown open and the air-conditioner switched off. It would be a rare treat, this time of year. Even at that late hour, the surrounding sidewalks were dotted with pedestrians. Many were headed home after an evening out, while others were just getting the day under way. All of them were young. It was a few years now since Dante first realized that New York had become the property of the next generation. They were the ones with boundless if often aimless energy; with ambitions still fresh and dreams still vivid in imagination's eye.

At the corner of West Eleventh and Hudson, he started past the low black iron railing that separated the sidewalk dining area of the White Horse Tavern. Dylan Thomas, who drank himself to the brink of death here, would no longer recognize the place. Tonight it was filled with leisure-time lawyers and bankers, not the Village bohemians of old.

"Hey! Lieutenant!"

Startled from his reverie, Dante glanced up to find Brennan's new model waving at him. With a drink tray in one hand and an apron tied over her blouse and skirt, Linda Fletcher was working her way between the double row of picnic tables, picking up empties. She stopped on the other side of the rail from where he stood.

"Remember me?"

There was the same puppy-dog enthusiasm in her voice. More of that boundless energy he'd been thinking about. She couldn't have meant what she'd just asked. He just met her four hours ago.

"Of course, Linda. It looks like you're busy."

She rolled her eyes and blew a wisp of hair from her forehead.

"I probably shouldn't complain. The tips've been great."

Dante bet they were. "How do you like working for Brian? He seems real pleased with the new project."

Again, that roll of the eyes. Joe got the feeling that in spite of her apparent sweet nature, it was a habit that could get on a man's nerves.

"How do I *like* it? God, I still can't believe it's *real*. One night, Charles Fung—the painter?—was having drinks here with another artist friend. He says that if I ever want to do any modeling for him, I should give him a call. He gave me his number, I sat for him a couple of times, and now *this*. It's unreal."

Dante suppressed a chuckle. So Charlie Fung was the connection. An old friend of Brian's from their SoHo starvation days in the late sixties, the Chinese-American painter had since carved himself one reputation as a technically masterful literalist, and another as a connoisseur of female beauty. At one time in their respective careers, he and Brennan fought over who would lay claim to model Diana Webster's limited time.

"Just don't let them work you into the ground," he warned. "I like the idea of having you here in the Hudson Street scenery."

The young woman actually blushed. He hadn't meant to embarrass her and reached quickly to touch the hand gripping the tray.

"Take it as a compliment from an old cop who enjoys running into a friendly face on the way home from work. And call me Joe, huh?"

She nodded, normal color returning to her face. Those huge brown eyes lit with warmth again. "Sure . . . Joe. I guess I'd better get back to work. You got time for a drink? It's starting to thin out down at the other end."

"Thanks," he begged off. "Long day tomorrow. I'll take a rain check."

SEVEN

Wednesday morning began like all other mornings for the new, slimmed-down Jumbo Richardson. He was up at five-thirty, pulling on sweats. After a fifteen-minute stretch, he hit the pavement for an eight-mile run through his Brooklyn neighborhood. The routine was always the same and always torturous until he broke a sweat. Then he fell into a rhythm and could remove himself mentally from the pain his body experienced. Always, Jumbo listened to jazz. He was particularly fond of saxophonists. Johnny Griffin, Coltrane, Benny Carter, Charlie Parker, and Sonny Stitt were particular favorites. He could get lost with them as the wind burned in and out of his lungs; float away on those waves of melody.

At seven minutes a mile, the eight took him precisely four minutes less than an hour to complete. At the end of the run, he slowed to a cool-down trot and then a walk. He passed his house to continue on up Lafayette to the nearest corner deli. There, he purchased a copy of *Newsday*. Later, he'd catch up on the sports scores over coffee. It was rare when he read the front section. If the news was important, the job grapevine tended to buzz with it.

Today, as the sweat-drenched Richardson walked back from the deli with his newspaper in hand, he took a moment to survey his neighborhood with feelings of pride. Just ten years ago, Fort Greene teetered on the brink of extinction. Back then, these very blocks of Lafayette were lined with gutted and boarded-up brownstones. Today, every last one of them was restored to its original condition. The tree-lined blocks were pristine and litter-free. Young professionals, fleeing the high real estate prices of Manhattan, had come here in their Turbo Saabs and BMWs, infusing the local economy with badly needed capital. Jumbo and his wife, Bernice, their two kids both away at college now, bit the financial bullet and bought their three-story town house here two years ago. Their old East New York neighborhood, over on the far side of Brooklyn, had deteriorated badly since Richardson's childhood. With Bernice working full-time and Jumbo pulling down sergeant's pay, they needed the tax shelter a mortgage could provide. Still, neither had imagined the sort of civic pride they found here, the atmosphere of friendliness and neighbor watching out for neighbor. The fact that they were black meant less to their upwardly mobile white neighbors than the fact that they had a cop in residence. They liked that; respected it. Shortly after moving here, Bernice was elected to the board of the Neighborhood Watch committee. Instead of the hour it once took Jumbo to travel between his old home and downtown Manhattan, it now took him less than twenty minutes.

The predilections of his yuppie neighbors notwithstanding, that Ferrari Testarossa parked at the hydrant in front of his next-door neighbor's place stuck out like a sore thumb. Richardson slowed as he approached it, pausing to examine those sleek, sexy lines and stooping to peer in the passenger-side window. He'd never seen a package like this up close: two hundred thousand dollars worth of sleek red fiberglass, unlimited horsepower, and supple beige leather. The dashboard looked like the cockpit of a jet fighter: all gleaming gauges, knobs, and toggle switches. The Italians had produced one mean-looking machine.

While straightening from his examination of the Ferrari, Jumbo focused again on that enormous price tag. What the hell was a car like this doing parked out here? Was it stolen? The plates were from New Jersey, the registration stickers current. The fact that it was parked at a hydrant wasn't so peculiar; there wasn't an empty space on either side of the street. Eventually, as he began to move off, Jumbo's gaze settled on the house adjacent to the car. Just two weeks ago, a young Hispanic couple moved in there. Rumor had it that he was some sort of hotshot computer software designer and that she worked on Fashion Avenue. So far, they'd kept to themselves, but this was New York. People took time to feel out a new environment. Still, Jumbo found his detective's curiosity piqued. That car wasn't parked there when he'd wandered out for a six-pack of diet soda late last night. He hadn't seen the computer guy's Accura Legend around the past couple days. Could be the man of the house was away on business, that the little lady had something going on the side. He figured what the hell, if you were going to play while the cat was away, why slum it?

Jumbo had reached his own walk and was leaning forward to release the latch on the low iron gate when the front door of his new neighbor's place opened. A casually dressed young Latin male emerged, carrying a bulky duffel bag in each hand. No scanty-negligee-clad lady of the house followed to plant lingering kisses on his lips. To judge from the amount of luggage this guy had with him, Jumbo doubted he was witnessing the aftermath of any stolen moments. The man's act seemed furtive, but not of the diddle-another-man's-wife sort. While the Ferrari roared to life and slithered away from the curb to disappear up the block, Jumbo let his imagination freewheel. Computers. There was big money in state-of-the-art technology. He knew that software was forever being updated, the latest breakthrough packages selling for large sums. There was that visionary kid out in California who got bought out of his own company for more than a hundred million bucks and then started another. That was the kind of cash that could easily support a life-style including fancy Italian road machines.

So who was this guy? The competition? And if he wasn't, if he was here on the up-and-up, why had he acted like he was raiding someone else's cookie jar? Out of habit, Jumbo made a mental note of the Ferrari's plate number. Once he got to work, he'd have Central Records run it. He didn't trust the arrogance of an act like that: leaving a two-hundred-thousand-dollar car parked on a Brooklyn Street.

For the second day in a row, the Operations Desk caught Dante in the middle of feeding his cat. This time, the bowl had actually hit the floor. He was replacing the can of food in the icebox when the telephone rang.

"Dante."

"Morning, Lou. Sergeant Lewis. Op Desk."

"Yeah, Phil. We gonna make this a habit?"

Moments earlier, Copter the cat had been yeowling up a storm. Generally the noise stopped once he was fed, but today the old guy was electing to cop an attitude. Instead of diving in, he just stood there, sniffing disdainfully at the contents of his bowl.

"Sorry, Lou. We just got a call from some eager beaver over at the lab. They've stumbled across something they think you should know about."

Dante scribbled the technician's name on the notepad next to the phone, thanked Lewis, and cut the connection to dial the lab. By the clock on his oven, it was seven forty-five. In another couple minutes, Mr. Coffee would be delivering a topped-up pot of life-giving java. Meanwhile, he could only hope that the forensics crew wasn't set to serve up another emergency.

"Police lab. Horvath."

"Bernie. Joe Dante. Op Desk says some guy named Bobby Byrd is trying to connect with me."

Horvath, the former lab director, still worked for the Department part-time as a consultant. Dante was surprised to find him on hand so early in the day.

"*Gal* named Bobbie, Cowboy." Bernie had his own nickname for the Major Case whip, dating back to wilder times. The fact that Dante hated it didn't seem to much matter. "She's the dedicated individual who agreed to come in early with me and see if we could make some headway through the backlog around here."

"And?"

"It's one of the blood samples taken from the Mott homicide scene. It's every bit as fresh as the dead man's, but while his is O negative, this is *AB* negative."

Dante's pulse quickened. "You wouldn't, by any chance, have checked that second type against Dewayne Muncie's?"

"One step ahead of you, Cowboy. Muncie is O positive. And another thing. A scrape of Mott's right hand reveals that he fired a gun quite recently. When they found Muncie in possession of Mott's gun, there was an extra empty in the cylinder."

"Yeah. I was aware of that."

"Recently fired," Horvath added.

"And so now we've got a third player for sure," Dante mused.

"Yep. I'd say it looks like there's someone stumbling around out there with a bullet in him, doesn't it?"

"Or her."

"Granted."

"Thanks, Bernie. I owe you one."

"No sweat. You seen the *Post* headline this morning?"

"Jesus. I just got *up*."

" 'Martyr Cop.' With a picture of Mott, edged in black. You've got some rough riding ahead, Cowboy. The mayor's office is speculating that Mott was bushwhacked. They got two perps: Muncie and the evil drug Crack. That's all they seem to need to call this case *made*."

A moment later, Dante was back on the line with Phil Lewis at Operations. "New development, Phil. Get your people on the horn and have them contact every hospital Emergency Room in the tri-state area. We're looking for reports of treatments for gunshot wounds in the past thirty-six hours. Anything you get, I want Chief Lieberman notified of it immediately."

When Rick LeFevre's wife had gotten pregnant, the captain's men friends with children assured him that a positive response to paternity was inbred into the species. That it was chemical. They contended that the minute his own little bundle of joy appeared, he would embrace the idea of fatherhood with open arms. He wanted to believe it, but those deeper emotional attachments still eluded him. Shortly after Monica revealed her condition to him, she'd cut LeFevre off sexually. It was two and a half months since the baby was born, and he still hadn't gotten laid. Nightly, his baby girl roared with the agony of gas trapped in her tiny belly. By day, she dripped, crapped her diapers, yeowled demands for satisfaction of an insatiable hunger, and stared at her daddy with a head-rolling, wide-eyed, *absolute* failure to recognize. His once-adoring wife had withdrawn into her own impenetrable realm. In the wake of quitting her job, their bills had piled up. Last night, Rick spent most of the evening trying desperately to figure some way to make ends meet. The numbers insisted on adding to the same bleak sum. LeFevre felt trapped, angry, and alone.

The captain was not prepared for what greeted him

when he got off the elevator and entered his investigative offices that morning. The squad room had been invaded. The big central table, with piles of files stacked atop it, had been commandeered by that prick lieutenant from Major Case and his big black partner. Nearby, Deb Glenmore paced like a caged animal.

"What the fuck is this?" LeFevre demanded. He closed fast on the table to grab a folder off the top of one pile. It confirmed his suspicions. These were the documents confiscated yesterday from Warren Mott's Manhattan FIAU office.

Dante sat with one leg thrown over the corner of the table and his jacket hung on the back of his chair. He glanced up to regard Rick with a cool, emotionless stare. "*This* is a homicide investigation, Cap. Difficulty recognizing one?"

His fury barely contained, LeFevre whipped a copy of the *Daily News* from beneath his arm and slapped it on the table, headline prominent.

OPEN & SHUT
—Cop Killer Gets It at Deli Owner's Hand—

"There *is* no more homicide investigation, Lieutenant!" And then he whirled on Glenmore. "You gave them access to this stuff, Sergeant?"

Wordlessly Glenmore passed across a single sheet of paper. It was a directive, typed on the commissioner's letterhead. Scanning its short, succinct text, LeFevre realized he was reading an authorization granting the Detective Bureau's Major Case Unit access to all of Captain Warren Mott's files and papers, dating back two years. At the end of it, the infuriated man looked up in confusion.

"The mayor's media people jumped the gun, Rick." Glenmore's tone was measured. She sounded no more pleased about the current situation than he was. "They don't have all the pieces . . . and nothing *concrete* against Muncie. Not yet, anyway.''

"He had the fucking *gun!*"

"Mott's gun, not the murder weapon,'' Dante corrected. "Until my chief and the PC decide this case is closed, it's still wide open, Cap. If you don't mind, we've got a job to do.''

Blood pounded in LeFevre's ears. All he surveyed was tinted red. Snatching his newspaper off the table, he turned toward his office. "We'll see, Lieutenant. Get me Chief Liljedahl, Sergeant.''

It was at times like this that young Marcus Harkness wondered if maybe he'd chosen the wrong line of work. Two years ago he left the South Bronx to move downtown. Manhattan was where the living promised to be easy. Up in the Bronx, there was an economy of sorts, with food stamps exchanged for money, nickel-dime rip-offs, and a drug trade, but midtown Manhattan looked to be where it was *really* at. White kids flocked here from all over the burbs to score and get high. Tourists from all over the world walked the streets with unprotected handbags, nice cameras, and no common sense. An enterprising young man could get rich down here. Or so he'd thought.

Last night Harkness was busted for selling crack for the third time since January. The little blond bitch with the fat ass and big blue eyes didn't look to be more than eighteen or nineteen, en route toward the Lincoln Tunnel after a tough day in some honky corporation's secretarial pool. When she pulled her Nissan Maxima to the curb next to Marcus's station on the corner of Thirty-ninth and Ninth Avenue, he sold her one shitty little ten-dollar vial and learned, too late, that the honky corporation she worked for was NYPD.

Harkness had managed to beat one arrest last winter when the arresting officers screwed up logging their evidence. After his next arrest in May, he'd cut a harmless little snitch deal and gotten off with probation. This time, it didn't look good for him. The blond bitch'd done it all by the book. In addition to these arrests, he had another dozen on his sheet from his misspent youth in the Bronx. Most of them were sealed with his juvenile file, but others still remained. The courts weren't looking kindly on his sort of repeat offender. Marcus was due to do some time.

Last night was an active one all over the five boroughs for the cops. All of the prearraignment detention facilities down on Centre Street were filled before Midtown South could transport Harkness to Corrections custody. Then Midtown South filled to capacity and Marcus got a little change of venue when they shifted him to the Midtown North lockup. It was here that he'd spent the night. Just after breakfast, he heard the exchange between those two cops. Their shifts finished, they were loitering in an office across the hall from the detainment area.

"Died, huh?"

"Yeah. Guys in the squad just got the news. Tough little monkey, wasn't he? Me? I didn't think he'd last so long."

"*You* didn't? I saw the sorry sumbitch. Had a hole in him big enough to chase a cat through."

"You think he's really the guy got Mott?"

"Do I *care*? Muncie was fuckin' scum an' now he's *dead* scum. Mott's some Gold Shield's problem."

The light of salvation suddenly came on in Marcus Harkness's mind. He knew Dewayne Muncie'd gone down, but word on the street had him still alive. Just yesterday morning, before Muncie went off to try and hit that deli, he and Marcus had shared a pipeful inside a derelict warehouse over on West Forty-fourth near the railroad cut. The whole area was crawling with cops, and Dewayne was getting off on smoking it right there under their noses. Dewayne was one crazy nigger and always had been, ever since they were kids. Yesterday he'd shown Marcus the dead cop's gun, and right now, Marcus knew something the cops didn't know. It was no longer a question of ratting out a brother, a brother who might recover and who had one mean-ass temper on him. Now, Marcus would use what he knew to buy his freedom.

Dante and Richardson worked to separate the two years of Warren Mott's investigative activity into categories. There were 106 case files in all, and certain of them were destined for the dead-end pile. These were generally investigations of the bare-bones sort: short on follow-up documentation; petty in nature. After reading the cover sheet and final entries on each case, the name of the officer under suspicion was noted on a running roster. If an allegation wasn't substantiated and the last activity in the file was at least a year old, it joined the ranks of least likely leads. More recent cases fitting the same criteria were given the next-lowest priority. From there, it got more interesting.

"I remember this pair'a creeps," Jumbo murmured.

Dante watched his partner come up out of a tedium-inspired slouch to lean forward over a file fat with promise.

"Who?"

"A sergeant an' his patrolman partner outta the one-oh-three. Mark Gaskill an' Nestor Pelar. They were big news, remember? Busted runnin' that chop-shop op outta some garage in Queens. They stole cars from the long-term lot at Kennedy an' cut 'em up for parts."

Dante frowned. "I remember it, but that case's gotta be at least five years old. What's it doing in here?"

Glenmore, since retreated to her office cubicle just opposite, looked up from the report she was typing. "Warren reopened that file when Nestor Pelar took a shiv between the ribs up at Greenhaven last year. Gaskill was in protective custody, but Nestor couldn't hack the isolation. The minute his old partner died, Gaskill started making noises about getting even.''

''Even with who?'' Jumbo asked it distractedly while still poring over the contents of the file.

Glenmore scowled. ''Even with Warren . . . for putting them away in the first place. Warren had evidence that Gaskill and Pelar were homosexual lovers. Gaskill was single; Pelar and his wife had three kids. Pelar's wife divorced him after the bust. Warren never actually used that particular information, but some reporter got it from somewhere else. Rumors about those two were flying all during the trial, and both of them blamed Warren for starting them.''

''So *did* he?'' Dante asked. He'd met Jumbo here instead of downtown this morning and hadn't yet briefed him on the nature of Glenmore's past relationship with Mott. It was interesting now to hear the way she repeatedly referred to her dead ex-boss. It was always Warren; never Captain Mott.

Glenmore shook her head. ''Now that he's dead, we'll never know, Lieutenant. If it could have helped his case, he might have. Warren rarely worked on only one level when more were available to him.''

''Information about their sexual proclivities? How could that help him bring charges of criminal misconduct?''

''Gaskill was the brains behind the operation. It seemed like Pelar just went along for the thrill of the extra cash at first. Once Nestor compromised himself on that one front, he was open to being compromised on others. Warren may have thought that presented with the right evidence, Pelar would be frightened enough to make a deal. A queer in prison is everybody's meat. A queer *cop* walks in the front gate with a death warrant tacked to his back.''

Dante swallowed hard on the bile of disgust. ''And Mott would have tacked it there if it served his ends, right?''

"But it *didn't*, Lieutenant. I don't know for a fact whether Warren ever tried that avenue, but Nestor Pelar never confessed. He refused to even testify."

As Glenmore and Dante conversed, Jumbo had continued his pawing through the file. Now he produced a news clipping stapled to a sheet of white paper. "Interestin'. I don't remember it, but it looks like the Pelar homicide was big news, too. Just t' be on the safe side, Corrections got Gaskill the hell outta Greenhaven an' transferred him downstate t' Sing Sing. This feature writer from *Newsday* took a trip up the river t' do this piece on him. Right after it all went down, I guess. You read this, there ain't much doubt about the bitterness he was feelin'."

He handed the article across to Dante, who in turn pointed at the stacks of files on the table before them. "Bitterness? There's bitterness behind every one of these investigations."

"Prob'ly," Jumbo agreed. "But how many of them guys seen their partners killed as a result? In that thing there, Gaskill's claimin' he an' Pelar was railroaded. Says the Queens DA built her whole case on hearsay."

"Bullshit." It was Glenmore again. "Our investigation caught the two of them dead to rights. When Queens Borough Command finally dropped the net, they caught both Gaskill and Pelar in the suspect garage. Inside. Dressed in mechanic's coveralls. Gaskill tried to fabricate some fairy tale about the two of them going undercover on their own time. It was an obvious crock and nobody bought a word of it."

The phone at the sergeant's elbow rang and she paused to pick up. After a brief exchange, she held the receiver up for Dante. "For you, Lou. Operations Desk."

As Dante rose to take the phone, he glanced over the progress made in the past two and a half hours. All of the files were now neatly categorized. They'd compiled a list of nearly two hundred names, each classified by priority. Mark Gaskill was the only one who'd gone on record with an overt threat against Mott. So far. Once they did a little digging, others would surface. Most troubling right now was the absence of Sal Onofrio's name on that list. There'd been no file on the nuisance investigation Viki Onofrio described last night. Viki was loud and obnoxious, but she wasn't crazy. So where was it?

"Yeah."

"Lou? Sergeant Lewis. We just got a call from Midtown North. Detective Sergeant Brickman. He says there's something come up that he thinks you'll want to hear, firsthand."

EIGHT

Marcus Harkness was like a joker dealt into a serious game of stud poker. When Dante and Richardson arrived at the station, Dave Brickman was still trying to figure how seriously he should take this swaggering peacock's story. The sheet Brickman called up from Central Records read like a road map to loserville. At the ripe old age of twenty, Harkness was already a well-seasoned street crook. Penny-ante stuff. No weapon nastier than a knife; no dollar amounts bigger than a few hundred. Still, the kid was steady. Today, he was vying to be man of the hour.

It wasn't noon yet and already Dante looked harried: tie loosened, jacket slung over his left shoulder, and sleeves rolled back halfway to the elbow. Brickman didn't envy him this case. The media focus was intense, and the mayor's team hadn't helped much by already calling it a wrap. And now up pops Marcus Harkness. If his story held water, the mayor wouldn't just pardon him for peddling crack, he'd probably invite the young man to Gracie Mansion for lunch.

"Morning, Dave," Dante greeted him. "You know Beasley Richardson? We hear you've got a little bird with a song we've got to hear."

Brickman nodded and shook hands with Richardson. "*Cute* little bird," he replied. "Most'a his variety end up flockin' t'gether on Rikers. Here, take a look." Dave handed over the Harkness rap sheet and dug into his drawer for the key to the holding cell. As a standard precaution, Dante and Richardson handed over their weapons. No officer went armed into a detention area.

Richardson read over Dante's shoulder and let out with a low groan. "Oh, good. A real *model* citizen."

"We've managed t' substantiate one part'a his story," Brickman reported. "Central Records ran some background. They established that Harkness an' Muncie both grew up in the same project on a Hundred Thirty-fifth Street. Bronx. Both their mothers still in residence."

"He's claiming to've known Dewayne?" Richardson asked.

Brickman nodded. "Brothers under the skin; whole shot. But why hear it from me? I want youse t' get it from him."

"What exactly's his claim?" Dante pressed.

"Okay." Dave gestured toward a couple of chairs. "Round eight this mornin', Harkness starts houndin' one'a the uniforms supervisin' the lockup. Says he's got information 'bout the Mott thing. Wants her t' put him in touch with someone up the ladder, pronto. For an hour, this officer—one'a our new kids on her first permanent assignment—shines him on. Then he starts makin' so much racket that she calls the desk. They send the watch commander, who's just gettin' set t' swing out. He listens t' Harkness, thinks maybe we'd better have a listen." As he spoke, Brickman wandered to the coffee machine, poured himself his fourth cup of the morning, and paused now to take a sip. "Soon as we get t' the holdin' cell, Harkness goes all paranoid on us. It's like if the other guys in there hear what he's got t' say, they'll cut his balls off. So okay, we drag his ass up here, sit him down, an' tell him it'd better be good. Accordin' t' him, he works the early mornin' rush-hour dope trade on the corner'a Forty-fourth an' Tenth. Claims he can clear better'n three hunnerd 'tween six an' nine. So Tuesday mornin' the commuters are just startin' t' trickle inta the city when Dewayne Muncie comes along. He says Muncie's all jacked up, an' not from smokin'; that Muncie claimed to've tried t' take off some unsuspectin' white man behind the wheel of a passin' car an' it went sour. White man turns out t' be a cop.''

"Tried to take off somebody behind the wheel of a car," Dante interrupted. "A *passing* car. How?''

"The old con man's trick. Step off the curb like you ain't payin' attention. Slap the fender hard an' then fall down like you've been hit. When Mott stopped, Harkness says Muncie suddenly realizes he's a cop and bolts. Mott gives chase, followin' him inta that alley. They tussle an' Muncie gets the drop. Harkness says Dewayne showed him the cop's gun an' shield."

Richardson asked the obvious next question. "What about the gun he shot him with? What'd he do with that? No, wait a minute. Don't tell me. He threw it inta the fuckin' river, right?''

"Chapter an' verse.''

"Jesus Christ," Richardson complained. "Any asshole could'a made up that story, just from readin' the tabloids."

"Not quite," Brickman cautioned. "For starters, he claims t' know where Muncie ditched the shield. He's keepin' his mouth shut till we get him an assistant DA up here. He wants t' cut a deal."

"That's in the works?" Dante asked.

Brickman nodded. "But Marcus don't know that. We tol' him he's gotta convince the detective runnin' the Mott investigation that it's worth the gamble. Right now, I'd say Harkness is ready t' become putty in your hands, Joe.''

* * *

It was an hour since the other detainees in the Midtown North holding cells were transported out. No other local arrests had been made, and Marcus Harkness was alone. Without the aid of a pipeful to fill his imagination with delusions of grandeur, the solitude was unsettling. The tentacles of paranoia squeezed at the pit of his stomach.

Finally the door down the hall from his cell opened. That first cop, the one he recognized from earlier, crossed to where his keeper sat and dismissed her. Marcus was glad to see that ugly bitch gone. He'd grown sick of looking at the way her fat ass spread side to side across the seat of that battered folding chair. But through the dismissal and her departure, his attention was riveted on those other two dudes.

The first was a brother. Big. Built wide, with close-cropped hair, a battered, mean face, and eyes Marcus couldn't read. His first hope, that the brother was somebody from the district attorney, guttered and went out as he watched him move. The dude didn't borrow space, he *owned* it. A cop. There was no misjudging the tall white man who trailed in the brother's wake. This one had maybe an inch on the gangly Harkness and also had him by at least thirty pounds. All that weight was spread rock-solid over a long-legged athlete's frame. Even in those loose-fitting slacks and shirt, it was easy for a kid with a trained street hustler's eye to spot these things. They spelled trouble. This pair looked to be the next hurdle Marcus would have to hop, and that hurdle looked more imposing than he'd imagined.

"Marcus," the familiar cop barked. "Meet Lieutenant Dante and Sergeant Richardson. I told 'em your story an' they've got a few questions."

Even though the cell behind was empty, Harkness glanced back nervously over his shoulder. He didn't like the feeling of exposure, the way the bars of his confinement were so wide open to all ears.

"Here?"

The lieutenant, with his shirt cuffs rolled back and hands dangling loose at his sides, stepped up to peer in and lock eyes.

"Our apologies, my friend. The presidential suite at the Plaza was all booked up."

Those eyes almost hurt, the way they bore in. Blue like old denim; and cold.

"What we want to know is *how* your old buddy Dewayne knew the man he tried to rob was a cop. Anybody could feed us this bullshit story. I'm talking *details*."

"How?" When his voice quavered slightly, getting it out, Marcus was angered with himself. God, he wished he could have a quick smoke; bolster himself from the balls on up. "Dewayne seen plenty'a you Five-O's afore, man. Probably smelled it on him, just like I can smell it on you dudes right now." That was better. He wasn't going to let those eyes bother him. No way. "He prob'ly weren't payin' the right attention at first. He was in a bad *jam*, man. Owed his man a debt an' his man was gonna have his ass if he didn't get the bread up fast."

"So he tried to rip off the first driver who happened along West Forty-fifth Street at five in the mornin', huh?" the big black cop asked. "Just outta curiosity, why'd he owe this *man* this debt he was so desperate to pay back?"

"Man was his *supplier*," Marcus answered. "Fronted him fifty vials, which means he gotta come back with the bread fo' twenty-five. Sunday, he meet this fine-lookin' uptown bitch took him to a party? Him, he lookin' t' get laid an' starts playin' the dude holdin' the dope. 'Fore he knows it, all them freeloadin' niggers smoked up thirty vials of his shit. He already smoked a few on his own. He needs a couple more t' get hisself through. He ain't sold but ten by Monday, an' Tuesday he gotta get square with his man. He didn't know that suit in the car was no cop till the dude was out an' all over his ass. He's plannin' t' rip the motherfucker off, an' all of a sudden he's gotta make a break or get his ass run in for attempted.''

The mean-looking brother leaned in closer now, his beat-up face right close to the bars. ''We heard it from Sergeant Brickman here, but now we wanna hear it from you, Marcus. Tell us how Dewayne said it all went down. Exactly.''

Harkness shrugged. ''I guess the dude get outta the car, not scared at all that he hit somebody, an' stoops down t' get a closer look. Dewayne realizes the dude ain't reactin' like he should. He's either gotta make his play or get the fuck *gone*, an' he realizes he don't have the *complete* upper hand. The smart street nigger knows when it's stupid t' press on. Dewayne said he tried t' dodge this motherfucker by hittin' the jets an' then meltin' inta that alley. Didn't fool the Five-O none. Man come right inta that alley for the showdown.''

''And?'' It was the white man with the eyes again.

''An' *what*? Some middle-age honky motherfucker pulls heat in your face, what would *you* do? It don't matter if it's a cop or not. At five in the fuckin' mornin' he could shoot your ass dead right where you stand an' wash his hands. Prob'ly go home an' eat a nice big breakfast.''

''So Dewayne shot *him*.'' Blue eyes.

Harkness nodded. ''Far as that crazy nigger's concerned, the worse news is that the man don't have a *dime* on him. Dewayne was mostly still in a state 'bout his man an' that money. Half hour after he tell me this story, he try t' strong-arm that scum-hole deli on Fiftieth an' gets *hisself* blowed away.''

When the black cop shook that big, ugly head, it was unclear to Marcus whether it was in sadness or disbelief. ''All so's he could pay a two-hunnerd-dollar debt, right, slick?''

Harkness's nostrils flared. ''You don't fuckin' *know*, Jim. Man would'a cut his dick off if he didn't pay.

Brothers onna street want t' stay healthy, they stay square with the man in the fancy wheels, Jim. Man in the wheels can't 'ford t' let one slidin' nigger slip through. Word gets 'round too fast. Do that an' he's yesterday's meat.''

The white cop grunted. "A philosopher. So what did your friend Muncie do with the other gun?''

Harkness shrugged. "Prob'ly pitched it inna river. When I seen him with that badge, I tell him he's *crazy*, carryin' shit like that 'round with him. I seen all the pigmobiles. Heavy heat. 'Fore he split, I watched him ditch the dead cop's wallet.''

"Where?'' It was the white cop again.

Marcus gave him a tight, smug little grin. "You-all get me a someone I can cut a deal wit', I show you where the wallet stashed.''

The white cop smiled back, turned to the other two, and tilted his head toward the door. "Maybe, Marcus. Meanwhile, you enjoy your stay.''

"Sorta blows my hooker/rip-off theory fulla holes, don't it?'' Brickman complained.

The three cops passed into the outer hall at the station house and began mounting the stairs toward the squad room. As Dante climbed, he shook his head.

"I like your theory a whole lot more than I like the fairy tale I just heard.''

"Few holes in it,'' Jumbo agreed.

Leading the way, Brickman reached the landing first and held the door. He frowned, eyes moving from Dante to Richardson and back.

"I don't wanna believe him, just on principle. Sheet on him alone'd make me doubt his mother's first name, even if he swore t' it onna stack'a Bibles.''

Dante followed Dave in and grabbed the first convenient chair.

"For starters, he made no mention of anyone else being in the passenger seat of that car. He made no mention of Muncie ever being in it before the engine was switched off. The belt position tells us that seat was occupied.''

''Malfunction?'' Brickman asked. ''The fuckin' electric windows on my car is *always* breakin'. That shit happens.''

Dante shook the suggestion off. ''Lab boys checked it. That belt mechanism is in perfect working order. My second problem with the story I just heard is that no mention was made of Muncie being shot. I've got to believe that the one unexplained empty in Mott's gun, combined with the residue scraping from his hands and the blood the lab found at the scene, all add up to somebody else being hit. The type of that blood says it wasn't Muncie. How he got Mott's gun and shield is open to spec. Maybe he *was* working in tandem with someone else. That would give us a better fit. It's hard to imagine what Mott was doing over there at five in the fucking morning if he *wasn't* cruising whores.''

''You realize what sorta shit's gonna break loose once the mayor's office gets an earful'a this kid's story?'' Richardson asked. ''Hizzonner wakes up this mornin' t' have his eager-beaver press people tell him they might'a *accidentally* jumped the gun on Dewayne Muncie. Marcus Harkness is gonna look like the fuckin' tooth fairy.''

''We either gotta call in the DA or ship him downtown,'' Dave told them. ''We keep him under wraps much longer without playin' his game, we start havin' trouble with due process. The bust they got him on was clean. We fuck up her case an' we're gonna have one pissed-off lady narc t' contend with.''

''Either way, he'll tell the same story to his public defender,'' Dante admitted. ''Once he does that, there's no way we can keep a prosecutor from catching wind. Mind if I use your phone?''

* * *

Lunch came and went before an assistant district attorney and a public defender showed up outside the holding cell. It was nearly twenty-four hours now since Marcus had done a hit. His moods swung like a wrecking ball, the emotional impact battering his confidence. After sitting on ice for another hour and a half since talking to those downtown cops, he was steamed. Barely able to control that anger, he told these lawyers the same story he'd already told twice this day. Then, when the prim-bitch prosecutor stepped aside to huddle with his geek public defender, Marcus threw a fit.

"I tryna *help* you people! You treatin' me like a pile'a *dog* shit; like dey's some question who gonna pick me *up*. Lock my black ass in here an' feed me shit. Fuck wit' my mind. You think I can't *see* what you-all doin'?"

The lady prosecutor, a little red-haired butterball with cream white skin and big green eyes, tried to look tough when she turned back to him. "Okay, Mr. Harkness. Your attorney, Mr. Dunmire, and I are going to accompany you to the scene where you claim Dewayne Muncie hid Captain Mott's wallet. If, and *only* if, that part of your story proves accurate, the district attorney is prepared to drop these most recent charges pending against you."

The geek, Dunmire, stepped up to the bars of Marcus's confinement. "It's a good deal, son. You walk."

The corner was precisely as the prisoner described it. To the northeast, a huge Hess filling station ran street to street between Forty-fourth and Forty-fifth, fronting Tenth Avenue. Back behind it ran a green and white fence, separating the station from a north/south railroad cut, thirty feet below street level. On Forty-fourth, Harkness was led handcuffed out onto the sidewalk.

"That be the buildin' there, what we smoked our pipe in," he told the detectives and lawyers. The ramshackle, three-story warehouse he indicated with his chin was evidently abandoned. Its street-level windows were bricked up, and all those above, boarded over. Around on its back side, where it fronted the rail cut, broken brick and an access hole to the interior were visible. Harkness then turned, indicating the other side of Forty-fourth Street with a nod.

"Over there. Up 'long the top, 'hind the fence. You see them tires? Dewayne put the wallet inside'a one o' them."

Dante, standing a little to one side with his fellow cops, let his eyes travel along the fence to a heap of discarded tires lying among other dumped debris. "You care to be a bit more specific? There's gotta be over a hundred tires there, Marcus."

"It's one'a the first ones on this side. He didn't go that far in."

Dave Brickman volunteered to squeeze his way through a hole in the chain link. Dante watched as the detective picked his way along the trash-strewn lip of that man-made granite canyon and stooped to upend the first tire he encountered. A look of disgust was discernible, even from fifty or sixty yards, as a wash of brackish water covered his shoe tops. He was more careful with the second and third tires he overturned. It was the fourth that yielded Warren Mott's shield case. Brickman held it aloft, and Harkness beamed.

"I *tole* you, now din' I? So how 'bout you get these fuckin' cuffs off me. I believe I'm a free man."

Mott's shield case, with both his tin and photo ID still intact, were sealed into an evidence bag for lab analysis. Dante called in the Crime Scene Unit to pick over the immediate area. Harkness was taken away to Centre Street for processing. Together, Dante and Richardson stood on the Forty-fifth Street sidewalk where they had good vantage of the progress being made by the Crime Scene team. To the south and slightly below the street, half a dozen technicians were pawing through garbage, with little enthusiasm. The

July heat was at work on a lot of it, and any disturbance made it stink even more.

"I'm getting some bad vibes about what's happened today, Beasley. *Real* bad vibes."

"Mayor's sure gonna love Harkness," Jumbo agreed. "Kid come gift-wrapped, just when City Hall's all set t' eat crow."

Brow knit, Dante bit his bottom lip and slowly shook his head. "Something else you and me haven't talked about yet. There was something missing in those IAD files this morning. It bothers me. Last night when I took the run over to Bensonhurst and talked with Theresa Mott?"

"Yeah. I been meaning t' ask you how that went."

"Sal Onofrio's wife, Viki, was there. The two of them are sisters, right? Well, Viki lets slip that once Mott and her sister split, Mott launched an investigation into Sal and his Night Watch squad. Claims it was hung around some trumped-up extortion allegation. We compile a list this morning of names culled from those files and Sal's name ain't on it. Why?"

"Because there weren't no file."

"That's right. So where is it, Beasley? And if it's missing, how many more are?"

"You're sure this story ain't the product of an overactive imagination? Lotta cop wives is like that, Joey. Somebody's always out t' get their man."

Dante shook his head. "Theresa's a whole lot more level-headed than her sister, and she didn't dispute it. The two of them appear to be close, and I can't believe it's the first time the subject's come up."

"Interestin'. Maybe you an' me should talk t' Sal. If he can back it up, then we got us a problem. Free access ain't free access if somebody's holdin' somethin' back."

"I was thinking the same thing. But right now I can see a more immediate problem. This Harkness guy and his story are gonna be trouble. There's no way the mayor's office'll hold back on feeding it to the press. Hell, it vindicates their sticking their necks out. If Tony Mintoff buys into it, our access to Mott's files could be a dead issue. There's only so far we're gonna get with a story about a seat belt, some funny blood, and a gun with a missing round.''

"Yep. The belt was temporarily jammed, the blood's from some bum cuttin' his hand onna broken bottle. The missin' bullet's easy. Mott got one off an' missed.''

"And what've we got to counter that?'' Dante grumbled. "A trail growing colder by the minute. Mel and Napier've got to find us that pimp. He's laying low for a reason.''

"Maybe.'' Jumbo didn't sound hopeful. "An' I s'pose while they're uptown searchin' *that* haystack, we oughta have Don 'an Rusty start in on that list o' names. They could take a run up the river. Talk t' Gaskill. We know he's got motive an' he *did* make threats.''

Dante sighed. He was looking down the street now, on past the public school to that Fire Department outpost. It was freshly painted a dark cream and well maintained, the sign along its roofline proclaiming it headquarters of the Manhattan Field Investigation Unit. "We're running out of runway, Beasley. There was a reason the new mayor kept Mintoff on as PC. They thought they could work together. There's no way Big Tony's gonna step on administration toes because we're unhappy about a few loose ends. Outside of the possible pimp/whore connection, we've got no witnesses. I talked to that fire captain last night; the one who went home with the flu bug. I doubt he was sneaking off to screw his girlfriend. He looked like shit and he didn't *see* shit. Nobody did.''

Gus Lieberman hadn't heard a lot he could get enthused about in Dante's update. Then, only minutes after receiving it, his exec leaned his head in the door to say that Tony Mintoff was on the line. No doubt to gloat.

"Gustav! What's this I hear? Op Desk reports your guys found Mott's shield?"

"It ain't the murder weapon, Tony."

The PC ignored this reminder. "And they tell me that the guy who led them to it can put Muncie at the homicide scene; that he's fingered him for it, and the DA's cut some sorta deal."

"Deal or no deal, the story's hard to corroborate with Muncie dead," Gus replied. "My people think it's got quite a few holes in it."

Again, what he was attempting to convey didn't seem to register. "I've got the mayor calling up to congratulate me on one line, and Jerry Liljedahl all over my fanny to plug the breach in his security on another. Time to congratulate Dante and his team on a job well done, Gus."

Lieberman lit a smoke, the snap of his Zippo lid echoing off the walls of his office like the report of a light-caliber weapon.

"Tony, you can't pull out. Not just yet."

"I've got the mayor ready to give everyone in your Major Case Unit citations, Gus. They don't want them?"

"Citations? You don't know Dante like I do, Tony. Right now, he'd probably tell him where to stick his citations. He's got a gut feeling about this guy Harkness; thinks a lot of the tale he tells is bullshit. I respect those instincts of his, and so should you. We've both seen the man's track record."

"Gus, Gus. I respect your respect. I guess you don't understand the problem *I've* got. This new administration is backing up its pro-cop rhetoric with allocations. I can't afford to piss them off."

Lieberman took a deep drag; so deep, he nearly choked. "What kinda problem am *I* gonna have if the best people in my Bureau are told that a thorough investigation ain't the top priority of this department any longer? There's no murder weapon here, Tony. We've got conflicting evidence comin' out our ass. Damn it, *I* ain't satisfied.''

"Get satisfied, Gus."

To Lieberman, the message was all too clear. When he spoke, his tone was measured but hard as nails. "Sorry, Tony. I won't do that. You pull the plug on this, my resignation's on your desk by five o'clock. A good investigation team's got the same sorta spirit as a good racehorse. I won't help you break it; not with this one."

Down the line; dead silence. Lieberman counted eight before he heard Mintoff clear his throat. "I don't like being threatened, Gus."

"You know as well as me that I don't need this job, Tony. I want another day."

More silence, then an audible sigh. "Twenty-four hours. Dante better bring you something soon, Gus. I don't have your sort of patience."

NINE

The fact that Captain Bob Talbot once worked as an Action Desk administrator at Internal Affairs had little to do with the visit he was about to make. The story *SPRING 3100* editor Rosa Losada related to him over lunch had frightened him. An indignant Deborah Glenmore, dissatisfied with the way her superiors were handling the results of a rape investigation, had contacted the magazine editor about other possible avenues of action. She'd talked about going to the media with it, and that made her a loose cannon. If she fired such a broadside, she could blow Tony Mintoff's tenure as commissioner right out of the water. As the PC's exec, Talbot was responsible for making sure the commissioner's ass was covered. And because his own career was tied hip to hip with Mintoff's, Bob was covering his own ass as well.

From the south, clouds had begun to accumulate, threatening one of the Northeast's typical summer downpours. What began as a sparkling clear and relatively cool day was quickly turning muggy. As he parked and left his car on Poplar Street, Talbot thought momentarily about the umbrella beneath the front seat.

His preoccupation got the better of him. He continued on, empty-handed.

Back when he'd run the Action Desk and Deborah Glenmore first came aboard at IAD, she'd been the object of more than passing fancy. Tall and lithe like he preferred his women, she was also bright, apparently resourceful, and certainly dedicated. But in those days, Deborah Glenmore was also green, with enough rough edges to dissuade a man of Talbot's ambition. She was Queens, with that horrible back-of-the-mouth accent, heavy eyeliner, and tortured hair. Then, as now, Talbot picked his associations with care. With his eye always on the next political prize, pragmatism always managed to win out over lust.

Today at lunch, when Sergeant Losada showed him that profile in the upcoming issue of *SPRING 3100*, it seemed evident from the accompanying photograph that Glenmore had changed. There were leaner and more mature lines in that face. The hair was cut short in a style accentuating her bones. The glint of determination was still in those eyes, but the makeup around them now helped soften it a bit. Detective Glenmore was a full-fledged IAD investigator now, working her own cases; a detective sergeant. She'd no doubt hung on to that accent, but Talbot might revise his position on that. There were an awful lot of middle-class, blue-collar voters who would identify with the outer-borough touch, the same voters who instinctively mistrusted affluence, prep-school educations, and families with Park Avenue addresses.

Glenmore seemed surprised to hear from him when he called. Now, as he entered the third-floor squad room, she rose from behind the desk in her office cubicle to cross the room, hand extended. There was frank firmness in her grip, but he thought he detected a wariness in her cool blue eyes.

"To what do I owe the honor, Captain? You're a very busy man."

Talbot beamed his best disarming smile. "This is my job, Sarge. Over lunch today, Rosa Losada outlined the basics of this problem you're having and gave me the file. I thought it demanded immediate attention. In my experience, that's the best way to *minimalize* my workload . . . in the long run. Is there someplace private where we could go and talk?"

"Not a problem, Captain. They're all off digging dirt somewhere. Coffee?"

Talbot shook his head and followed as she led him toward her desk. That accent was still there, but without the old look, it seemed less strident. As they settled into chairs, Bob motioned toward a bank of trophies lining the top of a low, lateral file.

"I read that article Rosa did on you. How do you see your chances in Cleveland?"

"My chances? If I don't get this other stuff cleared up, lousy. I can't focus."

"You're serious about this? Taking it to the media? Just to see your idea of justice done?"

Glenmore bristled at his implication. "*My* idea, Captain? And just what is yours?"

Talbot summoned his best look of Socratic serenity. "There may be mitigating circumstances that you're unaware of, Sarge."

"Like what?" she retorted. "That those guys are *family* men? That was Chief Liljedahl's line. They're rapists, Captain."

"I read the file." Again, he had that politician's serene, placating tone.

"Good, then you know there *are* no mitigating circumstances."

"There could be some question . . . concerning those women's reliability as witnesses."

"Then you only read half the file. I've got hospital photographs. Forensic evidence. You order DNA prints, you'll nail those two. Cold."

Their eyes had locked, Glenmore's glowering with the heat of disgust.

"You like it here, Sarge?"

"What does *that* mean, Captain?"

Talbot shrugged. "That you've been here long enough to know how Jerry Liljedahl runs things. The Internal Affairs agenda is *his* agenda. You cross him in a way that hurts him in the eyes of his boss and the public, he'll have you inventorying traffic barriers for Support Services."

Glenmore smirked. "I thought all transfers and promotions came down from the PC himself, Captain."

Talbot smirked back. "When was the last time you had drinks and lunch with Commissioner Mintoff, Sarge? Chief Liljedahl had that pleasure just this afternoon."

"Did you come here to lecture me on the dangers of political suicide, Captain? I'm a police officer, confronted with a moral dilemma. That dilemma is compounded because I'm also a woman. Cops are sworn to uphold the law, and we're not doing that here. As a woman, I live in mortal fear of men like Ahern and Escobedo. So what do I do? Turn my back and let them walk? What kind of message does that deliver? Or isn't the South Bronx part of the community we're sworn to protect?"

As she spoke, Talbot had begun to shake his head. Slowly. "I came here today because I wanted to hear it straight from you, Sarge. Given the evidence in that file, and how strongly you insist on standing behind your investigation, I'm convinced that Jerry Liljedahl is making a mistake. That's off the record and between just you and me."

"So what's on the record, Captain?"

For the first time since greeting her on arrival, Talbot allowed himself to smile. This woman was like an alligator. Once she had her teeth closed on something, you couldn't pry or shake her loose. He liked that. "On the record, I'm going to be apprising the PC of the situation, as it stands. In exchange for that promise from me, you won't take it to the media.''

"I want action, Captain.''

Talbot smiled again. ''Stay close to your phone, Sarge. Within the next day or two, you'll be hearing from the Bronx DA.''

"Either that or a call from Jerry Liljedahl, transferring me to Traffic's Barrier Section, huh?''

"Unlikely. Right now, your boss has his hands full. He's in the middle of trying to win a turf battle with Chief Lieberman. Damn shame about Warren, by the way. I know you two worked pretty closely there for awhile.''

"Damn *shame*? You used to work here, Talbot. You know what the real shame is.'' Gone was the more deferential ''captain.'' ''An IAD investigator is murdered in cold blood and we're excluded from the investigation. I don't understand it, but I do know how strange it feels to be left out in the cold on a thing like this.''

Glenmore stood abruptly and strode out into the squad room to pour herself a cup of coffee.

"Five years, Captain.'' Her back was to him now, her tone more subdued. ''I worked with Warren Mott for most of the time I've been here. It doesn't make any sense to me. If the perp is somebody from the past, somebody Warren brought down, then some piece of evidence that might mean nothing to Dante and his unit might trigger something inside IAD.'' She turned, confronting Talbot from catty-corner across the squad room. ''Is it too much to ask to be kept abreast of their investigation? It's not like we want to step on anyone's toes.''

Talbot had picked a rubber band off her desk and twirled it idly between opposing index fingers. Now he took aim at a framed citation, shot, and missed. ''Excluding IAD was the commissioner's decision, not mine, Deb. Don't forget where I come from. I've got certain loyalties, linked to the past. And no, I don't think it's asking too much to be kept abreast. Maybe I can help you there.''

''You?''

''Why not me? I see everything that goes across the big man's desk. For instance, I know that the mayor may have been premature in jumping on the Dewayne Muncie solution. Then again, just this afternoon, something else surfaced which may prove all we need to close the book.''

As her eagerness transformed her, Glenmore crossed the room to reclaim her position behind her desk. ''I'm listening, Captain.''

''How long have we known each other, Deb? Eight, nine years? Try Bob. It may grow on you.''

She tapped her blotter nervously, betraying her impatience.

''Fine, *Bob*. Tell me about this new development on the Muncie front.''

''A witness. His name is Marcus Harkness. Grew up in the same project with Muncie in the South Bronx. He was busted for sale of crack just six blocks from where Warren got it. Today, he's claiming to have been with Dewayne Muncie yesterday morning between the hour when the homicide took place and the time when Muncie hit that deli. He led Dante and an assistant prosecutor to the spot where Muncie hid Mott's shield case. He claims Dewayne bragged about having to kill Mott when Warren tried to bust him.''

''Really. And Dante's bought it?''

Talbot lifted his hands. ''Who cares? The Manhattan DA's office did. They released Harkness an hour ago. Straight deal.''

It had been hanging in the air between them all day, and it was starting to get on Melissa Busby's nerves. Along with pounding on doors and following up dead-end leads all over Harlem, she had the nearly palpable guilt of her partner to contend with. Now, it was getting on toward the end of the day. Henry "Honey" Lucas continued to elude them. Melissa was taking her turn behind the wheel as they made for the barn. Beside her, in the passenger seat, Napier sat slouched, his eyes averted to stare vacantly out at the storefronts of St. Nicholas Avenue.

"All right, Boy Wonder. Want to get it out of your system before it eats a hole in your stomach lining?"

"I couldn't tell her." It came out as a mumbled murmur.

"You couldn't *tell* her? Tell *her* what?"

"We promised to be honest with each other . . . about *everything*."

"Ah. You mind me asking you a personal question?"

Napier glanced over now, the hurt obvious in his eyes. "What?"

"When was the last time you got laid? Before last night."

It was like she'd slapped him. "Jesus *Christ*, Mel! What makes you think that's any of your business?"

She shrugged. "Don't know, Guy. Twenty-seven-year-old man has needs. Seems to me that you were pretty primed last night. Not that I'm complaining, but you came like your balls were going to explode. If a woman can't take time to make love to the man she's going to marry, I don't see where she gets off demanding honesty from him. Not about where he goes to get his rocks off."

Napier jerked around in the seat to face her. His eyes narrowed. "Where the fuck do you get off, telling me how to live my life?"

Melissa smiled. "We got a little toasted and wound up fucking, Guy. I had a lot of fun. You did, too. We parted friends. Then you went home and let a lot of guilt fester. Today, you feel like you should take it out on me. But I'm not the one who's making you feel unhappy. Think about it."

Some of the steam went out of him, but he continued to frown.

"It's not that simple. I've made a commitment."

"Has she?"

"What do you mean? Of course she has."

"Really? You work your ass off all day. Risk your life protecting the public. Come home at night and try to leave the job behind you. Am I right?"

"That's right. I'm not one of these guys who takes it home with him."

"Good for you. That's healthy. So what about Jennifer?"

Napier scowled. "She ain't even *in* the job."

"But she has *a* job, am I right? And the reason we had drinks last night was because her job is so important to her that she'd rather stay late at the office than be home with you."

"You're twisting this all up."

"Am I? Or are you walking into something blindfolded?"

Napier sat forward with his head in his hands, his words muffled. "Ten minutes after you drove out of that garage last night, I got this knotted-up feeling in my stomach that hasn't gone away since. I took a fifteen-minute shower as soon as I got home, and when Jennifer crawled into bed, I swear she could still tell."

"Bullshit."

"Huh?" He'd looked up, surprised by the amusement in her tone.

"You heard me. Guilt does funny things to our sensory receptors, buddy boy. Rubs 'em raw. Makes a fart seem like an earthquake. You think about it a minute. On the nights when she gets home late, it's always the same story. She's too tired to talk and too tired to fuck."

"Jesus, Mel."

"Am I right or am I right? We had fun last night,

Guy. So get over this bullshit guilt. If I were you, I'd be doing a little thinking about my priorities instead. Get 'em straight, *and fast*, or you're gonna be just another disillusioned dipshit, your dick in your hand and no steam left in your dreams.''

Central Records Division, on the fifth floor of One Police Plaza, is the clearinghouse for most of the job's information requests. As Dante visited one office to consult with the division commander, Beasley Richardson wandered down the hall to yet another. They'd come here in an effort to obtain information on Marcus Harkness's history inside the criminal justice apparatus, but that Ferrari parked at the hydrant in front of his new neighbor's house was also on Jumbo's mind. Its Jersey plate number was scribbled on the folded piece of paper he now handed Mabel Huggins across the top of her computer monitor. Pleasingly plump, Mabel was five foot two inches and 130 pounds of flirtatious fun poured into a purple knit dress that fit her like a sausage casing. She was also known throughout Central Records as *the* wizard at cross-linking files from the various data banks: National Crime Information Computer, FBI files, state records in Albany.

''What's this, baby? Mash note?''

Richardson grinned. ''Keep dreamin', Huggie; though if I do say so m'self, you look good enough t' eat t'day. That's the plate number of a car I'm curious about. Do me a favor an' give it a quick check, would'ja?''

''Good enough t' *eat*? Be still, my flutterin' heart.'' Mabel had unfolded the notepaper, and already her hands were flying across the keyboard. ''I know I've asked before, Sergeant, but you met any nice single men lately?''

''Black? At least six foot? Own place? Own car? Steady job? High five-figure income?'' Richardson shook his head. ''I'm a cop, Mabel, not an investment banker. You do better takin' this show downtown some. The pickin's be more your style.''

"What can I say? I'm kinky. I like men who carry handcuffs. Ferrari? Nineteen eighty-nine Testarossa?''

"Model's right. I got no clue 'bout the year.''

"This one's registered to a Hor-hay DaSilva. Old County Road, Closter, New Jersey.''

Jumbo pointed to her hands, poised over the keyboard. "Do me another favor an' check that name with the National Crime linkup.''

Again, the fingers flew. Then Mabel Huggins sat back to wait a moment, eyes still glued to her screen. "Oh ho. Name's flagged here, Sergeant. We're bein' dumped into the DEA data base.'' She leaned forward, plenty of cleavage leaning out there with her, and her finger pointing to the characters now starting to parade before her.

Richardson read along, his excitement growing. His Ferrari owner was one Jorge DaSilva, Colombian national. He was born June 22, 1946, in Cucuta. Suspected connection to the Cali cocaine cartel. There were no arrests. His background profile listed him as an electronics merchandiser with import/export operations based in Paramus, New Jersey. He operated two other outlets, in Miami and on Sixth Avenue in New York City. As Jumbo waited for more, the data bank stopped feeding it to him.

"That's it?''

"Yep. All she wrote. Your Mr. DaSilva might smell funny, but they ain't been able t' find any shit on him yet.''

Jumbo stooped to kiss her on the cheek. "Thanks, Mabel. I owe you one.''

"Yeah? What're you doin' after work, handsome?''

"Goin' home t' my wife, babe.''

She gave it a reluctant but philosophical tilt of the head.

"Why're the good ones always spoken for, Sarge?''

* * *

After half a dozen phone calls, Central Records was finally able to get Dante the information he'd requested of the Manhattan district attorney's office. A rap sheet on a habitual criminal was one thing, and the whole story, quite another. The sheet provided description, mug photos, modus, arrest dates, and a concise history of convictions. What it didn't provide was a glimpse behind the scene: at deals made, strings pulled, and favorable considerations granted. Only the DA could do that, so in the matter of Marcus Harkness, Dante was going to the source. It ended up being like pulling teeth, but those people in Central Records could be persistent. Once the file was faxed office to office and Joe finally had it in hand, he left and encountered Jumbo in the hall outside.

"You got it?" Richardson asked.

"Eventually. So let me guess. The guy dicking your neighbor's wife is blond, fleshy, and owns a lot of casinos and skyscrapers with his name on them."

"Swarthier. And you left out possible dope kingpin."

Joe stopped to regard his partner with a less amused expression. "Serious?"

Jumbo nodded. "That Ferrari's registered to a Colombian suspected by the DEA of bein' hooked inta the Cali cartel. They ain't been able t' pin nothin' on him yet, but his setup sure looks tailor-made. He imports and exports electronics. Three outlets, one of 'em in Miami."

"You want to chase it a little?"

"Bet your ass." Richardson glanced down at his watch. "Lissen. I just called the deeds registrar at Brooklyn Hall o' Records. She was gettin' set t' call it a day but said she'd stick 'round if I'd get my fanny in gear. You mind?"

"No. Go ahead. I'll circle the wagons back at the squad and then run the latest past Gus."

* * *

Chief of Detectives Gus Lieberman was sitting alone in his office when Dante arrived. With his back to the room and feet up on the window heating unit, Gus left his eyes lingering on the view outside. "Looks like more rain," he growled.

"Started to get muggy again, a couple hours back," Dante replied. "That nice breeze we've been getting just stopped dead."

"You didn't come here t' talk with me about the weather, right?"

"Nope."

"You *did* come here t' tell me more about why you're not buyin' Marcus Harkness."

"Yep. I'm not buying because I'm a detective, Gus. I believe an eyewitness like Neil Armstrong when he says he's been to the moon because he's got the video-tape and moon rocks to prove it. Marcus Harkness is a different sort of spaceman altogether."

Lieberman dropped his feet and turned slowly in his swivel chair. "Better make it good, Joey. The mayor's office don't wanna hear fuck-all about blood types and seat belts. They've got a dead cop and another corpse in possession of the dead cop's gun. They've got a story of how it all went down and the dead cop's shield case to tie it all up, nice an' neat."

"Nice and neat, huh? Without even having a murder weapon. I like that, Gus. What *they* like is the fact that their perp is dead; that a dead man can't pop their bubble with something as inconvenient as the truth. So what about Mintoff? Where's he stand?"

"One foot on either side'a the fence, which makes his balls ache. He wants me t' get him down offa there, ASAP. Meanwhile, Jerry Liljedahl's crawlin' up his ass about IAD security breaches. As of two hours ago, Tony's given me twenty-four hours to pull our rabbit outta the hat."

Dante crossed to toss the DA's Harkness file onto the chief's blotter.

"What's this?"

"Take a look. It makes interesting reading; the Manhattan DA's half of the Marcus Harkness story. The other half's somewhere up in the Bronx DA's office. A call made to the DA's Investigation Squad would probably be enough to get it dug out. I just tried from Central Records, and everybody up there'd already closed down for the day."

"You wanna feed me the essence here, or is this hide'n seek?"

"In simple terms? Harkness has a history of selling prosecutors on his active imagination. Twice in the past year he's been arrested on crack sales charges. He's yet to go to trial. First charge, they blew the evidence. Second time, he cut a deal in exchange for information. Weak stuff they couldn't do anything with."

"Do I hear you suggestin' that the information was *bad*?"

"Just weak. It looked good up front but didn't have enough glue in it to hold anything together."

"He *did* know where Muncie hid the shield case, Joey."

"Sure he did. And someone else stole Mott's shoes. The ME thinks the corpse was left lying there for at least an hour and maybe more before our team got to it. Once rush-hour starts up, that whole area is crawling with windshield washers and crack peddlers. Anyone can pick a dead man's pockets."

Gus patted his shirtfront for cigarettes and came up empty-handed. "I gotta give it to you that the blood sample an' the seat belt thing are inconsistencies. I don't know what the hell t' make of the break-in over in Bay Ridge. But let's toss all that out a minute. Say some homeless guy *did* cut himself; that Mott *did* have a whoor in there with him, coppin' his joint. Maybe her head was down an' Muncie didn't see her. He's concentratin' on the game. Once Mott gets outta the car after Dewayne pulls his stunt, there's a chase an' the whoor hears gunfire. She spooks an' melts inta the sunrise. What's wrong with that?''

Dante was now staring out that big window himself. ''What's *wrong* with it? What's wrong with a desk-softened IAD captain chasing some petty street punk without backup? His dick still wet. In the wee hours of the morning, out in the middle of *no*where.''

Lieberman broke into a broad grin. He finally located his smokes on the corner of his desk and lit one. ''I'm with you, Joey. I just needed t' hear it from you; hear how serious you are about your position. You think the Harkness kid's story is a crock; that the DA an' the mayor bought themselves the easy out. As long as you persist in believin' that, I'll take the heat.'' He paused to flick ash into his PAL ashtray. ''An' by the way, there were five reported gunshot treatments in the metro area yesterday. Four were drug-related; one domestic. All of them were checked out, and none of the times are right. I take it you'd like me t' see what the Bronx has on Hizzonner's model citizen?''

''The sooner the better. If we can discredit this creep, we buy ourselves more room, right? I've got too much on my plate to be worrying about Big Tony's aching balls.''

''Mintoff's not your problem,'' Gus growled. ''That's why we got us a chain of command. When my balls start t' ache, that's your problem. When it's the Maltese midget's, the problem's mine.''

TEN

In the eyes of the job command, Detective Sergeant Rosa Losada was an affirmative action dream come true: female, Hispanic, and a Bennington College graduate in economics. In the eyes of every red-blooded male in the Big Building, she was also the best-looking woman to ever graduate the Police Academy. Hands down. Recently she'd been promoted from Public Information Division's press liaison to editor of the job's glossy bi-monthly publication, *SPRING 3100*. She was just wrapping up another day of trying to get the late summer issue to press when Joe Dante poked his head into her outer office.

"Busy?"

Dante was her ex-partner from those days on the street just after she earned the Gold Shield. He was also an ex-lover, and the sight of him still did funny things to Rosa's heart.

"Nope. Just finishing up. Come in."

Dante entered, that summer-weight wash-and-wear suit looking a bit rumpled but still good on him. She'd dragged him to Brooks Brothers to purchase that suit and listened to his protests every block of the way. To no avail. Rosa considered it a crime to waste that kind of build on off-the-rack stuff. With those long legs, slim hips, and squared off, angular shoulders, even a few wrinkles couldn't detract from the way good clothes hung on him.

"For a guy who works just two floors away, you've been making yourself pretty scarce lately," she observed. "Something I said?"

Across the desk from where she sat, Dante pulled up a chair and gave the comment a no-big-deal shrug. "I heard about you and Bobby Talbot splitting. Thought maybe you'd want a little space. I was just over talking to Gus and thought I'd stop by, see how you're holding up."

Shortly after moving out on Dante and into her current East Village digs, Rosa had taken up with the PC's executive officer. Last May, after nearly two years, she and Talbot admitted that the idea of spending another summer together was more than either could face. They'd called it quits.

"What's to hold up?"

"You two still on speaking terms?"

She smiled. "A man who wants to be mayor or maybe governor someday knows he can't afford to make lasting enemies."

The notion tickled something in Dante. "News to me. I guess I'm the exception, huh?"

"There's one to every rule," she agreed. "Plenty of people have had occasion to piss Bobby off, but you're the only one I know of who seems to *relish* doing it."

"Only when I'm right, which is most of the time. It ain't easy for a street cop to listen to a glorified secretary tell him how to do his job."

"You've taken great pains to point that out to him."

Joe smiled again. "No pain at all. It's him that the truth seems to hurt. But I didn't come here to talk about Talbot, Rosa. I dropped in to see if I could lure you away from here. Congratulate you on the promotion. Maybe buy you a drink."

The beautiful lady cop chuckled. "Don't feed *me* your bullshit, Dante. You want something."

Joe wondered if paying his old girlfriend a visit might be a mistake. On the other hand, she was profiling Deborah Glenmore in her upcoming issue, and right now, he needed a read. Captain Rick LeFevre was never going to be an ally, access to certain IAD files could become crucial to the success of the Mott investigation, and Glenmore looked like his only hope. On leaving the Big Building, he led Rosa past the several off-duty watering holes on Dover and Front Streets and on toward the South Street Seaport. The Fulton Street Fish Market was locked up tight at that hour, but the persistent odors of the place had no trouble insinuating themselves into the heavy summer air. Gus had been right; it did look like rain.

"No drinks in cop dives for the people's cop, right, Joe? When he drinks, he drinks with the citizenry he's sworn to protect, right out here in the real world."

They were crossing South Street beneath the elevated FDR Drive. Dante ignored the barbs in Rosa's comment and glanced around them. "You call a bunch of yuppie investment bankers playing after-work grab-ass the real world?"

"You eat, sleep, and drink the job, you risk letting the job eat *you* . . . alive. Dante's third law of upright living. Correct?"

"You looking to fight or relax after a tough day?"

He watched her shake her head. "The old habits die hard. You've got something on your mind. Maybe I'd better hear it before I make up mine."

The sharp edge to her words gave him pause. Picking people's brains was what he did for a living. Assemble facts, mull them over, discard the incongruous, and use the rest to build a theory. How he got those facts was often shameless. This evening, he'd intended to ply Rosa with a few drinks and work his way around to the problem he was having with IAD through the back door. He should have known better. "That obvious, huh?"

"Like Bozo's nose, Dante. And give me a little credit. I haven't seen you for nearly two months. I'm supposed to think this is strictly a social call?"

They'd reached Fulton Street and joined the evening migration from the financial district to stroll the Seaport cobbles. Gianni's looked as good as any place and they settled there, choosing a window table in front of the bar. Once again, Dante was struck by how young the crowd around him was. Even the battlements of enterprise were being manned by children, masquerading as war-weary veterans. Young turks in tailored suits and silk power ties were everywhere here, bristling confidence and ambition. Few were much over thirty. They were the same people who populated the high-rent apartments in his neighborhood, who drank in its taverns and ate in its restaurants.

"I heard today that your upcoming issue profiles an IAD investigator, name of Glenmore. You're the one who did the interview?"

What was behind the frown that flashed for only an instant across her face? Irritation? Jealousy? Or was he flattering himself? Just as quickly as the frown appeared, she recovered and sat studying him. Cool. Maybe even a bit distant now.

"That's a leading question if ever I've heard one, Lieutenant. What's behind it? I run a magazine. I'm not a meat inspector."

It *was* jealousy. Dante couldn't help but smile. "Wrong read, Rosa. I won't deny she's attractive, but her ass isn't what I'm after. I'm having trouble with her bosses over on Poplar Street and I'm looking for a friend. She seems the most likely candidate. What can you tell me about her?"

Rosa continued to eye her ex-lover suspiciously. "What am I missing here? The way I've heard it from at least half a dozen different media people, the Mott case is a wrap.''

Their drinks arrived, and as Dante took his first sip, he studied her. At thirty-three, she was even more beautiful than when they first met five years ago. Tall, at close to five foot nine, she had a face that was all exquisitely defined bones, full lips, and hot black eyes. ''I'm afraid your pals in the press may have jumped the gun. There are still a dozen unanswered questions. We don't have the murder weapon . . . or a motive. Meanwhile, we've turned a few curiosities which demand explanation. Somebody broke into Mott's Bay Ridge apartment. We doubt it was Dewayne Muncie. Our search of the place turned up an envelope stuffed with over eleven thousand dollars. We've turned evidence of an investigation Mott conducted that isn't in his files.''

Rosa's body language had changed. The defensively hunched shoulders were now relaxed. Her fingers ceased their nervous fidgeting with her drink straw. ''It's funny that you'd ask about Sergeant Glenmore right now. I got a call from her just this morning. It seems that you're not the only one having trouble with her bosses. While I was interviewing her, she refused to talk about any of the current work she's engaged in, so I was surprised when she called to ask my help with one.''

''*Your* help?''

''That's right. She's put together evidence substantiating rape and sodomy allegations made against two uniforms from the Four-Four. Unfortunately, the allegations were made by a number of those cops' female arrests. Mostly prostitution. When she submitted her findings, Chief Liljedahl sat on them. She's confronted him with the fact that he seems to be stonewalling and he's thrown it back in her face. According to her, he claims that these two guys are both family men, that he doesn't want to see them dragged through the mud by a prosecution based on unreliable testimony.''

Dante was more than a little surprised by these revelations.

"Wait a sec. She called and *told* you all this? Jesus. If Jerry Liljedahl finds out she's telling tales out of school like that, he'll have her run outta there on a rail."

"She knows that, Joe. She also believes that those two characters up in the Bronx are guilty as a pair of smoking guns. What she was doing was using me as a sounding board. The way she sees it, she can either let it die and live with the knowledge of those two running loose up there, or work with me and do an exposé."

"Not through the magazine."

"Hardly. Sergeant Glenmore remembers who I was before I became editor of *SPRING 3100*. She knows I've got extensive media contacts."

Dante hadn't quite recovered yet. "She'd actually risk it? I mean, *seriously* consider that course of action?"

"She's very angry, Joe. Two nights a week, she teaches female self-defense. Half her pupils are mugging victims. We're talking about rape here, by guys with guns and badges. If pushed to the wall, I honestly think she *would* risk it."

"Sounds like she's already been pushed to the wall."

"Not quite. I managed to convince her that I've also got a few contacts inside the PC's office. She promised not to go off half-cocked until I talked to somebody who's got Tony Mintoff's ear. I'm hoping there's a way to defuse the situation before it explodes in everybody's face."

Joe had to admit he was impressed with Glenmore's dedication to principle. The idea of going to an outside organ and leaking the details of an Internal Affairs investigation in order to see justice done was unprecedented. Seeing it through would take extraordinary courage. Glenmore would risk losing a lot more than her job as an IAD investigator. She'd risk losing her shield.

"That somebody who's got the PC's ear wouldn't be one Captain Bob Talbot, by any chance?"

Rosa lifted her glass and gave the suggestion a smug little smile. "Bobby and I had a falling out on the romantic front. We also had lunch today. On a professional level, he's just as interested in seeing the Department dodge a media shit-storm as I am."

"Is Glenmore willing to give him the time he'll need?"

"I hope so. I don't know how it went, but Bobby planned to see her this afternoon."

"Well, I hope she bit. She won't do me any good if Jerry Liljedahl has her tarred and feathered." And as Dante said it, his beeper went off. The call-back number belonged to the cellular unit in Gus Lieberman's car. He picked a quarter out of the change left in the middle of the table. "Excuse me a sec, will you?"

Once again, Jennifer wasn't yet home when Guy Napier returned to the roost. He'd showered to wash away the city's grit and grime, pulled on a pair of jeans, and was searching the contents of his freezer for possible dinner when the phone rang. In a true test of both quickness and speed, he managed to tear the carton on a dozen frozen burritos, pop four into the microwave, and punch up the timer before grabbing the receiver on the fifth ring.

"I know. You're tied up. No sweat, Jenny. I can feed myself."

"Spare me the kink in your sexual proclivities, Boy Wonder. And bad news about dinner. It'll have to wait a few hours." There may have been a hint of humor in the way Lieutenant Dante made his pronouncements, but Napier was too busy recovering from his surprise to hunt it out. "How soon can you pack a bag and get your ass to LaGuardia?"

"It's packed. I'm on my way, Lou. Where to? What's up?"

"The Atlantic City PD got your Henry Lucas APB on the wire, and two hours ago he turned up in their morgue. We've got a chopper scrambled for you and Mel at the Marine Air Terminal. I want everything they've got, so go sic 'em, big guy."

In preparing himself a light supper of pasta primavera, Bob Talbot had himself a clever shortcut. Over on Third Avenue, just a block from his East Sixty-third Street apartment, the local Korean greengrocer featured an extensive salad bar. On the way home from work, he picked up fresh chopped broccoli, bell pepper, carrots, onions, and shelled peas. No fuss with slicing and dicing. No extra veggies to rot in his crisper drawer. A package of spaghetti, a can of button mushrooms, and a half pint of light cream completed his shop. Once home, he had little more to do than boil water and run through a quick sauté.

Talbot had a daily regimen which included an hour and a half at his health club and keeping a close eye on his diet. He didn't smoke, rarely drank, and tried to limit his intake of animal protein. The results of his conscientiousness were evident. Of medium height and spare, he had the musculature of a distance runner. If he saw any drawback in his build, it was the fact that he tended to carry most of his power in his legs. That was something he was currently working to correct, with lifting aimed at adding mass to his delts, traps, and pecs.

Tonight, dressed in a pair of gym shorts, he had the door to his terrace open to catch the breeze. For atmosphere, he had a little Herbie Hancock in the CD player. His recent workout had left him feeling loose and decidedly mellow. Life was good. For the moment, he was free of any ongoing sexual entanglements and he was beginning to believe he preferred it that way. The AIDS thing was a drag, sure, but the drawer of his night table was well stocked with condoms. In this town, attractive women were in anything but short supply. Why get tied down? Bob had healthy appetites, but he also had a master plan. Those appetites and that plan had to be made to dovetail. He'd gotten his twenty in on the job. Next year he'd make inspector. Once that happened, he'd quit the job and run for City Council. From there, he could pick and choose: Congress, borough president, something big on the state level. He had the social background, he'd served at the grassroots level, and he'd sucked his share of hind end. The world of New York politics was going to be his oyster.

The doorbell rang just as he'd dumped the pasta into boiling water and started to sear the vegetables. He removed his skillet from the heat and hurried to answer. Timing, he reflected as he tugged the door panel inward, was so often everything.

"Captain." Deborah Glenmore, still dressed in the same suit he'd seen her in this afternoon, delivered the greeting with a distancing coolness.

"Hi, Deb. You caught me right in the middle of making dinner. Come in, come in."

As she stepped tentatively into his entry hall, her pale eyes, with their unnerving ability to penetrate and judge without words, flicked first over him and then over her surroundings. Talbot questioned his calculated decision to invite her here, but instead of letting his apprehension slow him, plunged straight ahead.

"That's Chief Lieberman's progress report on the Mott investigation." He pointed to a manila envelope set out on the coffee table in his living room. "From where my office stands, it looks like a wrap, but you go ahead and have a look. Take your time. I'm afraid I've got to excuse myself. My pasta will turn to mush if I don't keep an eye on it."

Glenmore gave him a tight little smile. "No apologies please, Captain. You're the one stuck his neck out to do me the favor. Go cook."

"Get you something to drink? I've got a bottle of San Pelligrino opened. There's also white wine or beer."

"Mineral water, thanks." Glenmore was already halfway across the front room, her eyes still assessing her surroundings. "You've got a beautiful apartment. Mind if I take this stuff onto the terrace?"

"Be my guest."

Fortunately, the spaghetti hadn't suffered from the interruption. With three or four minutes to spare before it was cooked, Talbot hurried to fill a glass with ice and mineral water. The skillet went back onto the burner and he disappeared for a moment to grab a shirt.

"There you are," he told Glenmore, placing the glass before her on the terrace table. It was nice out here, with a slight breeze coming in off the East River. The afternoon's mugginess was vanished after a brief rain squall. Daylight would hold for yet another hour. The lanky blonde had her shoes off and her feet up on the chair opposite, the contents of the envelope removed into her lap.

"Have you eaten?" he asked. "I'm throwing together a simple primavera and there's no way I'll be able to eat it all."

That smile again, but not quite so tight this time. "I'm famished, actually. Thanks."

Inspector Mike Hanniger, Atlantic City PD Homicide, met the New York chopper when it touched down opposite his jurisdiction on Brigantine Island. Napier and Busby were briefed en route over the Route 87 causeway. It was cooler out here on the open ocean than it had been on departure from LaGuardia. Melissa had her window run down. Up front, while his driver got them under way, Hanniger turned in his seat.

"It's sorta a surprise that New York's Finest got a broad workin' Major Case. That must mean you're the cream'a the cream, toots."

"Either that or I bought my way on," Melissa replied. "There's a rumor going around downtown that I give terrific head."

Something caught in the driver's throat. He made a gagging sound clearing it as color drained from the florid, overweight inspector's face. Melissa reached across the seat-back to pat his shoulder. The smile on her face was as soft and sweet as fudge.

"That's okay, Inspector. You're not the first puncher I've met who had a glass jaw. Can we talk Henry Lucas? My partner and I haven't eaten and it's been a long day."

Wariness. "My guys assumed it was drug-related. That's based on location, the way he was dressed, an' how it was done. One 'hind the left ear. Light-caliber. Corpse still had on half'a ton'a gold jewelry. Looked intact. Same wit' the room. Suite at the Nugget, not a *towel* missin'. The sheet we pulled offa the National Crime computer says this guy Lucas's got half dozen priors for sale and possession."

"What about associates?" Melissa pressed. "Our information had Lucas running a string of at least three and maybe four transvestite prostitutes."

Hanniger had completely recovered his composure.

"Joy boys, huh? Come t' think of it, this Lucas did bear a strikin' resemblance t' Little Richard. Considerin' the location an' the way he was dressed, my people thought at first that they might have a celebrity homicide on their hands. One'a them suites is high-roller heaven. Staff said he was pretty much behavin' himself but that there was always a few good-looking party girls around the place. Could be they was mistaken 'bout them. I seen a couple guys with tits in my time where you couldn't tell the difference."

Melissa wasn't warming to this guy.

"I take it that none of these party animals were still on the premises?"

"Cleared out."

"How about evidence that it *was* drug-related?" Napier asked.

"Y'mean actual, *physical* evidence? That slug in the brainpan is a pretty good indicator. That's the way you get done down here when you cross one'a the big boys. We got all the usual ears down out on the street but ain't heard nothin' back yet. We got the sheet on him sayin' he's had problems in that area in the past. Inside'a the suite, all we found was one lousy set'a works inside a shaving kit."

Melissa glanced to Napier. "Those hookers of his are likely to stick out, even in Atlantic City. How hard can they be to find?"

"Can I ask you somethin'?" Hanniger asked. "This APB. Says Lucas was wanted for questionin' in connection to a ten-thirteen homicide. You mind fillin' me in a little there?"

"We had an IAD investigator killed on the west side of Manhattan yesterday," Napier told him. "Heavy prostitution area. Lucas was working the same block. One of the theories we're working right now is a possible rip-off gone haywire. When we went looking for Lucas to ask him some questions about it, we found him cleared out."

Hanniger frowned. "Hooker rip-off? This Internal Affairs joker was gettin' his wick waxed?"

Napier shrugged. "It's one theory."

Deborah Glenmore was surprised to discover this other side of Bob Talbot. Back when he'd worked for IAD, he was meticulous both in his work and in the way he presented himself. Tonight she'd gotten a glimpse of something else: a casual side. Catching him in his gym shorts like that was fun. He didn't drink, had proven himself a fairly decent chef, was in better than decent shape, and was going out on a limb right now to show her this file.

"I don't see how they can call this case anything *but* closed," she asserted.

Across the table, Talbot pursed his lips and smiled, his eyes making frank, friendly contact. "Dante's still got reservations. That's nothing new. I've seen something of the way he does business, and believe me, it's pretty normal."

They'd eaten Talbot's primavera outside on the terrace table and lingered now over cups of decaf cappuccino.

"He's got that kind of free rein?"

Talbot grimaced. "Chief Lieberman thinks highly of him. Dante's first squad assignment was under Lieberman when the chief was the whip at the Sixth. Dante's made him look awfully good in a number of tough investigations. Some say that Lieberman might never have made chief without the headlines Dante helped him grab."

"You can't be telling me that the chief of detectives doesn't question the decisions made by a subordinate special unit commander."

"I might be. Dante gets an awful lot of latitude from up the chain of command. If he's got a problem with some aspect of an investigation, Lieberman will generally cut him the slack he needs to chase it down. Within reason."

"And what's reasonable in a situation like this?"

Talbot resumed smiling. "Right now, it's out of Chief Lieberman's hands. Mintoff's given him twenty-four hours. There's just too much pressure building at City Hall to call it a job well done."

Glenmore handed the envelope back across the table and checked the time. "I was hoping to see something in there that I could help with. Something IAD could do better than Major Case. I guess I should be pleased, huh?" She pushed back her chair.

"You're hitting the road?"

Did she detect a hint of disappointment in Talbot's tone?

"Afraid so, Cap. I'm an early-to-bed, early-to-rise type. With those national championships just a few weeks off, I'm doing extended morning workouts. That means being there when my trainer opens up. Six-thirty sharp.''

"I've scheduled a meeting tomorrow morning to brief the PC on your Bronx investigation. This afternoon I took an hour to read that file again . . . the *whole* file. You did some very good work.''

"Thanks. When do you think I'll see some action?'' Talbot was confident. "Right away.''

"Okay. I gave you my word that I won't do anything without talking to you first. Don't disappoint me, Bob.'' She was on her feet now and gathering up her handbag.

Talbot stood to move with her as she made her way inside and toward the front door. When she reached it, she turned to extend a hand.

"I didn't expect dinner, Bob. Thanks.''

His face lit with an easy grin. "My pleasure, Deb. I expect that come this weekend, you'll have reason to celebrate your own job well done.'' He paused as though something had just occurred to him. "All this early-to-bed-and-rise stuff. That doesn't mean all work and *no* play, does it?''

"Depends.'' She kept it coy.

"I was just thinking that I've got my family's place outside Southampton all to myself this weekend. Why not drive out Saturday after your workout? After all the hard work you've done, you could relax with a swim. Get a little sun.''

It evoked a wistful smile. "A beach with less than a hundred thousand other people on it? You tempt me.''

"That's the idea. We can talk Friday, once the Bronx DA's given you a call. Meanwhile, I'll fax you a map.''

In the world of club owner Bryce Weller, Wednesday night was the beginning of the weekend. And to the inhabitants of that world, the weekend would stretch all the way to the wee hours of next Monday morning. His sleep-by-day, play-by-night clientele didn't live by the working world's standards or the working world's time. They milked trust funds for sustenance and slept only when they were too tired to move or when the drugs ran out.

It was early yet, at only a couple ticks past ten-thirty. The real action wouldn't get cooking until well past twelve. Still, he had a good dinner crowd downstairs, and already a dozen or so early arrivals were lounging at tables around the second-level dance floor. Weller could feel the heavy, thumping pulse of a bass riff tickle the soles of his feet up here in his third-level office. The weekend at FLOTSAM, downtown Manhattan's current toast of the night life, was off and running. Tonight's agenda had two postmidnight acts on the bill, both with big cult followings. Weller was looking forward to having all three levels, from the ground-floor dining room to the sprawling video lounge outside his office door, jammed by one o'clock. There was no sweeter sight than supplicants lining the Crosby Street sidewalk downstairs.

Meanwhile, Weller had his own agenda working, and she was a sweet sight of another sort. A bit of a plain Jane but with a high-energy little body on her, the woman who called herself Ursula Worst was one of the perks Bryce liked most about his job. The tip on her had come from an aging rocker with a taste for life's finer offerings. He'd pointed her out to Weller, and Bryce had pointed her out to the guys working the door. For nearly a month now, she was allowed to jump the line and wasn't charged cover. On a couple of occasions, Weller just happened to bump into her at the bar. He bought her drinks. Last time, he'd passed her a little folded packet fat with a full gram of his personal stash. She'd returned the packet half-empty. The aging rocker reported that she'd walk barefoot through a snake-infested pit for a snort. He also described what she'd do for a man once she got what she wanted. Tonight she'd shown up early. Weller had asked her to join him for dinner. Over their meal, he'd plied her with wine and once again passed her a taste of the gusto dust. But this time, there wasn't anywhere near a gram in there. When she expressed an interest in more, he'd explained that he had plenty more, upstairs in his office.

"Where do you *get* this shit?" the little bleached blonde marveled. In two deft runs, Ursula Worst got every speck of coke laid out before her on the glass top of Weller's coffee table. Two twelve-inch lines, each in excess of a quarter gram.

Now she lay sprawled across his Italian leather divan, head thrown back and eyes roving the ceiling above. Her Adam's apple bobbed seductively. That blouse, loose-fitting and so translucent that he could make out the shape of tiny, upswept breasts, was unbuttoned halfway to her navel. And just below the hem of her ultrashort red leather skirt, he could make out the clasps of garters. The legs, loosely crossed at the ankles, were dynamite.

"It's one of the advantages of having special friends," he boasted. "I'm glad you like it."

She giggled, eyes still on the ceiling. "*Like* it? I fucking *love* it."

Time to play the next card. "Listen, Ursula. I've got a pile of paperwork I'd better get to before all my liquor suppliers get pissed about not being paid. Maybe we'll run into each other later, huh?"

That head, with its chop-cut platinum coif and heavily made-up eyes, came off the back cushion. "Work? You just said a really ugly word, Bryce." Her ultralong, black-painted nails fluttered over the last two buttons of her blouse. Fingers closed on the slinky fabric to pull it from the waistband of her skirt. "I was just thinking, here I am in the office of this totally happening club, with the owner, who just happens to look like he might be a stud. I was thinking what a waste it'd be if we couldn't somehow get *together*. You know what I mean?"

Weller played it nonchalant, slipping out of his jacket and taking a moment to hang it neatly. He was en route toward his little coke-fiend seductress's side on the sofa when the door he'd neglected to lock suddenly swung open. Thwarted in midapproach, he whirled on his unbidden guests. "Who the fuck invited *you* in here?"

Two men, definitely not late night club types, stood just inside the door. Weller, a touch nearsighted and too vain to wear glasses in public, didn't get a good look at them until he faced them straight on. Further protest stuck in his throat. Both were imposing specimens, dressed in summer-weight slacks, jackets, shirts, and ties. While one, a thirtyish, towheaded giant with a bodybuilder's bulk, eased the door closed, his darker and older friend pointed to Ursula.

"Why don't you get dressed and get lost, sweetheart?"

Bryce turned back to her, apology in his tone. "Later, okay? I'll meet you at the downstairs bar."

The young woman stood, making no attempt to hide herself as she slowly did up her blouse, one button at a time. The zipper and waist clasp were undone, allowing her to carefully tuck the slinky fabric and straighten it while watching herself in the full-length mirror mounted opposite. Weller took another step in her direction.

"Sorry, babe. It's an appointment that totally slipped my mind. Later, okay?"

One black-nailed hand went to her head, fingers primping the carefully contrived unruliness of her hair. "Maybe, Bryce. This isn't exactly a turn-on, you know." She exited then without a backward glance. Weller was left rooted and staring at his two visitors in obvious fury.

"What?" he hissed. "I don't see you two for *six fucking weeks*. I've got your money rotting in my desk drawer. You bust in here like it was *me* missed a fucking payday."

"Sorry about that, Brycie." The older of the two raised his chin toward the door. "Nice set on her, if you like your titties tiny. You really oughta lock up if you don't want to be disturbed."

"What I *ought* to do is call the fucking cops."

The big blond guy, leaning with one shoulder against the door, chuckled. He and Weller were about the same age, but this guy was a good six inches taller and outweighed the club owner by as much as eighty pounds. "But, Bryce. We *are* the cops. And you're the crooked little weasel who rakes more cash off the top in a month than either of us makes in a year. Not to mention that bag of dope you've got sitting out on your desk over there. Or the wetbacks you've got working in your kitchen. *Or* the two dozen code violations we choose to ignore."

Weller abandoned the offensive. Instead, he stalked to his desk, dug the key from his pocket, and unlocked the bottom right-hand drawer. A carefully folded brown paper sack came out of it and the half-ounce bag of cocaine went in before he kicked it shut and relocked. The paper sack was hurled in the general direction of his visitors, where it hit the wall behind them with a thwack. Neither man moved to retrieve it as it fell to the carpet.

"Why are you looking at me like that?" Weller demanded. "That's what you came for, so take it. And you don't have to count it. It's all there. Six thousand."

"There's been an internal shake-up, Brycie." It was the older guy addressing him again. "That's what the six weeks downtime was about. And with the shake-up comes a slight change in the rules."

The face on the corpse Inspector Hanniger showed them in the Atlantic City morgue was the face in the photograph Napier and Busby had been circulating for the past two days. The word was put out to local car-rental agencies asking them to report any contacts with apparent transvestites. Lucas's Jaguar Vanden Plas had been located in the Golden Nugget garage. Exhausted, the two visiting detectives had seen no reason to go any further after inspecting the homicide scene. They took a couple of rooms on the Nugget's sixth floor and made arrangements with Hanniger to meet him in his office first thing the following morning. After checking in and dropping their bags, the partners had taken a table in the first restaurant they passed.

"You got enough energy left to think about tomorrow's plan of action?" Melissa asked.

Service was quick. Within minutes of being seated, they had a drink. Once they placed their order, the salad course arrived inside ten minutes. Napier figured the management saw no percentage in encouraging customers to linger over their meals when the real money to be made was in that big, bright, noisy room down the hall.

"You think looking for a pimp in Harlem was tough, looking for three or four transvestite hookers in a city full of them is going to be next to impossible. It might be nice if we knew who they are."

"Or at least what they look like. What do you make of our host?"

Napier grinned. "Hanniger? He's got no idea *what* to make of you, Mel. I think one of his priorities is to spare this hotel and casino any embarrassment. You find a dead guy in one of the high-priced spreads, you play it as close to the vest as you can. Once you learn your victim's a Harlem pimp, you try to sweep it under the rug. He'll go through the motions with us, but I doubt he'll deplete the city treasury assigning extra manpower."

"That's my read, too. Lucas's wallet had money in it. He had all that jewelry on him. Whoever killed him didn't do it to rob him. In my experience, a whore is completely dependent on her pimp. If Henry's own string offed him, they would have taken everything they could get their hands on. I think they found him dead, freaked, and ran.''

"Be my guess," Guy agreed. "A.C. isn't all that far from New York, and if something hadn't scared them away in the first place, I'd think they might already be back home. If they aren't, then they'll probably go to ground somewhere around here. I doubt they'll be renting any suites. We should concentrate on the cheaper motels and rooming houses.''

"If we're lucky, Hanniger can get us a list.''

"Wonderful," Napier groaned. "More legwork, and my feet are already killing me.''

"At least you're in better spirits than you were in this afternoon.''

Napier's expression sobered. "What you said to me was a little more on target than you probably realize, Mel. I haven't been too happy lately.''

"You want to talk about it?''

He shrugged. "What's to talk about? I need to *do* something.''

"You're not convinced you're in love with her, are you?''

A shake of the head. "I *was*, Mel. Head over heels. What I'm not convinced of now is that she's ever been in love with me. She likes superficial things, like the way we *look* together. Everything in her life is contrasts. I'm big and she's tiny. She went to Bryn Mawr, I went to City College. Her father's a career diplomat and mine's a high school history teacher. She likes feeling superior in little ways. I didn't mind at first because I thought she *was* superior.''

"Why?''

"Her world's more sophisticated than mine. She's beautiful. A lot of bullshit reasons, I guess.''

"Sounds like you don't believe them anymore.''

Guy's expression lightened and he was grinning again. "I'm not getting married this spring, Mel. I don't

149

know what else I believe, but I don't think Jenny and I are going to work."

"You've told her that?"

"I haven't seen her. When I do, I will."

Busby now sobered. "I hope it wasn't that stunt I pulled the other night that's brought you to this. I'm thinking maybe I made a mistake."

"You didn't see me kicking and screaming, trying to get away."

"I had to spend a whole day believing you hated me for it anyway."

Napier shook his head. "Naw, Mel. I think I liked it so much, it scared me. It forced me to answer a few questions I've been too chickenshit to face."

An hour later, the pair of them stood in the middle of the corridor between their two rooms.

"G'night, Boy Wonder. I asked the desk for a six-thirty wake-up. See you about seven?"

"The minute you started toward that ambulance, I thought you'd read my mind."

"Forget about it, big boy. The City of New York rented you that room, it's gonna get full value. G'night." Melissa turned for her door.

Napier stood admiring her backside and figured, shit or clover, it was time to take a roll in it. "I'd been fantasizing about fucking you ever since the lou made us a team."

Melissa had her key in the lockset. She turned it, pushing the door inward. "Go figure. I thought it was all my idea."

"G'night, Mel."

Napier was fumbling in his pocket for his key when Melissa turned. This time, it was her admiring his backside. "All right, you wild stud, you. And God help me. Get your ass in here."

ELEVEN

Time was too short and the clock was ticking. Dante was forced to concentrate his manpower in two directions. While the report from Mel Busby wasn't positive, he instructed them to keep plugging. Maybe Lucas's death was drug-related, but there were a few too many coincidences surfacing around this case. Sooner or later, one of them would prove otherwise. Meanwhile, on a second front, they would continue to search out Mott's enemies. The possibility of a missing investigation file was still disturbing. Something was amiss there, and it needed follow-up. The convicted chop-shop cop, Mark Gaskill, was an avenue in need of exploration. Grover and Heckman would chase that one, taking a trip up to Ossining to question the imprisoned man. In an early morning brainstorming session, the four unit members in attendance debated the merits of calling out the Harbor Unit's scuba team. If Dewayne Muncie was their perp and he did throw the murder weapon into the river, it was most likely lodged somewhere in the ten blocks of mud south of the passenger-ship terminal. The kind of underwater manpower needed to conduct a search like that was expensive. Dante nixed the idea. The PC was already antsy enough.

A call to Manhattan South Borough Command revealed that Sal Onofrio had already swung out and headed home. Joe and Jumbo saddled up for the trip down to Staten Island, with Dante taking the first turn at the wheel. As he drove, Jumbo fiddled with the AM dial in an effort to learn who would replace the most recently fired Yankee manager. A particularly inane caller was making a fool of himself on all-sports radio. Beasley switched it off.

"I been thinkin' a bit 'bout that Bay Ridge break-in, Joey. If what you say 'bout the wife suspectin' Mott had a nest egg stashed is true, then she had motive."

"Yeah?"

"Sure. She breaks inta his place lookin' for his cash. Let's s'pose she got a call, tellin' her that the daddy of her little girl was dead."

"From who, the Op Desk?"

"There was plenty other people knew. She was a cop's ex-wife. Maybe someone who hated Mott's shoo-fly ass an' felt sympathetic."

"Like Sal Onofrio."

"Why the fuck not? Don't sound like there was no love lost. She gets the word early, an' Bay Ridge ain't all that far from Bensonhurst. She drives over there lickety-split, tears the place apart, and don't find shit. Me? I feel sorta sorry she didn't."

Dante shook his head. "One thing wrong with that. Once she found out about the splash pad—how, I don't know—she told me she walked right in there and caught him in the sack with Glenmore. Wouldn't that mean she had a key? Our guy kicked the fucking door in."

Jumbo scoffed. "Think, Joey. Your wife catches you with your Johnson where he don't belong, you at least change the locks. Me? I'd up my life insurance; start wearin' Kevlar Fruit o' the Looms."

"Okay," Dante relented. "We'll call Motor Vehicles and have them send her thumbprint to the lab. They dusted the hell out of Mott's place. It's interesting how Sal's name keeps popping up, isn't it?''

"That's 'bout all it is. We may not like him all that much, but I got no reason to believe Onofrio ain't stand-up.''

"Me neither," Joe agreed. "So how'd you make out yesterday at the Hall of Records?''

"Brick wall. Least for the moment. It ain't a *person* bought the house next door, but a fuckin' corporation. The deeds clerk's doin' me a favor there. She's callin' the state attorney general. Gonna find out who the principals are. Once she gets me some names, I'll have Huggie chase 'em for me.''

"Any more Ferraris parked out front?''

"Nope. All quiet on that front. Lady of the house come home just after me last night. Then *he* put in an appearance 'round nine. First time I seen him in a couple days. Maybe he heard DaSilva's screwin' his wife. Came home t' protect his investment.''

"She look to be worth the trouble?''

Jumbo purred like a hungry jungle cat. "Oh yeah.''

"So what's she doing in Fort Greene? Couldn't find Fifth Avenue?''

"I doubt it. She looks like she could find Fifth Avenue just fine. An' judgin' from that set o' wheels I saw, I bet she could even find somebody t' drive her there.''

Viki Onofrio was forever on Sal's ass to get off the Homicide Task Force's Night Watch detail, but Sal liked working nights. He argued that the extra money came in handy, but that wasn't really it. On nights, the squad was small: four guys. Sal was his own boss. Every day, he showed up a few minutes before midnight, spent the next eight hours tagging stiffs for the morgue, and was generally home by nine-thirty the next morning. Sal wasn't much of a sleeper. Pulling regular duty, he could expect four or maybe five hours shut-eye a night, tops. Night Watch duty suited his sleep patterns perfectly. A

quick breakfast, nap in his den for a couple of hours—
or on a nice day like today, out by the pool in his
trunks—lunch in his robe, and then a couple more hours
sack time in the late afternoon. He was always awake
by six, hungry again and all set to enjoy his evening
before heading back to work, internal clock ticking right
as rain.

"What a day, huh?" He called it across the yard to
where Viki stooped fussing with her petunia beds. Why
she insisted on gardening in those silly high-heeled san-
dals was beyond him, but he did like the way the velour
of her burgundy warm-ups stretched tight across her
ass. Before the morning was out, he thought maybe he'd
like to have a piece of that.

Viki ignored his enthusiasm for the day, much like
she ignored most of what he said. It wasn't out of mal-
ice, but over the twenty-two years of their marriage, his
wife had developed a convenient deaf ear. Anything of
real importance filtered through, but the rest of it went
right on by. While she continued with her gardening,
Sal killed the last half of a breakfast Budweiser, heaved
himself onto his side, and rolled directly from his
lounge into the water. Several months back, his doctor
told him he needed to get his cholesterol down fifty
points, and start getting some exercise. Sal loathed exercise but didn't so much mind paddling around the
pool for half an hour or so. To keep Viki off his back
about it, he pretended to be making an effort. The water
was nice and cool. Minimal exertion propelled him in
lazy laps. When he emerged, soaking wet, it was difficult to prove whether or not he'd raised a sweat. Once
the weather turned cool, he'd have bigger problems on
his hands. Viki had ordered one of those stair-climbing
contraptions.

At the terminus of his twenty-fifth lap, Sal's breath
caught when a finger tapped him on the top of the head.
His surprise saw him snort water clear through his nose
and down the back of his throat. The searing pain of it

set his sinus cavities afire. As he surfaced, sputtering and furious as a wet cat, he found Viki squatting on her heels overhead.

"Jesus fuckin' *Christ*! You fuckin' near drowned me!"

"Sorry, Sallie. But look who just walked inta the yard. First I run inta him at Terry's the other day and now he's here."

Recovered now, Onofrio kicked upright and began treading water. There on the pool deck behind Viki was Joey Dante and that nigger partner of his.

"Hate to bother you off-duty like this, Sal," Dante apologized. "Something's come up and we need your input."

Onofrio immediately got suspicious. "My input? So you drive all the way down here t' Staten Island? You couldn't fuckin' call?"

"It's a little touchy," Dante explained. "Is there someplace we could go, sit down and talk?"

Sal knew Dante meant inside the house, and he'd be damned, cop or no cop, if he'd invite that nigger Richardson into his home. On the job, he lived by one set of rules, but down here on the south end of Staten Island, he lived by another. This was white man's land. Living with the Irish was bad enough, but there was one thing the micks and the guineas agreed on: the niggers could run roughshod over the rest of the city, but not down here.

"What's wrong with right out here, Joey? Sun's shinin'. Pull up a chair. Viki'll bring us some iced tea." He grabbed hold of the pool ladder and hauled himself out. When Viki handed him a towel, he slapped her on the ass and nodded toward the house. "Thanks, babe. An' lotsa ice, huh?"

While Dante and Richardson got settled in a couple of chairs around a patio table with its Cinzano umbrella, Onofrio took his time toweling off. "Touchy, you said? I thought you was still wrappin' up the Mott thing. What could be touchy? Ain't it all pretty straight-forward?''

Dante smiled. "Not quite everything. We spent yesterday morning going over Mott's files. Night before last, when I paid your sister-in-law Terry a visit, Viki mentioned something that since strikes me as odd. She said Mott had investigated *you*, and the strange thing about it is that no record of that investigation exists. Not that we found.''

Sal had to sit so hard on his outrage that his sphincter muscles started to cramp. Viki had a fat yap on her. "Maybe that's because this so-called investigation never amounted to any more than it was in the first place, Joey. A pile'a shit.''

Dante eyed him steadily. "You care to elaborate?''

Sal shook his head in disgust. "I'm convinced that prick was diggin' around for some way t' stick it to me, an' up pops the Civilian Complaint Review Board. They'd passed along some crock'a-shit story that some coke-freak club owner told 'em.'' He paused to shrug. "Or maybe it wasn't a crock. All I know is that it didn't have nothin' t' do with me. Mott didn't care. He had a hard-on for me, and now he had a place to put it.''

"What's the exact nature of this crock of shit?'' Dante asked.

Sal scowled. "This crazy was claimin' that a group'a maverick police an' Fire Department guys were conductin' a major shakedown op. It's unfounded, far as I know. Thugs with shields targetin' trendy night clubs in midtown; extortin' payoffs. Maybe it *wasn't* bullshit, but me'n my guys never heard nothin' about it.''

Richardson seemed to be spending more time gawking around than paying attention to the conversation, but now the big monkey leaned forward. A frown of consternation knit his brow. "You call the complainin' owner a coke freak. That just your assessment of club owners in general, or did somethin' come up t' support it?''

"Come up? Only the daisies, wherever they buried his sorry ass. I got little experience with that breed 'cause it was never my beat. All I know is this one's dead. Overdose. It happened a month or so back an' my squad caught it. Ugly fuckin' scene. This guy an' some little bitch with her face'n tits all scratched up; both bought it on a mixture'a coke an' heroin."

"Joint cop and Fire Department op," Dante mused. "And you're saying nothing ever came of Mott's probe? Not that you're aware of? Did he even bother to look into the Fire Department allegations?"

"You're askin' me? Who the fuck do I know in the Fire Department? IAD comes snoopin' around and talkin' extortion, you got enough on your mind, coverin' your own ass."

At that juncture, Viki arrived with a tray of tall, ice-filled tumblers and a pitcher of iced tea. As she set the glasses out and filled them, she avoided Sal's eyes. When Dante and Richardson expressed their appreciation, she muttered something unintelligible and beat a hasty retreat from the field. Watching her, Sal reflected on the fact that she *knew* she had a fat yap. That served to only further incense him.

"So tell me, Joey," he pressed. "Why you muckin' around in this pile'a shit when you already got your perp in the bag? I've heard'a chasin' a few loose ends, but this is busywork."

Paisan or not, the smile this Palace Guard prick flashed him was phony as Hamburger Helper.

"Your so-called perp had pretty thin motive, Sal. There's that, and a few other odds and ends we can't get to add. Right now, we're interested in anyone who might hold a grudge."

Onofrio snorted. "I thought Warren Mott was an asshole—and Warren *knew* I thought he was an asshole—the day we met. Like I say, he had a hard-on for me. But once he got it in his mind to crawl up my ass with it, he shot nothin' but blanks. Why should I hold a grudge when he couldn't hurt me?''

Dante drained his glass and started to rise. ''Sorry again about disturbing you like this, Sal. You understand how it struck us when we heard about it. An investigation and no file. If Mott had any other *hardons*, it was one for detail. It's hard for me to believe he didn't keep a few notes. But—'' he shook his head, the expression on his face saying *who the hell can figure?* ''—the investigation's only three days old, and already there's a lot I can't believe.''

Richardson rose with him. ''Mind if I use your bathroom, Sal?''

Onofrio sure as hell *did* mind, but he couldn't very well tell the man to use the bushes. Distractedly, he gestured toward the open patio slider, dead ahead. ''Help yourself. First door onna left, past the kitchen.'' He never once made eye contact with the black man, turning instead to address Dante. ''Tell you the truth, I ain't surprised Mott didn't keep no file. CCRB gets crackpot complaints about cops all'a time. Terry caught Warren gettin' his dick damp an' threw his ass out. He decides t' strike out at her family. The idea that he was conductin' an extortion investigation is bullshit. Not one that was legit. It was a personal vendetta; him sniffin' 'round for the stink'a shit where there weren't none.''

Richardson had offered to give Dante a break from behind the wheel, and Joe sat with his knees wedged against the dash, head thrown back against the rest. For a moment, they'd debated taking the ferry back to downtown Manhattan and tossed that option over as too time-consuming. Now, en route back over the Verrazano Narrows, Richardson started to chuckle.

''I bet he's got his old lady in there sprayin' that toilet seat an' maybe the whole bathroom with Lysol. Ol' Sal sure don't like us colored folk, *do* he?''

Dante stared off into some unseen distance as he

shook his head. "Sal's dad, Marty, was a cop, so Sal's a cop. Marty used to talk about the 'niggers' like he was running for Grand Wizard of the Klan. Sal's just like his old man: not very well educated, not all that bright, and he's got to have somebody he can look down on. You're black; Sal and his dad are white. If they're looking for somebody to feel superior to, they figure why look any further than that?''

"You gotta love the simplicity of it,'' Richardson murmured. "What would you say that house would run? In-ground pool, nice-sized lot, at least three, maybe four bedrooms?''

"Down here? Two and a quarter; maybe two and a half.''

"Toshiba big-screen TV, Joey. One'a them thirty-two-inch jobs with power swivel. The speakers on his entertainment system are Boston Acoustics; top o' the line an' heavy bread. I know 'cause I priced a pair last Christmas, just for the hell of it. He's got not one but two'a them eye-talian leather sofas—the kind you see in the window of Maurice Villency?—glove-soft an' at least three or four big a pop. An' all that shit was just in his fuckin' den. I didn't get a look at the *rest* of the house.''

Dante turned to watch the side of his partner's face. "What you're saying is that Sal Onofrio lives pretty high for a guy who draws the same pay as I do, am I right?''

Jumbo kept his eyes glued to the road. "That woman in them silly little high heels got a job? She work?''

"Not that I know of. No.''

"My wife works her ass off. New York Public Library don't pay quite so much as the Police Department, but it don't pay peanuts neither. We got two kids in college, granted, but they's state schools, not Ivy League. We got one five-*hunnerd*-dollar sofa, not two at four *thousand*. We got us a Sony Trinitron nineteen-

inch that cost me more'n I should'a paid for a fuckin'
TV. End of every month, we're barely scrapin' by.''

"You're saying you think Warren Mott's extortion investigation might not've been the pile of shit Sal would
have us believe.''

"Sounded good, didn't it? Personal vendetta? Coke-
freak club owner? We might not be able t' find Mott's
file, but I'll bet the CCRB's got somethin' on it. They
generally check them coke-crazed complaints out before they pass 'em along.''

Sal was incensed, and Viki knew it. If he'd told her
once, he'd said it a hundred times: his life inside the
job was separate from their life at home. She didn't talk
about it to the other wives in their Staten Island neighborhood. She didn't talk about it to anyone. Sal had
tried to impress her with the fact that he often did work
of a delicate nature, work that could be compromised
by loose lips. That's what being a cop's wife meant.
Loyalty, confidentiality, control.

There was no sense dodging him on the issue. As
soon as Joey and his partner left, Viki emerged from
the house with her patio tray to collect empty glasses.
Sal still sat where she'd left him, and now, as she approached, he glowered, his head down like an enraged
bull.

"You just *happened* t' mention your scum-fuckin' ex-
brother-in-law's extortion investigation?'' It came out
low and throaty; almost inaudible. "Before or after you
tol' him about the laser surgery I had on my fuckin'
piles?''

When Sal got mad like this, Viki knew there was
little more she could do but play penitent and hope it
passed. She leaned over the table to pick up the black
detective's glass, tray hand trembling. "We was talkin'
about how rotten Warren was t' the whole family after
the divorce, Sallie. I didn't think it was no big—''

The blow from Sal's open hand caught her flush on

the side of the head and sent her flying backwards. When she landed hard on her backside, the tray flew clattering in one direction, and that lone glass shattered on the terrazzo.

"No big *what*?" he snarled. "Deal? Secret? How many times I gotta tell you it's none'a your fuckin' *business*?" In his rage, Sal swept his hand in a crazed, jerky arc around the yard before him. "All'a this is yours, earned by the sweat off'a *my* fuckin' balls. I ask only one fuckin' thing. About what I do in'a job? You keep your fuckin' mouth *shut*. That's too fuckin' much to ask?"

From where she sat, sprawled on the deck and now starting to bleed from a tiny cut made by broken glass, Viki was on the edge of hysteria. "I'm *sorry*, Sallie. I swear t' the mother'a Jesus God, I'm *sorry*. It was Joey Dante we was talkin' to. A guy from the neighborhood."

Sal sneered at her. "The neighborhood was more'n twenty years ago. Joey Dante's been gone from the neighborhood a long fuckin' time. Most'a that time he's been asshole buddies with Gus Lieberman, who's now our glorious chief. Joey ain't on our side no more. He's on the side'a them fuckin' vipers in that snake pit downtown." Sal stood with frightening abruptness, his chair falling over backwards. If he noticed the blood on her hand, he paid no attention. Viki was left sitting where she was as he started off across the lawn toward the house. "Clean up that fuckin' mess," he snarled. "Somebody's gonna cut his feet."

As her husband disappeared inside the house, Viki sat there a moment, trying to get hold of herself. The sting of that wallop he'd fetched her was starting to subside, and the cut wasn't so bad. Her right ear was still ringing, but judging from where his hand impacted, there wasn't likely to be any visible bruising. Over the years since they were first married, Sal had gotten a lot better with his placement.

After taking pains to get upright without cutting herself further, Viki retrieved the tray to collect the empty iced tea pitcher and two remaining glasses. The broken glass had to wait until she returned with the broom and dustpan from the kitchen utility closet. When she entered the house through the patio slider off the family room, she could hear Sal on the phone in his den.

"What'dya mean, *how* do I know? Joe fuckin' Dante was just here with his nigger partner, *askin'* about it. What I'm tellin' ya, pal, is that this guy Dante ain't your garden-variety snake. When he bites, it ain't long before everything *but* your dick starts t' stiffen up."

As Viki crossed to place the tray on the counter next to the kitchen sink, Sal paused. He seemed to be listening for a moment and then he exploded. "Whoa, pally! You think that because there ain't a file no more that it ain't a fuckin' problem? Get your head outta your ass! I'm tellin' you, it's startin' t' heat up all over again."

Neither Major Case detective had ever been to a prison before. They'd seen the way Hollywood romanticized them in the old black-and-whites with James Cagney and Edward G. Robinson, but no film had ever portrayed the cold, brutal *presence* of the place they now entered. Sing Sing was not what either Don Grover or Rusty Heckman had pictured. Both partners assumed this would be more boring than anything, that they'd gotten the short end of today's stick. While Dante and Richardson made a milk run south to visit Sal Onofrio, it fell to the only other available Unit members to rattle a pathetic felon cop's cage. Neither pursuit looked all that hopeful, but Staten Island was closer than Ossining, and a blowhard like Sal Onofrio was sure to offer more amusement.

The law requires cops to carry their duty weapons at all times on the job, unless they are handling prisoners in lockup. Here, the State of New York had more than twenty-three hundred hardened bad guys under key. When the deputy superintendent in charge of security met them outside in the parking lot, his first order of business was to impound their handguns. Just inside the front gate, they were asked to empty their pockets, shed their jackets, and remove their belts before passing through a metal detector. A red and white sticker was affixed to their breast pockets, identifying them as "Escorted Visitors." Only then were they allowed to proceed further inside.

Grover was impressed with their escort: a tall, steel-hard-looking character who was addressed by guards at every turn as "Dep": "Mornin', Dep." "Sign my log book please, Dep?" As they awaited the unlocking of yet another gate, Don leaned over to whisper into Rusty's ear.

"He was in the job, I know just what they'd call this guy."

"Yeah?"

"Sure. Captain Marvel. Look at him. He fucking *shines*."

Grover realized he'd used the aside as a diversion, a means of establishing contact with the familiar. Inside, this place was making him feel anything but confident. All around him were bare, enamel-painted walls, tiny barred windows, and clean-swept concrete halls. Shine or not, he had no idea how this man and his corps of guards could stay sane under these conditions. Here and there, green-suited inmates passed, their walks listless and faces frozen in *give-a-fuck* sneers. As far as Grover was concerned, Captain Marvel and his blue-uniformed legions could have the place. The bars, the echoing clang of gates, the walls glistening sweat in the summer heat; all of it gave him the willies.

In the movies, Grover didn't remember the cells being as small as these in the maximum-security wing. No more than five feet wide and eight feet deep, they were crammed with a narrow bed, a tiny eight-by-ten-inch wall sink, and a Spartan pressure-flush toilet. The more ingenious occupants had rigged tiny tables. Most every cell Don peered into was hung with a clutter of memorabilia from the outside world. One was decorated entirely in red: bedspread, tablecloth, towel, and washcloth.

Former NYPD Sergeant Mark Gaskill—pale, narrow-shouldered, bald with a gray-flecked fringe—sat hunched over a small portable typewriter. Even with bars separating them, he looked to Grover like a New Age monk. His surroundings were stripped bare, reflecting a meticulous neatness embraced by choice, not compliance. Indeed, most of the cells they'd passed were cluttered. Here, the only possessions in evidence were that typewriter and a sheaf of clean white paper.

"Gaskill. Company." The Dep didn't bark it like an actor playing the part might. His delivery was cool, undramatic, and even.

The inmate looked up from his two-fingered hunt-and-peck typing. A pair of intense dark eyes flashed with anger at being disturbed. "I don't *want* company, Colonel."

The rank insignia worn on the deputy superintendent's collar was the same rampant eagle worn by an army colonel. Grover found it interesting that Gaskill would assign the man his corresponding military rank.

Heckman removed his shield case from his inside jacket pocket and dangled his tin before the bars. "We're police officers, Mark. This ain't a social call."

Gaskill squinted to get a better look, and Grover realized the man was nearsighted. He didn't wear glasses, but then, why should he? Here in protective custody, he was shut off from everything that stood at any distance. He'd lived nearly five years like this.

"Let me guess. It's about Warren Mott, isn't it?"

Rusty pointed to the cell door. "Mind if we come in?"

"What if I did? Could I stop you?"

When the door was unlocked with a hollow, metallic clunk, it swung wide. Don and Rusty entered. As their escort locked up after them, he indicated another gate, just up the corridor.

"There'll be an officer stationed right up there, gentlemen. You want back out or need any assistance, just give a call."

Once the three of them were left alone, Gaskill surveyed his visitors more closely. "Go ahead. Sit on the bed. You two got names?"

"I'm Detective Sergeant Heckman and this is Detective First-Grade Grover. Major Case Unit," Rusty introduced them.

When Gaskill smiled for the first time, Grover noticed that there was no warmth in it. The man wasn't quite as tall as he was, but had that same gangly build on him. Don wondered if Gaskill ate like he did.

"Ah. Palace Guard hotshots. Should I be flattered or just impressed?"

Up and down the corridor outside, a cacophony of conversation and television programming filled the air. Don noticed that everywhere they'd gone, the place hummed with a constant, restless din.

"Your choice," Heckman supposed. "Go with your gut instinct, Mark."

Gaskill shook his head. "Better not. I want outta here in another two weeks, and right now my gut instinct tells me to either spit at you or throw something."

Rusty grinned. "It's nice that five years upstate hasn't dulled your sense of humor."

"I don't *have* a sense of humor," the defrocked cop snarled. And just as suddenly as he flared, Gaskill recovered his cool. Watching him, Grover thought the way he could turn it on and off like that remarkable. Spooky. That death's-head smile even returned. "Then again, I got a *good* laugh when I heard some street nigger finally put that shoofly scum where he belongs."

Grover looked to Rusty and frowned, shaking his head like he was confused. "I read an interesting interview: the one *Newsday* did right after your old partner Nestor got it, Mark. You talked about making sure you saw Warren Mott dead. I'd think you'd be disappointed that someone beat you to the punch."

Gaskill continued to beam that smile. "Talk is cheap, Detective. I was mad as hell. Nestor couldn't do the time like I can. He couldn't stand this kind of isolation. Being a cop inside is bad enough. Then there was the shit Mott let slip about the two of us being queer lovers. Nestor was meat the minute he took a cell in with the general population."

Grover's look of confusion only intensified. "He didn't know that?"

"Of course he knew it. But what the fuck did he have to lose? His wife had divorced him. Took his three kids off to Puerto Rico. Everybody from the old neighborhood in Spanish Harlem had him pegged for a *maricón*. What did he have to go back to?"

"Was it true?" Don pressed.

Gaskill's dander was up again. "What the fuck business is it of yours?"

Grover gave it a slight tilt of the head. "None, really. You wouldn't know anyone inside who knew Dewayne Muncie, would you?"

When Gaskill spoke, it came out through clenched teeth.

"There's twenty-three hundred inmates inside this hellhole, Detective. Eighty-five percent of them are niggers, and ninety percent of *them* are from New York City. From what I hear, Muncie was a nigger from the Bronx. How were you with probabilities in high school math?"

Seated alongside Grover, Rusty clucked his tongue. "You wanted Mott dead, and we think Muncie might've done it for you. If we can connect those two facts, you'll *never* see the light of day again, Mark. The door of probability swings both ways. The way we see it, the chances of you meeting somebody inside who knew Muncie are pretty good.''

Gaskill sneered. As he spoke, his tone dripped disdain. ''You're jerking yourself off, Sergeant. For starters, the whites and niggers don't exactly hang out together here. Then there's the fact of where I've been. I'm locked away in isolation, pal.''

Rusty pursed his lips as though seriously considering the points made. ''You still have some contact, don't you, Mark? The Dep told us that much. And a smart guy like you, knows how to use a typewriter; he's in a position to do somebody a favor. Type a brief. Help formalize a complaint against staff. What would you trade for a favor like that?''

Gaskill stared straight back at Heckman now, that mask of indifference no longer behind his eyes. ''Don't get me wrong, Detective. I *wanted* to see him dead. Sometimes the karma wheel spins and comes up justice. I'd like to believe it always will, but sometimes it takes too long for my liking. It took nearly five years this time. You can bust my balls over this all you want, but I never heard of Dewayne Muncie until Tuesday, on the news. Talk to your friend the Dep and see how many briefs I've typed for niggers. I've got a deadline I'm up against.''

''How's that?'' Rusty asked.

''On my book.''

''No shit. A book, huh?'' Heckman looked over at the typewriter. ''About what?''

Just as quickly as he'd shifted earlier to anger, Gaskill now oozed pride. ''It's a novel. Three life-term inmates run a sort of in-house firm. Together with this bleeding-heart civil liberties guy on the outside, they work up cases, do all the research, and he argues them in court.''

Rusty looked impressed. ''You got a title?''

''I like *Pro Bono*. My editor likes *Due Process*.''

''Your editor?''

"Sure." Gaskill stopped; a hint of disbelief dented his scorn. "You mean you don't know? Six months ago, Simon and Schuster paid me a two-hundred-and-twenty-thousand-dollar advance. That's about twice as much as I ever made chopping cars."

Rusty turned to Don, shaking his head. "I guess that means Mark here is rehabilitated."

TWELVE

As the postlunch meeting convened in the Major Case Unit squad room, Tony Mintoff's twenty-four-hour grace period had less than an hour left. Grover and Heckman were fresh returned from Sing Sing and looking subdued. Dante and Richardson had encountered a jackknifed tractor-trailer at the mouth of the Brooklyn-Battery Tunnel and had spent an hour and a half trapped in traffic. Gus Lieberman was the only member of the assembled group who seemed pleased with the progress of his day. He was just returned from a lunch in Chinatown with the commander of the Bronx district attorney's Investigation Squad.

"You first, Chief," Dante suggested. "You're the only one who looks like he might have good news."

Lieberman glanced around the table and opened his notebook.

"As far as the Bronx DA's office is concerned, Marcus Harkness is a pathological liar. Based on his re-cord'a past performance, they'd no sooner cut a deal with him than George Steinbrenner. Accordin' to the DA's squad commander up there, it was a bright little assistant prosecutor who first identified the trend. She got Harkness on a car-boostin' beef three years ago,

169

spotted all the times he'd walked in exchange for information, an' took a little deeper look. Seems the kid'd been feedin' 'em shit for years.''

"What kind'a shit?" Jumbo asked.

"That's the interestin' part. Apparently, he kept his eyes an' ears open, managed t' glean just enough to put together somethin' plausible, an' then used his imagination t' fill in the blanks. Once that lady lawyer caught him out an' refused t' play ball, the next judge who got him in his court gave Marcus six months upstate in a youth camp. Once he did his time, Marcus got wise an' took his act to another DA's jurisdiction.''

"Could your squad commander document it?" Dante wondered. "It sounds like just what we need to buy ourselves a little space.''

Gus shook his head. "It ain't that easy, I'm afraid. Everything but Harkness's list of priors is sealed. This is all oral history.''

"Can we talk to this lady lawyer?" Joe asked.

"We're workin' on that. Name's Yolanda Vega. Went to the Bronx DA straight outta St. John's Law. Sharp little cookie like that don't spend much time workin' the public sector. Not with all the majors downtown droolin' for good affirmative-action talent. Female. Hispanic. On the plus side is the fact that she's no longer an interested party. I got my office try'na find her through the New York bar. What I got now ought'a be enough to get my boss off our backs.'' He paused to look toward Dante. "So what'a you guys got for me, Joey?''

Dante occupied his usual chair down at the window end of the table. His jacket was hung on the nearby coat tree, and one leg was up, his clipboard resting on his thigh. "Talked to Mel down in AC about twenty minutes ago. Homicide down there is still calling the Lucas hit drug-related. Until something else turns up, there's no reason they shouldn't. She and Napier spent the morning looking for the dead man's stable. We had the Two-Eight up in Harlem go by the pimp's crib and see if any of them were dumb enough to just go home. No such luck. Mel sounded tired. It's her opinion that the inspector in charge of Homicide down there would still be pounding a beat if he was one of ours. Guy name of Hanniger.''

Gus shook his head. "Never heard of him. What about this felon cop? Don? Rusty?''

Heckman grimaced as though the mere mention of Mark Gaskill gave him gas. "Man's got a chip on his shoulder nearly as big as his ego, Chief. No doubt the grudge he held against Mott got bigger once Nestor Pelar got it, but we seriously doubt he had Mott done. If anything, he's pissed that somebody else got him.''

Lieberman turned back to the man at the head of the table.

"You got anything else, Joey?''

"One other thing. What do you know about an investigation into Sal Onofrio's Night Watch squad? Allegations of them engaging in extortion. Mott would have launched it right after he came over to work Detective Bureau FIAU.''

"An *extortion* investigation?'' This was obviously news to the chief.

"Thought so. What would the procedure be on a thing like that? Does the field IA unit notify your office when they *commence* an investigation, or only once it turns a bad apple in the barrel?''

"Technically? I should be informed straight off. The way it usually works, with them feelin' their loyalties are divided between us and Inspection Services, they usually don't inform me until they've dangled the hook and got a bite.''

"So they've got a lot of leeway.''

"Plenty. Not that it really bothers me. I don't wanna know about all the candy-ass complaints made against my cops unless there's evidence to bear them out. What's this about the Night Watch?''

"Something we stumbled on through the back door. Then we sorted through every scrap of paper from Mott's office and didn't find the file. Sal wasn't too enthusiastic talking about it, but he did confirm that an inquiry was launched. He claims that Mott's singling out his squad wasn't motivated by anything in the Civilian Complaint Board's evidence. Mott was married to Sal's sister-in-law. She threw him out when she caught him cheating. Sal claims Mott carried a grudge against the whole family."

Gus looked skyward and shook his head. "Who made the allegations in the first place?"

"Some disco owner. Sal says he's since died of a drug overdose. The claim is that a joint group of renegade cops and firemen are shaking down club owners for protection payoffs."

Lieberman's interest was piqued. He'd torn the foil off a fresh pack of butts but now left them at his elbow. "You say you talked to Sal. Aside from proclaiming his own innocence, did he have anything else to say about it? Did he know where it went from him? How far Mott actually got?"

"Nowhere," Richardson growled. "Right where Sal says he should'a got."

"You said that with a certain amount of disdain," Gus noted.

"Beasley's got a problem with the way Sal manages to live," Dante explained. "For a guy who claims he's innocent of taking payoffs, Sal's living pretty high up the hog. I know enough about his background to know there's no money in either family. Where he gets the dough for a new Cadillac, an in-ground pool, and state-of-the-art sound equipment is a good question. There may be no relevance here, but his finances bear looking into."

"You say the file on this investigation doesn't seem to exist," Gus pressed. "Any idea why that would be?"

Dante shook his head. "If Mott was anything, he was

meticulous. If it wasn't for the fact that the file is missing, we never would have chased it this far. If it wasn't Dewayne Muncie who killed him, then we figure the next best bet is a cop who either hated Mott enough to want him dead, or *feared* him enough.''

Gus reached for his Carltons. "A good investigator, one with as much experience as Mott had, would take care to lay his groundwork and be in a position to drop the net before his subject even knew he was in jeopardy.''

Dante smiled. "Unless he *meant* the guy to know he'd been caught.''

"What are you drivin' at?''

"I'm saying that here's an instance where a stickler for detail kept no file. It's missing, so that's possible, right? Or maybe it's missing because Mott wasn't keeping it in his office.''

"The burglary,'' Jumbo murmured.

Dante set his clipboard on the table and came forward in his chair. "That's right. The burglary. The evidence suggests that the burglar was frantic to find something. Our search turned up eleven thousand dollars concealed in a clever place. We assumed that was what the perp was after, that he missed it. But was it?''

A silence fell over the squad room. Through it, the chief of detectives drew thoughtfully on his cigarette and blew smoke through his nostrils. "The logic's good, but it's still a pretty wild shot in the dark,'' he said at length. "Sal Onofrio an' his whole squad was at the homicide scene.''

Dante didn't disagree. "Yep, they were. And without that file, we've got no idea how far Mott's investigation ranged; who *else* might've been implicated.'' Dante pointed at the note Gus made during his lunch with the commander of the Bronx DA squad. "But shot in the dark or not, this investigation is now three days old, Gus. Your Bronx guy just convinced you and us that Marcus Harkness is a bullshit artist. Mel and Napier are down in AC looking for either three or four whores. This new angle is the only other thing we've turned. Where else—''

"Don't forget t' mention that the club owner who made that original CCRB complaint's since turned up dead,'' Jumbo interrupted. "Drug overdose.''

"You've already looked that far inta this?'' Gus asked.

"Sal told us that much,'' Richardson said. "There was a girl died, too; looked like she might'a been the victim of some rough play, so Sal an' his squad caught it. We don't even know their names yet.''

Dante was on his feet and pacing now. "If we can't read Mott's file on it, then let's get the CCRB file on the original complaint. Sal claims he was being picked on because of the family tie-in. We just don't have enough information to know if that's plausible or not. I want to get financial work-ups on Sal and his Night Watch guys, Gus. See if we can find anything out of whack there. If you can locate this lady lawyer and use her to get the PC off our backs, we can chase this thing a little. See where it runs.''

Dante sent Grover and Heckman off to the Civilian Complaint Review Board with a request for files on any Manhattan club owner making shakedown allegations. Beasley was dispatched three floors up to Central Records, where he would attempt to ferret out death reports on anyone who died of drug overdoses inside nightclubs since the first of the year. While he was at it, he would collect the Mott financial work-up they'd requested from Support Services and ask them to do similar profiles on Night Watch detectives Salvatore Onofrio, Craig Palmer, Stewart Beal, and Howard McGraff. Alone in the privacy of his office, Dante placed a call across the river to Captain Rick LeFevre's IAD investigation unit. A gruff male voice he didn't recognize answered and asked him to hold. A moment later, LeFevre came on the line.

"What is it, Lieutenant? I've got an appointment on your side of the water in forty minutes, so make it short."

"A fine afternoon to you, too, Cap. When we culled through Captain Mott's files yesterday, we didn't find Lieutenant Sal Onofrio's name in there anywhere. You got any idea why we might've missed that file?"

"What file?"

"The missing file on Mott's investigation into allegations of extortion, made against the Manhattan South Task Force's Night Watch squad."

"Chief Liljedahl tells me that your further access to any information from this office is going to be restricted, Lieutenant."

"Going to be, Cap? That's curious. I distinctly recall being granted access to Captain Mott's case files."

The comment drew a protracted silence from down the line.

"Right or wrong?" Dante pressed.

LeFevre's voice came back icy; tight in his throat. "I hope you're not implying that we withheld documents from you, Lieutenant."

"I implied nothing, Cap. The question was simple and straightforward."

"Sergeant Glenmore and I turned Warren Mott's Manhattan office inside out. Every scrap of paper in that office ended up here on Poplar Street. We barely had time to get them out of their trans-file boxes before you people arrived here to paw through them. If you didn't find a file on a particular investigation, then there *was* no such investigation."

"Or no such file."

"I beg your pardon."

"There *was* an investigation, Cap. Why Mott wouldn't have documented it is one of a dozen questions I want to see answered right now."

"Warren Mott never conducted an investigation without documenting it, Lieutenant."

"Never's an absolute, Cap."

"Go fuck yourself, Lieutenant." LeFevre broke the connection.

So much for inter-Bureau cooperation. Dante stood, emerged from behind his desk, and was headed for the coat rack when the phone rang. He reversed field. "Major Case. Dante."

"It's Beasley, Joe. It's gonna be a while 'fore these guys can dig through all the overdoses an' narrow it down. I've got one'a the Central Files clerks hand-carryin' Mott's financial picture up to you. Meanwhile, the Brooklyn Deeds Registrar got a couple names for me. Managed t' pierce the corporate veil—I swear t' God that's how she said it. While I'm down here, I'm gonna have Huggie run 'em through NCIC. You got anythin' else?"

"Not here. Why don't you stick with those death reports. See if you can dig anything out once they get you something. When Don and Rusty get back, you can compare notes."

"Sounds like you're off somewhere."

"I am. I've got an idea I want to explore. Anything comes up, beep me. I just talked to LeFevre at IAD, and he says that if we didn't find a file, it's because there wasn't one. Even went so far as to say that if there wasn't a file, there couldn't have been an investigation."

"Ah. Must be nice, always bein' so sure of yourself."

Them two cops, the big, baby-faced dude and the feisty little freckled bitch, gave Lawrence Kipp quite a start when they showed him that ugly mug shot of the Honey Man. Kipp and Junior Murphy had been working this stretch of Ventnor, south of the boardwalk, since just after lunch. The other two were still back at that fleabag motel, way down on Jerome in Margate. They'd agreed to work shifts, two and two. One pair would generate cash while the others slept and tried to score dope. Kipp already knew how hard it was to try and look his best when he was hurting. They'd left New York in a hurry, the Honey Man's stash dangerously low. The situation had gotten nothing but worse since.

Long ago, Lawrence learned that the best way to work his way out of a tight spot was to play outrageous. "Show me a picture of him with his pants down. *Then* ask me if I knows him. Y'all look like you might be hung pretty well yourself, big boy." Kipp was up on his tiptoes, that tight corset pushing his tits up high and proud. He moistened his lips with a slow, languorous sweep of the tongue. There beside him, Kipp noticed that Junior had started to sweat. He thought fast. "Picture like that don't tell me nothin'. You seen one bad-boy nigger been in stir, you seen 'em all. I tell you one thing. He ain't pretty enough t' work our side'a the street."

The lady cop took a step forward and tried to get a little taller. "You from around here, sweetheart?"

Lawrence let himself down off the balls of his feet just a bit. Now that beautiful set of his with all that glorious cleavage was right in the bitch cop's face. Better tits than hers, by the look of things. "Philadelphia. The city of *brotherly* love." He hit that brotherly hard and batted his eyes at big boy. Philly was the closest big city, forty-five miles to the west.

"Where in Philadelphia?"

Kipp kept those tits aimed at her and smiled pleasantly enough.

"Camden, actually. Dudley Park. I'll even give y'all my address if you promise t' get big boy here t' come visit."

The big one didn't look like he was enjoying this exchange one bit. "We want to know if you've ever seen this guy. We don't give a fuck if his pants were on or off at the time. Better yet, we're looking for anyone who might have worked for him. You know anybody like that? His name is Lucas. Henry Lucas. Nicknamed the Honey Man.''

''The *Honey* Man? Worked for him doin' *what*, gorgeous? Robbin' beehives?''

The bitch cop scowled and looked on up the street to where the next group of hoes was wiggling their fannies at passing traffic. One skinny blond white girl and a couple fat niggers. All bitches. If they had a pimp, he was nowhere in sight. There was disdain in Kipp's eyes as he followed the bitch cop's gaze. Street trash. As far as he was concerned, *anyone* could suck cock, but he was an artist. It took somebody who had one to know how good he could make a man feel.

''C'mon, Guy,'' the bitch cop muttered. ''This is a giant waste of time.''

Kipp didn't think her heart was in it, but he was happy to see her on her way. As they started to move off, he gave those tits a jiggle in the direction of the big man and told him to have a nice day.

Brennan was off at a meeting with the owner of his gallery, but Diana had just returned from a mixing session when Dante called and asked if he could drop by. When Joe stepped off the elevator a half hour later, Diana was recently emerged from a shower, her hair still wet. Barefoot and dressed casually in T-shirt and shorts, she kissed him on the cheek, handed over the bag of corn chips she carried, and led the way to the cavernous front room.

''What's up, copper? I just brought home what I think is the final mix of our new album. Wanna quick listen?''

''Maybe later. First I want to run something past you. Something Jumbo and I stumbled on this morning.''

Diana indicated the sofa behind him, took a seat herself, and tucked her bare feet up to sit on them. "Okay. Shoot."

Dante took a moment to gather his thoughts. Diana absorbed the way those penetrating blue eyes of his made frank, easy contact. She'd always liked that about him. When he talked to her, there was no one else in the world. It had to either frighten or flatter the object of his attention, depending upon the nature of the exchange.

"Let's see," he started out. "A little background first, I guess. You've heard of the Knapp Commission."

Diana nodded.

"Well, back before Knapp, there were a lot of cops with their fingers in a lot of pies. Envelopes full of money were just another part of the job. Knapp saw a lot of heads roll. For the most part, those envelopes full of cash became a thing of the past. For the *most* part. Every once in a while, a little stink seeps out. Then somebody does some digging, and before you know it, the Department's got something nasty to confront. Dope-dealer cops. Pimp cops. Extortionist cops. Twenty years ago, small business owners who were operating right on the edge of the law would give the local bulls a little something to turn a blind eye. What I'm wondering now is what you know about that kind of situation existing in the club scene."

Diana took a couple beats to absorb all that information.

"You mean shakedowns? Sure. It goes on, Joe. I guess I've never talked to you about it because I assumed you knew."

When he smiled, Diana thought she detected a hint of sadness there. "Not about this one, Di. Nobody's ever been fool enough to try and cut me in. There's a certain kind of cop who thinks he can't trust me. He's usually right." Dante reached into the bag of chips to grab a handful and then passed them back across. "I need a name. Or an introduction if that's the way you'd

179

rather work it. I need a club owner who'd be willing to talk to me.''

''About *shakedowns*?''

He moved to reassure her. ''You might know about them, Diana, and everybody else on the inside of the club scene might know, but believe me, the rank-and-file cop knows nothing. If there is such an operation, it's being run by a small group of renegades.''

''Why would any owner in his right mind want to talk about it? Wouldn't he be putting himself in serious jeopardy?''

''I don't think he'd be likely to *want* to, but once we move in and shut this game down, he's the guy paying bribe money to crooked cops. That's a felony. The city and state'll revoke licenses right and left.''

''You're offering some sort of protection from that?''

''If he plays ball? You bet. Immunity.''

Diana took a moment to think and carefully word her response.

''If club owners were a separate species of animal, I might liken them to barracuda, Joe. You go diving off any of the leeward islands down in the Caribbean, you see these schools of the brightest, most beautifully colored fish imaginable. And all the while, you've got shark in the back of your mind. You don't really expect trouble, but you're always aware of the possibility. And then, right in among the other fish, swims this long, lean-looking guy who might even be attractive if he didn't have those rows of wicked-looking teeth. He's not a shark, Joe. He doesn't have to keep moving to breathe. A barracuda can drift around looking for all the world like he's enjoying his surroundings. You know the fish population is safe as long as he's eaten recently. Otherwise, he can rip anything that catches his fancy to shreds.''

''Club owners, huh?''

''You got it.''

''I need to meet one,'' he pressed.

Reluctantly, she shrugged in acquiescence. "Okay. It's probably going to take a little legwork. I can't say I'm *friends* with any of them, but I know a few. Let me dig around and see what I come up with."

"Hate to push, but I'm on a tight schedule. It could be that this is tied to the homicide I'm working."

"Fine. Most of the guys I'd want to talk to are only just getting out of bed at this hour, but I've already got a couple ideas. I'll get on it tonight. *Now* do you want to hear my tape?"

For a change, Dante got home to the Village at an early hour. After parking his car, he stopped at the deli to replenish his beer supply and then grabbed a loaf of french bread from the patisserie next door. There were an inordinate number of pretty women parked at the little café tables inside the bakery this evening. The sight of them lifted his spirits. Tonight he was going to order in Chinese, open a beer, and put his feet up. At some point he'd take a look at Warren Mott's financial profile, but for the most part, he intended to relax. There came a point in every investigation when Joe knew that his subconscious, left to its own devices, could be counted upon to make a major contribution. A good night's sleep helped, and so did distraction. A month ago, the administration at John Jay had asked him to teach a night class in investigative technique next semester. He'd put off working up a course proposal. Tonight it looked like he might finally get started.

As he strolled up the tree-lined Perry Street sidewalk, dodging an unscooped pile of dog shit, the lieutenant was surprised to find Sergeant Glenmore loitering outside his place, perched on the front fender of a parked Mazda Miata.

"Evening, Sarge." He shifted his groceries from one arm to the other and dug for his keys. "Should I be surprised, or did I miss a message somewhere?"

Glenmore hopped to her feet, and once again Dante

was impressed with the way she moved. Fluid, perfectly balanced.

"I tried to reach you downtown, but they told me you'd already left for the day. I'm sorry to bother you at home like this, but I think there's something we need to get straight."

Dante released the latch on the iron gate and nodded toward his building's front door. "I realize you're in training, but I'm gonna have a beer. There's cold seltzer in the fridge. Join me?"

Glenmore followed him into the building, waited for him while he checked his vestibule mailbox, and entered his apartment ahead of him as he held the door. He excused himself a moment to pry the cap off one beer and pour his unexpected guest a glass of seltzer. The sergeant accepted the glass offered her, took a sip, and nodded her appreciation.

"Thanks. This isn't at all what I expected. It's a curious place for a karate-fighting cop."

While Dante threw open the shutters over the windows to the street, Glenmore found a place and sat. He was justifiably proud of this place. Situated on the ground floor, it ran back from the street to a private little garden. The living room was big, with an ornate marble fireplace and two walls lined with books. The decor was an eclectic hodgepodge of predepression furniture. There were several pieces of Brian Brennan sculpture, and above the fireplace hung a Charles Fung oil of Diana Webster. The painting dated back to the period when the hungry young singer posed for a series of nudes. In this one, she sat with her back to the viewer, one leg tucked beneath her, and the other stretched out behind for balance as she reached for something unseen.

"I'd like to think that karate-fighting cop is a little limiting. I've got a few other interests."

"Obviously. Have you actually read all these books?"

"Most of them. So what is it you tried to get hold of me about that couldn't wait until tomorrow morning?"

Glenmore set her glass on the table before her, using the moment to center herself. "I'm still not sure how this is gonna come out, Lieutenant, but here goes. I overheard Rick . . . uh . . . *Captain* LeFevre's half of the exchange he had with you this afternoon, and I felt like I needed to try and explain something. Rick's been under a lot of pressure at home lately. It's why he's been acting the way he has. I'm not here to make excuses for him, but you should know that. What I came here to tell you is that we very much want to see Warren Mott's killer apprehended."

"That's good to hear, Sergeant."

Glenmore frowned at the edge of sarcasm Dante inserted into his tone. "I think that what you're seeing in Rick's attitude, and probably in mine, is resentment at being excluded from the investigation. Warren was one of ours. We feel it's only right that we be involved. I came here to ask you to let me help; to tell you it's making me nuts, being forced to sit out in the cold like this. Warren Mott and I worked shoulder to shoulder for five long years. I don't want to see his killer go unpunished."

"You were lovers." He said it matter-of-factly, to see how it would hit her. She took it almost like she'd been slapped awake after drifting off.

"You know." Subdued, almost defeated. "Mind if I ask how?"

"I'm good at my job, Sarge."

"It ended right after she caught us together."

"I heard about that, too. If you want to help, tell me what you know about that money we found. What was he up to?"

Glenmore retrieved her glass and took a slow sip before shaking her head. "We had an affair, Lieutenant, but there was a side of Warren I never got to know. It was like there was a door to one part of him that he

183

kept locked and bolted from the inside. The discovery of that money was as much a surprise to me as it was to you. Maybe even more so.''

"What surprised you? The money's implications?''

"You mean that he might have been dirty?''

"Bingo.''

"I still won't believe that, Lieutenant.''

"Did he ever tell you about a shakedown investigation? About a scam being run by renegade cops against midtown night spots?''

Her gaze clouded. "What investigation was that, Lieutenant? I've been all over those files and—''

"It wasn't there, but we've got reason to believe such an investigation did exist.''

"Who are the cops?''

He shook his head. "Not important.''

Glenmore sank back into her chair, obviously frustrated. "Once Warren moved across the river to take over the Detective Bureau's FIAU, we only spoke once or twice . . . on the phone. They were more the how's-it-going sort of thing than anything else. I think he still felt uncomfortable with how it ended between us.''

"How *did* it end between you?''

Now there was an edge of sadness in her voice. "It just sort of petered out. Once his wife broke in on us, it killed something in it for him. Maybe it was the thrill of keeping a splash pad and having a mistress. I never thought that was all there was between us, but . . .''

From down the hall toward the bedroom and bath, Copter the cat ambled into the living room. A glutton for affection who always recognized a potential admirer, he made a beeline for the chair occupied by the attractive blond stranger.

"What an interesting-looking cat. What is it?''

"It's a he. Name's Copter.''

"I mean, what *breed*? He's got *spots*.''

"Egyptian Mau. Listen; I was planning to order in

184

some Chinese tonight. There's always too much. Care to join me?''

Glenmore looked up, both surprised and apparently pleased by the invitation. "I can't, Lieutenant. But thanks. My trainer just got a batch of competition films he wants me to watch with him. It's nice of you to ask.''

Tonight some of Glenmore's hardness was gone. The gesture she'd made was obviously conciliatory. Maybe Rosa was right about her. Shoofly or not, Joe liked what he'd just seen. As they approached the front door, she paused, a mischievous smile surfacing.

"You know, I'm wondering if you'd be interested in getting together on the mat sometime. I think it would be good experience for me. Most people I spar with are my size or smaller. I don't think I've ever fought anyone good who has your leverage.''

"Might be interesting,'' he admitted. "Let me think about it.''

Once she was gone, Dante sat with the cat in his lap and finished his beer. In a mind that was supposed to be freewheeling in neutral, he was experiencing anything but a slowdown of cerebral function. Instead, he was actively entertaining the idea of going to the mat with Deborah Glenmore, and it wasn't inside any dojo.

Diana Webster waited until after dinner to contact her manager. Johnny Hopper was out on the coast negotiating the details of a Christmas tour being planned in conjunction with release of her band's new album. She reached him at his Wilshire Boulevard hotel, and when Hopper heard the details of what Dante had in mind, he gave it a long, low whistle.

"Then all of 'em are up to their tits in shit, hon. The only way *anybody* gets paid in that world is under the table.''

"Is there any one of them we're particularly fond of? Somebody whose ass you think might be worth saving?''

Hopper could be heard to chuckle down the line. "Maybe we could work this to our advantage. I can think of half a dozen people who are gonna be hurt, but I like Bryce Weller best. You remember him?"

Weller was the owner of FLOTSAM, a club in SoHo on Crosby, off Grand. It was currently in vogue with denizens of the downtown scene. If Diana remembered correctly, this establishment was the second Weller had fronted in the past half dozen years. The last one, opened on a shoestring, had gone like a house afire for a few months and collapsed under its own weight. There was too much overhead; too much cash skimmed off the top. There were too many wild, private drug orgies . . . or so the scuttlebutt had it.

"Why Weller?"

"How soon you forget. Remember his grand opening last New Year's Eve?"

"Sure."

"But you've probably forgotten that Queen of Beasts played that gig for half the usual fee."

It all came flooding back. One of FLOTSAM's backers was the son of their record label's CEO. With the new album set for release later this same year, Hopper's strategy in accepting the deal presumed that a little back scratching would be repaid in kind. If a label elected to skimp on a new release's promotional budget, that album was doomed before it got out of the gate.

"Howard Lowenstein's son."

"You got it, hon."

"Everyone with money in FLOTSAM is exposed right now, Johnny. I know Dante, and I know this is serious."

"Let me make a call," Hopper suggested.

"Dante's in a hurry."

"I'll get back to you within the hour. Just sit tight."

At eleven o'clock that night, Sal Onofrio left the house through the garage and climbed behind the wheel of his IROC Z-28 Camaro. As he prepared to make the nightly run into Manhattan South Borough Command, he still had that prick Dante heavy on his mind. Every man in his squad knew how much he had to lose, and knew enough to keep his mouth shut, but the proximity of a hard-nose like Dante still scared him. The man had now been to his house. He'd seen how he lived. That fucking nigger Richardson had been inside. There wasn't much Sal could do about it now, but he could make damn sure that the others knew of the danger, and where it lurked.

The Genie opener started the big door rolling up and out of the way as Sal started the engine and tugged the shift lever into reverse. Prudence demanded he make sure he was well clear of Viki's Caddy before easing off the brake. The way the bitch parked in here sometimes, it was like trying to get a sardine out of the tin with bare fingers.

Sal never saw the shadowy figure who slipped in beneath the rising door. His head was turned away, his eyes focused on the car beside him as the figure slid alongside. A .32-caliber American Derringer "Ultralight" came up in line with the back of his head. When it was directly behind his left ear, the shadowy figure pulled the trigger.

Sal never heard the report of that shot, but inside the house, where his wife was watching the closing credits of "Knot's Landing," it sounded like somebody had pitched a firecracker into the garage. Viki hurried through the kitchen to peer out beyond the pantry door.

The light on the Genie threw a dim, eerie illumination over the scene. She'd been riding Sal about putting in something bigger than a twenty-five-watt bulb. She worried about creeps lurking in the shadows when she made a late run to the 7-Eleven for cigarettes. Sal explained that this was Staten Island—*White* Staten Island—and she was thinking like they still lived in Brooklyn.

There was still plenty enough light for her to see the sparkle of shattered glass from Sal's side window where it littered the garage floor. And there was enough light to create a soft glow behind the crimson sheen coating the inside of the windshield. In a heartbeat, it hit home like a sledgehammer blow to the solar plexus. When her guts heaved, she nearly choked on the surge of puke. Then she started to scream.

THIRTEEN

Instead of climbing into the sack and getting a good night's sleep, Dante had Warren Mott's financial work-up spread before him. Sergeant Glenmore's visit helped strengthen his resolve to make sense out of Mott's movements on the night of his death. Joe hoped something here in the dead man's finances would show an irregularity: a suspicious check written; an unusual deposit made; anything. He'd been at this stuff for four hours and it was now eleven-thirty. He'd found nothing. These figures, like every other aspect of this case, had become blurred.

Dante wondered if he'd nodded off when he started suddenly at the ringing of his phone. As he hurried into the kitchen to get it, he peered at the oven clock. It wasn't going to be any news he wanted to hear. Not at this hour. "Yeah."

"Gus, Joey. Somebody just hit Sal Onofrio. In his car. In his garage. One in the head. Exec down at the One-Two-Three just called. Caught me on my way home from the PAL awards banquet."

"Just the one bullet?"

"It was plenty. Half his gray matter's on the windshield. The wife says he'd just walked outta the house

189

on his way t' work when she heard the shot. Thought it was kids fuckin' around with firecrackers. It sounded so close, she took a look.''

"I'm rolling." Dante's guts felt like he'd crested the big peak of the Coney Island Cyclone. He'd lost the only puzzle piece he had toward solving the Mott homicide. Breaking the connection, he dialed the Operations Desk. When the duty man picked up, Joe asked him to roust Jumbo, Don, and Rusty, telling them to move at 10-13 speed.

The streets of his neighborhood seemed busier tonight than they were last night at this same hour. As Dante trotted diagonally across Hudson and up onto the opposite sidewalk, he saw that the White Horse was once again jammed with the usual summer night clientele. He also saw Linda Fletcher at about the same time as she spotted him. She waved and started toward him, looking delectable as ever.

"Hi, Lieutenant."

He barely slowed. "Joe, remember? Emergency call. I'm on the run."

She threw a quick wave as he disappeared in the direction of his garage. From up the block, Dante flashed the high sign at the lounging garage attendant. On his arrival, his Plymouth was parked idling at the curb. There was no problem with traffic at that hour, and he drove distractedly, depending on the roof flasher and an occasional blast from his siren to clear the way. A mental picture of Viki Onofrio discovering Sal's body lodged itself front and center in his mind's eye. By nature, she was as nervous as a novice nun teaching junior high. This would drive her right to the brink. He wondered if the more delicate and level-headed Theresa Mott would be on hand to help calm her sister.

The scene Dante found in Sal Onofrio's suburban Staten Island neighborhood was typical in scale for a crime of this nature. The news teams were starting to trickle in and get set up. Neighbors stood clustered in their bathrobes on adjacent lawns. The yammer of a dispatcher's voice and the flashing red and white lights of a half dozen parked radio cars filled the balmy night air. Joe spotted the chief's Buick as he picked his way forward toward the foot of Sal's driveway. Several uniforms were monitoring traffic there at the curb. A heavyset brunette with her hair tied back in a ponytail gave his shield a glance and waved him under the yellow tape.

"You seen the C of D?" he asked.

"Back there somewhere, Lou. The guy who got it; you know him?"

"A long, long time. Where have they got the wife?"

"Last I heard, she was still in the house. Poor lady. She's a mess."

Dante nodded his thanks and pressed onward. He'd noticed that the crowd at the top of the drive was standing clear of Onofrio's Camaro. Some loitered at the edges of the lawn, and others stood clustered around the back end of Viki's Cadillac. There was nothing nastier to look at than a man missing half his head.

Bits of broken glass gleamed on the concrete floor of the garage below the driver's door. As Dante approached, he slowed to take a few deep breaths and ease his hands deep into his pockets. The area surrounding the car was well ordered and seemed undisturbed. A lawnmower, weed trimmer, and host of other gardening tools were arranged along the side wall. Aside from the glass shards, the floor was clean. Neither car had a speck of dirt on it. So Sal and Viki were neat freaks. Their back gardens, lawn, and pool area were groomed with that same precision. If anything, the Crime Scene Unit might get a little break on account of these conditions. Joe took another deep breath and moved alongside the driver's seat.

The impact of the slug had pushed the dead man forward and to his right, where he now lay hunched over the shift console. From that angle, it was easy to see the bullet's point of entry behind the left ear and difficult to see the exit wound. Joe figured he should be grateful for that. The damage was evident enough in the amount of blood and blackened flesh coating the windshield.

"They tell me the car was runnin' when they found him. Shift lever's in reverse. He died with his foot on the brake."

Dante straightened and turned to find Gus a few feet behind him. "Nasty way to go, boss." His gaze moved to the automatic door mechanism. "Sal starts the door rolling, the perp slips beneath it, and . . ." He let it trail off.

"Yep. All nice'n neat. Wanna make any bets on the caliber'a that slug?"

Dante shook his head. "I'd rather bet baseball."

Fifteen years ago, when Diana Webster first moved to New York, she might have idolized Bryce Weller. Back then, her ambition was still raw, and a hunger for success rumbled in her belly. Weller owned *the* happening club. The atmosphere created and nurtured there was the toast of the downtown glitterati. FLOTSAM was where stars with hungry egos came to be seen. It was where tomorrow's hopefuls believed they had to be. Tonight, as Diana stepped from her cab at the corner of Crosby and Grand, a hundred such hopefuls lined the sidewalk outside FLOTSAM's velvet rope: eighteen- and twenty-year-olds, hairstyles and clothes worn like battle dress as they stood out here beyond the pale, on the fashion frontier.

At the ripe old age of thirty-three, Diana now only made this scene occasionally. Gone were the days when she had to stand in the crowd out front, hoping the doorman might spot her familiar face and wave her on. She wasn't the kid from Pittsburgh with a remarkable build and a rowdy mouth anymore. Today she was a star. Doormen fawned and cleared the supplicants from her path. Now, as she approached that crowd on the sidewalk, she braced herself. She wasn't dressed to dazzle like she would onstage, and managed to saunter along the curb undisturbed until she reached a point opposite the door. Fortunately, one of the two guys working up front noticed her instantly. He and his partner moved like their routine was choreographed. The bigger of the two stepped forward to plant himself between the entrance and the people at the head of the line. His partner unhooked the street-side rope from its stanchion and nodded discreetly in Diana's direction. It wasn't until she'd drawn opposite of these two, inside the protective confines of the cordoned area, that the squeals and oohs erupted.

"Evening, Diana," the smaller doorman greeted her.

Diana was plenty familiar with this unctuous little weasel. He was a fixture on the circuit, moving from club to club as one fell from favor and another took its place. The business demanded the presence of a discriminating eye at the gate; one who knew all the players, regardless of how obscure they might be. This character was not only paid well to perform his function, but mistakenly believed that he, too, was a star. Not content to just be downtown's preeminent doorman, he also called himself a poet. Diana had seen some of his work and found it both offbeat and inaccessible. On several occasions he'd plied Queen of Beasts with song lyrics. Terrible stuff.

"You got any idea where I can find Mr. Weller, Zowie?"

The weasel smiled. "Matter of fact, he just called from his office, wondering how the gate was."

Before he could say any more, Diana thanked him and hurried inside. At quarter past midnight, the dining room there on the ground floor was jammed. Upstairs on the second level, the first live act had yet to appear on the main stage, but the huge dance floor was filled to overflowing with bobbing, frenzied patrons. The hot new Holy Hell release pulverized the atmosphere through enormous ceiling-hung speakers. Like a boat, Diana created a wake as she started along the bar toward the third floor. Heads turned, elbows nudged, and mouths moved to ears.

FLOTSAM's video lounge on the third level was an environment of arcade games, large-screen televisions, sofas set about in intimate little groupings, and a long, neon-lit bar. The noise level up here was marginally lower than downstairs, and it was here that the real lounge lizards held court. Anyone hurting for a coke high could probably get one snorting the crud off the restroom floors. And it was down the hall from the rest rooms that Diana found Bryce Weller's office.

One of FLOTSAM's bartenders answered the singer's knock. His face lit with recognition as she slid past him. Weller was on the office sofa, hunched forward over the coffee table and carving a steak. A second plate of food sat alongside the club owner's. There were glasses of red wine as well as a small pile of cocaine. It appeared that she'd interrupted their dinner.

"Diana." Bryce said it with his mouth full. Eyebrows raised in question, he tapped the bottle of wine with his steak knife.

The singer shook her head. "No, thanks. You got a call telling you to expect me?"

"Yeah. What's this about?" He was still chewing.

She shot a quick glance at the bartender. "Privately, okay?"

Weller finally swallowed, following it with a swig from his wineglass. "Sure. Sure. You mind if we finish up here? Randy's got a long night ahead. You want a snort? Go ahead and do yourself."

"Not my brand, friend."

Weller shrugged and started carving again. "To each his own, babe. It's fine shit, right, Randy?"

* * *

The way Napier eased his big hands across her skin was the closest Melissa Busby figured she might ever come to being worshiped. It almost made her crazy with pleasure, all that size and strength so controlled, floating along the length of her like velvet. She knew this was insane, the two of them carrying on like this, but right now she didn't much care. This was ecstasy; a man in no rush, a man who understood that an imaginative journey was every bit as exciting as the journey's end. And God, what an imagination Guy Napier possessed. They'd fallen into bed exhausted over an hour ago and there was still no end in sight.

When the phone on the nightstand rang and her lover's tongue abruptly ceased flickering across the contour of her rib cage, Melissa let out a low, irritated growl. "We gonna get that?"

Napier, over on one hip and head propped in his free hand, traced a finger around the nipple of her left breast. "We got any choice?"

Melissa groped, found the receiver, and dragged it to her ear on the pillow. "What?"

"Dante, Mel. Sorry to wake you up like this."

"Yeah, Joe. No problem. What's up?"

"You remember me telling you about that missing file on Mott's extortion investigation?"

"Sure. Sal Onofrio and Night Watch. Something about shaking down disco owners."

"We confronted Sal about it this morning, and tonight somebody put a bullet in his brain. It's hard to imagine the two aren't connected."

"You think maybe Lucas is connected, too?"

Napier saw the look on Melissa's face and stopped his tinkering. Wedging her feet beneath her and using one elbow, Busby managed to get herself into a sitting position.

"We don't think anything yet," Dante replied. "But Gus wants to upgrade NYPD's interest in the Lucas homicide. He'll be talking to the brass down there, first thing in the morning. For now, we'll put the search for Lucas's string on the back burner. You'll be working directly with AC Homicide on their investigation."

"*What* investigation, Joe? They couldn't get the file closed fast enough. A Harlem pimp with a record for drug arrests gets killed inside one of the high-roller suites at the Golden Nugget. That gets out and they won't be able to *give* that suite away, let alone rent it. Gamblers are superstitious."

"We're talking about a possible connection to not just one but *two* ten-thirteen homicides," Dante reminded her. "Ride herd on them if you have to. I'll bet you won't once the NYPD chief of detectives explains the situation. First thing, I want our lab people to see copies of all their forensics reports. Coroner, Ballistics, the works."

"Consider it done."

"Thanks, Mel. How's the Boy Wonder holding up?"

Melissa's eyes roamed across her lover's naked torso and on down to the earlier focus of her attention. Remarkably, the interruption had done little to diminish his ardor. "Guy? Oh, he's holding up just fine, boss. Not a whimper out of him. Matter of fact, I think he's enjoying the change of scenery."

"So. Diana. What's so important that we've gotta go all hush-hush? I hated to make Randy eat and run like that."

As Bryce Weller asked it, he carefully cleaned the tip of his steak knife with his napkin. After inspecting the job he'd done, he reached out to scoop a neat little pile of cocaine onto the tip of the knife and draw it toward his nose. One quick sniff and the coke vanished.

"What's so important? I don't know. Maybe it isn't important at all." Diana was seated adjacent to Weller in a leather-upholstered tub chair. The dinner dishes were stacked off to one side, with the napkins wadded atop them. As she spoke, Weller twirled his knife and continued to eye that pile of coke. "I have a friend who's a cop. That friend dropped in to tell me an interesting story this afternoon.''

Weller set the knife down on the table almost simultaneously with the word ''cop.'' She had his attention now. Undivided.

''That a fact? A friend, you say?''

''A detective lieutenant. Runs a special unit out of police headquarters. He tells me they're getting set to come down hard on cops involved in the shakedown rackets.''

Weller was confused. ''Why tell *me* this?''

''Why? Because my friend knows I'm pretty well connected into the club scene. He knows I may have friends I want to protect. The shakedowns they're focusing on involve cops on the take from club owners. When I heard that, I got a little concerned.''

''I appreciate it, babe, but those guys are the crooks and I'm the victim. If you're worried about it hurting me later, don't sweat it. That kind of negative publicity is just what a place like this thrives on.''

''Dream on, Bryce. They plan to put undercover people into the clubs and bust both the bag men *and* the people paying them. Anyone indicted risks losing city permits and his state liquor license.''

She had more than Weller's attention now. He was stunned.

''Goddammit! That's exactly what I'm paying them to protect me *from*.''

Diana shook her head. ''Not anymore. Not the way my friend tells it. Somebody killed the Internal Affairs guy investigating the shakedowns. That's kicked it all upstairs, and the big boys've turned the heat up.''

The club owner's eyes narrowed slightly as he raised his chin, regarding her down the length of his nose. ''You say your friend knows you have people you might want to protect. *How* do they get protected? Gimme a for-instance.''

''They want a cooperative owner on the inside . . .

197

to help them set up the sting. The party who agrees to cooperate walks. Everybody else goes down as far as the district attorney can take them.''

It was two o'clock before the Crime Scene Unit finished going over the Onofrio garage and the immediate area. Door-to-door canvassing of the neighborhood produced no useful information. When Viki Onofrio failed to come off a hysterical crying jag, her doctor was summoned to sedate her. A search of the house revealed nothing but a lot of expensive furniture and high-tech playthings. Now, once he'd ordered the scene wrapped, Dante summoned the members of his squad to a powwow in the relative privacy of Sal's backyard. With Gus also tagging along, they gathered around the same poolside table used eighteen hours ago by Joe, Jumbo, and Sal.

"Okay," Dante addressed them. "Don. Rusty. Beasley tells me he got hung up in Central Records this afternoon. You guys never got a chance to compare notes.''

Heckman had his notebook already in hand. He thumbed back a few pages and cleared his throat. "Our copy of the Review Board file is back in the squad, but Donnie and I can probably piece most of it together. Man who made the complaint's name is Daniel Ironstone. Owns a club called Heebie-Jeebie on West Seventeenth.''

"Owned," Jumbo corrected. "Ironstone an' some bopper name'a Jane Doe are the pair'a overdoses Sal told us about. Night Watch caught the squeal, mid-June.''

"Jane Doe?" Grover asked. "It's been a whole month and they still haven't got an ID?''

"Nope. Prob'ly a runaway. ME puts her age at around sixteen or seventeen. I read the file front to back, an' there ain't jack shit on her.''

"But the beef was legit?" Dante pressed. "At least so far as the CCRB was concerned?"

Heckman nodded. "You bet. The way Ironstone filed it, a pair of guys would show up once a week—one cop, one fireman—to collect a cash payment of five hundred bucks. He claimed they first approached him about a month after he opened the club in the fall of 1987."

Dante turned back to Richardson. "What else was in the ME's report?"

"He don't paint a pretty picture. Girl was found with her blouse torn off her. Lotta scratches on her face an' the front of her torso. Both of 'em died injectin' high-balls. Lab analysis of the cocaine toxicity levels were high, but that wasn't what killed 'em. The traces 'a heroin they found mixed in with the coke in the syringe was unusually pure. They were playin' with dynamite."

"Sal said he and his squad didn't suspect foul play. What does the report say?" Gus asked.

"Wasn't really conclusive, Chief. After Sal's guys did the initial report, the regular squad at the Thirteenth caught it. They went through the motions, but it don't look like they had their hearts in it. Nobody asked where Ironstone got his hands on horse with that sorta kick to it. The ME didn't challenge the cause 'a death. No witnesses stepped forward t' stir it up." He shrugged. "Some dumb-shit doper kills hisself an' some little girl with no name. Case closed."

Lieberman looked at his watch and closed his eyes. "It's late, gentlemen. We don't get some sleep, none of us is gonna be able t' think worth a damn. Where you wanna head with this, Joey?"

"My first instinct? Hit the guys in Sal's squad. Tear apart Sal's office at Borough South. We didn't find diddly here, and I'm betting he's hidden something somewhere." Dante gestured toward Richardson. "Jumbo's right about one thing: Sal lived awful high on the hog. We need to find out how."

Grover pointed to Dante's notes. "I doubt those financial work-ups we ordered are gonna help, boss. Too obvious. I think we should check into safe deposit; see if any of them have boxes.''

''And not just the banks they use for their up-front business,'' Heckman added. ''*All* the banks near their homes. The banks close to Borough South. Those financial work-ups are only gonna reflect accounts they've got under their real names. They'd be fools not to keep that action clean.''

Dante's gaze roamed back and forth between the two partners. It was obvious they'd discussed the pros and cons here. ''It's your ball, gents. Go ahead and run with it. If they rented under other names, it's gonna be a bitch to ferret them out. Go on home and get a few hours. You can get started on it first thing.'' He turned to Gus. ''You're right about being too tired to think straight. Can you stall the Night Watch? Hold them over at the end of their shift?''

''Could be arranged. What time?''

Dante glanced to Beasley. ''Eight-thirty?''

Jumbo nodded.

''They'll be there,'' Gus promised.

FOURTEEN

Manhattan South Borough Command was less than a mile and no more than ten minutes from Dante's place. In the interest of squeezing in the most sack time possible, he'd gotten his Mr. Coffee all ready before turning in and setting the alarm for eight. When his head hit the pillow and he closed his eyes, he was all set for a full four hours sleep. When he found himself wide-awake at seven, he realized he'd omitted one important presleep step. He'd forgotten to lock the cat in the oven. Starting in at about six-thirty, the elderly Copter began his accustomed caterwauling. It was a bad habit he'd developed as he got on in years. The heavy-sleeping Dante was able to sleep through it at first, but lately it had increased to a volume only the dead could endure. By seven-twenty, he gave up tossing restlessly to plant both feet on the bedroom carpet. There was murder in his heart.

Copter was smart enough to sense the hostility in the air. He beat a prudent retreat as the boss moved on to splash water in his face and stare a moment at the medicine cabinet mirror. What Dante saw there were the red-rimmed eyes and stubble-coarsened chin of a sleep-deprived wreck. He questioned his will to go on and decided he'd settle for orange juice and coffee rather than suicide. Copter had taken up position alongside his bowl in the kitchen. He looked up expectantly as the boss padded barefoot from the bathroom to the fridge.

"Open your mouth and I'll rip your kitty fucking lungs out," the master snarled.

"Meoooow!"

It was difficult to get any respect. As Dante grabbed the OJ, he also withdrew an open can of elderly-cat cat food.

By quarter of eight, Dante had managed to shower, shave, and dress himself presentably. While three hours sleep wasn't enough to revitalize him physically, it and a few cups of coffee left him mentally refreshed. He was on his way out the door, figuring he'd grab carbohydrates at the patisserie, when the phone rang. Nobody ever called him at eight in the morning with good news. He groaned inwardly.

"Joe? It's Brian. Diana left me this note asking me to give you a call."

Dante's sculptor buddy had no idea how relieved Joe was to hear his voice. "Brennan. Where's the Queen herself? She's got you doing her phone work now?"

"Still sawing 'em. Late night."

"Do tell."

"It says here that you've got a lunch date with her and Bryce Weller. One o'clock at FLOTSAM. She wonders if you can give her a ride."

"Tell her good, yes, and thanks."

Howard "Crime Dog" McGraff was none too happy about being detained here at Borough South. His regular Night Watch shift ended at eight. Like all of them, it had been a long one. For starters, they'd gotten word of the hit on Sal. And before they could follow up, maybe get clearance to lend a hand, they'd gotten a call of their own down on Pell Street. Two rival Chinese gangs had a run-in outside a Chinatown social club. It turned ugly when some idiot emptied the clip of a 9-mm Beretta at the opposition. When the stink of cordite cleared, there were two dead and eight more in need of emergency medical attention. Night Watch was six hours sorting out the wreckage.

Dante and the colored guy, Richardson, both showed up at quarter past eight to interview the squad. Instead of doing it en masse, they were isolating each man to question them one at a time. They had Wally Mansker in there behind the closed door of Onofrio's office right now. McGraff had just left them to join Stewie Beal out here in the squad room. Some of the Task Force day shift was around, but after expressing their condolences, they steered clear. There was a creepy tinge to the air in here that Howard didn't like. Stewie seemed to like it even less. He hadn't been in there yet, and right now he was anxious.

"What'a they got t' ask that they couldn't've asked us all t'gether, Crime Dog? What *is* this bullshit?"

"Might not be all bullshit," McGraff countered. "They want to know what *we* know about Warren Mott's extortion investigation."

Beal looked more anxious than ever. "What'd you tell 'em?"

McGraff's smile was smug. "Fuck-all, Stewie. Same as Wally's doing right now. Same as you're gonna do, too."

"It sounds like they know sump'n, don't it?"

"Nothing they're telling, Stewie. That door's gotta swing both ways, right?"

Beal scowled. "I got a kid in fuckin' *law* school. 'Nother seven months an' I'm vested. I already done the first interview with the security director out at Rockwell. Ain't no way them Palace Guard pricks is gonna fuck up my retirement, Howie. No *fuckin'* way."

McGraff smiled. "Glad to hear that, Stewie. We three stick together, there's nothing to find no matter how deep them bastards dig."

This last Friday in July was going to be a hot one. With the sun already cooking the pavement of East

Twentieth Street, Dante and Richardson paused in the shade on the Academy complex driveway to remove their jackets before proceeding out onto the sidewalk. Joe folded his and set it atop the trans-file carton he was straddling. Along with actual Homicide case files, the carton contained every other scrap of paper found in Sal Onofrio's office.

"You feel like you needed a pair'a rubber boots in there?" Jumbo asked.

"More like a rubber boat. Pretty hard to put the squeeze on a guy when you don't have anything to squeeze him *with*."

"I don't think it was a total loss, Joey. I got the feelin' that maybe we spooked 'em. That was a good idea, isolatin' .'em like that. Plant seeds of suspicion. Every one'a them three is gonna be lookin' over his shoulder now, waitin' for one'a the others t' stab him in the back."

Dante sighed. "I hope that isn't just wishful thinking, Beasley. I'm too tired to've spent two hours beating my head against a brick wall like that. Let's hope Don and Rusty find us something we can wedge into the cracks." He squatted to hoist the file carton and move on toward his car. "So tell me about the name the Deeds Registrar got for you. How did it check out?"

Richardson gave it a vague head shake. "Mystery t' me, what's goin' on there. The president of the corporation that house is registered to? 'Nother Colombian. I had Huggie run him through NCIC, an' she didn't find even a parkin' ticket. Same with the DEA an' FBI. Man's a clean-Gene."

"You think he's the new neighbor? Your computer whiz?"

Again, the shrug. "Beats me. This corporation's got a high-tech-soundin' name. Syner-Calc or some such shit. Anyway, he's got no drug connections, least so far as anybody knows. I got no idea how our boy in the Ferrari fits in. Maybe he's a buddy from down there an' maybe he's a relative. Who the fuck knows?"

"Not every Colombian is a drug czar," Joe reminded him.

Jumbo scowled. "That ain't the point. The parkin' in my neighborhood's a bitch. I like t' think'a that hydrant out front as my own personal slot."

It was too late for Sal Onofrio's financial work-up to either hurt or help him, but Grover and Heckman included it in their survey anyway. None of the Night Watch files were proving at all extensive. Cops just didn't make enough legitimate money to have more than one or two bank accounts and file anything but the IRS 1040 Short Form. Both Don and Rusty knew that only the dumbest cop in the history of the modern job would put dirty money in a bank account or declare it on his taxes.

"We're wasting our fucking time here," Rusty complained.

Heckman had shown up cranky this morning and was showing no sign of changing his tune.

"Maybe," Grover allowed. "And then again, maybe not."

"No hand jobs, Donnie. Please. I can't take it."

His partner shook his head. "These work-ups tell us where the Night Watch guys bank."

"Or banked, in Sal's case. Yeah? So?"

"So it stands to reason that each guy would be known at his own bank . . . which makes *that* bank the wrong place to take out a safe box for the purpose of stowing dirty money. For one, I doubt they used their own names. For two, if they *didn't* use their own names, then any one of them would be a moron, walking into his own branch and trying to rent a box as Joe Schmoe. He'd go somewhere else. I'm betting he'd go somewhere convenient either to his house or work."

Heckman brightened only slightly. "What you're saying is that we can throw all these banks out. That we've wasted the past two and a half hours."

"Not wasted. I needed that time to come up with this brilliant theory."

"I'm afraid it ain't shining like maybe it should. Take it a step further."

"Okay. What I'm also saying is that the banks where they *did* rent boxes are probably pretty close to these ones. I'd draw a radius of no more than a mile around them and look inside those circles first."

"What about around Borough South?"

Grover wiggled his eyebrows. "Good point, but let's treat that possibility as secondary."

"Why?"

"Because they show up for work at midnight and swing out at eight. Then they've got all day, during the usual banking hours, to visit a branch more convenient to home. I ain't had breakfast yet. You hungry?"

The sudden shift of subject, from illicit banking to food, was not a surprise to Rusty Heckman. When his partner got hungry, an alarm went off. That alarm interrupted all rational processes.

"I could eat," Rusty replied. "You mind if we bring along a city map? It might be interesting to draw some of those circles you're talking about."

The big news in the early editions that morning was the arrest of two cops in the South Bronx on rape and deadly weapon assault charges. From his desk in the commissioner's office, Captain Bob Talbot was happy to see Deb Glenmore getting some action on the results of her investigation. He was also happy to see something other than the Mott homicide dominating the news for a change. That was before Bob saw the headline carried by the *Post*. A so-called afternoon paper, the *Post* was printed and released a few hours closer to dawn than the *Daily News* and *Newsday*. The paper had held its press run long enough to get a picture of Lieutenant Sal Onofrio's garage and the back end of his Camaro. It dominated nearly all of the tabloid's front page. The accompanying headline was equally subtle.

#2

SECOND COP GUNNED GANGLAND-STYLE
THIS WEEK!

While Deb's rapist cops were still news, their story was buried inside on page four. Bob was disappointed but suspected Sergeant Glenmore wasn't likely to care where the *Post* carried the story of those arrests. She was going to be happy they'd been made, and grateful for Talbot's assistance toward that end. She would be in a mood to celebrate. He'd already faxed her a map to his family's Southampton beach house. This afternoon he would call her. Hopefully she would accept his invitation.

Meanwhile, fantasies of what Deb Glenmore looked like in a bathing suit weren't going to help Bob through the business at hand. Tony Mintoff was on the warpath. In the wake of the Onofrio homicide, Chief Lieberman's people were making a strong connection between it and Warren Mott's murder. The scab had been picked away from the earlier investigation, and now they had an open wound twice the original's size. The mayor's office was having fits. The police chief in Atlantic City was less than pleased with the pressure the New York job was exerting on his jurisdiction. Mintoff was demanding to know what the hell the death of some dope addict in Atlantic City could have to do with the murders of two cops up here. Talbot had been working his ass off all morning, trying to get the boss some answers.

As Diana Webster emerged from her building, the clothes she wore were the type she preferred in her private life: jeans, a T-shirt, and canvas flats. When she wore what she termed her "urban camouflage," fans rarely recognized her on the street.

"You two are really gonna hate this guy," she announced. She'd barely gotten the Plymouth's passenger door closed, and offered the comment instead of greeting.

"I probably will," Dante replied. "That's why Jumbo's along. He's so even-tempered."

Joe had the wheel, and Richardson had given up the shotgun seat to their guest. Diana turned to grin at the big man behind her.

"Beasley, you see Joe getting that look in his eye, don't get in his way. Please. You'll be doing the whole human race a favor." She returned her attention to her friend. "When I fed him your story about the police being ready to come down all over the club scene, he didn't really start to quake until I mentioned the city and state pulling licenses. That scared him. He's got heavy backing in the venture."

"You mean it's like the old movie cliché?" Jumbo asked. "He blows this one, he'll never work in this town again?"

Diana nodded. "You bet. Bryce blows this one and he might as well move to Spokane."

"So he'll cooperate." Dante didn't ask it but stated it flatly.

"He's the one who suggested this meeting, Joe. I fed him all the ifs and buts; let him figure it out. When I told you guys were looking for a cooperative player in exchange for immunity, he jumped all over it."

FLOTSAM, like most downtown clubs, didn't look like much on the outside. At that hour the velvet ropes and chrome stanchions were stored inside. There was no awning, and the only sign was an unobtrusive pink neon one hung from a middle window on the third floor. Dante parked the Plymouth in the yellow zone out front.

"Don't look like he's got much lunch trade," Jumbo observed.

Diana chuckled. "Lunch trade? Most of FLOTSAM's clientele are still in bed."

Bryce Weller met them at the door. The madras shirt with the collar buttoned and tails hanging out over baggy black knee-length shorts was no doubt a statement on the cutting edge of fashion, but Dante thought he looked like a bookie from Miami Beach. The thinning black hair was slicked straight back. The way he had it tied in a little ponytail was getting to be standard issue on the downtown scene. There were even little hairpieces available: clip-on hair extenders. Dante was tempted to tug at Weller's to see if it was real.

"Gentlemen. Please come in." He didn't offer to shake hands, but as Diana passed, he insinuated himself in close for a quick peck on her cheek.

Within minutes, the four of them were seated around one of the forty or so tables in FLOTSAM's empty dining room. Weller's chef and one of his waiters had evidently been asked to work this little private party. The group was presented with menus offering all the same selections the dining room would serve for dinner later that Friday night. Dante was impressed by the choices; nearly as impressed as he was with the astronomical prices. Both he and Jumbo refused drinks while Diana ordered a Campari and soda.

"I understand that you already know the basics of our plan," Joe opened up. "And what we're prepared to offer for your cooperation, Mr. Weller." As he said it, he made direct, steady eye contact. It was pleasing to see the way it made the club owner squirm.

"I'd like to hear it again in your own words, Lieutenant."

"You mean what we're up to? Or what the deal is?"

"The deal."

"The deal's immunity, Mr. Weller. You help us bait and trap the bag men, you walk."

"No strings?"

"You could be called upon to testify in court."

Weller continued to shift nervously in his chair. In the process, he broke eye contact. "I assume this plan's got details?"

Dante nodded. "But the less you know about them, the less nervous you'll be when it goes down. From your end, we want it to look like business as usual. You just tell us when they make the pickup and where.''

Weller took a deep breath and let it out. Slowly. His eyes wandered first to Diana and then back to the two detectives. "Saturdays. In my office up on the third floor. Usually around midnight."

"Ever much earlier?" Jumbo asked.

The club owner shook his head. "If anything, later. Once or twice it's been as late as one."

"Help us out with some history," Dante prodded. "How long has the squeeze been going on?"

"How long? Since a month after I first opened the club. That's about how long they give you. Once they're pretty sure you're on your feet, they move in. Same story four years ago when I opened my first club."

"You ever compare notes with other owners?" Jumbo asked.

"Not at first, I didn't. I was scared shitless. These guys with badges were walking in here and pointing out all the ways they could shut me down. Next thing I knew, I was handing people cash in paper bags. That isn't something you brag about to the competition."

"But you've talked about it since," Jumbo pressed.

"I've been in the business long enough to've met just about everyone." Weller paused and shrugged. "Sure. I've compared some notes. All of us are getting hit in the same way. Some more, some less. It depends on how successful these leeches think your operation is."

Dante moved in. "You say some more and some less. What sort of range are we talking about?" In the back of his mind were the swimming pool, the big-screen TV, and all the other goodies they'd discovered at Sal Onofrio's place.

Weller got a funny look working, a twisted perversion of a smile. "Interesting you should ask that, Lieutenant. From the middle of June until just this week, I didn't hear a thing from them. There were no collections and no contacts. Then they showed up again

Wednesday. They tell me the rules have changed, that they've reorganized."

Dante stopped him with a hand gesture. "You say they didn't show up for what? Six weeks?"

"That's right. Then they feed me some crock of shit about reevaluating their accounts. I'm doing so well here that they decided I should double my contri-fucking-bution. I've been jumped from a grand a week to two."

Dante flicked a glance at Jumbo. It was six weeks ago that Sal claimed to have learned about Warren Mott's investigation. A week later, the original complainant died of a drug overdose. Shortly thereafter, Mott was reported to have dropped the case. Joe didn't much like this self-important little troll, but his information was crucial. Weller's story fit.

Jumbo leaned forward, planting those huge forearms of his on the table. "Describe these dudes. You say *they*. How many? What kinda badges?"

"Two. Always the same pair, ever since they first showed up last February. Both big; one older, with dark hair, and one about my age. Blond, with a build on him like he lifts weights. The older guy carries a police sergeant's badge, and the blond one is from the Fire Department."

As Weller spoke, Dante extracted file photos of the four Task Force Night Watch detectives from an envelope. Once he'd laid them side by side atop the table, he motioned to them. "You recognize any of these guys?"

The club owner took a moment to contemplate each of them before shaking his head. "Nope. Can't say as I've ever seen them, but then, I meet a lot of people. Who are they?"

Dante pressed ahead, ignoring the question. "How do you know the blond guy is from the Fire Department?"

That got him an impatient scowl. "He carries a wallet with a shiny little badge inside it, just like the other guy. Only this badge says Fire Department on it."

211

"He carry a gun?" Richardson wondered.

Weller scowled again. "How would I know, Sergeant? They weren't robbing me at gunpoint, and since when do firemen carry guns?"

"You'd be surprised who carries guns in this city," Jumbo murmured.

When Rusty Heckman and Don Grover returned from breakfast, they took their maps and circles to the basement offices of the Printing Section and had blowups made. From there, they took copies to Central Records and requested the names and addresses of every bank branch inside those four outer-borough areas. Now they were back in the squad room. Grover had tacked copies of the four areas up on the corkboard.

"You look at all those streets and get a sinking feeling like I do?" Heckman asked.

Grover had a full stomach. He was feeling content, and that made him feel confident as well. He shook his head. "I've been giving this a lot of thought, Rust. Looking at it from as many angles as I can imagine, crazy or not. These guys wouldn't use just anybody's name. They'd know they've got to be careful as all hell, and with a name pulled outta a hat, there's too much implied risk."

"You wanna expand on that?"

The team's eating machine shrugged. "Sure. It's the sort of thing a guy on the street might think is an impossible long shot, but a crooked cop's got to indulge a little healthy paranoia. I'm talking about coincidence; another guy using the same name to rent a box in the same bank. Take this guy Mansker for instance."

Grover stepped up to one of the four enlargements: an area of Broadway bisecting the Riverdale and Kingsbridge sections of the North Bronx. The job duty roster listed Detective Walter Mansker's home address as 3671 Irwin Avenue, four blocks west of Broadway on the Riverdale side. The financial work-ups told them Mansker did his banking at a Chemical branch on the corner of Broadway and 232nd.

"I'm trying to *think* like a crooked cop. I'm Mansker. What I've gotta do is rent a box in a bank branch other than my own, under a *name* other than my own. What do I do? Pick a name at random outta, say, the Brooklyn phone book? Make up some bullshit Social Security number and walk into an Anchor branch to take out a box?"

Heckman thought he was following now. "Might be a problem with another guy who has the same name already being there in the card file. Draw undue attention to himself."

Grover nodded. "That's part of it. If I'm Mansker, I wouldn't want to risk making such a simple, bonehead mistake. Then there's the next consideration. Let's take it a step further. If I'm setting up a stash for a lot of crooked cash, I've gotta at least consider the possibility that the game I'm playing might unravel someday. My job is already at risk. Do I want to risk all my sweet, ill-gotten gains, too?"

Rusty was lost again. "Throw me a bone or something, Donnie."

"I'm talking about phony names and manufactured Social Security numbers. We don't have Mott's case file on that investigation, so we'll never know for sure, but I've gotta assume he'd indulge in the same exercise we're working our way through right now. There's no telling how far he got, but I think he would have hit all these banks, subpoenaed lists of all their box tenants, culled out the Social Security numbers, and sent them to the SSA. He would've asked them to generate their own list of names, and then he'd see if they matched up."

Heckman groaned. "Jesus. That's got to be what? Six or seven thousand names?"

"At least. But I don't see as we have any choice. Fundamental or not, we can't just assume that Mott got that far. So we'll use that avenue as our backup direction."

"Backup? You lost me again."

"I think that Mott probably *did* get that far. I think he didn't find anything in those lists because there *wasn't* anything to find."

Exasperated, Heckman threw his pen onto the table and slumped back, staring at the ceiling. "If there wasn't anything outta whack, then who rented the boxes, Donnie?"

"You've been in and out of the Task Force offices up at Borough South. What've they always got pinned to that corkboard outside the whip's office?"

Heckman frowned, thinking back. Then he shrugged, shaking his head. "You got me."

"Newspaper clippings, right? Put up there to remind them of homicides they still ain't shut the book on. That's the Night Watch beat, Rust. Homicide."

It was like a cartoon bulb went on inside Heckman's head. "Dead men. I *like* it. God*damn*, buddy."

Grover had moved away from their maps and circles to pace excitedly. "Sure, we've gotta go through the lists of box tenant names and Social Security numbers, but I think we should give this the inside track. Compare that list of tenants to a list of homicides the Task Force has investigated over the past five or six years. I'll bet you a hundred bucks right here that we find at least four names that match."

"I think I'll keep my money." Rusty was already reaching for the phone. "Let's call records."

FIFTEEN

The New York Fire Department's equivalent of One Police Plaza is located at 250 Livingstone Street in Brooklyn. When Dante contacted Chief Lieberman with Bryce Weller's tale of badge-bearing firemen and a joint extortion venture, Gus contacted the Fire Department's Bureau of Operations. Once he was apprised of the situation, Op Bureau Chief Francis X. Ryan cleared his calendar. It was nearly three o'clock before Joe and Jumbo could drop Diana back at her place and hurry across the Manhattan Bridge to lower Flatbush.

Like most everyone from the fire ranks prior to the advent of the Fire-Fem and the lowering of physical qualification criteria, Chief Frank Ryan was huge. Standing as tall as Dante, he was nearly four inches broader through the shoulders and outweighed him by at least seventy pounds. The chief's introductory handshake would have shamed most blacksmiths. Dante was fortunate to have anticipated it. He was able to give back some of what he got. Jumbo was more Ryan's size, plenty capable-looking and black. The Op chief worked him a little less aggressively and offered them chairs.

"So what's this I'm hearin', gentlemen? I've got a rogue in my ranks?"

"We don't know that for a fact, sir," Dante replied. "Only that certain evidence suggests it."

"What certain evidence would that be, Lieutenant?"

Dante sensed that Ryan was accustomed to taking the high ground, both by right and natural inclination. Joe planned to meet the chief at any level he chose. "Before I answer that, let me give you some background. My unit is investigating the homicide of the Internal Affairs investigator killed this past Tuesday morning."

Ryan nodded. "This Mott fella. Hard to miss news o' that one."

"Recently, Mott was looking into allegations made to the CCRB that cops were shaking down Manhattan club owners for protection money. We're curious to know what you've heard about firemen being involved in the same sort of thing."

The chief's eyes probed deep into Dante's gaze. He slowly shook his head. "I don't get it. You said Mott's investigation was into cops."

"The CCRB complaint only specifies cops. Mott's file on his investigation is missing. Twice now in our investigation, we've had involved parties report that Fire Department personnel are also involved."

"First I've heard of it," Ryan replied. "You mind me askin' *how* they're involved? Excuse me; *alleged* to be involved."

"We've got a report of a man who presents Fire Department credentials, sir. Specifically, a shield. If I'm not mistaken, that would make him a marshal, correct?"

"If his credentials are legitimate, Lieutenant. Not too many people've seen a fire marshal's shield. It would be easy enough to dummy one up."

"That occurred to us, Chief. We've narrowed the cop side down to guys working the Task Force Night Watch at Manhattan South Borough Command. There could be other guys from some of the local squads involved, but we doubt it. This is the sort of thing they'd want to keep close to home. I commanded the Borough South Task Force for two years. I know every squad commander in Manhattan South, and I've met most every detective working below One Hundred Tenth Street. I can't fit any of them to the description we were given. I'm wondering if any of your Manhattan marshals are big, muscle-bound, blond guys.''

Ryan was still trying to loom from the lofty heights. ''We've got a lot of big men in our Department, Lieutenant. A lot of them are blond. Hundreds of 'em lift weights. The answer to your question is no; I haven't heard one goddamn word about any o' this.''

''We'd like you to check your personnel files, Chief. Just a routine search to see if there are any men fitting the description who work as marshals out of Midtown.''

''So you can go on a witch-hunt?''

Jumbo hopped in here. ''We're worried about a connection t' two *homicides*, Chief. It's gone way beyond extortion an' witch-hunts.''

''Homicide's a nasty word, Sergeant. I'd need to know how my man might be tied in.''

Dante took it over again. ''I'm afraid we can't get too specific, sir. Right now the ice is still pretty thin. What we can promise is that you'll be kept abreast as we go. If anything on your side of the street surfaces, you'll be one of the first to know.''

Frank Ryan seemed to soften some. ''I'll get you your list, gentlemen. But I'll tell you now that I intend to be brought aboard. Up front. Officially.''

As Dante and Richardson departed, Joe enjoyed beating Ryan to the leverage point as the chief once again attempted to crush his knuckles. There was satisfaction in the way the muscles of the bigger man's face tightened. He and Jumbo had returned to the ground floor and were crossing the lobby toward the street doors when he spotted Captain Marty Schoenfeld from the Midtown Investigation Unit. The man was back on his feet, having exchanged his bathrobe for a navy jacket and gray slacks. Judging from the man's color, Joe guessed he was still moving a step slow.

"Hey, Cap. I thought your beat was west of here."

Schoenfeld's head came around. His eyes focused on the source of this vaguely familiar voice but registered no recognition.

"Dante. PD's Major Case Unit. We talked on your front stoop the other day."

Recognition and surprise. "Right! Sorry, Lou. I guess I was pretty far out of it that night. What brings you to our humble home?"

Dante introduced Jumbo and pointed at the ceiling. "Business with the brass upstairs. How you feeling?"

Schoenfeld shook his head in disgust. "Bitch of a bug, this flu. Night I saw you, I thought I'd have it licked in a day. Fucker won't let go."

While waiting for their hosts to package the Lucas homicide forensics for shipment north, Guy Napier and Melissa Busby worked the streets again that morning. After lunch in a Ventnor City diner, they reported back to police headquarters to hear some surprising news. Inspector Mike Hanniger had a middle-level dope dealer under arrest for the murder of Henry Lucas. Everyone in the homicide command seemed relieved that the suspect was strictly local; not some hotshot trigger man from the Big Apple. Apparently the Atlantic City criminal element had gotten upset about the increased heat on the street. They'd put the word out. Anybody who could help the cops with this one would be doing them a favor, too. In Atlantic City, there are as many wise guys on the way up as there are addicted gamblers on the way down. A gunslinging local heroin merchant named Lucho Avila was ferreted out and offered up in near record time. The way he told it to his interrogators, Henry Lucas had made a pass at him. When Lucho arrived at the door to the Honey Man's Golden Nugget suite, Lucas answered it wrapped in a towel.

Halfway through their business transaction, Lucas let the towel drop and asked if Lucho fancied a piece of *his* action. For all his generosity of spirit, he'd gotten a bullet in the back of the head.

Napier was still wrestling with the disappointment of hitting a brick wall. He and Melissa were waiting out front of headquarters for a ride to their hotel and then the heliport. "*Back* of the head. Makes you wonder if our pal Avila might have taken Lucas up on his offer, doesn't it?"

Melissa grinned up at him. "You've got a dirty mind."

"C'mon, Mel. You love every synapse."

By the time five o'clock rolled around, last night's lack of sleep was taking its toll. There was no way Dante was going to sort through the day's developments and plan his next moves without rest. He knew that if he went to bed now and tried to sleep through until morning, he'd be awake at three and twiddling his thumbs until sunup. The answer was a nap. He brought the Mott case file home, planning to review it later. Tomorrow was Saturday: the weekend for most people. In the wake of two 10-13 homicides, Gus and Tony Mintoff had authorized unlimited overtime. Don Grover and Rusty Heckman would spend Saturday culling through stacks of computer printout. With the return of Napier and Busby, the rest of the squad would devise a strategy to net them a couple of bag men. Dante was in bed by five-thirty, the alarm set ahead three and a half hours, to nine.

The sun was just setting when the shrill, electronic pulsing of his clock awakened him. From his bed, Joe drew the curtains back from the glass doors to the garden and lay there a moment watching the way the shadows fell. The sky had gone a soft persimmon, bathing everything in the faint glow of it. He hadn't had time to putter in any of the beds this week, but Tuesday's rain was doing its job. The petunias, impatiens, snapdragon, and dianthus were all in full bloom. Their colors, a riot in the midday sun, were muted now. This little private world was Dante's escape valve. He'd let it go for years, everything growing up tangled and wild. Then one of the women in his life had taken it on as a project. She'd taught him the therapeutic value of digging the earth, planting, and watching things grow. The thought of that woman led to thoughts of other women and finally to food. He was suddenly hungry for a burger.

With August just two days away, the evenings had turned uncomfortably warm. Dressed in a gift T-shirt from the NYU Blood Donor Center, a pair of loose-fitting shorts, and flip-flops, Dante could feel the pavement and buildings radiate the heat stored through a day of bright sun. He found the sidewalk tables outside the White Horse Tavern jammed with people either in for the duration or waiting for the traffic to thin before departing for weekend beach retreats. Joe couldn't be bothered with cooling his heels until something opened up. It was going to be cooler inside anyway. At the bar, he'd be closer to a steady supply of suds.

As he entered and mounted a stool down at the short end of the bar, Dante was surprised to spot an old veteran of yesteryear seated nearby. Fifteen years ago, when Joe stopped in here more or less regularly, he'd met and swapped lies with a dozen or so people who he assumed had moved on, just as he had. This guy was a merchant seaman; a deck officer who worked container ships and tankers.

"Hey, Mike. Long time no see."

The seaman looked up from his drink and squinted across the corner of the bar. He looked older now and was probably a lot more senior in his work, but weren't they all? "Dante? Jesus, Joe. How the fuck are ya?"

"No complaints."

"Buy you a drink? This new Brooklyn brand's pretty tasty. You still in the neighborhood?"

"Thanks, Mike. Yep, still here."

As the merchantman was flagging the barkeep and ordering them a couple of Brooklyns, Linda Fletcher emerged from the kitchen. She was halfway through the room, headed for the outside tables with a tray full of food, when she spotted Dante there at the bar.

"Hey, Joe. You don't even say hi?"

"First I've seen of you, Linda. Thought I'd see if the burgers are still as good as you say they are."

Her free hand went to her hip and she gave him a leer of mock suspicion. "You mean you didn't come to see *me*?"

He snapped his fingers. "Of course I did. I mean, I can get a burger most anywhere, right?"

"God, you're a lousy liar. Listen, I worked happy hour, and I'm off as soon as my relief shows. Maybe we can have a drink when I finish up?"

He thought that would be fine and watched her sashay away through the front door.

"You're a friend of that little broad?" the merchantman marveled. "Jesus, Joe. Every guy in the joint's been trying to get into her pants since she came to work here."

Ten minutes later, Dante's long-lost drinking buddy drained his beer and made his excuses. It was another ten before Linda's relief arrived. Meanwhile, Joe ordered a burger and fries. His three and a half hours sleep had helped. He was feeling relaxed. It was another twelve hours before he had to put his nose back to the stone, and a beautiful young woman had just offered to join him for drinks.

When Linda emerged from the kitchen, she had his burger and fries on a plate in one hand, had gotten rid of her apron, and was carrying a knapsack over her shoulder. Dante bought her a margarita and, as he ate, asked her to tell him about working for Brennan. Talk soon turned to her aspirations as an actress. She was serious about her career. This seemingly naive, fresh-off-the-farm girl was a graduate of Carnagie Tech. She'd worked summer stock in the Berkshires throughout her college career and had come to New York to train at the Actor's Studio. She'd already signed with an agent and was auditioning for commercials, television, film, and stage roles.

"How old are you, Linda?"

She pretended to be taken aback. "Isn't that a question no man is supposed to ask a lady?"

"I'm a detective, remember?"

"Twenty-three. Today, as a matter of fact."

"Say again?"

"I'm twenty-three today. It's my birthday."

Dante's surprise became solicitude. "It's your birthday and you had to work? So where's the singing staff and the cake? What's happening to this world?"

She got a mischievous smile working and leaned down to retrieve her knapsack from atop the foot rail. "My boss gave me something better than a cake." And with a flourish she produced a bottle of Perrier Jouet brut.

"Champagne? Nice. Your boss is forgiven."

As she sat there cradling the bottle, she looked at Dante's nearly empty plate and then at her empty glass. "I suppose we could get Gary to open it, but I've been here since three o'clock, and to tell you the truth, I'm sorta sick of the place. Maybe we could go somewhere else."

Dante thought about that file he'd brought home just long enough to dismiss it. All work and no play was already making him a dull enough boy. "You're sure you don't want to keep that? Have it with a few friends or something?"

She smiled. "I graduated in May, moved to New York in early June, and I've either been working to keep up with my outrageous rent, taking classes, or going to auditions ever since. When have I had time to make any friends?"

She was so good-looking that a part of him couldn't imagine a beautiful young woman like her ever being lonely. But that's what she was right now: lonely. This was her twenty-third birthday and she was alone in a city of eight million strangers. He reached for the check and then for his wallet.

As they emerged from the White Horse, Linda took a deep breath and sighed, putting plenty of drama into it. "It's too bad I'm not your type."

Dante saw amusement in her eyes. "What's that supposed to mean?"

"Your T-shirt. It says you're O positive. I'm B negative. Shame, huh?"

"Shame?" I'M YOUR TYPE was the message emblazoned across the chest of his shirt. Beneath it, all the blood type categories were listed. The nurse at NYU had checked the box next to Dante's type in red marker pen. "You know what they say about us O positives. We're *universal* donors."

As she laughed, Joe took her hand to hook it through the crook of his arm.

"Didn't Diana say you only live a block from here? Any chance you've got two clean glasses?"

When they reached his place, Linda explored Dante's living room while he got out a pair of flutes and put her birthday present on ice. Just yesterday, Deborah Glenmore had given his lair the same sort of going over. For some reason, Joe felt a bit more self-conscious about the current survey. It seemed more personal. Linda recognized the Brennan pieces and picked one up to stroke its smooth, polished lines. When Joe eventually led her back through his bedroom to the garden, she stopped to pick Copter up from where he'd been sleeping on the bed.

Between sips out there in the night air, Linda sat with the cat in her lap, her head thrown back and eyes staring at the starless sky. "I've never lived in a place where you couldn't see the stars on a clear night,'' she said at length.

Dante chuckled. "I've never lived anywhere you could."

Linda's head came down from the heavens to regard this man across the table from her. "I asked Brian and Diana a little more about you yesterday."

"Oh? How's that?"

She hesitated and then seemed to make a decision. "Well, I started off by mentioning that the most attractive man I've met since moving to New York is a cop . . . and how odd that seems."

He grunted. "Odd, huh? Well, two months ain't all that long. You did say you've been awfully busy."

She got serious. "I meant that as a compliment."

"I'd like to think so."

"But you don't want to acknowledge it. Diana told me that it might be best if I kept it to myself. Why?"

"Why? I'm twice your age."

"Not quite. I checked. You're nineteen years older than I am."

"Fine. A beautiful young woman needs friends in this town, Linda. Not ex-lovers. I like to think I can be a pretty good friend."

"*Ex*-lovers, huh? They can't ever be friends?"

"I didn't say can't. In my line of work, you get so you hate absolutes. They've usually got something to do with death."

Linda was looking at him differently now. She took a moment before she spoke. "You came down to the White Horse tonight because you wanted to be my friend?"

"Didn't I mention something about being hungry?"

"I'm supposed to believe that?" She was quickly getting impatient with him. "You know what I *do* believe? I think you're having second thoughts now that I'm sitting across from you here in your back garden . . .

probably because you've decided you don't want to hurt me.''

He admired her candor. "So how does someone who just turned twenty-three get so wise?''

The smile creeping across her face had a little sadness in it. "What choice did I have? I've had sleazeballs hitting on me since I was fifteen. Not flirting; hitting. I didn't get the difference at first. Most men see me—or my body—as a commodity.''

"If you hate that, why are you letting my buddy Brian turn it into bronze for all the world to ogle?''

She shook her head. "Some men hate women. They just want to exploit. Brian loves women. All you've got to do is watch him at it to see that his art is a labor of love.'' She paused to smile, her eyes locking with his. A hand came across the table, finding his fingers and intertwining. "I may be only twenty-three, but I've made a few mistakes learning the difference.''

"Just a few? You're lucky.''

"Probably. I've also learned a little about knowing what I want when I see it.''

Two hours later, Dante found himself lying awake in his bed for the second time that night. This time, a beautiful girl-woman slumbered alongside him. Even in the dog-day heat, Linda wouldn't let him switch on the air-conditioning. She preferred a lovemaking lubricated by the sweat of exertion. Now she lay on her side, back to him, the sheet drawn across her at the hip. There was little wonder why Brennan chose this body to immortalize. It was a pity there was no way to isolate and capture the rest of her: the directness, the faith she had in her own judgment, the enthusiasm she had for life. The combination of them in her took his breath away.

Linda had drifted contentedly off to sleep. In Dante's experience, sex tended to jack most women wide-awake. He, on the other hand, wouldn't be able to drop off for at least another hour. At half past midnight, all that good exertion had left him not exhausted but flushed with vitality. He knew he'd be content to just sit propped against the headboard here and watch the breath move in and out of her, but there was that file sitting on his dining table. There was probably no better distraction for putting him into a mood for sleep.

As Joe slipped from between the sheets and back into his shorts, he noticed that Copter was not only there on the bed but nestled asleep against his new friend's stomach. She even had an arm thrown over him. The sneaky little devil couldn't be faulted on his taste. To ensure that neither of them would be disturbed when the light came on down the hall, Dante eased the door almost closed as he left.

The noise of shattering glass startled him. He turned to cock an ear. The French doors opening onto his garden were secured before he and Linda went to bed. The iron security gates were bolted and locked. Someone or some*thing* had just broken one of those glass doors.

He was just reaching for the knob when the force of an explosion blew the bedroom door off its hinges. It came at him, face-on. He heard nothing and saw only a blinding flash of light before the impact propelled him backward like a discarded rag doll. He was thrown hard into the heavy oak dining table. It caught him at mid-thigh, his momentum flipping him backward into the air. When the back of his head hit the floor, the full weight of his body drove him into it. He went out cold. Twenty feet away, his bedroom was a raging inferno. Linda Fletcher and Copter were trapped inside.

SIXTEEN

Brian Brennan's pulse was still pounding in his ears as he pulled away from the street-level loading bay. Diana sat huddled on the seat beside him. Their restored 1956 Dodge pickup hated being kicked to life and asked to perform without a warm-up. The engine sputtered and coughed as Brian jammed it into gear and shoved the accelerator to the firewall. Fewer than five minutes had elapsed since Jumbo's call interrupted their sleep. There'd been an explosion and horrible fire. Dante was knocked unconscious and had suffered from smoke inhalation before a neighbor could drag him from his apartment. He was refusing to go to a hospital.

The scene they found on Perry Street did nothing to allay their fears. Dante's block was choked with fire equipment, police, and EMS vehicles. They were forced to park in a yellow zone on Bleecker and walk. Rubbernecking passersby and occupants of neighboring buildings crowded the street and sidewalks adjacent to Joe's smoldering, fire-gutted building.

"Holy *shit*," Diana murmured.

As they approached the area cordoned off with yellow plastic tape and started into it, a uniformed patrolwoman from the nearby Sixth Precinct moved to intercept. "What are you, blind? Get the hell outta here!"

"Sergeant Richardson called us," Brian explained. "We're looking for Lieutenant Dante. Do you know if he's okay?"

The feisty watchdog's demeanor softened. "Last I saw him, he was still coughing and choking a lot." She pointed up the street past the front bumper of a hook and ladder. "I think he's sitting in the back of that ambulance over there. You can go ahead."

As they proceeded, Brennan regarded his friend's building in awe. "Jesus, Di. Look at it. It's *gone*."

They found Joe sitting on the back bumper of that ambulance instead of inside it. He was barefoot and dressed only in a pair of shorts, an EMS blanket draped over his shoulders. Soot dirtied his face, chest, and legs. His hair was matted where blood caked over a cut on the back of his head. Beasley stood alongside, clutching an ice bag that Dante was apparently refusing to use. Brennan winced as coughing racked his friend's lungs. And then he saw the gleam of tears.

Richardson lifted his hands in a gesture of helplessness. "Will you see if you can talk some sense inta him? I can't. He needs stitches. The paramedics want an Emergency Room doc t' check him over."

As Diana hurried to her injured friend's side, Brennan joined Jumbo. "You said on the phone that it was an explosion. Of what? Gas?"

"We wish," Richardson muttered. "Fire marshal's sayin' it looks like some kinda incendiary device; gasoline used as the accelerant. Bastard pitched it through Joey's back door. He was standin' in the hall when it blew." Beasley's expression was grim, but Brennan thought he detected a hint of sympathy in the big man's eyes. "A woman was trapped in there, Brian. Joey tells me you've been workin' with her; that he met her at your place."

Brennan felt himself go light-headed. "Linda?" He could barely get the name out.

Richardson nodded. "Curled up asleep with the cat. Caught in the blast. There's no way she could'a known what hit her. Joey was *outside* the room, and he don't hardly remember a thing. Them shorts he's got on is all he's got left. Whole fuckin' buildin's nothin' but an insurance adjuster's nightmare now. We're lucky nobody *else* died."

"Who pulled him out?"

"Kid from 'cross the street. Blast woke him up. When he sees all the flames, he cuts through Joey's front door with a fuckin' *chain saw*. Says he brought it with him when he moved up here from Highland County, Virginia. Been keepin' it in his hall closet. Sounds like 'nother crazy, but the mayor's gonna end up givin' this one a medal."

Brian turned to look at Joe. Diana was down on her knees in front of him, both his hands in hers. "That cut on the back of his head?" he asked Beasley. "Looks nasty. How bad is it?"

"Bad enough. He should be at St. Vinnie's, but he won't go."

Dante was so numb that he could hardly feel the hands now gripping his. He could hardly see Diana, nor could he hear the words she spoke. Behind that numbness was despair.

"She trusted me, Diana. A girl young enough to be my own daughter." The words rang hollow through a void. He was trying hard to focus, Diana's eyes and her earnest expression slowly coming clear. "I killed her. That was supposed to be me in there."

He watched as Brennan squatted down beside his wife and said something in her ear. He watched her eyes widen in simultaneous jolts of surprise and horror. Now she knew who was killed. He fully expected those hands to release their grip. Instead, she leaned closer.

"She wanted to be there, Joe. I know that much."

He shook his head. "We talked about her hopes and dreams, Diana. That's almost *all* we talked about. I feel sick."

As Dante was racked by another fit of coughing, Brennan leaned down to rest his big hands on his friend's shoulders. "You can't blame yourself for what happened, Joe. Wherever Linda is, I don't believe she's blaming you."

"Bullshit." It came out half croak, half gasp.

"C'mon, Joe. They tell me that's a nasty cut you've got. You took a serious shot to the head. We're taking you to see a doctor."

When Dante was hit again by a fit of coughing, his seared lungs screamed as he doubled over. It probably lasted no more than a minute but seemed like an eternity. "What good's a doctor gonna do me? I'm fine."

Brennan grunted. "And I'm the next president of Ethiopia. You're going to see a doctor and then you're coming home with us."

Dante was summoning the strength for further protest when Gus appeared. As he pulled up alongside Jumbo, the chief shook his head. "You heard him, Joey. Sometimes your friends know better'n you do. There's nothin' you can do here. I've got Don'n Rusty keepin' an eye on the lab people. You get some rest an' we'll talk tomorrow."

"You know what this is about, same as I do, Gus. We've scared somebody. You expect me to just walk away?"

"Nobody's askin' you t' walk away, Joey. Look at yourself. You took a shot that knocked you out *cold*. Go on home with your friends an' we'll talk in the mornin'."

Dante finally gave up and let himself be led away. The EMS people transported him to St. Vincent's Emergency in the ambulance while Brennan and Diana followed in their pickup. The gash in his scalp took a dozen stitches. He lost a little hair in the swab-and-prep process. By the time they reached West Twenty-seventh Street, it was three o'clock. All of them were exhausted, but no one was going to be able to sleep quite yet. A few years back, Brennan had given up drinking the hard stuff but still kept a bottle of decent Irish on hand for emergencies. Once Dante emerged from a shower, Diana handed him a tumbler full of whiskey and pushed him toward the living room sofa.

Joe sat, closed his eyes, and took a good-sized slug of the whiskey. When he started to throw his head back, Diana anticipated the move and gasped. He caught himself in the nick of time. "God, my head hurts."

"The way you were talking to Gus before we left, it sounds like you've got an idea who threw that bomb." Instead of the Irish, Brian had a beer. "Is it something to do with that club owner Diana took you to see?"

"All part of the same picture, yeah. And you got me wrong. I *don't* know who. We've managed to narrow it down to a handful of people, but that's not good enough." Dante took another gulp of whiskey, its velvety warmth quick to join the turmoil already at work on his stomach lining. "She was so *young*. God knows I've got a weakness for beautiful women, but . . ." The tears welled and threatened to roll again. "I keep asking myself if I really intended that she end up in my bed tonight. It all happened so fast."

"It generally takes two willing partners to dance that dance, Joe." Diana's voice was husky with emotion.

Dante stared into the depths of the amber liquid left in his glass. "She was twenty-three. Did you know that today was her birthday?"

Located on the spit of land between the Atlantic and Shinnecock Bay, the Talbot family's beach house and its surrounds were a whole different world for a girl from Kew Gardens, Queens. Rising before dawn, Deborah Glenmore had gone through a brutal two-hour workout with her trainer and gotten on the road by nine. Considering it was Saturday and she was headed for the beaches of eastern Long Island, she and her little Miata made excellent time. She drove with the top down and the tape deck cranked loud, the warm highway breezes whipping her hair. The morning's exertion had her feeling alive all over. Those two bastards in the Bronx were finally behind bars. Regardless of how the Onofrio homicide had stolen her thunder, she was feeling deep satisfaction.

It was eleven before Deborah left the Montauk Highway and found her way south to the ocean and Meadow Lane. She knew Talbot was from money but had no idea it was *this* kind of money. All of the houses she passed en route were at least as large and ostentatious as the sprawling cedar-and-glass home she found by following Bob's map. Out front, just across the road to the south, sat Southampton Beach and the Atlantic Ocean. Behind, across the dunes, lay Shinnecock Bay. Between the Talbot place and the houses on either side ran fifty yards of beautifully landscaped grounds. There was a hedge-wall of twisted evergreen isolating it from the road-front and running back to the bay. An electronic gate controlled access to the drive. Wow. It gave her goose bumps just to look at it.

Once the gate was released, Deborah proceeded up the drive to park alongside a Seven-series BMW. Talbot emerged from the house to greet her. Today he was wearing only a pair of bikini briefs, but out here, that didn't seem all that odd.

"You made good time, Deb. I wasn't expecting you for another hour."

"I did like you suggested and took the Jericho out to the Veterans Memorial. Missed all the Jones Beach and Fire Island traffic." She paused to look around, taking a deep breath of the tangy sea air. "This is great, Bob. I can feel my batteries recharging already."

"You brought a suit, I hope."

"You bet. How's the water?" She'd noticed as she approached up the beach road that, unlike the public beaches farther west, all that glorious sand out front was virtually empty. With a light breeze coming in off the Atlantic, it was at least five degrees cooler here than it was at her home in Queens. Still, it was plenty warm enough for swimming and sunbathing.

"Water's great," he reported. "We've got a couple hours to kill before lunch. What say we hit the beach?"

The smell of coffee greeted Brennan when he opened his eyes. Nobody had set any alarms, and now, as he awoke, it was already eleven o'clock. Diana slept on as he eased from bed and slipped into a pair of sweatpants. He didn't find Dante in the kitchen, where he discovered a topped-up carafe in the coffee maker. Neither was he in any of the other rooms in the living half of the loft. It wasn't until Brian carried his cup of coffee into his workshop that he discovered their houseguest in the drawing studio.

Joe was sitting on a stool in there, the one Brian generally perched on while he worked. Before him was the wall covered with sketch studies of the *Aerodite* project. A half dozen were detail sketches of the model's face and head. The rest were of her body from all angles. Two weeks' work had yielded most of what Brian needed to get started on the next phase. He hadn't gotten to the hands and feet, but Diana would no doubt sit for those. She and Linda had similar builds, so any final execution problems could be overcome. Last night *Aerodite* became more than another commission. It was personalized now: Linda Fletcher's project.

"Too bad you probably won't be there when I get the bastard." Dante's voice was cold and even.

Brennan moved forward, his coffee cup cradled in his hands, to stand before his work. "I'm gonna do her justice, Joe. I'll work my ass off to see to that."

"You can't bring her back, Brian. No one can."

Brennan turned to face him. "Diana and I talked it over. We want you to stay here. We already planned to go up to our place on the Sound on Monday. We'll be there all of August and maybe some of September. As soon as you can get away, maybe you'll come up and stay awhile."

Dante drained the rest of his cup and stood. He was dressed in the sweatpants and T-shirt Brennan had lent him last night, along with a pair of flip-flops. He and Brian were almost the same height, but most of their physical similarities ended there. Brennan was large-boned but less filled-out; more wiry. His feet were two sizes larger than Joe's, and his jackets, one size smaller.

"Can't think that far ahead right now, Brian. But thanks. I've gotta go. Day's half-shot already. I've got to meet with my squad and I've got to get myself some clothes."

"How do you feel?"

"Physically? My head hurts, my neck's stiff, and my lungs feel like somebody ran sandpaper through them."

"If you need anything, all you've got to do is ask. I hope you know that. It's what friends are for."

The smile on Dante's lips was wan, but he was trying. "I owe you one, Brian."

Brennan shook his head. "I don't think so. That blow to the head's affected your memory."

Talbot's eyes popped when Deborah emerged from one of the guest rooms. She'd purchased the string bikini just yesterday from a Forest Hills boutique. It was black, what there was of it, and when she first tried the suit on, she was a little embarrassed by the way it contrived to crawl up the crack of her behind. But what the hell; she worked hard on her body and could see no reason not to showcase it. Women who could carry it off were wearing this sort of thing now. She liked the way a bikini left her abs exposed. Her stomach was one of her best features: flat and tight as a drumhead.

"Nice suit," Talbot complimented.

"Nice *suit*? The suit I bought yesterday, Bob. I've been working on the body inside it for over ten years."

His eyes roamed, appraising. "Karate, huh? I think the sport just won a new fan."

Deborah grinned. "You ever see one of those fighting posters of Bruce Lee? Hot damn. Arnold Schwarzenegger, eat your heart out. Bruce wasn't big, but that man was *tuned*. You might want to try taking it up yourself, Bob."

Talbot chuckled as he turned to lead the way toward the front door. "I'm forty-one years old, Deb. Maybe in my next life."

"My trainer's got a grandmother of sixty-three in one of his intermediate classes. She started in her late fifties."

They moved down the drive and across the road to the sand. After a quick dip in the ocean, Deborah sprawled facedown in the sun on one of the towels Talbot provided. He opted for a beach chair, no doubt preferring the view from higher ground.

"So what's the latest on the Mott homicide?" Eyes closed, she asked it into the crook of her left arm. "I gather Dante thinks it and Sal Onofrio are somehow connected?"

"You didn't hear?"

Eyes open now. "Hear what?"

"Somebody firebombed Dante's apartment last night. Whole building went up. A woman was killed."

Deborah was up on her elbows now. "Jesus. No, I *didn't* hear. I haven't seen a paper yet today. It's been on the news?"

"Everywhere."

"Who was the woman? Another tenant?"

Talbot shook his head. "Tenant of Dante's bed. An actress named Linda Fletcher. Just a kid, from what I hear. Trapped in the bedroom when the bomb was tossed through the garden door."

235

Deb frowned. "In his *bed*? So where was he?"

Talbot related how Dante had been in the hallway when the bomb went off; that the bedroom door had thrown him twenty feet. "A neighbor heard the blast, saw flames, and pulled Dante out."

"He's okay?"

"Scalp laceration. Smoke inhalation. I doubt he feels too good this morning. His building was gutted; a total loss. It's awful about the girl."

Talbot went on to tell her that little progress had been made connecting anyone to either the Mott or Onofrio killings. They'd abandoned a related investigation into a homicide down in Atlantic City. No connection. "So how do you feel about Ahern and Escobedo being behind bars? The judge at the arraignment ordered those DNA prints you wanted. The Bronx DA will have the results by Monday."

"How do I feel? Castration wouldn't be justice enough for those guys. The way the system's been working lately, we're lucky if they get more than their fingernails clipped. I appreciate what you did for me and those women, Bob. Don't get me wrong. But I'm not optimistic. It's a first-offense situation. In today's climate, they wouldn't convict Attila the Hun on a first offense for sacking Rome."

Rusty Heckman and Don Grover managed to make it to One Police Plaza by ten o'clock Saturday morning. Like the rest of the team, they'd been summoned to the scene of the Dante firebombing and were understandably slow getting a start on their work. By the time noon rolled around, they'd been poring over stacks of computer printout nonstop for almost two hours. Grover had eaten a hearty breakfast, but his stomach had no recollection of it. Across the squad room table, Heckman was unconsciously pushing a red pencil in and out of the springy texture of that flaming red hair. Neither had spoken in more than half an hour, and neither rose to refill empty coffee cups. There was even an untouched box of donuts next to the coffee maker.

"Eureka."

Grover didn't shout it. Instead, it slipped out as a distracted murmur. Heckman stopped fiddling with his pencil to look up.

"You got something?"

Grover lifted the two sheets he'd been comparing and turned them in Rusty's direction. So far this morning, they'd been working with a handicap. Central Records had compiled lists of branch banks in all four of the circled areas surrounding Night Watch personnel's homes, but only three banks had responded with the subpoenaed lists of safe-deposit tenants. They'd started with those.

"Here." He pointed to the list of victims from the Task Force Homicide files. "And here." The bank was a Chemical branch on the Hempstead Turnpike in Franklin Square, Long Island. It was just outside the one-mile radius drawn around Howard McGraff's home in Elmont, east of the Belmont Park Race Track.

Heckman read the two names Don had circled. Both names and the accompanying Social Security numbers were identical.

"Clyde W. Parsons." Grover had the cover sheets from every Task Force investigation file and had dug this one out of the "Ps." "Killed by his brother-in-law during a domestic squabble in 1987. June sixteenth. One-thirteen West Houston Street, third floor rear. Name of the investigating detective who signed the report?"

"Nickname 'Crime Dog'?"

"This is your lucky day, partner. I'm buying lunch."

Talbot had proven his skill as a short-order chef at his apartment the other night, but Deborah thought today's lunch put him at a whole other level. What he'd done with a boneless chicken breast was remarkable. After boiling down nearly half a quart of tarragon vinegar, butter, lemon juice, and who knew what else to a mere few tablespoons of thick marinade, he tossed the chicken in this sauce and then onto a hot barbecue grill. The butter in it produced a lot of flame, causing Deb to wonder if her host knew what the hell he was doing. But Bob explained that the butter was burned away in the process, while the chicken's juiciness was sealed inside. And he was right. It was fabulous.

As they ate, Talbot looked up from his plate to watch his guest enjoying herself. "You think this is tasty, wait till you try the seafood at the place I'm taking you for dinner. It's right on the water in Sag Harbor."

"Tonight? God, I'm sorry, Bob. I should have said something. It's my sister's birthday. I even packed what I've got to wear so I could squeeze in as much time out here as possible. I've got to be at a restaurant in Queens Village by seven-thirty."

Talbot had trouble masking his disappointment. She'd pulled on a pair of shorts for lunch but didn't bother with a shirt. He hadn't been able to tear his eyes off her all day, and it was fairly obvious what sort of hopes he was entertaining.

"Why the long face, Captain?" she soothed. "I don't have to leave for a few hours yet." Part of what she enjoyed about karate competitions was the audiences. If you had good stuff, they got excited. "You've sure got a touch with food, Bob. Everything's wonderful."

Talbot tried to smile modestly, but it was obvious he was pleased. "Thanks, Deb. I guess I hoped you'd be able to stay longer."

"I'm here now." She eased her chair back and moved gracefully to her feet. One quick tug at the bow behind her neck saw her bikini top come loose. She whisked it off and sent it floating through the air to land on the table before him. One of the straps fell into his water glass. "And I don't have to leave for *hours* yet."

She was proud of the way her pectoral development kept her breasts riding high, like a young girl's. Her words were an invitation, but the pose was a challenge. Most men seemed to enjoy that. Warren had certainly enjoyed it. Challenge made the lovemaking hot and furious, the way she liked it. Bring the horse into the stretch already lathered, give him the right sense of urgency about the task at hand, and if you've done your job right, you don't have to go to the whip. Talbot had been champing at the bit for three hours. The way he came around the far corner of the table, she would swear she could hear the thundering of hooves.

SEVENTEEN

Over on the New Jersey side of the Hudson, the neon light of the giant Maxwell House sign reflected off the river. The sun had set beyond the Hoboken skyline half an hour ago. Now Dante waited, the night falling quickly over the world outside his temporary home. The new clothes he wore felt strange: cream-colored linen jacket, pearl gray silk shirt, and slightly darker pants. They weren't the sort of threads he would normally rush out to buy when his wardrobe was wiped out, but Gus had authorized their purchase for tonight's sting operation. Because of time constraints, everything had come from Ralph Laurèn, all the way down to the shoes. A loose weave of light gray kidskin in a casual loafer configuration, they were the most comfortable shoes Dante had ever worn.

Back in the guest room, more new clothes were hung in closets and stuffed into drawers. Practical things: underwear, socks, a few cotton dress shirts, several pairs of slacks, and a couple off-the-rack jackets. Nothing on hangers fit very well, but Joe didn't care. These were stopgap purchases. When he had more time, he'd begin rebuilding his wardrobe the same way he'd rebuild the rest of his life. Step by step.

Emotionally drained, Dante saw little in the day's events to fill his cup. The Grover-Heckman discovery tying Howard McGraff to a fraudulent safe-box rental was the high point. A definite coup. Then again, with half the banks still dragging their feet, it was going to be Monday before they had the data they needed to complete their survey. Joe wished he'd been able to lend a hand, but most of his day was consumed by meetings with the job brass and people from forensics. Then he'd made his mad dash uptown to Ralph's, followed by a stop at the Buyer's Factory Outlet on lower Fifth Avenue. When he returned to Brennan's, there was no hungry cat to feed and scratch between the ears. Those sketches still covered the drawing studio wall, haunting him with memories of last night. When he tried to steady himself, to reach for something familiar, it hit home time and again that all of it was gone.

"Ahem!"

Startled from his reverie, Joe turned from the window to see Mel Busby standing with Diana across the living room. Both women were turned out for a night on the town.

"What do you think?" Diana asked. It was made in reference to the job she'd done on Mel's hair and makeup. The rest Mel had pulled together on her own: the ultrashort skirt hugging her fanny like a best friend, the silver lamé heels, and a shoulderless silver sequined top. Dante was surprised by Mel's legs. On the job, she always wore jackets and slacks. He'd had no idea what she was hiding: a pair of legs that were better than passing decent.

"Think about what?" he wondered. "I hand you a pretty fair lady detective, you turn her into Cyndi Lauper. What *should* I think?"

Mel stepped up and twirled. "You like it?"

Sure he did. And if he thought Mel looked good, he thought Diana might well need police protection before the night was out. Dressed in skintight leopard capri pants over a white halter-neck swimsuit, she was pushing the rock star persona almost as hard as she did onstage.

While Joe was busy enjoying the scenery, the elevator bell rang. Diana hurried to release the car while Melissa crossed to admire the cut of her date's linen jacket. A moment later, Jumbo and Gus Lieberman stepped into the living room. While the chief was casually acquainted with both Brian and Diana, this was the first time he'd ever been to their loft. He paused a moment to survey his surroundings. Then he spotted Melissa.

"Jesus. Did *we* buy that?"

"Just the shoes, sir," Busby replied. "Rest of it I dug out of my closet. Diana did the hair."

Gus turned to their host. "Appreciate what you're doing for us here, Diana."

"My privilege," she replied. "Anyone want coffee? It's likely to be a long night."

The chief declined, while the rest of them thought it sounded good. When Diana turned for the kitchen, Gus got a look at the backside of her outfit for the first time. His eyes popped. There was nearly no back to that top, and the way her gait moved the mock-leopard fabric covering her behind was something to behold. Watching his boss watch Diana's progress gave Joe a badly needed lift.

"I hope you know what the fuck you're doin'," Gus growled. He had a brown paper sack clutched in his right hand and held it out now in Dante's direction. "Two grand. Serial numbers sequential and all the bills marked. Nice threads. I s'pose we bought 'em?"

"Yep." Dante took the sack, flattened it, and slipped it into his inside jacket pocket. His gaze left the chief's face, moving to admire Beasley. A rock star wouldn't go out in public dressed like Diana without a bodyguard. Jumbo was decked out to fit the bill. He already had the size and that battered, mean-looking scowl. To complement them, he'd found a white suit, black silk shirt, white shoes, and a snappy Panama. There was enough gold jewelry around his neck—on loan from Narco Division's confiscated property vault—to immobilize a hyperactive three-year-old.

"Bought that rig, too," Joe told Gus.

"Ever'thing but the gold," Jumbo corrected. "Damn shame I gotta give it back. I could get me a franchise in the old neighborhood, lookin' like this."

"I'm outta here," Gus told them. "Bring me a prize. I'm in a mood t' nail somebody's balls to a wall."

To avoid their standing out on the sidewalk in front of FLOTSAM with the usual horde of hopefuls, Diana had arranged for limousines from the company that handled her record label's account. Saturday nights tended to get busy a little earlier than other nights, and by the time they pulled up out front, more than a hundred people already lined the Crosby Street sidewalk. En route, Dante told Melissa about his days working undercover for Narcotics Division. During that time, he'd learned something about the ins and outs of the late seventies and early eighties club scenes. He explained now that it was all in the attitude as you approached the front door. Once they climbed from their limo, he took her elbow, ignored the line, and moved on the doorman; moved like he was *somebody*. He'd confided that while the guy at the gate was paid well to know all the somebodies, there were always high-rolling strangers flying into the city from Europe and the other coast. If a person was a stranger who looked and moved like a somebody, he always got the nod.

Ten-thirty was still early enough for them to get good position upstairs. As they moved through the place, Melissa was conscious of people watching: women with their heads together at tables; men clustered like loitering bachelors on the Italian Riviera. Everybody got sized up here. Some were dismissed out of hand. Others were watched with keen interest. Down on the second level, they passed Napier playing the part, too. Leaning on the end of the bar, he looked to be having a ball ogling tits and fannies in tight dresses. He and some muscle-bound kid from Special Frauds Squad had arrived at nine and eaten dinner just to make sure they got in without having to draw attention. Melissa thought Napier looked like he was having a bit too much fun.

Dante chose a spot in the video lounge with sight lines down the hall to the owner's office as well as a view of the stair landing. They ordered drinks, Melissa choosing Bloody Marys tonight instead of martinis. As they waited for their drinks, Joe checked the tiny radio unit secreted in his jacket pocket. Parked half a block away in a second limo, Jumbo and Diana acknowledged receipt of the signal, their return transmission lighting a red indicator.

At eleven-thirty, Dante handed Melissa the folded brown sack.

"Okay, cuteness. We don't want to cut it any closer than this. If Brycie gets nervous, he gets nervous. I've already spotted him buying people drinks at the bar twice, and he looks like he's feeling no pain. You just wander down there and give him that. Tell him as little about the game as you can."

As Melissa took the bag, she nodded in the direction of Weller's office. "Diana says he has a reputation he thinks he's got to work hard to maintain. If he goes for a handful, how hard can I hit him?"

"Hard as you want," Joe replied. "Just make sure the bruises don't show with his clothes on."

Melissa stood and made like she was headed for the ladies' room. Weller appeared to be alone in his office when he answered the door. The look of relief flashing across his face quickly turned peevish.

"Do you mind? The ladies' room is the one with WOMEN on the door."

"Detective Busby, Mr. Weller. Let's talk a minute." She saw him trying to decide what to make of this.

Both the content and tone of her message caught him off guard. Instead of giving him a chance to consider his alternatives, she pushed her way inside.

"You had lunch with Lieutenant Dante and Sergeant Richardson yesterday, Mr. Weller. Welcome to phase two." She tossed him the bag of cash and watched with amusement as he snatched for it and missed. Definitely drunk. "You keep your money tonight and give them that. It's legal tender, and don't worry about the count. It's correct."

"You're planning to come busting in here?" An obvious protest, it came out as a mixture of whining and disbelief.

Melissa knew her best reassuring smile was no prizewinner, but it was all she had. "Relax, Mr. Weller. The plan's to catch them on the way out. You play it cool, do everything the way you've always done it."

"Cool? Jesus, that's rich. You obviously haven't seen these guys yet. I've *never* played it cool around them."

"Just make sure you give them *that* bag."

With the alcohol at work on him, Weller's confidence came back in a rush. Yesterday it was all just talk. Tonight he was going to help trap the monkey on FLOT-SAM's back.

"This is fast. I didn't expect you to move quite so quickly. You caught me off guard."

"I could see that."

"You've got nice legs for a cop."

"For a *cop*?" Melissa wasn't going to give him any more room. She threw it back over her shoulder as she turned for the door.

The minute those two economy-size fellas got out of a Lexus sedan pulled up to the fire hydrant across from the entrance to the club, Jumbo knew it was showtime. Those two were *not* headed inside for a night of FLOT-SAM fun. One was too old by a mile, and both of them moved the same way the law moves everywhere. The crowd they approached was a little bigger now than it was when Jumbo and Diana arrived here, but they ignored its existence and walked straight in the front door.

"Let's start her up," he told the driver. "I'll tell you when to roll."

He noticed confusion register on Diana's face. The little radio unit lay on the seat between them. It hadn't chirped yet.

"I think I just spotted 'em goin' in," he explained. "You all set?"

She patted his knee. "You think I can get some sort of commendation out of this?"

"Prob'ly. If you want one. Me? I think you can start a fire just as easy with plain newspaper. You can get a newspaper at any corner stand, an' you don't have t' waste time shakin' some asshole's hand, neither."

She took a deep breath, started to pull a compact from her purse, and paused. "That picture your friend Melissa's gonna take? There's a chance it'll end up in court, right?"

"Good chance."

"So how do I look . . . for a white woman?"

The big man chuckled, his eyes taking their time as they roamed over her.

"I meant my makeup."

"Who's gonna be lookin' at your face?"

She clipped her bag shut. This time, the pat she gave his knee had a little sting to it.

The tiny black box between them suddenly emitted a sound like an electronic alarm clock. That meant the quarry had passed Dante's position en route toward Weller's office.

"Okay," Jumbo told the driver. "Don't rush it, but get us right up at the curb in front'a the door." He checked the time. It was 12:06. *Punctual* bag men.

Once the driver parked, he got the back door open in a hurry. As Jumbo emerged, he slipped the man an extra fifty. The two guys working the door were already peering curiously into the limo, and Jumbo gave them a curt nod. When Diana appeared, there were oohs and aahs of recognition. Richardson planted one of his huge hands on the small of her back and hustled her forward. As the crowd closed in for a better look, Diana moved closer to her protector's chest.

Forging ahead, it was hard for Jumbo to keep his mind on the job. Diana Webster just might have the best body he'd ever seen on a woman, black *or* white. His nostrils were full of her scent, and his fingers registered every muscle twitch along her sacrum. God, there were times when he loved his work. The plan had them making their way to the second level and casually crossing it toward the third floor stairs. Everywhere they moved, Diana proceeding directly in front of him, Jumbo was aware of the crowd's attention. Stardom had a price, and he was getting a feel for just how high that price was.

It wasn't until they approached the end of the huge second floor bar that Jumbo spotted Guy Napier with the man on loan from Special Frauds. Joey had gone outside Major Case for this extra manpower rather than drag Grover and Heckman along. Those two were completely wrong for a scene like this, both in age and appearance. Besides, they'd worked their asses off today.

Now, directly above them, Beasley spotted the quarry starting down from the third floor and Bryce Weller's office. That meant the deed was done. They had the marked cash.

"Okay," he muttered into Diana's ear. "This is our cue."

When the bag men hit the second floor and started along the bar, Mel Busby emerged from the dance floor with an excited squeal. Just as the targeted pair was passing between, Diana stepped directly in line with Mel's camera lens. The squeal drew their attention, and the flash temporarily blinded them.

The younger of the pair, a big blond guy carrying some impressive muscle mass, was the first to realize the implications of their being photographed. Blinking furiously, he turned to see who this squealing photographer had *meant* to shoot. Diana was standing so close behind him that he could easily have touched her. A vague recognition was registering when his partner plunged ahead onto the dance floor. Bingo. An assistant DA had explained to Dante that to ensure a conviction, they should force the suspects to show their hand. Joe had come up with the photograph idea. Two men in the act of making a collection wouldn't want to have their presence documented.

Napier and the Special Frauds man were down off their bar stools and moving into position on either side of the blond man. This action freed Jumbo up to follow the older suspect onto the dance floor. He arrived just as Mel was being grabbed.

"Sorry, sweetheart. I'm gonna have to have the film in that camera."

"Get your hands off me, you bastard!"

The confused crowd reacted by clearing back. Mel and the bag man were isolated in a circle about ten feet in diameter. The suspect pulled his captive close and took a swipe at the camera. To no avail. Mel held it at arm's length as Dante emerged from the crowd to take it.

The air around them pulsed with deafening rock and roll. It was impossible to hear what was said, but the bag man could plainly see Joey drop that little idiot-camera into his jacket pocket. Height-wise, Dante and this other character were about even. By the looks of him, Jumbo figured the suspect to have seven or eight years on Joe, while outweighing him by a good twenty or thirty pounds. But Joey was a veteran of twenty years spent warring on a dojo mat. Just last night he'd seen his home firebombed and a woman killed in his bed.

The suspect threw himself at Dante, coming ahead like an inside linebacker. One second Joey occupied the area his opponent aimed to hit, and the next instant, he'd vanished. The suspect's feet were suddenly swept from beneath him. He crashed hard to the floor, hitting down on his chin and chest. The momentum of his flying tackle attempt did most of the damage. Before the man could recover from the impact of his fall, Joey was on his back.

Jumbo watched his partner get the cuffs on that one before turning back to the bar area, wondering if he was needed to assist with the Incredible Hulk. He didn't wonder for long. When the second bag man saw his buddy go down on the dance floor, he immediately started in that direction. From each side of him, Napier and the Special Frauds man pounced. The Boy Wonder had a height advantage but didn't have the suspect's bulk. Special Frauds had some of the bulk but nowhere near the leverage. When the Hulk saw their attempt to restrain him coming, he flat out poleaxed the Special Frauds detective. The fist impacting with the Frauds man's chin caused his eyes to roll back. Then, as Jumbo hurried to close the distance between them, a knee caught Napier in the solar plexus. The air went out of him in a rush as FLOTSAM patrons scattered like tin roofs in a hurricane. Napier was going down anyway, but the blond hulk hammered him upside the head for good measure.

Less than thirty seconds had elapsed since Joey kicked the other suspect's feet from under him. The first live act hadn't hit the stage yet, and with a group of oversized men brawling out front of the bar, the disc jockey cut the music. A hush fell. The blond guy crouched and spotted Jumbo coming for him. Beasley knew this gold around his neck was going to be a problem. And pimp rig or not, it was clear enough from the way he was moving that he was on the other team. He only had a few seconds to size up the competition and didn't like the odds at all. At six four and a good two-fifty, the blond man had a four-inch height and thirty-pound weight advantage. Jumbo watched as the man came forward off his heels and started slowly to his left. That was a useful tip. He was probably right-handed. His power or "plant" foot was trailing.

"Let me do this, Beasley."

The words were spoken low and soft from just behind him. Jumbo's eyes never lost contact with the blond man's as a smile slowly stretched his lips.

"Sure you don't wanna flip for him?"

"Nope. I might lose."

"I guess you're the boss, huh?"

"That's right."

Dante moved into Jumbo's peripheral view. He had his jacket off and had handed his weapon to Mel.

"You got him?" Jumbo asked.

"Oh yeah." Dante was riveted on his quarry. "You're under arrest, pal. The other two officers didn't have time to identify themselves, but . . ." He had his shield case in his left hand and let his tin dangle for the bag man to see. "You push this any further and you've got a charge of assaulting a police officer tacked on top of extortion. Pretty boy like you ain't gonna like prison much. Why extend your stay?"

"Suck my dick." The words dripped contempt.

"No, thanks." Joey's words were calm.

The smile on Dante's face infuriated his opponent. "I'm gonna kick your candy ass, you little cunt!" The man launched, throwing a carefully aimed haymaker.

Dante worked him like a matador. A quick skip-step to his right brought him directly into the path of his opponent's momentum. It caught the other man by surprise. He was off balance, and as he took a half step to steady himself, he walked directly into a vicious whip-kick. The force of it caught him flat across the chest, landing so hard that he staggered back a step. That gave Joey room to flex down on his right leg and throw a heel up toward his target's head. In the silence fallen over the dance floor, a distinct crunch was heard as nose cartilage gave way. The man screamed and grabbed at his face, but Dante wasn't finished. He had a choice of targets across an exposed lower torso and legs. A snap kick to the groin brought the Incredible Hulk sagging to his knees.

Jumbo was ready with the cuffs. ''You pulled that last shot.'' He'd leaned close to get Joey's ear. ''Why?''

Dante jerked one of the groaning man's arms behind his back and offered Jumbo the wrist. ''We'll want to talk with him later. I'd rather question him on our own turf. You know how I hate hospitals.''

EIGHTEEN

A frisk of the two bag men produced the specially marked cash, two fire marshal's shields, one police sergeant's shield, two pistols, and a blackjack. Considering circumstances, the cops were grateful that neither man had gone for his weapon inside the crowded club. As it was, the Special Frauds detective appeared to have sustained a broken jaw. He was taken to the Emergency Room at Beekman Downtown for X-rays. It took some doing, but Melissa finally persuaded Napier to follow and get himself checked over. He seemed fine now, but the blow he took to the head had rendered him momentarily unconscious.

Once Chief Lieberman was contacted with news of the arrests, the prisoners were transported to the Fifth Precinct station house on nearby Elizabeth Street. It was two o'clock before they were booked. Formal questioning could not begin until representation was called. Lieberman contacted the district attorney to request he roust a prosecutor. He then informed Commissioner Mintoff of the night's events, and in turn, Mintoff saw it as his duty to contact his opposite at the Fire Department. Then, anticipating a possible jurisdictional squabble, Mintoff called the mayor.

Dante was in an interrogation room with the senior of the two suspects, now identified as Lieutenant Tom Neeley, when a florid-faced man with a bulldog's loose jowls and watery eyes strode in without knocking. He glanced quickly at the faces around the room and stopped before the Major Case commander.

"You in charge here, mister?"

"It's Lieutenant Dante. Who are you?"

The bulldog looked like he might blow a gasket. "Who *am* I? I'm Lewis Cole, mister. The *fire commissioner*. Lieutenant Neeley, you're coming with me. Where's Mr. Potts?"

Before Neeley could respond, the young brunette sent over by the district attorney rose from her chair at the end of the table. "This man is under arrest, sir." The woman had managed to get herself dressed and run a comb through her hair, but that was about it. She addressed the fire commissioner with irritation in her tone.

"And who the hell are you?"

"Leslie Blumenthal. Manhattan district attorney's office, *sir*."

At that point Chief Lieberman entered the room. "Problem here?"

Cole whirled, but as he sized Lieberman up, some of the wind came out of his sails. "You are . . . ?"

"Chief of Detectives Lieberman."

"Commissioner Lewis Cole, Chief." They shook hands, brass to brass, with Cole nodding to Leslie Blumenthal. "Miss Prosecutor? Would you be kind enough to accompany us?"

The assistant DA gave Dante a *be patient* glance and followed these two heavyweights out into the hall. As soon as the door closed, Joe left Neeley sitting with his attorney and beckoned Jumbo into the opposite corner.

"I'll keep an eye on things here. You get on the horn and call Don and Rusty. Tell 'em it's time to go on the offensive. I don't know *how* Night Watch is connected to this, but I aim to find out."

"At this hour? Rusty says the branch vault where McGraff's got that box rented is under a time lock, Joey. There ain't no way t' get inside until Monday."

Dante winked at him. "You know that and I know that."

A sly smile crept across Beasley's face. "But Crime Dog don't know it."

No sooner had the interrogation room door closed behind them than the fire boss let some of the heat out from under his collar. Gus got the full force of the blast.

"Commissioner Mintoff said something about a sting operation, Chief. If FD personnel were suspected of being involved, why wasn't my office informed?"

"Call it what you want, Commissioner," Gus replied. "The extortion game your people been playin' is somethin' my men stumbled on in the course of a homicide investigation. The nature of their primary interest dictated we play it close t' the vest."

The mention of homicide set Cole back on his pins. "Those two are fire personnel with police powers, Chief. The crème de la crème. Homicide's a nasty word. I hope you can back it up."

"Don't tell me how to do my job, Commissioner."

Lieberman's hard line infuriated Cole. He turned to the lady prosecutor, a scowl fixed on his face. "If I understand the current allegations correctly, my men are being held for extorting payoffs in exchange for protection from Fire Code enforcements. That would make this a problem between Fire and the district attorney, would it not?"

Leslie Blumenthal shook her head. "The action taken against your men was the direct result of a complaint made by a club owner to the police, sir. It's not an inner-departmental disciplinary problem; it's a criminal matter. Lieutenant Neeley was found carrying a police detective's shield. He was also found in possession of an alleged extortion payoff. Two of the policemen involved in the arrest are in an Emergency Room right now. Before the night's out, I may be tacking criminal assault to the list of other charges. They've been booked, printed, and delivered to my custody for arraignment. Signed and sealed, Commissioner.''

At that juncture, Tony Mintoff and the mayor appeared at the head of the stairs down the hall. Behind them came one of Hizzonner's trusted advisers and the Manhattan district attorney. Leslie Blumenthal looked grateful to see the DA climb into the ring. She was tough, but she was fighting way out of her weight class.

Fire Investigation Unit Commander Marty Schoenfeld paced the confines of his West Forty-fifth Street office. It was now two-thirty, and his guys were overdue. They should have reported in over an hour ago. He was convinced that something had gone wrong. The first thirty minutes of his vigil had been easy enough to handle. They'd been a few minutes late a couple of times in the past. But this past half hour had been hell on his nerves. He'd begun impatiently flipping the lid of his Zippo lighter about twenty minutes back. Open and shut. The crisp crack of steel on steel bit the surrounding stillness. It helped calm his nerves.

Schoenfeld was so wound up that the phone bell startled him. He pounced, snatching the receiver in the middle of the first ring.

''Arson Unit.''

''Captain Schoenfeld?''

''Speaking.''

''Commissioner Cole, Captain. You've got a lieutenant named Neeley and an investigator named Potts in your command.''

''Yes, sir.''

''Any idea where they are at the moment?''

''Making the usual weekend rounds, sir. Occupancy Code enforcements; routine stuff.''

''The police seem to think they've been taking a little

255

something under the table *not* to enforce those codes, Captain. The cops caught your people in a sting net; taking payoff money from the owner of some jiggle joint in SoHo. Serious charges, Captain. I suggest you get your ass down here and help me straighten this thing out.''

''There's gotta be some sort'a mistake, sir. Where are they bein' held?''

''The Fifth station house. Nineteen Elizabeth Street, just north of Bayard.''

''I'm on my way, sir.''

As Schoenfeld slowly replaced the receiver in its cradle, he let it all sink in; the feeling that every trapped animal must ultimately know. While one side of his awareness confronted it, another side still refused to believe that *he* was caught. This game was up, but Marty was a survivor. He'd survived two tours of long-range reconnaissance in Vietnam. If that experience had taught him any life lesson, it was that the puny and weak were trampled by the machine of civilization, while the strong and willful rode that machine to their advantages. Right and wrong weren't moral choices, they were survival choices.

Schoenfeld had chosen carefully when he assembled his tiny team of Manhattan arson investigators. Potts and Neeley were like him in that most important regard. Neeley was awarded the Silver Star for acts of heroism while defending Saigon through the January Tet Offensive in 1968. Craig Potts was one of just a handful of marines who walked away from the October 23 suicide attack on his barracks at the Beirut Airport in 1983. Both men had seen adversity. Both were strong. They were capable of ruthlessness in pursuit of their dreams of prosperity. Like Marty, they were destined within the natural order of things to survive.

''Those two won't say dick,'' he muttered to himself. ''Hell'd freeze over first.''

It was Sunday. There was no sense holing up and

waiting for the Citibank vault at nearby Manhattan Plaza to open. Schoenfeld kept some mad money stashed at his place in Forest Hills. He would need it if he wanted to make a run. Right now, he saw no other option. Once he could hurry to the street level and back his T-bird from the building garage, he circled the block to Forty-sixth Street and started east toward Queens with his emergency flasher pushed out onto the roof.

At Dante's request, Chief Lieberman ordered Howard McGraff, Stewart Beal, and Walter Mansker to report here at the Fifth. The two fire marshals, still sealed up tighter than a pair of cherrystone clams, were escorted away to detention cells downstairs. When Don Grover and Rusty Heckman appeared, Joe briefed them on developments and explained his current strategy. The whole squad was exhausted, but their investigation finally had a focus. That buoyed them. It was going to be at least another day before Don and Rusty could ferret out the goods on the Night Watch's Mansker and Beal, but they had Howard McGraff. He was the wedge they would drive to break this case.

Word of the punch-out at FLOTSAM and the arrest of two fire marshals had been circulating on the late night grapevine for almost two hours. By the time the three Night Watch detectives arrived at the Fifth station house, they already had a good idea of what the score might be. The idea turned fact when Chief Lieberman invited Howard McGraff into the interrogation room. Alone. As he took a chair, the man his squad called "Crime Dog" was sweating everything but blood. Dante took up position, looming over him with his knuckles planted fist-down on the table.

"You know why the chief's here, Howard? He's here preparing to launch a special internal investigation, based on information Don and Rusty are putting together for him. Financial information, Howard. Places you guys've stashed dirty cash."

257

"You're crazy," McGraff protested. "What dirty cash?"

"The cash you guys took off midtown club owners over the past four years," Dante replied. "Big cash, judging from what those two clowns were carrying tonight."

McGraff wasn't much at bluffing, but at least he was game to try. He shifted back in his chair, feigning ease. "Those guys are *fire*, Joe. What've they got t' do with me an' *my* squad?"

"And you've never heard of Clyde Wilbur Parsons, right, Crime Dog?" It was Heckman, sitting behind Dante and slapping a manila folder against his knee. "You've got no idea who might've rented a bank box in a dead man's name at a Chemical Bank in Franklin Square. And to think we'd assumed all the money in that box was yours."

McGraff's eyes widened. There was no question the man was having trouble drawing breath. Dante took over again.

"I guess a handwriting analysis of Clyde Parson's signature and the other stuff he put on the file card is gonna leave you smelling like gym socks laundered in Tide, huh, buddy?"

Across the room, Richardson was lounging against the wall in a chair, rocked back on two legs. "Maybe Howard don't quite understand what's at risk here, Joe. Maybe he ain't readin' his *Newsday* like he should. I think he already *knows* we got him on the extortion beef. What he's doin' is blowin' smoke so we don't think he's involved in fuckin' homicide."

"That right, Crime Dog?" Dante had backed away as Richardson spoke, and now he was looming again. "That you maybe don't understand we're talking about murder one here? Two counts?"

"None of us *killed* anybody," McGraff blurted. "Anybody who told you we did is a goddamn liar."

The Major Case team had softened him up, and now

it was Lieberman's turn to jump in. "It sounds like you know who did, Howard."

McGraff tried to be emphatic as he shook his head. He wasn't much of an actor. All that feigned ease was vanished. "I *don't* know, Chief."

"But you've got a good guess, don't you, Howard?"

McGraff looked trapped.

"Murder one, Howard," Gus reiterated. "Two counts."

"Okay. Let's say I've got some suspicions. That don't mean I know nothin'. Suspicions don't mean shit."

"You care t' share 'em with us?" Gus wondered.

A man defeated, Howard stared down at his hands. "Ain't nobody gonna hang no homicide on me or anyone else in my squad. Not for that prick Mott. An' for *sure* not for Sal. He was our friend. He was in it deep as we was, right on through. Deeper."

"Into what, Howard?" Gus prompted.

"The shakedowns. It was Sal made that deal with the marshals inna first place. Set it up. We split the work: leanin' on the club owners; makin' the pickups. Split ever'thing fifty-fifty. Then that shoofly fuck Mott starts snoopin'; diggin' for dirt."

"*They* killed Sal?" Dante demanded. "Why? Just because we showed up asking a few questions?"

McGraff snorted. "You got it, ace. For them assholes, a few questions was a few too many."

"You talk like it was Fire that made all the high-level decisions," Gus pressed. "That ain't like most'a the cops I know; playin' second fiddle to a bunch'a firemen?"

McGraff shook his head. "It weren't that way at first. No fuckin' way. It's just that once the deal went sour, we got out. Once Mott started stickin' his nose in, the whole deal was s'posed t' be dismantled. That's what Sal an' the other side agreed. Then we start hearin' rumors that them guys had it goin' again. On their own. Sallie was pissed."

"How's it going to go when we reopen the file on that dead club owner?" Dante asked. "The one who filed the original complaint. If there's any evidence of foul play and the DA thinks you had any knowledge of intent, he'll charge you as an accessory. Same goes for your connection to the Mott homicide."

"Lick mine with your knowledge of intent, Dante. None of us knows who Sal's opposite was at Fire. We *still* don't. It was safer that way."

Across the room, Richardson chuckled. "You 'spect anyone t' *believe* that?"

McGraff glared. "If we *did* know, you think he'd still be alive? After what he did to Sal?"

Dante pushed himself away from the table and shoved his hands deep in his pockets. In the silence, everyone in the room could hear the jingle of change as he started to pace. "According to Commissioner Cole, the investigation unit headquartered on Forty-fifth Street only works three men at night. We busted two of them. Tom Neeley and Craig Potts. You know them?"

"Negative. We always worked separate."

"But you can add, right? Three minus two leaves one. A guy name of Schoenfeld. Captain Marty Schoenfeld. Ever heard of him?"

"He's the fuck who did Sal, ain't he?"

"You tell us, Howard."

Marty Schoenfeld stood in the bathroom of his Forest Hills home and stripped out of his uniform shirt in front of the washbasin. As he reached to tug the sleeve from his right arm, he winced and bit his lower lip. Shirt removed, he tossed it into the tub. Schoenfeld was a well-muscled specimen, lean and tight. If he saw any flaw in his physique, it was the lingering evidence of overdevelopment in his upper body. After his army discharge twenty years ago, he'd done some lifting for bulk. Kid's stuff. He'd been working ever since to burn it off. Just as he suspected, the dressing covering the wound where Mott creased him had bled through. The bullet's ricocheting off a rib had been a lucky stroke. His liver was right there in that same area. Instead of going deep, the bullet ripped a nasty six-inch trough along his right side and broke that rib in at least one place. Not only had it bled a lot, it also hurt like hell.

While watching in the medicine cabinet mirror, Marty unwound the gauze wrapping. When the wound was exposed, he gingerly sponged the area off and poured what was left of a bottle of peroxide into it. There was a fair amount of foaming, meaning that some primary infection had set in, but he had no time to waste contemplating the fortunes of war. From the cabinet came antiseptic and a new sterile pad. He smeared one on the other, eased it into place, and rewrapped the wound. The bloodied sponge and dressing went into the bathroom trash.

Before he dressed, Marty dug out the money belt secreted beneath loosened floorboards in his bedroom closet. As he strapped it on, he was happy to see how the weight of the Krugerrands forced it down away from his rib cage. The diamonds didn't weigh as much and would take a little longer to negotiate, but they'd net another ten grand. The belt also contained some cash and several current credit cards. Total: thirty-five thousand dollars. In fact, it was no more than a safety net. Thirty-five grand wasn't going to take him very far. Sooner or later, he'd have to get his safe-deposit box.

Once Howard McGraff spilled his guts, nobody in the interrogation room believed that Captain Schoenfeld was likely to show up. It was thirty minutes since Commissioner Cole had called the investigation unit commander. At that hour of the morning, Forty-fifth Street was no more than a fifteen-minute drive.

"The closest station house to his Queens place is the One-Ten," Dante told Lieberman. "Let's send a squad car by, see if they can intercept him. If he left his unit offices when Cole called, he should be arriving home about now.''

"You think he'd go home?'' Gus asked.

Dante shrugged. "I've got no idea where he'd go. I got the impression he isn't married. He doesn't wear a ring, and he was alone that evening I stopped by his place. No reason to keep a splash pad, but it's possible he'd hit a friend's place. Who knows?''

Gus reached for the phone. "I'll have the Op Desk put out an APB. They can get us the make, model, an' plate number on his car; make sure special attention's paid t' airports, bridges, an' tunnels.''

Alongside Dante, Heckman shook his head. "If he ran for Jersey, he's already there.''

"We'll make it tri-state,'' Gus countered. "If we gotta, we'll put it out on the NCIC's national wire.''

Dante was on his feet and grabbing his jacket. "I want inside his house, Gus. It's always a good place to start.''

"Okay,'' Gus agreed. "Man in a hurry might overlook somethin'.''

"His office, too,'' Joe added. "Let's tear it apart.''

While Gus Lieberman's heart was on the street, there were political games left to be played. Only a fool would leave the mayor and two commissioners dangling without first satisfying them that they were at the center of the real action. Mayors and commissioners needed to believe they were in control. The chief's first order of business was to clear the way for an inspection of Captain Schoenfeld's West Forty-fifth Street office. Grover and Heckman were dispatched once a reluctant but ultimately pragmatic Lewis Cole finally gave his consent. Meanwhile, the mayor was prevailed upon to call a judge in night session at Municipal Court and request bench warrants. Leslie Blumenthal was hustled off to collect them. By the time Gus received the call telling him that the prosecutor had the warrants in hand, Dante

and Richardson had already arrived outside Schoenfeld's house.

When Joe and Jumbo pulled up out front, they found
two uniforms waiting in a parked radio unit. Once they
all converged at the foot of the drive, the ranking uniform pointed to the front door.

"No response when we rang and knocked, Lou," the
sergeant reported. "We checked the garage. No car."

"You got anything heavier than a tire iron in your
trunk?" Dante wondered.

The sergeant grinned. "Jimmy lad. Why don't you
run and get us that six-pound sledge we spotted in the
garage."

The younger cop hurried off as his partner and the
two detectives approached the side door off the drive.
In their collected experience, they'd all found kitchen
doors to be generally less formidable than the one out
front. The hammer bearer returned. He put considerable power behind his first blow and caught the knob
side of the panel dead on between the lockset and the
dead bolt cylinder. As the sergeant and detectives stood
off to each side, weapons at the ready, the door swung
inward.

Silence greeted them from within. Joe nodded to
Jumbo to make sure he was being covered and climbed
the two steps of the stoop. As he crept inside, Dante's
instincts about Schoenfeld being a bachelor were confirmed by the condition of his kitchen. The room was
spotless, like it was almost never used, but the remains
of the last coffee brewed in the Norelco hadn't been
dumped. Over next to the sink, one dish, one coffee
cup, and a few eating utensils had been set to dry in
the rack. Joe didn't open the dishwasher, but he would
bet money that it was empty. Marty Schoenfeld,
crooked or not, was a man wedded to his job. He
worked nights, slept here, kept his clothes here, and
generally ate out. As Joe entered the living room and

saw nothing to alarm him, he waved Jumbo and the uniforms ahead.

The place was empty. As the two uniformed men loitered out of the way in the kitchen, Joe and Jumbo started through, room by room. Dante was in the living room examining the contents of shelves on either side of the fireplace when Jumbo's voice came to him from down the back hall.

"Jackpot, Joey."

Dante hurried aft to find Beasley on his knees in the bathroom. The big man was using his pen to fish bloody gauze dressing out of the wastebasket beneath the basin.

"Warm in this house, Joey," Jumbo commented. "Hot even. Blood wouldn't be this fresh if he dumped this before he went to work. It'd be dry; at least most of it."

Dante squatted down next to him for a better look. "That's an awful lot of gauze, isn't it?"

Beasley nodded. "Like it was a leg wound or maybe somethin' up top."

"Some flu," Joe remarked. "Looks more like lead poisoning. Any bets on the type of that blood?"

"I'll take AB negative. You?"

"Let's get the Crime Scene Unit out here."

Dante was starting to rise when Jumbo put a restraining hand on his arm. "Let me do it, Joey. They get one more priority call from you that drags 'em out in the middle of the night, we're gonna be investigatin' *your* homicide." He dropped the bloody dressings back into the wastebasket.

NINETEEN

When the Queens Borough Task Force got wind of something going down in Forest Hills, they arrived to lend a hand. Jumbo had just phoned in the request for the Crime Scene Unit, and until they arrived, Dante was grateful for all the help he could get. He was busy dividing the house into sectors and assigning a detective to each when Gus arrived. And no sooner did the chief of detectives enter the house when Fire Commissioner Cole pulled up out front. Lieberman and Dante watched from Schoenfeld's living room as Cole emerged from his car and addressed one of the uniforms working crowd control.

"He don't wanna believe any of this," Gus murmured. "Not when our bustin' his boys might mean they're involved in homicide."

"Wait till he sees what Beasley dug out of the bathroom trash," Dante returned. "I'll bet he changes his tune once you let him sniff the bloody bandages. Mott gave a little of what he got, Gus."

"Fresh blood?"

"*Real* fresh."

"No shit. So Schoenfeld didn't run west after all,

even though the fuckin' Lincoln Tunnel was right around the corner.''

"It's just speculation, but we figure he came back here for something. Something he didn't want to be on the run without.''

"Like money? It's pretty hard t' go anywhere without it.''

"Either that or some piece of evidence that makes the shit he's standing in even deeper than we think.'' Dante yawned, rubbing his face. "Pretty wild night, huh?''

"How you holdin' up, Joey? You look whipped.''

"Forget it, Gus. I've got the scent now.''

Lewis Cole came bursting in the front door. "You didn't find him here, right?''

"He was here,'' Dante replied. "The two men the One-Ten sent 'round just missed him.''

"How do you know that, Lieutenant?''

Dante glanced to Gus. "Beasley's back there with some guys from Borough South. Have him show it to you.'' He turned back to Cole. "And whatever you do, don't touch anything . . . *sir*.'' Dante seemed distracted as he spoke. Something across the room had caught his attention. He left Gus and the fire commissioner standing where they were and crossed the room to a corner cabinet. It had a glass door and was filled with mementos from the captain's years of fire service. The top shelf was jammed with trophies.

Instead of taking Cole back to the bath, Lieberman started in Dante's direction. "What is it, Joey? What've you got?''

"Karate trophies.'' Dante murmured it distractedly. He had the cabinet door open and was reaching inside. Tucked up behind the gleaming golden statuettes on the top shelf was a framed photograph of contestants at a Bravest vs. Finest competition. This group looked to be medal winners from judo, boxing, and Tae Kwon Do contests. Marty Schoenfeld was pictured holding one of the trophies now on display in his living room corner cabinet. Down on one knee, directly in front of him, was Deborah Glenmore. She clutched a similar prize.

As he handed the photograph to his boss, Joe slowly shook his head. "And I thought it was that tight-ass LeFevre who was our problem at IAD."

Without his reading glasses, Lieberman had to squint to see what Dante had seen.

Dante moved away from the corner, his head down and brow knit as he tried to puzzle it out. "LeFevre told me there is no such thing as a missing file at Internal Affairs." He paused, an index finger raised to test the consistency of his next thought. "He said that if Mott was anything, he was a stickler for detail, a guy who always observed procedure. Well, he was wrong on that first count and probably right on the second." Joe's head came up, his eyes meeting Lieberman's. "God*damn*, Gus. She nearly got away with it."

"You're sayin' you believe Sergeant Glenmore stole that file?"

"That's exactly what I'm saying. And I think it goes deeper. The burglary at Mott's place the morning he died? We found that money and thought our dead shoo-fly was crooked. When we learned about the extortion investigation, that missing file made us think Mott was using Onofrio's shakedown game to pick up a little free money for himself."

Gus was right there with him. "You seem convinced now that he wasn't."

"Oh yeah." Dante's tone was almost admiring. "The burglary idea was brilliant. The perp didn't break in there to steal a file, or to *steal* anything. He—or she—was planting that cash."

Gus digested this slowly. "Those are some pretty big leaps, Joey. You think Glenmore'd *already* stolen that file?"

Dante shrugged. "Even though the romance was over, she admitted she and Mott stayed in touch. And if she didn't get it before the fact, she got it after; once she and LeFevre packed all Mott's papers off to Poplar Street.''

"Conspirin' with a cop killer. That's a heavy accusation. Glenmore's got a record smells clean as an Ivory girl's asshole. What've we got here? Her an' Schoenfeld posin' in the same picture? There's fifteen *other* cops an' firemen there, too.''

"It all fits, Gus. A club owner files a complaint with CCRB, and before IAD can get its teeth into it, the owner dies. That's pretty convenient. Then Mott gets wind of possible fire involvement in the extortions and meets with Schoenfeld in a Hell's Kitchen alley . . . at five in the fucking morning. That smells clandestine to me; like Mott was sneaking around looking for some confidential cooperation.'' He paused, shaking his head. "Warren Mott was a cautious man, Gus. I don't believe a guy like him would meet *anyone* out there at that hour without believing the meeting was safe.''

"You're sayin' you think Glenmore helped set him up.''

Joe nodded. "It's just theory right now, but it fits.''

Gus took a moment with all this theorizing, looking the conjectures up one side and down the other. "Okay. So let's say you're right. If we make a move on her, we gotta *know* we'll hit pay dirt, Joey. Right now I got Jerry Liljedahl ready t' blow any second. Man's got a fuse almost as short as his dick.''

Dante smiled. "So we set up on her and watch awhile instead. If she leads us to Schoenfeld, we're heroes. If she doesn't, we've squandered a little overtime. No harm, no foul.''

"Put her under surveillance.'' Gus was weighing the idea out loud. "Maybe hang a wire on her phone, see if he calls lookin' for assistance.''

"Sure. And if Schoenfeld's car is parked out front of her place when we get there, we go in. Otherwise, we sit tight. I'll even take the first shift.''

"You?" Lieberman snorted it. "You're half-asleep on your feet."

"So's everyone else in my squad. Beasley can run on home, get a few hours shut-eye, and relieve me after sunup. We'll set up a rotation from there. We're gonna get the bastard, Gus. *I'm* gonna get him."

Lieberman gave up arguing. "All right. You work that end your way and I'll try t' get a wiretap authorization. Where's she live?"

"I don't think it's far from here. Her karate dojo's in Kew Gardens." Though he was exhausted, Dante's eyes conveyed nothing but grim determination. "I'll get the address from Operations."

Beasley Richardson wondered when he'd ever been more tired. Endgame or not, the smell of a win in the air, he was still having trouble feeling satisfaction. In fact, feeling *anything* was difficult when it demanded all his energy just to keep his eyes open. As he entered his Fort Greene neighborhood, he thought about that hydrant out front of his neighbor's place. Because alternate-side parking was suspended Sundays, he knew that finding a legitimate space might take thirty or forty minutes. It was almost four o'clock, and he was due to relieve Dante at nine. An open slot a few feet from his front door meant an extra half hour of shut-eye. Right now, that looked to be worth every penny of a thirty-five-dollar ticket.

When he slowed on Lafayette Avenue, nearing his house, Jumbo spotted a beat-up Ford Econoline van parked in his space. And then he saw the commercial plates and the sign emblazoned across the street side:

SYNER-CALC *Our Deals Add Up To Savings!*
Rt. 4 & Rt. 17 Paramus   and   1310 6th Av. NYC
201-555-CALC   212-555-CALC

Richardson was scanning farther up the block, all the while hating his neighbors, when two women emerged from a house across the street, carrying a small cooler and beach chairs. He'd heard of getting up at dawn to beat the weekend migration out to Jones Beach, but four A.M.? When they hurried across the sidewalk and unlocked the doors of a late-model Volvo, he decided not to question his luck any further. If these gals wanted to sit naked in front of the rising sun, they could go wild. He wanted their parking spot. He wanted Bernice's backside spooned cool against his belly. He wanted sleep.

Within minutes, Jumbo had the job Dodge parked, his jacket slung over one shoulder, and was lifting the latch on his gate. He was on his way through, those visions of sugarplums really starting to dance, when a strange odor reached his nostrils. Chemical, like cleaning fluid. He pulled up short and glanced around. It was a strange hour for anyone to be removing spots from his ties. Then again, it wasn't such a strange hour to be operating a drug lab.

That smell was acetone. Three years ago, Jumbo attended a job-sponsored seminar on the detection of clandestine drug operations. Such setups are of serious concern for more reasons than just the manufacture of cocaine and crack. The chemicals employed in the process, generally either ether or acetone, are highly volatile substances. Anyone operating a lab in a heavily populated area does so at extreme risk to his neighbors. As Richardson looked up and down the block, trying to determine where the odor was coming from, he saw the open basement window.

The drapery hung over the opening behind his new neighbor's transom-type basement window was dark and heavy. A casual passerby wouldn't see that the window itself was ajar. Jumbo had a better angle from his stoop. He could see that the basement beyond was brightly illuminated. There was no question where that acetone odor came from and no question in his mind what his

270

neighbors were doing behind that street-level transom. Jumbo's exhaustion vanished behind a rush of hot rage.

The Emergency Room at Beekman Downtown wasn't equipped for quite as much business as it got that Sunday morning. It was located on the corner of William and Beekman between the financial district and City Hall, and the bulk of its business came through on weekdays. The southern tip of Manhattan was jammed during the work week. Beekman Downtown got everything from lawyers suffering stress-induced chest pains to runners on the floor of the Stock Exchange suffering cocaine-related heart palpitations. On weekends, the most they got was the odd drunk taking a tumble at the nearby Seaport or a tourist kid with something stuck in his eye. Only one physician had been on duty when Melissa had arrived with the two injured cops. The Special Frauds man was in much the worse shape, so Guy Napier was forced to cool his heels.

Twice now, Melissa had called the Op Desk checking to see what had developed from the FLOTSAM bust. The second time she called, the cop manning the switchboard patched her through to Dante's cellular mobile phone. She knew Joe was at least as tired as she was and was surprised to hear animation in his voice as he updated her. Once she heard what was in the wind, she experienced her own little rush of excitement. When he finished outlining his immediate plan, she asked what she could do to assist.

"For the moment? Stay where you are and make sure our Boy Wonder doesn't do something stupid," Dante replied. "I saw the way that knee caught him. It's possible there could be some internal bleeding. Don't let him outta there before he gets a clean bill of health."

"Not to worry, boss. How about later?"

"Try to get some sleep. We might need you rested and ready to roll at a moment's notice."

When she returned to the waiting area, she found

Napier champing at the bit. "They took my blood pressure over an hour ago," Guy complained. "I'm tired. I'm alive. Let's get the hell out of here."

"The minute you get the green light, buddy boy." She took gentle hold of his chin and turned the other side of his face toward her. "That's gonna be one good-looking shiner once the swelling goes down. Scared the shit out of me the way you went all blue like that."

"Serves me right," he grumbled. "How could I be so dumb? I mean, I walked right *into* that knee."

She smiled and patted him. "At least your instincts were good."

From across the room, the lone overworked physician emerged from a doorway carrying a clipboard. "Detective Napier? I'd like to get your BP one more time just to make sure it's consistent. Then you can go. Your head X-ray was clean. Get more ice on that face as soon as you get home. Most of the swelling should be gone by morning." He grabbed a blood pressure stand en route and wheeled it up next to Guy's chair. Once he had the cuff wrapped around Napier's bicep, he pumped it and took a reading. "No evidence of any internal bleeding," he murmured. "You're lucky you're healthy as a horse."

On her way out the door into the predawn gloom, Melissa turned to her charge and hooked an arm through his. An eerie kind of quiet gripped this part of the city from Friday evening until first thing Monday morning. At no time was the stillness more palpable than it was right now. Six blocks to the east, the Seaport had been closed for hours. Nobody lived down here. It would remain a virtual ghost town until the start of the business week.

"I told myself I wasn't going to do this, and here I am doing it," she said.

"Do what, Mel?"

"Invite you home. You go to your place, I doubt you'll be getting much rest. Once your fiancée gets a look at your face, you'll be up half the night trying to explain it.''

''I doubt she'd even wake up.''

''Really. Well then, let me drop you. Woodhaven, right? It's on my way.''

The Boy Wonder tried to grin, and paid for it. A sharp intake of breath described his pain. ''I said I *doubt*, Mel. Not won't. If I'm not there, she *definitely* won't wake up. Just tell me that you sleep in something bigger than a twin bed.''

She scowled and managed to check herself before elbowing him in the ribs. ''I'm a cop, you lummox, not a nun. And if I were in your condition, I wouldn't be worrying about the size of the playing field.''

''You heard the doc. I'm healthy as a horse.''

''Tell it to your veterinarian.''

As soon as he got inside his house, Richardson called the Fourteenth Division duty captain. A duty captain was one link higher in the command chain than the shift commander at the local station house. If this proved to be what Jumbo thought it was, he wanted any police action to be directed by the man with the most resources at his disposal. At this hour, it wasn't likely that the Eight-Eight had more than a handful of men on duty and one radio unit available. When Jumbo explained the basis for his suspicions, Captain Chuck Beatty's interest level skyrocketed. Colombians driving Ferraris meant big money was likely to be involved. A collar that involved quantity drugs and heavy cash meant glory for the cop who directed the strike.

''I got an idea, Cap,'' Jumbo told him. ''You call in a tow truck from Traffic. The van they got parked out front is on a hydrant. Have Traffic drop the hook on those wheels while your people watch from both ends of the street. I bet some hothead comes outta there like a bullet; raises hell about it.''

Beatty liked it. ''And one of our patrol cars just happens to be in the area,'' he expanded. ''When it gets a little loud, they pull up to assist.''

''Sounds right,'' Beasley agreed. ''An' I'll tell y'somethin'; if them guys in that basement are on a schedule—if they *need* them wheels—they ain't gonna be one bit happy 'bout seein' them go.''

''Hell yeah. They might even make a fuss; give us reasonable cause for a look into that basement.''

''I doubt you'll need that, Cap. The stink of that chemical is plenty strong cause as is.''

They settled on a staging area several blocks away, at the southeast corner of Fort Greene Park. As Richardson hung up, he found his exhaustion vanished. Before leaving again, he hurried upstairs to explain what was happening. There was no question that Bernice would be awake. Since the first night tour Jumbo worked as a rookie patrolman, she'd awakened each and every time his key turned in the front door lock.

Deborah Glenmore's residence in Queens, between Kew Gardens and Richmond Hill, was the bottom half of a two-family. That stretch of Myrtle, only a couple blocks west of where it intersected with Jamaica, was sort of a main drag through a quiet, middle-class area. From where Dante sat parked, he watched the shadows of houses and parked cars start to take shape in the dim early light. Far off to the east, the sky was just beginning to lighten with the approach of dawn. Most of those cars were fairly late model, just like those parked on Warren Mott's Bay Ridge block. The houses weren't dissimilar either, uninspired places to eat, sleep, and grow old.

Dante's physical weariness was being short-circuited by twelve cups of coffee, but the effects of all that caffeine were starting to tell on him. An excess of digestive juices was rubbing his stomach raw. His nerve endings fairly jangled. And yet he was appreciative of the downtime, the momentary solitude. When he arrived here,

Joe had driven up and down all the nearby blocks searching for the late-model Ford Thunderbird described to him by the dispatcher at Operations. He'd found only one car parked in Glenmore's drive, the same Mazda Miata she'd been leaning against the night he discovered her waiting for him on Perry Street.

The theory spawned earlier was starting to flesh itself out now. Glenmore and Mott had remained in touch even after their romance ended. They no doubt shared professional confidences. IAD was isolated from the rest of the job and saw itself as an exclusive society. Regardless of their past romance, Glenmore and Mott were still members of this tight-knit group. When she learned of the investigation Warren was launching into a joint PD-FD extortion scheme, she probably tipped Schoenfeld. Then Marty talked to Sal, and they'd shut their operation down. But what did Glenmore know of Schoenfeld's own complicity? And how deeply was she involved in the developments of this past week? Was she an unwitting accomplice or an accessory to extortion *and* murder? And if she was an accessory, then why? Everything he'd seen and heard told him she was a good cop. Dedicated. Principled. As he continued to stare at the front of her house, Dante still couldn't see the *why*.

Within forty minutes of their phone conversation, Jumbo and Captain Chuck Beatty were parked in the spot vacated by Richardson's beach-bound neighbors. Behind them to the west, two squad cars sat double-parked around the corner on Clinton. Just ahead, two more waited on Waverly. As the Traffic Department tow truck glided up next to the illegally parked van, Jumbo watched the basement transom window through a pair of field glasses. The sun was up enough now to provide fair illumination. In another half hour, a warm morning would turn hot. For the moment, both Richardson and Beatty were comfortable in shirtsleeves. It was nervousness that saw their backs and armpits soaked with sweat.

Beatty had directed the tow operator to leave the gain knob on his two-way cranked up loud enough to attract attention. When the door of the truck swung open and the driver stepped onto the street, the noise of radio squelch and a dispatcher's voice bit hard into the Sunday morning stillness.

No sooner had the operator gotten down on his hands and knees to hang his hook on the van's frame than two very agitated men emerged from the target house. New York City towing law was simple: once an operator attached that safety hook to the subject vehicle, that vehicle was gone. Many had tried, but few ever persuaded a tow operator to leave a car once his hook was attached. The driver was rising to head back to the truck cab as the excited Latins hurried around the front bumper in an attempt to intercept. He ignored them and climbed behind the wheel. With the two of them gesticulating wildly outside his window, he got the idling truck into reverse and lowered the tow cradle. All that agitation became outrage when the cradle made contact with the van. Jumbo watched one of the two Latins haul off and kick the tow truck.

"Looks like it's time to play our next card," Beatty commented.

"Uh huh." And as Jumbo continued to observe through the glasses, Beatty lifted the radio handset.

"Okay, Alpha. Nice and easy now. It's Sunday morning and you've just happened by. Keep an eye on each other's backs."

Taking the cue, a blue-and-white appeared to turn the corner off Waverly and roll toward the scene on Lafayette. Two excited men alongside a Traffic tow unit were cause enough to justify a stop. Jumbo watched as the squad car's left window came down. The uniform behind the wheel poked his head out. The tow operator, a middle-aged black man clad in the standard-issue brown jumpsuit, jerked a thumb backwards toward the van now nestled in his cradle. While both of the men on the street continued to rant in protest, the cop on the passenger side of the car emerged to confront them. Captain Beatty had made sure this man spoke Spanish. Short in stature but built like a bull calf from the ground up, he leaned across the roof of the car to engage the outraged citizens. One spoke with him, again gesturing wildly, while the other stormed off to inspect the way the tow cradle suspended the front of his van. When he crouched to peer up underneath, Jumbo spotted the gun.

"Pistol. Man by the van. Tucked into his pants under his shirt."

Beatty was on the horn again in a flash. "Beta unit. Suspects on the street are armed. Let's try to avoid spooking 'em, but I want 'em flanked. Go."

A second blue-and-white appeared, this time from around the corner off Clinton. Taking its time, it rolled to a stop at the scene of the altercation. Jumbo watched through the binoculars as the two backup cops parked behind the rear bumper of the van and emerged to approach on foot. It was neatly done. Now the two excited civilians were boxed, front and back.

At the edge of his field of view, the glimmer of incandescent light seeping from behind the basement curtain caught Jumbo's attention. When he turned the glasses directly on the light source; he saw the glint of the rifle barrel.

Any gun trained on fellow officers was alarming, but four inches of flash suppressor at the muzzle sent Jumbo's heart into his throat.

"Automatic weapon. Basement window." And as he spat it out, he was already reaching around for the pump-action riot gun lying on the backseat.

Chuck Beatty didn't have time to wonder what the detective sergeant was doing. No sooner did Jumbo get the gun in hand than he had the door open, one of his size-twelves already planted on the pavement.

"Stay off the hailer till I'm on 'em. Then tell everyone to get the hell *down*."

Jumbo was depending on the element of surprise as he sprinted pell-mell across the street and hurdled the low iron fence separating the subject house from the street. Back in the command car, Beatty was astonished to see how quickly the heavyset detective could move. The seven people now congregated on the street side of the tow truck had barely registered movement when that unseen sniper behind the curtain opened up. Out on the street, one of the recently arrived cops jerked spasmodically and crumpled. Everyone else dove for the deck. From where he lay sprawled on his belly, Richardson responded by pumping two quick twelve-gauge rounds into the basement. The burst of automatic fire was cut mercifully short.

When the shooting ended so abruptly, one of the suspects on the street went to the small of his back for his pistol. The Spanish-speaking cop pounced, jamming the suspect's face into the pavement and grabbing the weapon before it cleared the man's waistband. From both east and west, the other squad cars swooped. Jumbo, moving cautiously, was already halfway up the front stoop of the suspect house when Beatty directed four men to join him. While Beasley and the others crouched on either side of the front door, the Latino cop got on the hailer. First in English and then again in Spanish, he demanded that anyone remaining inside the house surrender. Moments later, the cops on the stoop heard movement behind the front door. As they pressed themselves to the brickwork, weapons poised, the thumb-latch clicked and the door swung inward.

Even with her hair tucked beneath a surgeon's cap, and a dust mask hanging beneath her chin, the first occupant to emerge was easy for Jumbo to recognize. She was half of the couple who'd recently moved in here. He didn't recognize either of the two who'd been arguing with the tow operator, but he did know the man who followed behind the good-looking Hispanic woman. This was the driver of the Ferrari, the man Mabel Huggins's computer had identified as Jorge DaSilva. He, too, wore a dust mask, as well as a rubber apron and gloves. Like the woman's, his protective clothes were covered with a fine white dust.

One of the cops across the stoop caught Richardson's eye, his own eyes wide and his fingers clutching nervously at the butt of his weapon.

"You got it," Jumbo told him. "That shit ain't baby powder."

When no one else emerged from the house, two of the cops took the prisoners into custody while the others followed Richardson inside. They moved cautiously through the first floor, stationed one man at the head of the basement stairs, and did a quick sweep of the floor above. Beasley could see why his new neighbors had been so standoffish. This wasn't a home; it was a crash pad. The living room furniture was all quick-purchase stuff. The kitchen was crawling with roaches and piled with garbage, the sink stacked with dirty utensils and glasses. Upstairs, there were mattresses on the floors, all covered with filthy sheets. A few garments were hung in closets. The rest were piled in suitcases.

Jumbo walked point as they descended into the basement. At the bottom of the stairs, they found a well-lit, full-scale cocaine lab. There were cartons stacked in one corner containing at least a hundred gallons of acetone in plastic bottles. More boxes, containing close to a ton of cocaine, all wrapped in kilo-sized clear plastic parcels, were stacked along one wall. And sprawled beneath the open basement window was Jumbo's next-door neighbor. The computer sortware designer was also clad in a rubber apron, a dust mask, and one rubber glove. He'd removed the other to better feel the trigger of the AK-47 assault rifle now lying on the floor next to him. At least Jumbo *assumed* this man to be his next-door neighbor. He had the correct height and build, but definite identification was otherwise difficult. One of those loads from the pump twelve had removed his face.

TWENTY

Captain Bob Talbot was not pleased to receive a call from his boss before dawn on a Sunday. He thought the commissioner sounded rattled. Somewhat out of character, Tony Mintoff expressed regret for disturbing him on his day off. More in character was the PC's failure to acknowledge having wakened him. There was a crisis afoot. The Major Case Squad investigation into the Mott homicide had turned nasty. Allegations of Police and Fire Department corruption were flying in all directions. The mayor was none too pleased about being caught out after declaring the Mott case closed. He was even less pleased to see scandals developing on two fronts within the public service sector. Mintoff explained that he needed his exec at his side to help with damage control. And throughout their conversation, Talbot had the feeling he was talking to the skipper of a sinking ship.

As he approached the outskirts of Queens, it occurred to Talbot that his route would take him just a few miles north of Deb Glenmore's address in Kew Gardens. He still hadn't gotten the taste of yesterday afternoon's frolic out of his mouth, and he had a hunger for more. Her interest in seeing Warren Mott's killer apprehended would provide another opportunity to ingratiate himself. He would invite her into the city with him for a ringside seat. She could work her appearance there to an advantage. The media was already responding favorably to the action being taken against those two cops up in the Bronx. A little high-profile hobnobbing wouldn't hurt Deb's career. Once Bob introduced her to the mayor, she'd be putty in his hands.

As he crossed into Queens and took the Van Wyck south to the Interborough Parkway, he entertained the idea of tearing off another quick piece like the one he got yesterday afternoon. God, that woman was a ball of fire in the sack. He figured that if he got lucky, he'd tell Mintoff he encountered a jacknifed tractor-trailer on the LIE. What the hell; there was *always* a truck accident somewhere along 495.

His mega-dose of caffeine notwithstanding, Dante was balanced right on the brink of sleep when Bob Talbot's 733 BMW eased into Deborah Glenmore's drive. While the BMW caught his attention, it was the captain climbing from behind the wheel that really kicked Joe's motor over. Bob was dressed casually in chinos and a polo shirt, suggesting that this wasn't some sort of official screwup. Dante watched him pause a moment to stretch the kinks out before striding toward Glenmore's front door. He moved with the bearing of a man who was at ease.

Talbot's appearance brought every element of Dante's carefully constructed theory into question. Deborah Glenmore's clandestine ties to Marty Schoenfeld had explained the missing files and Schoenfeld's knowledge of Warren Mott's intentions. Glenmore and Schoenfeld had some obvious things in common: the karate, a confident cockiness, a dedication to physical conditioning. Both were handsome in a clean-cut, hard-edged way. It was easy for Joe to picture them together. And difficult to fit Bob Talbot anywhere in their world. As Tony Mintoff's exec reached to depress the doorbell button, Dante snatched up the cellular handset. If it *was* an official screwup, Gus had access to the commissioner's office and could find out where Talbot had gotten his wires crossed. If this was something innocent, like a trip to the beach, then Joe had *his* wires crossed. There was a cop killer on the loose. He needed to know if he was wasting his time here. He needed to know it fast.

When Deborah Glenmore found Bob Talbot on her stoop, she had difficulty masking her displeasure. It was early. She'd been awakened from a fitful sleep. As she stumbled to the door, she'd been preparing to curse a gaggle of Jehovah's Witnesses to the depths of a pain-wracked hell.

"Bob! Wha . . . ?" One hand rose to rub her face and push at her hair. Without pausing to even look at herself in a mirror, she'd pulled on a T-shirt and climbed into a pair of shorts. "What did I miss? I checked my machine when I got home . . . or did I?" She drifted off and then came back once she'd organized her thoughts. "I don't get it." More forceful now. "It's Sunday morning. This is the only break I get in my training schedule. I get to sleep *in* on Sunday mornings."

Talbot appeared oblivious to her distress. "Dante broke the Mott case," he replied. "It's *big*. There are fire personnel involved as well as cops. They think it was one of the fire people who actually pulled the trigger . . . and not just on Warren. They think he got Sal Onofrio and was responsible for torching Dante's building."

"But what's that got to do with me?"

Bob was all smooth confidence. "Didn't you ask me to bring you along on this one? This is it. All hell's broken loose downtown. My boss ordered me back into the city to help organize his press conference. He's got the mayor there. The fire commissioner. I'm talking high-profile situation, Deb. I can introduce you around. Your name's been all over the grapevine the past couple of days, so let's put it together with a face. Career-wise, this could be a big break."

Glenmore brightened. "God, and I almost bit your head off. I'm sorry, Bob. I'm still half-asleep. Of course I want to be there." She paused to glance down at her bare feet and then back up at him. The smile she beamed was friendly, full of warmth. "But if you're pressed for time, maybe you'd better run ahead. I'll meet you. It's gonna take me a few minutes to pull this together."

Talbot shrugged. "What's a few minutes? I'll wait. It'll save you the drive."

She flashed him another grin and stood back, inviting him to enter. "Suit yourself, Cap. Make yourself comfortable. I'll be out in a jiff."

Talbot stood admiring that fabulous ass of hers and the dynamic, muscular turn of her legs as Glenmore disappeared behind her bedroom door. He'd had his hands all over that just fifteen, sixteen hours ago, and the memory was returning in a rush. If there was one thing that really turned him on, it was the way she'd come at him. Come on strong, stripping herself before him. She'd wanted it bad, and once she got a taste of it, she'd lost none of her enthusiasm.

It was as if his libido had a will of its own. Talbot left his polo shirt on the living room floor and headed down the hall toward the bedroom. He had his belt loose, his fly down, and was halfway through Glenmore's bedroom door when he realized she had company. Deb had stripped out of her T-shirt. She stood by the bed, engaged in whispered conversation with a heavyset guy sitting propped on pillows wedged against the headboard.

With the kind of net the cops would throw over the city now that he was a fugitive, Marty Schoenfeld wasn't fool enough to act out of desperation. He'd decided instead to lay low, giving himself time to sort through his options. By the time he'd abandoned his car outside a St. John's University dorm and Glenmore had come to collect him, it was already three-thirty. With the wound in his side giving him a lot of pain, he was too exhausted to think clearly. He needed sleep.

Earlier that week, he'd discovered the best way to avoid movement in his sleep was to prop himself slightly upright. He'd been sleeping in that posture for almost five hours when the doorbell woke him. It made him angry to feel the trickle of cold sweat tickling his sides as he waited for Debbie to answer. When she returned, she was in a state of near panic. She'd blurted out who it was, explaining why she had no choice but to go along with him, when Talbot walked in like he owned the place.

Surprised and embarrassed, the police commissioner's exec started back the way he'd come.

"Whoa there, buddy pal. Another step and I blow your nuts off."

Talbot saw the multiple muzzles of the little derringer Marty had trained on him and froze. With his pants hanging loose like that, he was forced to grab the waistband with one hand to keep them from falling down around his ankles. Schoenfeld lifted his chin toward the man in his sights as he addressed Glenmore.

"Why's this asshole think he can come prancin' in here half-naked like this, sweets? Jesus, he's got all but his dick in his hand."

Deb got defensive. "You told me to find out about Dante's investigation, Marty. If I might quote you, I think your exact words were 'do whatever it takes.' "

"So you fucked him."

"I found out, didn't I? And what good did it do, you arrogant son of a bitch? You didn't listen to me two months ago; why should I expect you'd listen to me now?"

Marty grinned at Talbot. "It's probably gonna be a little hard for a straight arrow like you t' understand the more complex *psychological* ramifications at work here, Cap. You see, a few years back, I'm gettin' into my car outside the local health club an' I hear this muffled scream. It comes from this parked van across the way. When I go over t' check it out, I find two mongrel mutts with Debbie here inside'a there, one with her head between his knees and a knife at her neck. The other one's got her bent over and is all set t' head in through the back door with his prize salami. I blew the blade-man's brains all over the fun-fur and drilled the wad jockey dead through the heart. You might remember readin' about it in the papers. You people never found the perp, but Debbie's been grateful t' me ever since; ain't you, sweets?"

Glenmore was hot as hell. She was standing there in nothing but her shorts, her feet set wide and fists planted on her hips. Her face had become a mask of fury. "I was in *shock* when you dragged me out of there, you son of a bitch!"

Schoenfeld grinned. "Debbie didn't see any reason why I'd want t' leave the scene," he told Talbot. "But the way I looked at it, a hard-on ain't generally a lethal weapon, and I'd just blasted a man who was unarmed. And don't let this act of hers fool you. She was grateful." He shrugged. "Why else would she wanna do me all them little favors . . . the ones she's been doin' ever since?"

"What *choice* did I have?" she snarled. "No, you didn't have to kill that other man, but I talk and I'm turning in the guy who saved me from being raped and maybe murdered. You used that *against* me, Marty. I don't do what's legally right, I'm an accomplice."

Schoenfeld was still all smiles. "That's right, sweets. You kept your mouth shut, and that got you into it, deep as me."

"So since when do you care who I *fuck*, Marty? Just

so long as I do you your little favors and keep my mouth shut? You never batted an eye when you needed me to get close to Warren. Hell, you wanted every juicy detail. So what's this? You're jealous now?''

Debbie still didn't know that it was Marty who'd sent Mott's wife that note. He'd borrowed the key to the splash pad from Debbie's key ring and copied it. She also didn't know that somewhere along the line, he'd started getting these odd feelings. The longer that affair went on, the more it ate at him. The idea of her and that prick Mott naked together, Debbie writhing and moaning, the sweat of exertion glistening sweet on her, twisted his guts up just like they were twisting now. He'd actually started to believe that maybe things could be different between them.

His free hand reached to grab one of the pillows from behind his head. From the corner of his eye, he saw Debbie's mouth start to work as he doubled that pillow over, pushed the muzzle of the derringer into it, and shot Talbot twice in the chest. The noise of the discharges was muffled, like the far-off backfire of an ill-tuned engine.

Schoenfeld stopped watching before his target hit the floor. His eyes were on Debbie now and not on the quivering body dying at the foot of her bed. ''Jealous, sweets? Maybe I am. But I think it's a dead issue now, don't you?''

Dante reached Gus back at the Big Building once the Op Desk located the chief in the PC's office. He was in the middle of reporting the most recent development when Glenmore's front door opened.

''Hang on, Gus. I've got movement.''

''Where? What's happenin'?''

''It's Glenmore. She's come out of the house and is crossing the lawn toward Talbot's car.''

''He with her?''

''Nope. She's carrying what looks like a beach bag

and has his keys. Just got in behind the wheel. Backup lights are coming on. It looks like we're going for a ride.''

When Dante said *lawn*, he was referring to a few square yards of sod wedged between the front of the house and the sidewalk. Space here, like in most of New York, was at a premium. The distance between Glenmore's front door and the curb was no more than fifteen feet. Now, as the IAD investigator eased the BMW around in reverse to sit idling at the foot of her front walk, Dante slumped down in his front seat.

''Must be good friends,'' he speculated into the phone. ''I doubt Bobby lets just anyone drive those wheels.''

''Sounds like you're beginnin' t' doubt your theory,'' Gus suggested.

''Maybe I'm getting old, Gus. You throw me a curve, there was a time I'd at least get a piece of it. This one fooled me.''

''Well, when she starts movin', let's play it out. It's the only theory we got, an' I still kinda like it.''

Across the street, Glenmore's front door opened once again.

''Movement,'' Dante reported. ''Whoa. Hold on.''

''Give it to me.''

''It's a guy, but it doesn't look much like Talbot. With his head down like that, I can't see who it is. The car's between him and me.''

''Jesus. Schoenfeld?''

''Really can't tell, boss. This guy looks shorter than Bobby. He's not wearing the clothes Talbot went in there wearing. Like I said, I can't see his face.''

''But you're pretty sure it's Schoenfeld.'' It wasn't a question.

''Who else? Goddammit, Gus; if Talbot's on the inside of this, then they've known our every move, every step of the way.''

''I don't want you makin' any move without backup,

288

Joey. Let 'em go an' then stay with 'em. I'll get some other people inta position.''

"I've got them rolling here, Chief. Let's see where they're going before you call up the reinforcements. Last thing we need is a parade.''

"Any sign of Big Tony's boy?''

"None. Better have the local station send some people around. Glenmore's smooth, Gus. She probably invited Captain Wonderful over here just to get his car. He's probably handcuffed to the crapper in there.''

Joe got the engine started as Talbot's BMW disappeared around the corner up the block. He jackrabbited out of his parking slot to take up the chase.

As Marty reached for the cellular phone handset, he was feeling pretty good. Next to him, gripping the wheel with both hands, Debbie was still white with shock. It was the same look he'd seen on her face the night he let the hammer drop on the rapist scum. Maybe this time he could make it turn out different. Start over with her.

"Nice car, huh?'' he offered. "What's a ride like this go for? Fifty, sixty grand? Maybe you an' me could get us one of these.''

His comments elicited silence. While Debbie drove them east on the Union Turnpike, Marty had the map of Long Island open on his lap. The map had come from her purse and had a smaller, more detailed map of Southampton clipped to it. The little map traced a route to the scene of Debbie's most recent infidelity. When he first saw it, Marty was tempted to wad it up and choke her with it. The reminder of her and that prick Talbot, together, made Marty's blood boil all over again. But then it had given him an idea. Phone in hand, he dialed the 201 area code and asked the New Jersey information operator for the number of a specialty air charter outfit in Ridgefield Park.

TWENTY-ONE

A half hour after Dante set off in pursuit of the black BMW, Gus Lieberman got back in touch. Up ahead, Glenmore was moving east on the Jericho Turnpike, with Joe holding a position three cars back. He picked up the phone as they rolled sedately through Locust Grove.

"I don't think Talbot was in on any'a this, Joey."

Dante had switched from handset operation to the speaker and overhead mike. "What'd they do?" he asked. "Leave him hog-tied in the bedroom closet?"

"Killed him. Two in the chest. Left him dumped in Glenmore's bathtub."

Joe knew it shouldn't have surprised him, but it still stung. "Jesus," he murmured.

"Let's still go slow an' easy, Joey. I got Mintoff talkin' extreme prejudice here. He's treatin' them two like Bonnie an' Clyde. Troopers an' local enforcement ain't good enough anymore. Last I heard, he was on the horn with the fuckin' FBI."

"I guess it hurts more when they start hitting close to home," Joe ventured. "Talbot was connected. Big Tony knows he's gonna have some heavy political heat coming at him now."

"I'm sorry 'bout the feds, Joey. I didn't want it this way. They stick their noses in, we risk losin' control."

"No choice now but to play it out," Dante replied. "I'll talk to you, boss."

The weary detective switched off and shifted the position of his seat back, trying to get more comfortable. The direction they were traveling seemed strange to him. Glenmore and Schoenfeld were heading east, not west. That was odd, because Long Island presented the same dilemma as a box canyon did in the old westerns. The island is over a hundred miles long. At its farthest reaches, out along either Orient or Montauk Points, the only route of escape is over the Atlantic. Because of that fact, Joe expected his quarry to head for one of the area's half dozen regional airstrips. When they eventually passed the Suffolk County Airport north of Westhampton, his imagination was scrambling like a terrier over wet boulders. Now there was only one airport left out here: a tiny facility on the outskirts of Easthampton. It was time to consider other options.

A boat would make sense only if they picked one up somewhere along the island's North Fork. Up there, they might set out across the Sound for Connecticut. But they weren't heading north. Instead they'd started south along the Montauk Highway. Down here, the closest land mass was the Jersey shore, at least a hundred miles to the west.

Any notion of them being headed for an airstrip vanished completely when Glenmore piloted the BMW south off the Montauk Highway at Southampton's Main Street. Dante had just made the turn to follow when the cellular console chirped. Once more, he flipped over to to the mike and speaker.

"Yeah."

"I'm directly in touch with both the troopers an' the Suffolk sheriff, Joey. What's the update?"

"What happened to the Bureau?"

"That's Tony's toy. They wanna give each other hand-jobs, they can be my guests. They got a sharpshooter team they're scramblin' outta JFK.''

"We just turned south toward the ocean in Southampton. I'm stumped, Gus. What're they doing headed for the beach?''

"Leave the line open,'' the chief directed. "I'm gonna talk to the locals an' get right back.''

"No cavalry charges, Gus. There's only two of them, and they're running out of real estate.''

"It's your show, Joey. Just tell me how you wanna do it.''

"Let's see where they're headed first. Then we give the local boys a rendezvous. Just a handful of their best. I'd rather go in like a surgeon than a meat packer.''

Up ahead, the BMW bore right at the intersection of Meadow and Gin Lanes. To the south, between lavish beach "cottages,'' Dante could see the sparkling surface of the Atlantic. While a seventy-thousand-dollar set of wheels was appropriate for this landscape, Joe wondered what its occupants were doing so far out of their element. Eventually Glenmore nosed the car off the beach road and up to the gate of a rambling beach estate. Perched on the dunes behind a lot of wrought iron sat a cedar-and-glass contemporary house of no mean scale. Single-story, it rambled east and west for close to two hundred feet. The lawns and shrubs out front were manicured. Dante's quarry waited no more than fifteen seconds before the electronically controlled gate rolled back. It wasn't until Joe pulled past to park out of sight on the same side of the road that he saw the sign on one of the stone pillars.

TALBOT

"You still there, Gus?'' He aimed the question at the mike mounted overhead.

"Uh huh. What's goin' on?''

"They just drove in through the gate of the Talbot family's beach house. Theirs is the only car in the drive."

"Where?"

"Dune Road. My odometer says it's three point three miles since I turned off Main Street. A quarter mile or so back, I spotted water behind here, over the dunes. I've got the open ocean here on my left." Dante flashed back to the drinks he'd had with the *SPRING 3100* editor Wednesday night. "See if you can contact Rosa, Gus. I think she can help with the layout here." He didn't know how she was going to take the news of her former lover's death and was glad it would be Gus who broke it.

"I'm lookin' at a map, Joey. If you're where you say you are, that water behind you's Shinnecock Bay."

"Bay? That would mean there's an outlet to the ocean." Dante was scrambling to conjure every possible move the suspects might make. This setting was relatively remote, and he had no reason to think his quarry knew of his presence. It could be that they intended to lay low here for a few days until the heat subsided. Then again, all that water would make it easy for them to get lost if they had access to a boat.

From the car, Glenmore led the way to the house and was set to enter using Talbot's front door key when she spotted the alarm system key pad.

"Great."

Behind her, Marty snickered. "What? You thought maybe a place like this *wouldn't* be alarmed? You been snoopin' around other people's dirty underwear too long, sweets. Welcome to the *real* fuckin' world." He turned to start off along a walkway leading around back.

"Why did you have to kill him, Marty?" Glenmore was standing her ground back by the front door. She called it to him from nearly fifty feet away. "It's not like you could cover anything up anymore."

Schoenfeld stopped and turned. "Once he saw us together, you were tied in, sweets. *Why* kill him? Because I didn't want you havin' any second thoughts, that's why."

"You're crazy, Marty. How far do you think you're going to get? What good is all your money, sitting in some bank? You've killed three cops now. They'll hunt you down like a dog."

He shrugged, and winced for his trouble. "If I were you, I'd shake a leg, sweets. They're gonna hunt you down, too. Maybe we can make a go of it if we try and stick together, huh?"

"I trusted you, and you *used* me, Marty. I was a good cop. Now I'm an accessory to I don't know *how* many homicides. Maybe we can make a *go* of it?" She laughed, her dry cackle filled with bitterness.

Frustration was evident in the way Schoenfeld shifted impatiently. "We can talk about all this later, Debbie. Maybe I did some things that I mighta done differently. Right now we've got more immediate concerns. There's a plane to catch." He tilted his head to one side and pointed skyward. Off in the distance, they could now hear the faintest droning of a single-engine aircraft, coming at them from the west. "You coming?"

Glenmore watched as he turned without waiting for her answer and disappeared around the corner of the house. God, just being this close to him left her feeling so dirty. All the women's self-defense teaching and fierce commitment to her duties within the job could do nothing to change that. Three years ago she believed Marty had rescued her from the worst violation a woman could endure. Since that time, he'd worked to destroy her life in a manner equally brutal. She hated his guts like she'd never imagined she could hate anything.

So what choices did she have now? She was trapped here, stranded in Southampton with the car of a murdered police captain. The idea of waiting on death row for the governor to start enforcing the death penalty did not appeal to her. Even if she could cut some sort of deal, turn state's evidence, her beloved career as a cop was still destroyed forever.

Because of the way the breezes played games down here along the beach, Dante heard the seaplane only seconds before he saw it making its approach.

"Hold the phone, boss. I think I just got it."

"Got what?"

"Seaplane, making its approach over on the bay side. No time to wait for the posse. I'm out of here."

Dante cut the connection and dug into the glove box for his old .38 service revolver. With its five-inch barrel and unaccustomed bulk, it felt strange in his hand as he checked the load. He yearned to have the PPK he'd lost in the fire. He hadn't qualified with a revolver in over five years.

No sooner did he step out of the car and start along the estate's shrub wall toward the eastern perimeter than the seaplane made a pass just feet off the water around back of the house. Joe rounded the perimeter corner, sprinting up the dunes in time to see the plane splash down and begin its turn in toward shore. Directly behind the house, a dock ran back from a private esplanade, ending a hundred feet out into the water. A cigarette boat was moored halfway along, flanked by a pair of handsome little day sailers. And hurrying down the length of that dock was the lone figure of Marty Schoenfeld. The fireman had a hand raised, waving to signal the incoming aircraft.

So where the hell was Glenmore? Shielding his eyes against the glare off the sand, Dante searched back from the esplanade and across the grounds to the house. There were several patio tables arranged around a big in-ground pool, a screened picnic pavilion, and a pool cabana back there, but no evidence of the fugitive shoo-fly. Meanwhile, that plane was now within a hundred yards of Schoenfeld's position. Without knowing where Glenmore was, Joe knew that any move he made toward the bay would leave his back exposed. It didn't make sense that Glenmore wasn't out here.

Dante's brain made that next leap. If Schoenfeld was on a homicidal rampage, what difference would another body make? Sooner or later, somebody would discover Talbot's car in the drive and call either the cops or the family. By the time they found Glenmore's corpse, Marty could be in Cancun.

The stretch of seawall where the esplanade met the bay shore looked like it would afford Dante good cover. From behind it, he would have a shot of at least seventy-five feet; not good range if he wanted to be sure Marty went down. On the other hand, he could try to draw return fire. It might discourage that pilot from coming any further ashore. He calculated the distance down the dune and how long he'd be exposed while traversing it. Then he was up and running.

The plane was still about fifty yards out when a bullet whizzed past Marty Schoenfeld's right ear. Marty's reflex reaction had already thrown him to his belly by the time he heard the gun's report. It shocked the hell out of him. He didn't think Debbie had it in her.

As soon as Marty dragged the artillery out of the waistband at the small of his back and crabbed around trying to determine where the shot came from, he heard the seaplane pilot throttle up and swing away from shore. Marty cursed the day that bitch was born. Back toward the beach and pool area, he could see no sign of her. He didn't figure he could draw fire from her without exposing himself. At the same time, he knew he'd better do something soon. That pilot had a radio in his plane. The County sheriff would no doubt respond quickly to a reported gunfight. If Marty could nail Debbie and do it quickly, that cigarette boat moored halfway back along the dock would be his ticket out of here.

For inside work, Schoenfeld preferred his little four-shot American derringer. He had large hands and could palm that piece, adding the element of surprise to his arsenal. But before he'd left his place in Forest Hills, he'd grabbed something with a bit more range and stopping power. With its six-inch barrel and .357 magnum loads, the Ruger revolver he now gripped in his right hand gave Marty confidence. That little .38-caliber pea shooter Debbie carried was no match for a gun like this. Debbie's snub-nose job was fine for carrying in a pocketbook and perfect for suicide, but it had no real accuracy beyond fifteen feet. In fact, he was surprised she got as close as she had with that first shot.

With effort, depending mostly on his left arm to bear his weight, Marty heaved himself to his feet and started back down the dock at a crouch.

"I don't want to kill you, Lieutenant."

Joe Dante froze as Deborah Glenmore spoke. Her words came from somewhere behind him, maybe twenty feet off. No more than that.

"Put the gun down. Slowly. Right there beside you in the sand. Then move to your left. Both hands out where I can see them."

As Dante moved to comply, he slowly shook his head. "I thought for sure you were dead. He's killed everyone else who got in his way."

"I guess I came in handier than they did."

Across the water, the seaplane had turned away abruptly with the exchange of gunfire. As the pilot gunned it and headed for safety, Dante prayed he'd have sense enough to radio the authorities. Meanwhile, up on the dock, Schoenfeld was running back toward shore. Joe assumed that Glenmore had functioned as their rear guard and now Marty was returning to do the dirty work. He was surprised, then, to see the fire marshal veer left as he drew abreast of the cigarette boat. There was nothing graceful about the way he threw himself into the open cockpit, but it got the job done.

Once Schoenfeld cleared the cigarette's gunwales, Glenmore scurried down off the lawn to Dante's side. As she stopped to snatch up his surrendered weapon, she muttered to him under her breath.

"I wanted to let you kill him, believe me. But I can't. He's my ticket. You kill him and I'm the one left holding the bag."

Joe flashed her one of his best disarming smiles. "I guess that means *you've* gotta kill *me*." And then he threw the fistful of sand.

The impact with the deck of the cigarette boat knocked the wind out of Schoenfeld, and he spent several agonizing moments trying to get his breath back. As the haze of pain cleared, he realized his movement back along the dock had drawn no fire. Perhaps the bitch was having a change of heart. As he dragged himself toward the helm and reached up to tear the wiring harness from its yoke, he hoped Debbie would try to beg his forgiveness. He didn't care how pressed he was for time; he would take enough to savor the look on her face when he shot her.

Dante had grabbed the sand with his left hand while Glenmore was concentrating on the gun in his right. As he threw it, he dove left and threw a kick at her feet. She lost both weapons trying to break her fall. She was clawing at her eyes with one hand and groping frantically in the sand when his instep impacted midtorso. He'd managed to get good purchase, even for soft sand, and caught her hard enough to crack ribs. It ended before it ever became a contest. Disregarding her choked gasps, Dante planted a knee in the middle of her back and slapped the cuffs on; tight.

"You've got the right to remain silent," he grunted. "The right to—"

From off at the west end of the bay in the general direction of Quogue, a familiar sound reached Dante's ears, coming fast across the water. A helicopter. And then, almost simultaneously, the power plant of the cigarette boat coughed and caught. Joe left Mr. Miranda and the declaration of rights for later. He found his revolver in the sand, thumbed the hammer, and spun the cylinder. With Glenmore left to moan and spit grit, he vaulted onto the dock.

Schoenfeld had one arm exposed. The blade of a penknife flashed in the sun as he struggled to saw his way through the bow line. It wasn't much of an angle, but Joe took what he got. Dropping into a combat crouch, he leveled the .38 and fired. Unfamiliar weapon or not, the shot was a good bet from twenty-five feet. He had good footing and time to set himself. As the gun jumped in his hands, Schoenfeld's knife bit through the remaining strands of that mooring line and flew end over end into the water. The boat immediately started to drift. Dante had no idea whether he'd hit his target or not. One moment the arm was exposed and the next it vanished. By the time he regained his feet and was moving again, the boat was a dozen feet from the dock.

Overhead, the approaching helicopter was less than a quarter mile away when Joe made up his mind. A team of FBI sharpshooters would have a field day from up there. It would be like shooting fish in a barrel. But this was personal. There was no way Schoenfeld would surrender. Not now. The swath he'd cut was too wide, the trail behind him painted with blood. Cop blood. The blood of an innocent young woman. When he reached the edge of the dock, Dante had most of the speed he wanted. The boat was still drifting away as he launched himself. He tried to lead it a little and was halfway there when Schoenfeld opened the throttle.

* * *

Marty knew from experience that the hole in his arm wouldn't start to burn for a few minutes yet. From the look of it, he guessed the slug had gone clean through the bicep without hitting bone. He had the nose of the craft aimed toward open water as he took the helm. The damn thing shook itself like a wet dog and all but stood on her ass end once he opened her up.

The chopper bearing down hard on his position from the west had Marty's complete attention when a dark form flew at him over the top of the windshield. He had no time to react before the barrel of a pistol caught him along the right shoulder and side of his neck. Already numb up high, his wounded limb suddenly burned like hellfire, clear to his fingertips. The hurtling shape's momentum took it all the way aft to land sprawled atop the stern bench seat. Schoenfeld was surprised by the audacity of the move. He spun and threw himself, fully prepared to rip the bitch's heart out.

Dante's impact with the top rim of the cigarette's windshield caught him hard across the abdomen and flipped him head over heels. He'd seen it coming and focused everything he had to land a blow before he lost the advantage. The combination of the contact and the force of his fall jarred his weapon loose from his grasp. When he landed aft, sucking hard for breath, he faced an enraged Marty Schoenfeld barehanded.

"You!" the attacking man screamed. His right arm hanging limp, he clutched a heavy-frame revolver awkwardly in his left hand.

Dante watched Marty's mouth move but barely heard him bellow over the roar of the cigarette's thundering power plant. Overhead, the rotor wash of that low-flying helicopter was generating a chop that pitched the speeding boat crazily. Then Schoenfeld was on him with the fury of a cornered and wounded predatory beast.

With his first swing, Marty managed to give back a little of what he'd gotten. Dante was still fighting for his wind and was barely able to parry the pistol whipped hard at his face. His forearm took the brunt of it as the gun discharged alongside his left ear. The fingers of his left hand went numb, his head ringing with the pistol's report. He had no time to assess or plot. Everything was on autopilot as he jerked a knee up hard at Schoenfeld's groin, rolled right, and came up throwing an elbow back into the man's exposed rib cage. He missed with his knee but got some good leverage on the follow-up. An elbow punch at close quarters and with a lot of shoulder and leg behind it, had bone-breaking power. Joe didn't have the footing but managed to use most of his upper body as a whip. He couldn't hear it, but he could feel the crunch.

Something was wrong with the engine of the boat. It coughed, started to clatter, and began spewing black smoke. Dante barely absorbed this along the periphery of his adrenaline-charged perception. He was busy pressing his advantage. With the force of that elbow shot, Marty screamed. Dante's own predatory sense remembered the old wound; the image of bloody bandages flashing before his mind's eye. Numb or not, he forced his left hand in there, gouging. It was clear that Schoenfeld was accustomed to overpowering opponents with his strength and bulk. A violently rocking boat gave such strategy certain advantages. It gave Dante little chance to exploit his superior grace or style.

Schoenfeld was trying to press his weight advantage, seeking to smother Dante as he bore in on him with flailing knees and his one good fist. Joe had been stung once with the initial onslaught and was stung again now. Marty managed to ram a knee into Dante's exposed right shin. Shin shots hurt immediately. The pain of it made Dante bite down hard and strengthened his resolve to end it.

In the twelfth year of Jae Doo Roh's tutelage, the master had taken his most gifted pupil aside for special training. His regimen was as much an exchange of social philosophy as it was advanced lessons in the deadliest techniques of martial arts combat. It was clear that Jae would not have opened that door to just any good fighter. He'd seen something special in Dante. As always, Jae's policeman-pupil applied himself diligently. And once those deadly secrets were learned, they were locked away in a safe place, out of reach of emotion.

Schoenfeld knew he'd stung his opponent. Now he got one foot planted behind him and, from a low crouch, brought the barrel of his weapon around. His numbed right hand reached to steady it, the action creating a tight, V-shaped zone of vulnerability between his outstretched arms and chest. Dante didn't need to see it. He knew it would be there. As Marty's move developed, Joe was already on his way to his knees, the fingers of his right hand snaking upward and curving inward, set as rigid as a carbon steel meat hook. The contact lasted no more than an instant, a wrist snap driving fingertips into the exposed throat to hook behind the windpipe. The vicious return jerk crushed the soft membrane against the larynx.

The Ruger discharged a second time, the slug going harmlessly wide. Schoenfeld straightened the rest of the way up, panic frozen on his face as he tried to get air and discovered he couldn't. He dropped the gun to clutch at his throat.

As Dante waved to the chopper, signaling for a towline, he patted his pockets for his penknife. Once Schoenfeld passed out for lack of oxygen, Joe figured he'd cut an airway down low in his trachea. It was a moment before he remembered he'd lost his knife in the fire. Marty's fire. His mind's eye saw the dying man's own knife flip into the water. Glenmore's words echoed. This guy was her ticket. If he died, she'd be left holding the bag.

As one of the Bureau men started a winch cable his way, Joe stood trying to steady himself against the violent rocking of the boat. By the time the cable was fastened to the bow cleat, Schoenfeld had gone still on the deck behind him. Once the boat was moving toward shore, Dante crawled aft to collapse onto one of the upholstered bench seats. Directly opposite him, a scar in the engine housing caught his eye. He leaned forward to trace it with his fingers. The placement and angle were about right. It was the hole the dying man's errant shot had drilled. It seemed both perverse and achingly pathetic that a gas hog's power plant had been the dying murderer's last victim. Soon, Joe knew he would travel south to rural Pennsylvania and try to explain all this to Linda Fletcher's grieving parents. Right now, he had no idea of where he would even start.

A loud *whump* startled him from his reverie as Schoenfeld's body shook with sudden, violent convulsions. Dante watched as the last of that life drained away. It was times like this that he hoped to God that there really was a hell. He wished Schoenfeld's soul to the hottest depths with the devil's speed.

EPILOGUE

Monday morning, Brian Brennan took the sketches of Linda Fletcher down off the drawing studio wall. Yesterday he and Diana packed most of what they wanted to take up to their house on the Sound, and today he was tying up a few loose ends. Instead of putting the *Aerodite* project on hold, Brennan wanted to press on while the image of his model was still fresh.

When Dante emerged from his room at close to noon, Brian was sweeping up in the shop. Joe had stumbled in late yesterday afternoon in a near-catatonic state of exhaustion. He'd slept right through both dinner and breakfast. Dressed in a pair of gym shorts, his sandy hair tousled in six directions and his face puffy with sleep, Joe padded barefoot to the shop fridge and withdrew a pair of beers. There was a network of scars covering the man's back, all of them whitened now, but many new since Brian first met him. After the way he'd looked yesterday, it was a relief to see he'd regained some of the accustomed spring in his step.

"You look like a man who might be hungry," Brian said to his friend. "How about a steak?"

"Hungry? What makes you think that? I had a big meal Saturday afternoon."

"All I've got to do is light the grill," Brennan reported. "Give me a minute to finish up here."

Dante handed over one of the bottles and grabbed the dustpan. As he crouched before Brennan's small pile of debris, he jerked his head toward the drawing studio. "You think the Nissan people might give you a deal on that Z in there?"

"Uh huh. Dealer cost. You in the market?"

Joe stared wistfully at that beautiful red machine. "Maybe. Ever since I lost the 'Vette, I haven't been able to decide what I want. That baby there's about as pretty as anything I've seen. I hear they'll blow the doors off most everything else on the road."

"You must be feeling friskier than you look, friend."

That drew a grunt. "Frisky? Maybe after I've eaten that steak. No, I'm looking at a new car as a token first step. I've gotta start thinking about rebuilding. My life's a fucking wasteland."

Dante rose from his crouch to dump the contents of the dustpan into an open plastic barrel. Brennan fished a book of matches from his shirt pocket and started for the stairs to the roof. Dante followed, and together they emerged into the brilliant midday sunshine. Up here, the spires of Manhattan surrounded them on three sides like the walls of a fortress. To the west sparkled the Hudson.

"Speaking of rebuilding," the sculptor murmured. He'd set a chunk of fire starter alight beneath the charcoal chimney and straightened. "Our tenant on the floor below us is moving his storage across the river to Jersey City. His lease is up. What would you say to us chopping a couple thousand squares off the west end down there and building you a loft with a river view?"

Dante frowned. "I don't know, Brian. I guess I haven't thought that far ahead yet."

Brennan waved at the backdrop of buildings behind them. "Have you checked rents on this island recently? The market might've softened some, but they're still brutal, buddy."

"It's a generous offer, Brian. But even if I went bare

bones with the decor, I doubt I could afford the construction costs. We've got to be talking at least a hundred grand.''

Satisfied that his fire was well established, Brennan backed away to stare off at the city. It was hot as hell out here, even with a light breeze coming at them off the river. ''Diana and I talked it over, Joe. You're our closest friend. We'd like having you as a neighbor. You figure out where you want the kitchen and bath, I'll have a plumber and electrician rough it all in. We'll help with the materials. I did most of the work on my place once upon a time, and you're pretty good with your hands. You and I can do a lot of the rest ourselves.''

Before Dante could finish swallowing a lump that had caught in his throat, the access to the roof garden swung open and Diana appeared.

''*There* you are. Am I interrupting man talk or can a girl and her fuzzy friend join you?'' She stood with one hand behind her back and now brought it forward with a flourish. Nestled in it was a six-week-old kitten, brilliant white with huge blue eyes. ''You looked like you needed a friend when you came in yesterday, copper. Meet Toby the Turkish Angora.'' As the singer crossed to place the kitten in the speechless Dante's cradling hands, her eyes had mischief in them. ''A lady engineer I know raises them. Says they're not dumb like Persians. This little guy is deaf, and that meant the kitty glue factory if I hadn't rescued him. Her daughter named him Toby, but I suppose you could change that. I doubt he's caught on yet.''

Dante lifted the tiny cat up to eye level, his hands cupping around him like he was a Ming vase. ''Toby's just fine. Deaf, huh? No sweat, little buddy. Ain't nobody's completely whole in my world. You'll fit right in.''

About the Author

CHRISTOPHER NEWMAN is the author of *Midtown South, Sixth Precinct, Manana Man, Knock-Off Backfire*. He lives in New York City.

✪ ✪ ✪

Look for these exciting precinct novels by

CHRISTOPHER NEWMAN

in your local bookstore.

MIDTOWN SOUTH

Dante was ready for light duty, away from the drug beat. But when your precinct borders on Times Square, easy police work is hard to come by. And when uncanny look-alike prostitutes are being murdered, the case is as hard as they come.

SIXTH PRECINCT

Newly assigned to the Sixth Precinct, Dante is working on the bizarre murder case of art collector Oscar Wembley, who was hacked to death with a kitchen knife. Another, more grotesque murder adds an unusual twist to the case and a new challenge to Detective Dante, who thought he had seen it all.

✪ ✪ ✪

⭐ ⭐ ⭐

KNOCK-OFF

A hot designer in the competitive world of high fashion is found bludgeoned to death. The stolen designs for the new fall line point to a piracy ring. The case brings Detective Joe Dante to Fashion Avenue for the toughest case of his career.

Also by CHRISTOPHER NEWMAN . . .

BACKFIRE

At the dawn of a presidential campaign, the secret buried a generation back suddenly surfaces. To one man it means enormous profit—and incalculable risk. To a second man it means solving one lethal mystery, only to uncover another as close as his own flesh and blood.

⭐ ⭐ ⭐

CHRISTOPHER NEWMAN

Look for these Fawcett paperbacks in your local bookstore.

To order by phone, call 1-800-733-3000 and use your major credit card. To expedite your order please mention interest code LM-3. Or use this coupon to order by mail.